THE
CROWNED
GUARDIANS

THE ARMOURED BUTTERFLY SERIES

THE CROWNED GUARDIANS

THE ARMOURED BUTTERFLY BOOK THREE

TRUDY ADAMS

The Crowned Guardians

The Armoured Butterfly, Book Three

©2023 by Trudy Adams

ISBN: 978-1-64960-412-5
eISBN: 978-1-64960-460-6
Library of Congress Control Number: 2023910689

This is a work of fiction. Names, characters, and incidents are all products of the author's imagination or are used for fictional purposes. Any resemblance to actual events or persons, living or dead, is entirely coincidental. Any mentioned brand names, places, and trademarks remain the property of their respective owners, bear no association with the author or the publisher, and are used for fictional purposes only.

Scripture taken from the New King James Version®. Copyright © 1982 by Thomas Nelson. Used by permission. All rights reserved.

Cover Design by Megan McCullough
Interior Typesetting by Dentelle Design

AMBASSADOR INTERNATIONAL
Emerald House
411 University Ridge, Suite B14
Greenville, SC 29601, USA
www.ambassador-international.com

AMBASSADOR BOOKS
The Mount
2 Woodstock Link
Belfast, BT6 8DD, Northern Ireland, UK
www.ambassadormedia.co.uk

The colophon is a trademark of Ambassador, a Christian publishing company.

To Tenille and Josie

· Cazarma

Sapphire Lake

Rydmarden River

· Rydmarden

· Hyandya

Hazmere Desert

Red Mountain

Jazmarda

The Red River

· Ellaway

· Keep

The Keeper's Mountains

Valley of Kesi

❖ Etarbelec

Kesi River

· Katurba

Jarren River

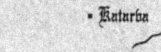

· Saltran

Red Bay

Kingdoms of the West

· Rorinhall

The Hewn Mountains

The Rhea Lands

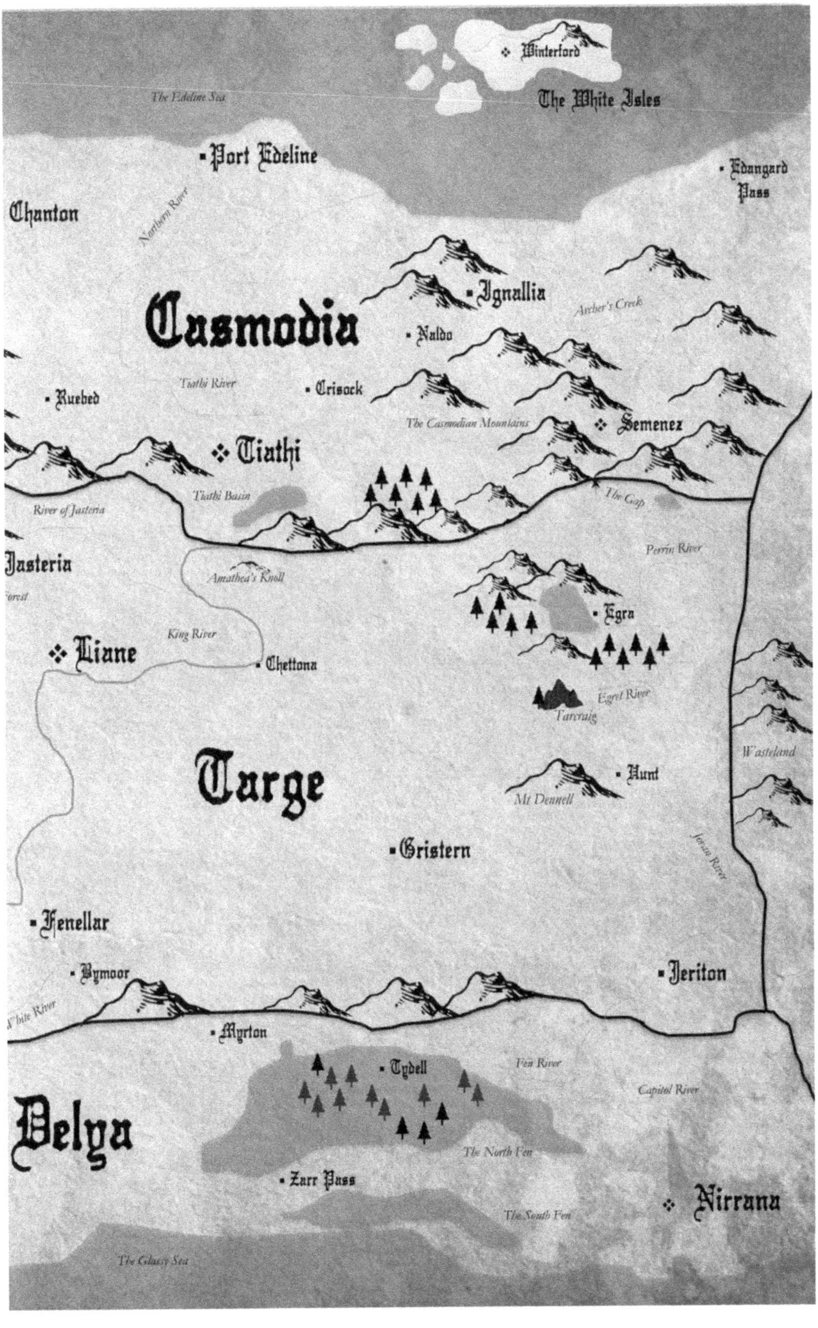

Winterford
The White Isles
The Edeline Sea
Port Edeline
Edangard Pass
Chanton
Northern River
Casmodia
Ignallia
Archer's Creek
Naldo
Tiathi River
Crisock
Ruebed
The Casmodian Mountains
Semenez
Tiathi
Tiathi Basin
River of Jasteria
The Gap
Perrin River
Jasteria
Amathea's Knoll
Egra
King River
Liane
Chettona
Egret River
Tarcraig
Wasteland
Targe
Hunt
Mt Dennell
Gristern
Fenellar
Bymoor
Jeriton
Myrton
Tydell
Fen River
Capitol River
Delya
The North Fen
Zarr Pass
Nirrana
The South Fen
The Glassy Sea

CHARACTER PRONUNCIATIONS

Adaliah—Ah-*dar*-le-ah

Amaz—Ah-*marz*

Anash—Ah-*nash*

A'zyon—Ah-*zigh*-on

Bagred—*Ba*-gred

Brzina—Brr-*zeen*-ah

Bylon—*Bye*-lon

Cades—*Kay*-dees

Cazine—Ca-zeen

Darj—Darge

Edangard—Ed-an-*guard*

Elhian—El-*high*-an

Elryane—El-*rye*-an

Engres—*En*-gres

Garrow—*Ga*-rowe

Hanequin—*Han*-eh-quin

Hazaka—Har-*zack*-a

Holormaza—Hol-or-mar-za

Izak—I-zack

Jenethea—Jen-*ee*-thee-a

Kadram—*Kad*-drem

Mirza—Mer-zah

Sirvan—Sir-*varn*

Telitha—Tell-*ee*-tha

Zalem—*Zay*-lem

Zavad—Za-*vard*

LOCATION PRONUNCIATIONS

Cazarma—Ca-*zar*-mah

Egra—*Eh*-gra

Etarbelec—Eh-*tar*-be-lec

Fenellar—Fe-*nel*-lah

Ignallia—Ig-*nah*-le-ah

Levanna—Leh-*van*-ah

Liane—Lie-*anne*

Naldo—Nal-doe

Rhea—*Ree*-ah

Rorinhall—*Roar*-in-hall

Semanez—*Sem*-a-nez

Sharlard—Shar-*lard*

For a full list of terms used in the *Armoured Butterfly* series,
please visit www.trudyadams.squarespace.com.

And the dragon was enraged with the woman

and he went to make war . . .

Revelation 12:17

PROLOGUE

I couldn't remember the name of the cave. Someone had told me about it only a day earlier, but a day earlier we'd been with Elhian and Darj. A day earlier we'd still had our belongings, including our clothes and weapons and horses. We'd been warm and uninjured and not caught in a snowstorm.

I didn't need to know the name of the cave, of course. I just wanted something to take my mind off the cold. Icicles hung from the ceiling. The air was still, but there was an unnerving whistling in the distance. The ground was a surly mixture of gravel, dirt, and snow. My feet were cut and blue. I wondered how long it would take for my toes to die. Would I have the courage to cut one off, if I needed to? Would I still be able to run? My back was sore from huddling against the stone wall. I wanted to sleep, but I had to remain alert. Even in the stormy weather, we could still be attacked.

But I had no sword. I wasn't wearing any armour, and I had no strength to put up a bare-fisted fight. I'd forgotten all that.

My cousin's lips were already blue. Her clothes were tattered, too. She'd dug me out of the snow and dragged me for several minutes before we reached the cave. She only managed to get us a few steps inside, just out of the wind. Teeth chattering, she tried to keep us awake by talking of our childhood memories. She stroked my arm in a distracted attempt to keep my blood moving, but I knew it wouldn't be long before we both fainted away. I imagined someone finding us generations later—two frozen women in a forgotten and nameless cave, only identifiable by the signet ring Alexia had hidden in her bodice.

She held me closer, joints stiffening. 'Keep breathing . . . dear cousin.'

A moment later, there was the blackness I longed for.

1
TWO PRINCES AND A PRINCESS

'It's another boy, and he's just as handsome as his brother!'

I was lying on my back when I heard the words, staring at the ceiling, crying. I don't know whether it was from the exhaustion, the fear, the excitement, or the relief. My body shook. I felt so weak, I was afraid I'd melt into the bed and never be separated from it again. Everything seemed accentuated—the musty smell of the sheets, the light flickering across the stone wall, the dusty fog on the window . . .

'They're beautiful!'

The bells rang outside, announcing the arrival of Casmodia's first-ever royal twins. I hadn't seen them yet, and already I could hear cheering through the castle window. Firecrackers lit the night, but all I could think was, *We're alive.*

I'd gone a week over my expected due date, and the fear had been worse than losing my memory or breaking the Dark Orb. Thoughts of my mother dominated my mind. She died with my younger brother only fifteen months after I was born. Died in a complicated childbirth, leaving me motherless and my father bereft. I knew Elhian thought about it, too. A lot.

But we survived. I will see them grow.

I waited for one of the midwives to place my sons in my arms. After two days of labour, the time it took for her to wrap them in cloths and bring them to me seemed stretched and slow. Elhian was slumped in his chair, white-faced and covered in a cold sweat.

'This is why men shouldn't be allowed into the birthing room,' one midwife muttered to another with an impatient glance towards him.

I thought of my friend Darj with a fond smile. He alone had helped my cousin bring Princess Eva into the world in the midst of a battle that had entered the very room they were in, no less.

'I'm fine,' Elhian said with an indignant tone, coming over to me.

Our second boy had cried just a little, and now he rested in my arms next to his brother with such contentment and innocence I wanted to stop time and stay there forever. Our firstborn was small and wrinkly, unaware that by being born an hour earlier, he was destined to inherit a kingdom that was becoming stronger and wealthier by the day under his father's care. I knew immediately within my soul that, if it came to it, I would die for them.

'Adaliah,' Elhian said, his eyes brimming with tears like dewdrops. He kissed my forehead. 'We are doubly blessed.'

Three days later, we received two notes by pigeon, both of which I had eagerly expected. Elhian brought them to me in the morning, just as I finished feeding our twins. He had caught up on sleep, his eyes no longer shadowed with exhaustion and worry but glistening with contentment. He was a tall, thin man, with long legs that made his stride swift. As usual, his smile was framed with dimples that gave him a kind and youthful look, yet he carried himself with a strength that made those around him feel protected and safe. His thick, unruly, brown hair was ever in need of a brush. He ran a hand through it now, making it sprawl in every direction. It never failed to endear me to him.

I handed the boys to him and sat on a chair by the window in the nursery to inspect the small letters. They both bore the Targian monarchy's seal—a crown set in a circle of twelve stars. The first one was a formal notification from the queen's court:

The Queen of Targe
is pleased to announce
that she safely delivered a daughter
on the fourteenth of this month.

'A princess!' I told Elhian, who had sat down on the edge of our bed in anticipation of the news. 'And born just a day before our twins. We must have been in labour about the same time.'

'Is Alexia well?'

'It doesn't say. Open Darj's note.'

Darj and Alexia had been married for just three months when Alexia discovered she was pregnant with her third child. I'd written to tell her I was expecting, and she'd sent me an almost identical letter at the same time.

The second note read:

Our daughter is born, and we have named her Nichole after my mother and Alexia after the finest woman I know. The queen is well after this her smoothest labour, and I couldn't be prouder of them both.

I read the note twice before handing it to Elhian, smiling as I imagined General Darj—or Prince Darj, as he was now—holding his first child. He was a kind father to Jeri and Eva, but holding his own little girl would have filled him with such happiness, I wished I could have seen it for myself. I thought of Alexia, humming to her newborn and managing the balance of mother, wife, and queen as elegantly as she always did.

I can only hope I will be able to do the same, I thought as Elhian and I waited near our castle's balcony, ready to introduce our sons the next morning. The last remaining maid fixed my hair with a clasp and laid it over my shoulder before hurrying away. Something caught my eye as she left: a piece of cloth, a sort of flag, nailed to the stone wall. It wasn't one of ours. It was black with red symbols. On one side was a crescent moon, the symbol of the evil spirit Anash, overlaid with an eye. Together, they made the symbol for the Zalems. On the other side was a simply drawn butterfly, one of its wings clearly detached.

The Zalems. A broken butterfly.

I pressed my lips together and swallowed.

The Zalems are finished. It means nothing.

But I'd seen that flag before.

Elhian squeezed my hand as the strident voice of the herald rang out across the crowd on the other side of the velvet curtain, returning my attention to the task at hand.

'The king and queen are pleased to introduce their sons, their Royal Highnesses Crown Prince Karlen Elhian and Prince Jovan Bagred!'

By the time we came back, the flag was gone.

2

THE BALL

King Hazaka of Jazmarda and his wife, Queen Telitha, were the first to arrive in Tiathi for the Winter Council. I stood next to Elhian at the castle doors, watching Hazaka ride up the main street and through the castle gate towards us. A retinue dressed in gold and red followed him, including a man-held carriage in which Telitha sat with her three young sons. Some of their party members were singing and dancing with gold and red ribbons. They fascinated the many people who lined the streets and castle forecourt. The ribbons flew through the air and shimmered in the sun like exotic birds. The dancers wore cropped shirts—not nearly warm enough for snow-covered streets and mountaintops.

You are not in the red desert here, Hazaka.

He dismounted his bay horse and landed masterfully on both feet. 'Your Majesties,' he said with great grandeur, 'thank you for welcoming us into your noble and prosperous kingdom.'

'You are welcome,' Elhian said with a grimace barely passing as a smile. Although he was more naturally congenial than the rest of us, even he struggled to stomach Hazaka's pomp.

Hazaka's queen and children disembarked from their cushioned chairs. As Hazaka introduced me to Queen Telitha, she eyed me with a brow raised, her lips twitching as if she were suppressing a snarl. She was decked in gold bangles and earrings and rings, even though her kingdom was said to be in drought with many people starving. There was something smug about her that I knew would grate my cousin, too. I found myself smiling at the thought. It was amusing to watch Alexia put someone back in their place, so long as it wasn't me.

The Jazmardian family waved to the crowd and went inside before I could come to any other conclusions about Telitha. Elhian and I remained where we were to greet the next carriage that was already approaching. There were no dancers or music preceding this one. It rolled through the people quietly and gallantly like a well-respected stag. The carriage was carved from chiefwood, a velvety, dark timber found in the southern region of Delya where the land fades into the Glassy Sea.

I hadn't seen King Thane Markus since he was sixteen, a shy and thoughtful youth. I was only twelve at the time, but I sensed even then I was too energetic for someone who preferred his own company. His brother, Prince Ren, maintained contact with Alexia and me after the Zalem Crisis, but the king communicated sparingly, as if each letter cost a kingdom to send. My memory of him was of a small, skinny boy who spent more time inside reading mysterious books than hunting or dancing. When he disembarked from his carriage, I could see he was taller and had added a thick, brown beard to his narrow face. Otherwise, he was the same pale boy I remembered.

'Your Majesties,' he said. 'It is a great pleasure to see you, but I'm afraid the journey has quite shaken me.'

His face was a sickly colour, and I thought he might empty his stomach at the door.

'You must go inside and rest,' Elhian said quickly, as if he feared the same thing. 'You have had the longest journey of all.'

'Indeed, it has been a slow and weary five weeks, particularly when I would have preferred to spend the winter in front of my fireplace.'

He took the lead of one of our servants inside. He had no wife or children to follow him.

'He seems as cheerful in person as he does in his letters,' Elhian whispered to me, waving to the people again.

'Alexia describes him as a rainy day.'

'Speaking of our dear cousin . . . ' He nudged me and nodded towards the castle gates, where the final carriage had just appeared. I squeezed his hand as the people started cheering again. I wanted to cheer with them. Alexia and I had only spent one short week together several months earlier, as part of one of my visits to the Keep in Kest. I had a few friends in the Casmodian court but no confidantes. I was tired of being careful with whom I trusted. I longed to be totally honest with another woman who shared my experiences and who genuinely cared—not just pretended to because they saw my friendship as an advantage.

In other words, I was starved of my cousin's company.

It was hard to remain composed and regal when the white carriage came to a stop in front of us. A footman opened the door and young Jeri disembarked first, now nearly nine years old. Everything about him spoke of his late father—his mannerisms, his walk, his face. He helped his little sisters down the steps. Eva gave me a heart-warming smile that was the image of her mother's, while Nichole stood shyly against Jeri, holding his hand. Darj followed them, as tall and handsome as ever and with a princely green cloak fastened to his shoulder. He bowed his head towards us before offering his palm to his wife.

A white-gloved hand slipped into it, and then she appeared, smiling, glistening.

As soon as the castle doors were closed and the crowd's cheers dulled, we greeted each other not as kings and queens, but as family. Alexia hugged me so tightly, I lost my breath, but I relished every second of it.

'I am so glad to see you looking so well,' she said, stepping back and cupping my face with her hand.

Eva tugged on my dress. 'Aunt Adaliah!'

I picked her up. 'How is my little princess?'

She wrapped her arms around my neck. 'I've missed you.'

'Oh, I've missed you as well.'

'It's good to see you both,' Darj said, grasping Elhian's forearm. 'Where are Karlen and Jovan?'

'Asleep,' I said. 'I would make the most of the peace, if I were you.' They laughed. 'Look how much this gorgeous girl has grown.' I stroked Princess Nichole's rosy cheek with the back of my finger, and she gave me a reluctant, shy grin before snuggling further into her father. Her face was a perfect blend of both parents—Darj's shape, Alexia's eyes.

'She's not always as placid as this,' Alexia said. 'In fact, I think she is the most restless of the three.'

'Well, that's no surprise when her father is a man of action,' I said. Darj chuckled quietly.

We spent almost an hour reacquainting over hot drinks and warm fruit cakes before Elhian and Darj took the children for a walk around the castle grounds, giving me some time alone with Alexia. As we sat down together in one of the sitting rooms, I had to restrain myself from asking her a thousand questions and divulging everything in my heart at the same time.

'Are you all right?' Alexia asked, apparently seeing this struggle in my face.

'Yes, I'm just so glad to see you,' I said. 'What do you suppose Hazaka meant by calling this council? And here, of all places?'

'Who knows what goes through that man's head? At least he has given us an excuse to see each other.'

'For that, I could almost hug him,' I said.

Alexia laughed. 'Let's not get carried away.'

I took in her blue eyes. They had changed. There was life there, when for so long, there had only been pain.

'Tell me, how are things in Liane?' I asked. 'Has it snowed there yet? Did I hear you say you've left Lord Fenton in charge while you're away? How are you and Darj?'

My questioning seemed to amuse Alexia, but her smile faltered at the last one. 'He is well, of course.'

'But?'

She let out a small sigh. 'He's still afraid I married unsuitably. Rumours have been rife in the court. In the beginning, some said I married him because I was already with child, but that at least was disproved by time. Now some are saying he shared my bed while Ethaniel was still alive, that both Jeri and Eva are Darj's children. Some say he blackmailed me into marriage, and still others say I only wanted him as protection. Most resent that he is common by birth and have forgotten all he's done for Targe, for me.'

'And what do the common people say?'

'They are much kinder. They remember all Darj has done for us. They believe the truth—that we married for love—and honour him wherever we go. He is not common in their eyes. I'm told performances are shown in the playhouses about our conquests and that his defeat of Sirvan is one of the favourite parts.'

'To them, he's their beloved queen's husband. To the council, he is still a soldier, the general. I'm sure they're jealous of his promotion.'

'Yes, you're probably right. I was angry to hear Ethaniel's memory dishonoured like that, but I really don't care what they think. It only bothers me because I know it bothers Darj. Their malicious rumours confirm his idea that he's not good enough for me. I have a hard time convincing him of the truth.'

'Which is what?'

'That I haven't doubted my choice for a second.'

She stood and peered out the window where Darj, Elhian, and the children walked through the frosty courtyard. Eva was swinging on Darj's hand. He was the tallest man I knew, his broad and muscular build offering the same feeling of security a strong house can when sheltering from a storm. He was completely unmindful of the regard every soldier in Targe and beyond held for him or the poems young maids wrote about his intense eyes and beguiling, albeit underused, smile.

'He loves you, Alexia,' I said. 'That will carry him through all of that.'

'I hope so. I just want him to be happy.' She sat by me again. 'Now, what about you?'

'I'm lonely, Alexia,' I said, instantly vulnerable under her gaze. 'And I can't escape the feeling that something hasn't settled within me. I feel driven by a sense of purpose I can't place. I love Elhian and my sons. I train the elite guards in sword fighting and keep myself fit, but it feels redundant. I feel like there's something more to be done in this world, and I don't know what it is.'

'I'm sure Elhian would refute the idea that you're not important to him, to Casmodia.'

'He would, but it's been two-and-a-half years since the Zalem Crisis, and I still don't feel like I've found my place in the normal world. How can you go on with life when you've seen the things we did, felt the things we did?'

'The way we do anything, I guess,' she said. 'One day at a time.'

The ballroom was warm the next night and filled with Casmodia's most elite residents. Everywhere, there were women in decadent gowns and men defying the weight of golden braids and ceremonial swords. They stood back and spoke in hushed tones as Elhian bowed to Alexia, the two of them the only ones on the floor. The Queen of Targe, wearing a dark magenta gown and a diamond tiara, curtsied in response. There was something about her that drew everyone nearer. Yes, she was well-celebrated in portraits for her well-cut figure, elegantly defined cheekbones set in a gently curved face, and piercing blue eyes that were capable of making you feel both enchanted and yet strangely *seen*. But aside from that, this was a queen with authority and a woman unburdened of the need for approval. It was her confidence and kindness that gave meaning to her beauty, that drew every eye.

Elhian began to dance with her, Casmodia's way of showing respect to a powerful ally. They chatted like they hardly knew they were dancing at all. The people encircled them, captivated. No one would have guessed, but it was a new dance for Alexia. We had sent instructions months before, and she'd been trained in it especially for the occasion. Her dress was perfectly suited for twirling. The many layers of her skirt fanned out in a lovely way whenever Elhian turned her.

Darj stood next to me with his eyebrows furrowed, watching his wife with an expression that held several emotions: pride, love, concern.

'Do you see the look on all of the ladies' faces?' I asked, searching for any change in his face. 'They all want to be her.'

A small smile tugged at his lips. 'I love seeing her happy like this. I think this trip is just what she needed.'

'What do you mean?'

He kept his eyes on her as he spoke. 'Sometimes, when she's laughing and talking to us, she drifts away to a place where I can't reach her.'

'But I thought she was doing so well.' I watched her gliding across the dance floor.

'Oh, she is,' Darj said, touching my arm. 'Considering where she was after Ethaniel died and Jeri was taken away, she is doing brilliantly. The wars have left their scars, that's all.' He sighed. 'On all of us.'

'Healing comes like rain, I think—a few drops, and then all at once.'

'Is that the sort of wisdom that comes from experience?'

Before I could answer, Elhian and Alexia completed one last turn together, the music finished, and we applauded them. The next song began, and countless couples started to dance, including Elhian and me and Darj and Alexia.

'A beautiful evening, Your Majesty,' Lord Stefan of Naldo said to Elhian as he and his pretty wife, Lady Elena, danced past us.

Lady Elena gave me a meek nod. 'You look beautiful tonight,' she said. 'We are most grateful to be here.'

Shoes clicked against the wooden floor. Darj and Alexia laughed together as they danced effortlessly on the other side of the room. There were flushed faces and smiles everywhere I looked.

'Did you and Elhian sort out all the world's problems while you were dancing?' Darj asked Alexia later as the four of us took seats at a table decorated with roast duck, curled butter, chutneys, and baked vegetables.

'All but who should be Thane's wife,' Alexia said.

Thane was across the room at a table with the Jazmardian royals. Hazaka and Telitha were not talking to him, so he was making a goblet of wine his sole focus.

'Perhaps not all men need a wife,' Elhian said.

'It hasn't done you too much harm,' I said.

Alexia nudged Darj. 'It's made this one a lot less prickly.'

'When was I ever prickly?'

'Always,' Alexia and I said together and laughed.

'Perhaps Thane was so heartbroken over your rejection, he's gone off the idea of women altogether,' Darj said.

Alexia rolled her eyes. 'He only offered out of duty. We both know that in reality, we would not have coped with each other. I would have been too much for him and he too little for me.'

'That's one of those comments we men aren't meant to understand,' Elhian said, taking a handful of nuts. 'When are we going to tell Alexia about the surprise, Adaliah?'

'I thought we were waiting until tomorrow.'

Alexia leant forward. 'What surprise?'

'We have a present for you,' Elhian said.

'What? Why?'

Elhian put a hand on mine. 'Can we show her now? Please?'

The four of us walked across the castle's forecourt towards the stables.

'My birthday isn't for months,' Alexia said.

'It was Elhian's idea,' I said.

'What was?'

We reached the stables, and Elhian opened one of the stalls. Behind the door was a flawless, golden mare with a white blaze and honey-brown eyes.

'Meet your new mount,' Elhian said.

'Elhian . . . She's beautiful,' Alexia said. 'I've never seen such a creature! But why? You know I have several horses at home—'

'But not one as strong and lovely as this,' Elhian said. 'The three of us all have our horses—Leuk, Bagred, Guntar. What good is it if you don't have a horse the people know you by and tell stories about, too?'

'Like Brzina,' Darj said.

'What?' Alexia asked.

'Brzina. You know, the fabled Targian horse. She was said to be the fastest horse known to man, but she escaped into the wild to run with the free horses in the north.'

'I thought that was a true story,' I said.

Darj shrugged. 'Perhaps.'

Alexia touched the mare's face. The horse gently nuzzled her hand. 'What's her name?'

'The stable boys call her Hazel,' Elhian said, 'because she was born under the hazel tree in the east paddock. What do you think? Do you like her?'

Alexia planted a spontaneous kiss on his cheek. 'I love her!'

3
ROSANA

Elhian was the only one who rose early the next day. The rest of us slept in, Alexia all the way to mid-morning. Still dressed in her bedclothes, she met Darj and me in the nursery, where our children were playing. Nichole clutched Alexia's leg, so she picked her up and cuddled her.

'Where's Elhian?' she asked.

'Giving Thane a tour of the city,' I said. 'I think it was an excuse to avoid Hazaka.'

A knock drew our attention to a servant at the door. 'Excuse me,' he said. 'There's a woman and her family here to see Prince Darj.'

No one said anything at first.

A woman to see Darj? In Casmodia?

My mind turned to Samela, the wife of Alel in Delya. She'd had a soft spot for Darj, but it couldn't be her. The servant had implied the woman had come with children, and Alel and Samela had none.

Alexia raised an eyebrow with a teasing glint in her eye. 'Is this your other family?'

'One of many,' Darj said. 'Did she give a name?'

'Yes,' the servant said. 'She called herself Rosana Odinel. A husband and several children accompany her.' The servant took a deep breath as if this had caused him considerable stress. 'She is quite insistent that she see you.'

Darj had fallen back a step as soon as he heard the name. 'Rosana?'

'Your sister?' Alexia asked.

Darj nodded dumbly. 'I haven't seen her since I was fifteen.'

'Shall I fetch her, sire?' the servant asked.

Darj opened his mouth, but no words came out.

'You two go down to her,' Alexia said, patting his arm. 'I'll get dressed and meet you there.'

I stood with Darj as he paced back and forth in one of our small sitting rooms.

'I haven't seen her for years,' he said again, running his hands through his hair.

'What's she like?'

Darj didn't speak much about his family due to his father's murder and his younger sister's suicide. Rosana was his elder sister, and I knew almost nothing about her.

'Well . . . uh, she was tall, slim, and quiet from what I remember.'

I smiled. *A military description.*

'She met an Islander merchant named Franc, followed him home, and married him. We still write to each other. I invited them to our wedding, but the seas prevented them from coming. She never mentioned she was coming to see me now.'

'Isn't it a good thing?' I asked gently.

He stopped pacing. 'Yes, of course. I'm happy to see her. I'm just shocked, that's all. And she's . . . ' He scratched the back of his head. 'Well, she's . . . '

'What? Missing an eye? Diseased? Only has one leg?'

He ignored me. 'She's a commoner, like me. She may not know how to act. I wish I had known she was coming. I could have . . . I don't know. I could have prepared for it better.'

What he was really saying was that he was afraid of embarrassing Alexia.

'Oh, Darj,' I said. 'It may come as a surprise, but we Elryane women do know how to talk to people beyond the castle walls. Alexia will not think less of you however your family behaves.'

Before he could answer this, the door opened, and the servant walked in with a noisy and boisterous tribe behind him. I backed up against the wall.

'Darj!' A plump and voluptuous woman wearing a loud, red jacket pushed everyone else aside. Two thick plaits of black hair lay over her shoulders. Bright pink spots filled both of her cheeks, and her smile showed a set of mostly oversized teeth. 'My dear brother! Or should I call you "Your Highness"?' She broke into laughter that sounded like high-pitched wind chimes blowing in a storm. It wasn't a mocking laugh but the kind people give when they're overly amazed at the situation before them.

Darj was unable to speak again. All he managed to get out was 'R-Rosana?' as if this was their first ever meeting. She threw her arms around him and held on for a long time, making showy, indecipherable noises.

My position at the back of the room gave me the view I needed to take it all in.

Tall and slim? Quiet? This woman fills the entire room!

Either Darj's memory was failing, or his sister had completely transformed.

'Franc!' Rosana grabbed the arm of the man in question and pulled him to the front of the group. He was a round man with a round face, and it was filled with a large smile. He wore a brown hat with a few tufts of fair hair visible at his ears. Snow had sprinkled on his overcoat.

'It is such a pleasure to see you again,' Franc said, bowing so deeply to Darj I was afraid his back would give way and he wouldn't be able to stand straight again.

'Children! Children!' Rosana spoke over the top of her husband. 'This is your uncle, Darj. Darj, this is Tomek.' She pointed to the tallest boy, whom I guessed to be about thirteen. He gave Darj a grin and opened his mouth to talk to him, but his mother cut him off as she introduced his five younger siblings, including two girls and three more boys, the youngest one aged about five. Four of them had fair hair, and the other two—Tomek included—had black, Targian hair.

'I can't believe we are finally seeing you,' Rosana said, clasping her hands together. 'We have been desperate, haven't we Franc—'

'Desperate!'

'—to see you since you became the husband of the Queen of Targe! Who would have thought?' Here, she elbowed Franc, who shook his head in wonder. 'I remember my little brother running barefoot through the streets, and now you're a prince!'

'And a general, Ma,' Tomek said, leaning over his siblings. 'He defeated Sirvan, remember?'

'Ah yes,' Rosana said with an air of solemnity, 'and revenged our dear father. And is this . . . ' She laughed nervously as she spotted me. She attempted to curtsey but bobbed up and down like she wasn't quite sure what to do. 'Is this . . . this . . . '

Darj hadn't yet regained the power of speech, so I introduced myself.

'My name is Adaliah,' I said, coming out of the shadows. 'I am your brother's cousin-in-law and friend.'

'The A'zyon Warrior,' one of the girls said.

The children talked over each other as they recounted what they knew of me. I heard the words 'Dark Orb' and 'swords' repeated more than once.

Rosana curtseyed three or four times. 'Such a pleasure . . . such a pleasure!'

A few more minutes of intense chatter followed before Alexia appeared behind them, wearing a lovely midnight-blue dress. She flashed me an expression that suggested the scene before her was not quite what she had expected.

Franc saw me peering across them and turned. 'Oh my goodness! Oh my!' He tapped his wife's shoulder until she noticed him and then Alexia.

Rosana gasped. 'Oh, Your Majesty, Your Majesty,' she said, all but falling on the ground. Even the children had silenced at her presence.

How does she do that?

Alexia stepped forward and tucked her hand into the nook of Darj's elbow. 'It's a pleasure to finally meet my husband's family.'

'The pleasure is all ours, isn't it, Franc?' Rosana nudged her husband again.

'All ours!'

'You are every bit as beautiful as they say,' she said.

'Every bit!' Franc said. Rosana slapped his arm.

'When I heard that my Darj had finally married—and into royalty, no less . . .' She wiped away tears and chuckled again. 'I can't believe the Queen of Targe is my sister-in-law! I've been telling everyone—haven't

I, Franc?—everyone at home that we are related. I don't think most of them can believe me.'

Her whole family laughed in wonder of it all. Alexia's face held reserved amusement, but Darj's was white. He stood as rigid as a castle. I couldn't help but feel a bit sorry for him. I had never seen him so embarrassed.

'Why are you here?' he asked in a small, croaky voice.

If there had been rudeness intended in his question, I felt certain Rosana wouldn't have noticed it.

'My dear Franc has come down from the Isles to trade with the Casmodians. And then I heard you were coming to Tiathi for a very important meeting, and I insisted we come to visit you.'

'I'm so glad you did,' Darj said, his smile becoming less and less convincing.

'You must stay,' I said.

Darj flashed me a pleading look that I ignored.

'Oh, we are, dear; we are! We have rooms booked at the inn in the city, near where Franc wants to do his trading.'

'Please come and visit us when you can,' I said. 'Darj, you should introduce your sister to her niece, Princess Nichole.'

'Oh, yes,' Rosana said, gasping again. 'Yes, the children are dying to meet their cousin. To think my niece is in line for the Targian crown!'

Darj narrowed his eyes at me.

'I am so sorry,' he said to us later, sitting on the sofa and hanging his head in his hands. Rosana and her family had left for their accommodations, and Elhian had returned from his walk with Thane, which he described as 'less thrilling than watching grass grow'. After

I filled him in on all the details about Rosana, he was disappointed to have missed the more entertaining show of the morning. 'Next time you can go with Thane, and I will host Darj's eccentric family members,' he told me.

Darj sighed.

'Come, Darj,' Alexia said, restraining a laugh and sitting next to her husband. 'It wasn't that disastrous.'

'That is not the woman I remember.'

'The woman you described is exactly opposite to Rosana,' I said.

'She's changed,' Darj said with an air of wonder.

'Clearly,' I said.

'It was her, wasn't it?' Alexia asked.

'Yes, of course. Franc hasn't changed a bit.'

'All families have members who require more tolerance than others,' Elhian said wisely.

'Exactly,' Alexia said. 'People think my life is perfect but look who I have for a cousin.'

I gave her a look of feigned hurt, and we all laughed.

4
THE WINTER COUNCIL

It was midday the next day when we assembled for the council. We met in a part of the castle Elhian and I had converted into one of three proper staterooms. It was nothing compared to Alexia's or Hazaka's palaces, yet it was something Elhian and I could take pride in. The walls were a Casmodian blue with delicate, white swirls patterned across them from floor to ceiling. We had removed some of the stonework to turn small windows into large ones. They now afforded a view not only of the immediate garden, but also of the Tiathi township. In the distance, exposed house frames stood dusted in snow, just a few of many that were being built. Tiathi had tripled in size since Elhian had declared it the new capital four years earlier, and still, it continued to grow.

Elhian, Darj, Thane, and Hazaka were already seated as Alexia and I came to the door. Telitha was walking down the passage away from the stateroom.

'Aren't you joining us?' I asked.

She stopped. 'I am a royal woman. Why would I want to involve myself in the common affairs of my husband's kingdom?'

'Because you are a queen and as responsible for your people as Hazaka is.' Alexia spoke her answer as if she'd had time to rehearse it.

Telitha folded her bangle-covered arms over her thin, gold dress. The bright colour complemented her smooth, dark skin. There was something about her—something in her eyes, perhaps—that reminded me of someone, but I couldn't place it.

'Is it true you have both performed great feats on the battlefield?' she asked.

I hesitated before answering. Her tone was judgmental. 'It's true we have fought hard against our enemies.'

'Royal women do not need to fight amongst the common people.'

I felt the tension rise in Alexia. 'My father taught me that leaders should never expect anything of their people they would not be willing to do themselves,' she said. 'My gender does not exempt me from that.'

'And yet you have both lowered yourselves by doing the work of servants,' Telitha said.

'What would you do if one of your children were under attack?' Alexia asked. 'Or if everything you believed in was under threat? Are you telling me you wouldn't take up a weapon and fight alongside your men?'

'I would never engage in such common pursuits.'

Alexia regarded her with disbelief. 'Wait until you are sufficiently motivated, and then see what you do.'

'It is true I have never seen war. Not yet. But if war ever comes upon me, I will not fight shoulder-to-shoulder with those whose job it is to fight for me.'

Now Alexia was angry. 'During the Northern Invasion, my people were either killed or enlisted in Cades' cause against their wishes. What kind of queen would I be if I stood by and did nothing, if I signed orders dictating their future from the safety of my private chambers? It is my job to protect the ones I rule and love, and it's yours, too.'

Telitha seemed unmoved. In fact, her expression suggested she found us ignorant.

'Are you coming?' Elhian called.

Telitha continued down the passage away from us.

'I'm sorry,' Alexia said to me, taking in a deep breath. 'I should not have given in to her deliberate provocations, especially not when I am a guest in your home.'

'I enjoyed every bit of it,' I said, and she smiled.

We stepped into the room. Thane seemed healthier than he had on his arrival but was holding his head like someone who had drunk more wine than intended. Hazaka draped his arm across the back of his sofa, showing off the extravagant, gold lining of his cape. His pants were tighter than they needed to be, and he seemed as impressed with his own importance as ever. Darj's face was hard to read as usual—perhaps he was still reflecting on his meeting with Rosana—but it softened as Alexia sat beside him. Elhian was the only one who appeared affable. His smile put me at ease as I joined him.

'Where should we start?' Elhian asked.

'Perhaps Hazaka should go first,' I said.

'Yes,' Hazaka said. 'I would like to see us reinstate the Cazinian Concordat. In full.'

'What?' Alexia leant forward to judge Elhian's reaction. His eyebrows had shot up into his forehead.

The Cazinian Concordat was the name for the agreement that took place when Hazaka's ancestor, Cazine, forged the four great swords to defend our kingdoms from evil. Delya, who had then just lost a struggle against the evil of Mors and the Zalems, refused its right to a sword. It was given to the province of Kest under the care of Targe instead or, most recently, under the care of my father and myself. There were many things I thought we would discuss: trade agreements, military placements, border management. The Cazinian Concordat was far from my mind. I was almost as shocked by the topic as I was by Hazaka getting to it so quickly.

'I want to tighten the alliance between all of us, including Delya this time.' Hazaka pulled out a scroll from a nearby bag. 'I have already had my scribe draw it up. This outlines the terms wherein we would support each other in all situations—militarily, economically—as far as we are able.' He laid the scroll down on the table. It took several seconds to unroll. The writing was small and tight, the paper full. Space had been left for four signatures at the end. Hazaka's name was already there, etched with an exaggerated flourish.

'Why?' Alexia asked.

'Why what?' Hazaka snapped as if he'd known Alexia would question him and had set himself up to be annoyed.

'Why is this so important to you all of a sudden?' she asked.

'Are you questioning my motives?'

'Well, yes, I am.'

'Is it not obvious?'

'If it were obvious, I wouldn't need to ask. Is this because your kingdom is in drought?'

'I am sure you can see the benefit—'

'I'm asking what you see as the benefit.'

Hazaka let out a loud groan, the kind I imagined him giving his children when they were trying his patience. Darj rested his hand over his mouth, not quite hiding the small smile that had appeared there.

And he didn't even see her arguing with Telitha.

'Elhian, Thane—what do you think?' Hazaka asked.

I caught Alexia heaving a silent sigh.

'Delya was not part of the Cazinian Concordat,' Thane said, 'but if there is an opportunity for us to be so now and the terms are reasonable, then I would gladly sign my name. I think we should support each other.'

Hazaka gave him a satisfied nod. He turned to Elhian.

'I'm all for alliances,' Elhian said. 'Casmodia would not be prospering so well without its agreements with Targe. But I would like to know the reasoning behind this one before I sign anything.'

'Are you under threat from a foreign army?' I asked. I knew Hazaka well enough to guess he was under some sort of pressure, one he was unwilling or unable to face alone. I also knew he wouldn't volunteer such information by himself—not if it meant admitting weakness.

'That's a constant possibility for all of us,' he said carefully, 'hence the need for an alliance.'

'That's two questions you haven't answered now,' Alexia said, leaning back in her chair. 'Jazmarda is under threat, isn't it?'

Hazaka leveled his eyes at her. 'No, it is not. Casmodia is.'

'What?' Elhian asked.

Hazaka smirked. 'I received information detailing a sea invasion. The King of the White Isles sent me a proposition wherein I would assist him in taking the northern section of Casmodia, from Ignallia up to the Edeline Sea.'

'That is the worst of Casmodia,' I said. 'It is cold, steep, and with only a few mining villages.'

'It is poorly defended and not nearly as harsh as the White Isles. King Engres Loren would bring an army on a fleet of ships, take those few villages in an easy battle, and go on to take the south of Casmodia.'

'When did you hear about this?' Elhian asked.

'When I requested this council.'

'And why are you telling me about it instead of taking Engres up on his offer?'

Hazaka didn't answer straightaway. In fact, he twisted in his seat like it had turned into a hard stone. 'Because whether I like to admit it or not, you have a strong southern ally.' He refused to look at Alexia, but she was certainly studying him.

Darj cleared his throat, drawing our attention to him. 'So, King Engres plans to reward you for your help with easy access to the precious minerals that are mined in the north, but you know that if you accept his offer, Casmodia, Targe, and possibly even Delya would turn against you.'

Hazaka nodded slowly. 'Jazmarda could stand against Casmodia, but not all three of you.'

'And that's the only thing stopping you from mounting an invasion?' Elhian asked. 'What happened to alliances?'

'Do not take it personally,' Hazaka said. 'Conquering land is just another form of trade, really, and this time the price is not in my favour. However, Jazmarda needs something to trade with and would indeed benefit from better access to minerals, given the fall in our agricultural production. I am hoping I can receive such access by fighting with Casmodia, rather than against it.'

Elhian's face darkened. 'What are you saying?'

'I do not appreciate that tone when I am kindly giving you options. If the four of us banded together under another concordat, we could defeat King Engres and even take the White Isles.'

'Take them for whom?' I asked.

'And when is this invasion supposed to take place?' Darj asked.

Hazaka hesitated. 'In twelve days.'

'Twelve days?' Elhian walked to the hearth and put a hand on the mantelpiece. 'I have to send men north now.'

'I already have a battalion there,' Hazaka said, 'by the village of Naldo, ready to go up to Ignallia when the time is right. But I have not yet instructed them whether to fight for you or for King Engres. That all depends on what decision is made here.'

5
MURDER

Elhian and I walked into our bedchambers, Alexia and Darj close behind. Darj shut the door.

'I can't believe him,' I said.

'We can't accept anything on his terms,' Elhian said. 'He's resorted to blackmail, and not telling us the whole truth. There's something here that doesn't make sense.'

'I agree,' Alexia said.

'Do I still have your support?' Elhian asked her.

'Of course.'

'Support or not,' Darj said, 'it would take too long for us to organise Targian soldiers to be in the north of Casmodia, especially in the dead of winter. Even if we sent for them now, it would be impossible. Hazaka knows that. That's why he didn't tell you until now. He's forcing you to rely on him.'

'Then we have no choice but to play his game,' I said.

'No,' Elhian said. 'We have to figure out who the true players are.'

We managed to get Hazaka to agree to a reprieve until the morning. I sat with my sons for some time after they fell asleep that night, stroking their hair while their father spoke to his officers of war. Karlen breathed peacefully, holding his blanket against his chest. Elhian had passed his favourite boyhood toy on to him—a stuffed horse. It was tucked under Karlen's arm.

Jovan was stockier than his brother. He was named after a Targian hero and my father Bagred, a Targian prince. Now, he was the more Targian of the two—black hair and the first Casmodian prince to have blue eyes. My eyes.

Nichole was sharing the room with them during her stay. Alexia and Darj had settled her to sleep before leaving to tell a story to Jeri and Eva further down the hall. She lay prettily under her covers, sucking her thumb.

Despite the obvious differences, I could see the blood tie between the three children. I hoped they would grow to be good friends as well as second cousins. I hoped, not for the first time, that we could leave them a world where this was possible, a world that was safe.

Why does such a world have to be fought for so continuously?

'Threats will always come,' my father told me once, 'and my sword will always come against them.'

'Come to bed, Adaliah,' Elhian said, appearing behind me and putting a hand on my shoulder.

I kissed our sons' foreheads and rose to my feet.

'Let's run away into the night,' Elhian said. 'Let's take the twins and find a small farm somewhere. I'll grow crops, and you can milk the cow.'

'Do you really think we could be satisfied with an ordinary life?'

'The longer I live, the more appealing it seems.'

I kissed him. 'I know you, Elhian. You couldn't abandon your kingdom.'

Elhian rested his forehead against mine. 'It's you I'm worried about, Adaliah. If this leads to war, what will happen to you, the one I love above all others?'

I cupped his face. 'With you by my side, I am prepared for anything.'

We walked into the hallway towards our bedchambers. Elhian turned the corner ahead of me but jumped back and stopped, nearly treading on my toe in the process.

'What is it?'

His cheeks were red. 'The Queen of Targe is in a somewhat . . . well, let's just say, a heated embrace with her husband.'

I grinned and peeked around the corner. Alexia was leaning back against the door of Jeri and Eva's room with Darj close against her, his hand under her ear, his thumb resting on her cheek, and the two of them exchanging several kisses.

'You do realise your bedroom is only a few steps more down the hallway,' I called out.

They broke apart without any urgency, but I saw the hint of shyness in Darj's eyes as they turned to us.

'I'm sure I caught you two in a hallway more than once,' Alexia said as we walked over to them.

'We weren't allowed to share a room then,' Elhian said. 'Prince Bagred would have killed us if we tried.'

'That's true. I remember when—'

Darj placed a finger on her mouth. At first, her smile widened, thinking he was being playful, but when I attempted to say something, he waved at me to be quiet, too. He cupped his ear with his spare hand, indicating for us to listen.

I noticed the other voices for the first time. Jazmardian accents. Hazaka and his wife were nearby.

'Which one of your dancers will you spend this evening with?' Telitha asked in a cool voice.

'Whichever one comes to me first,' Hazaka said. 'Do not pretend to be the victim with me, wife. If it were not for the fact they look like me, I would not even be sure who fathered our children.'

'I am careful. Are you? And when are you going to show me what is in your concordat? You have shown those other women. I have as much right to know as anyone.'

They were coming our way. I grabbed Elhian's hand, and we hurried back around the corner, out of sight. Alexia and Darj didn't move and pretended to be too engrossed in each other to notice anything else.

Elhian and I waited around the corner. He gave me a look that suggested he thought we were being ridiculous, but we both knew I couldn't help eavesdropping.

'Of course, I—' Hazaka said and stopped.

He's seen them.

'Hazaka.' I heard the subtle mocking tone in Alexia's greeting. 'I thought you would be moving into the north of Casmodia by now.'

'I have no interest in making a home amongst iron and snow.'

'Just in taking it from others then?'

He hesitated like he was striving to keep calm. 'Nothing has been decided yet. That is up to the young King of Casmodia. Let's hope his inexperience does not kill him.'

'That young king has achieved far more for his people than many other monarchs,' Darj said.

A rare compliment, I thought, *but a dangerous one, too.*

'He only achieves anything because of the support he has. But would that support be able to hold fast against both King Engres and me?'

'Oh, Hazaka,' Alexia said dismissively. 'Keep your threats for the morning.'

I held Karlen on my hip as we watched the snow fall from a window in the blue stateroom. The morning sun couldn't be seen at all, and the glass panes were fogged over. Karlen rubbed his hand across them, fascinated by his ability to leave marks.

'Pa?' he asked. The boys seemed to prefer Elhian's company now that they were one.

'Yes, darling, you'll see him soon.'

'Excuse me,' a young voice said. A small maid stood in the doorway. I didn't know her name; she must have been new. She looked about twelve, but we didn't hire anyone younger than fourteen. She was staring at her shoes, and her curtsey was coarse. 'King Thane.'

I realised this was an introduction, but only because Thane walked in a second later. The girl turned to flee.

'Wait,' I said.

She stopped and returned to studying her shoes.

'What is your name?'

'Reyna.'

'Reyna, please take Prince Karlen back to the nursery.'

'Me?'

'Yes.'

She stepped across the room like she was afraid she'd fall through the floor and into a pit of snakes. She took Karlen, set his feet down, and held his hand, tugging him along roughly. Karlen was unfazed. He waved to me as she took him out of the room.

'He is a healthy boy,' Thane said.

'They both are, and that is the most important thing.'

'Can you tell me what Elhian has decided about Hazaka's offer?'

Elhian and I had discussed it until after midnight. I'd hardly slept after that. The fears of war had come back to me—the uncertainty, the pain, the sacrifices. We'd never had a victory without sacrifice. My father, Ethaniel, Raggin, Zavad, almost three years of Jeri's life . . . Too many sacrifices.

The thought of Zavad returned to me as I stood by the window. I remembered for the thousandth time the last few seconds of his life, how he'd run across the battlefield and protected Darj from death. Tears pricked at my eyes. Frozen by the memory, a moment or two passed while King Thane waited for me to return to our conversation.

'Your eyes look as beautiful as the ocean in that dress,' he said in the end, his voice low but sincere.

This surprised me, and I uttered a quick thank you.

'I will do whatever you want me to, you understand,' he said. 'I am yours to direct. Our kingdoms fought together in the Zalem Crisis. The four of you saved Delya from the Zalems. I am not interested in war with Hazaka or Engres.'

'There will be war with one of them.'

'Will you fight again?'

I bit my lip. 'I don't know.'

Staying out of danger seemed more important now that I had children. But I thought of Alexia and how she had risked her life when she was pregnant with Eva and again in the Zalem Crisis, even leaving her beloved daughter behind to give herself up to the enemy for the sake of her kingdom. The one thing she and I often disagreed about was a monarch's priorities. I believed love for family had to come first; she believed a queen must sacrifice even that if it meant saving the people. Perhaps she was right. Perhaps she was braver than me. I had always fought for our people and would continue to do so, one way or another. But when I risked my life, it was mostly with my loved ones in mind. Their safety was what truly motivated me, especially now that I lived in a kingdom I hadn't been born to.

I loved Elhian and our sons. I'd resided in Casmodia for several years, but I couldn't honestly say that the people in our kingdom were more important to me than my family. Equally important, perhaps—such is the responsibility of those who wear a crown—but could I place the welfare of my people above the welfare of my husband and sons? I hoped never to be in that position, but what if I was?

Alexia had never expected to see Eva again in the Zalem Crisis. I couldn't imagine what pain that must have caused her, especially now I had Karlen and Jovan, but she'd suffered it for the greater good. I wasn't sure if I had that same strength. Now that I was a mother as well, I was afraid of failing in more roles than one.

Telitha didn't show any signs of attending the meeting, but I'd expected that. Elhian arrived and started discussing books with Thane while we waited for Hazaka. Alexia came in holding Eva's hand. The little girl's face was red and her eyes full of tears.

'What's wrong?' I asked her.

'Nichole jammed my finger in the door,' she said in between whimpers, holding up her little finger for me to inspect. It was red and swollen; Nichole had clearly shut the door with force.

'Oh, dear!'

'Mother kissed it better.'

'I've asked one of the servants to come for her in a few minutes,' Alexia said. 'I just didn't want to leave her screaming.'

'Of course. Where's Darj?'

'I'm not sure,' Alexia said. There was an edge in her voice.

We waited a few minutes for Hazaka to arrive, Alexia glancing towards the door every few seconds. If Darj didn't arrive on time, Hazaka would insist the meeting went on without him. Like me, Darj wasn't a ruling monarch. We would have no grounds to wait for him. But without him, we'd be like a carriage with a missing wheel on a rough road.

'Did you have a disagreement with him last night?' I asked.

'No, quite the opposite.'

Hazaka strode into the room, and I felt the mood change immediately. There was something about him that festered unease. He glanced around the room before shutting and bolting the door. Without a word to any of us, he crossed the floor and unraveled his long scroll on the main table.

'Well?' he asked. 'Who's going to sign it?' He held up a golden quill and thrust it towards us.

I realised I was reaching towards my hip, seeking a sword that wasn't there. Why did I feel so threatened? Maybe it was the fierceness in Hazaka's eyes, or the way Alexia had straightened next to me, or how Eva had suddenly stopped crying.

'Well?' Hazaka asked again. He glared at Alexia.

'I will not be bullied into anything.' Alexia spoke with strength and calmness, but I sensed her tension. Something was wrong. Eva was burying her head into Alexia's skirt the way she did whenever she was feeling shy or worried.

Elhian and Thane had stopped talking as soon as Hazaka had entered the room. Elhian peered at Hazaka's left arm, the one that wasn't holding the quill. There was a tear in his sleeve and blood.

'What's going on?' I asked as Elhian moved closer to him.

'You will sign it, won't you, Thane?'

Thane said nothing.

'Sign it, for your own sakes!' The violence had gone out of Hazaka's face. He was breathless and desperate. 'For the love of your people . . . For the love of your cousin!' Hazaka spoke that to Alexia but pointed at me. She gave me a troubled glance.

Is he shivering?

He coughed, and Lezan came to mind, the wise, old Jazmardian who had died during the Northern Invasion after he was grazed with a poisoned arrow.

'Elhian, we need an antidote,' I said.

'Antidote?' Thane asked.

By then, Hazaka was doubling over in pain. Elhian helped him sit on the floor and ripped his shirt back. 'How did you get this, Hazaka?' He took the torn shirt and tied it above the claw-like wound on Hazaka's upper arm as tightly as he could.

Saliva lurched out of the Jazmardian's mouth and onto our rug. His eyes rolled back into his head.

'We need an antidote!' I said again.

'For what poison?' Elhian asked.

'It's Dragon's Breath.' Alexia whispered it, as if the very name of the poisonous plant would kill us.

Elhian retracted his hands from Hazaka's wound. He hurried for the water jug that was sitting on the table. Drops of water and blood fell onto Hazaka's scroll as Elhian clumsily washed his hands.

'Sign it.' Hazaka was now lying on the floor, curling up like a dry leaf.

'There's no remedy,' Elhian said. 'He'll be dead in a second.'

I didn't appreciate his bluntness. I couldn't take in what was happening. Hazaka couldn't die. I didn't like him, but he couldn't die so young. He was a king. Apart from race, there wasn't much difference between him and Elhian.

'Get Telitha,' I said to Thane.

He moved to the door and began to unbolt it.

The King of Jazmarda is dying in front of me.

I could tell it was painful by the contorted expression on his face and the small groans he was emitting. I could also see how Alexia had identified the poison. The skin near the claw-like marks on his arm had gone scaly and red—the colour of fire—and blood-strewn puss leaked down his arm. I knew that if we were to look, his throat would be red and raw as well. A speck of concentrated Dragon's Breath in the smallest scratch could kill. That's why Elhian had rushed to wash his hands, why Alexia had picked up and tightened her protective hold on Eva.

'I can't get this to move,' Thane said, letting go of the bolt on the door.

'Hazaka locked it,' Elhian realised. 'I don't have a key in here; we never lock it.'

Hazaka reached his hand out to me. I took it. It was the most affection I'd ever shown him, and it felt awkward and forced. I wanted to feel more sorrow for what was happening, but I couldn't. When had I become so hard-hearted? Hazaka had three sons under five, and now they would never know their father. I felt sure I should feel pity for them.

'Jazmarda is made weak,' he said, his tongue struggling to get around the words. 'Jazmarda is made strong.' His eyes focused on mine. 'The Armoured Butterfly . . . must not be broken.'

He coughed, spraying blood and spit. He shuddered and stiffened. And then, with a tormented groan, he died.

6
TELITHA

Someone banged on the door so hard it shook.

'Alexia! Are you in there?' It was Darj.

'Yes,' she called back. 'We're locked in!'

The door moved again as he pushed against it. This went on for a minute or two until he muttered something about getting the key.

'Who would do this?' Thane asked.

We stood in a circle around Hazaka's body. 'We need to cover him,' Alexia said. 'His arm will rot and smell.'

I knew what she meant. Dragon's Breath ate its way through the flesh even after death. I'd only smelt it once when my father used it to kill a particularly wild pig that had taken up residence outside our Kestian Keep. I could remember walking near the corpse and retching.

Elhian pulled down one of the drapes near the window and spread it over Hazaka's body. It was a relief not to have the unblinking stare of his brown eyes upon me.

A key slipped under the door. Thane picked it up and unlocked the bolt. He turned the handle and pulled the door open.

In front of him stood not Darj, but Telitha.

My chest tightened.

How do we tell her? How will she react?

Somehow, I knew Telitha would not be the sort of woman who would throw herself at her dead husband's body, sobbing. I was right.

She saw the lump at our feet and remained silent. We didn't know what to say, and she didn't ask any questions. She knelt down and took his hand.

She's saying goodbye.

Just as I started to believe she cared for him, she roughly pulled the signet ring from his finger. She stood, strode towards the table, and smirked as she examined the unsigned scroll. Then, before any of us understood what was happening, she picked up the entire scroll in a messy mound and threw it into the hearth.

'What are you doing?' I asked as it went up in flames. I took a step towards her, but Alexia grabbed my arm. Her grip was firm.

She suspects danger.

She was right to do so. A king had just been murdered. There was no disturbance in the castle. It must have been a highly skilled assassin or someone he trusted.

I looked at Telitha's long fingernails. Three of them on her right hand were encrusted in blood.

She killed her own husband.

She knew I had seen her hand, but she didn't show any signs of fear, shame, or guilt.

'Why?' I asked.

She said nothing and walked back towards the door. I pulled away from Alexia and reached for Telitha as she passed, my fingertips just brushing her shoulder. The second we touched, she changed. She turned, hissed at me, and slapped me hard across the face.

Everything that followed was loud and intense. I fell down. Elhian shouted. Eva started crying. Telitha ran for the door again, but Thane grabbed her arm. She bit into his forearm so hard, he made an awful noise that sounded like a wounded dog. Without warning, Elhian pulled me to my feet, and my head spun. Eva thrashed about in Alexia's arms, trying to get away. In the confusion, Telitha made it out the door and ran.

We chased after her. She dropped something that looked like a small ball, and it cracked when it hit the stone floor, sounding like breaking pottery. The air filled with a fine, white powder that blurred all vision, and I couldn't breathe properly. The walls seemed to sway, and the carpet rose up at me like a wave. I floated towards the floor like a lost leaf. The last thing I saw was Telitha disappearing around the corner, the hem of her dress swishing behind her. On her ankle was the Zalem tattoo.

I felt queasy when I woke, and it took me some time to realise I was in Alexia and Darj's guest room. Darj was lying on the floor a few steps away from me. A red lump had risen on the side of his head, dressed in blood. Jeri lay limp on the bed, and I couldn't see Eva or the other children. I had to pull myself into a sitting position to see Alexia, Elhian, and Thane on the other side of the room. They were all on the ground, lying in awkward positions as if they had been tossed there like sacks of potatoes. Still dizzy, I crawled over and shook Elhian's shoulder. He rewarded me with a groan. I shook him again, and he rolled onto his back and blinked at me.

Within a few minutes, I'd roused Alexia and Thane as well. Alexia stood when she noticed Jeri. She calmly moved him into a more comfortable position and placed a pillow under his head; but her face paled, and she stiffened when she saw Darj and his head wound.

'Thane? Elhian?' she called, kneeling beside her husband. 'Can you lift him onto the bed, please?'

They staggered over to help and managed to lay the prince-general next to Jeri. This roused the boy, who opened his eyes.

'What happened?' he asked groggily.

Alexia ran her hand over his forehead. 'I don't know. Are you feeling all right?'

Jeri nodded. When he saw Darj beside him, he sat up, unnerved. 'I tried to get help, but they were too fast,' he said. Alexia put an arm around him and drew him to her. 'He was trying to get to you, but the people helping Telitha hurt him from behind.'

Alexia leant over Darj as he came around.

'Just as well you have a thick skull,' she said, kissing his cheek.

'Hazaka. Is he dead?' he asked.

'Yes,' Alexia said. 'How did you know?'

'I saw Telitha strike him. Jeri and I woke early this morning, so we went for a walk around the grounds. We came across a group of men, or women, perhaps both—it was hard to tell because they were all wearing dark, hooded cloaks. They were arguing, yelling. There was a shorter man there with a scar down the middle of his chin.'

'What?' Elhian asked sharply. We all looked at him. 'Cordale—one of the men who oversaw my imprisonment in Sharlard—had a scar there.'

'Yes,' Alexia said, remembering. 'I met him during my time with the Zalems. The High Zalem gave it to him as a mark of his servitude. I heard that Cordale wasn't satisfied with having a tattoo on his ankle. He wanted something more prominent as a sign of his commitment to the cult.'

'We never did see him again after Bylon and Sirvan's defeat,' Elhian said.

'Perhaps it was him, then,' Darj said. 'Telitha and Hazaka were both there, too. Hazaka was almost purple in the face, he was so angry.'

'What were they arguing about?' I asked.

'I don't know,' Darj said. 'They were speaking in Jazmardian.'

'It must have been something significant,' Elhian said, 'given it led to Hazaka's death.'

'Yes, she scratched him with the Dragon's Breath. I had to get Jeri out of there, so we stole away as quietly as we could. That's when I came to the door, but when I went to try and find something to break the door down with, one of them struck me from behind.'

'That's when I ran to get help,' Jeri said, 'but they caught me and hit me as well.' He rubbed the back of his head.

Alexia glared at the door, sending her contempt towards the Jazmardian queen. 'Perhaps Telitha didn't agree with Hazaka's proposal to develop a new concordat,' she said.

'She must have known that's why they were coming to this council,' Elhian said. 'Why let him propose the concordat and then kill him? If the concordat was the problem, she would have stopped him beforehand.'

'Remember what she said last night?' I asked. 'She wanted to read it. Perhaps she forced him to show her its content in detail, and she came across something not to her liking.'

Darj weighed this up. 'Yes, I think you're right. He must have managed to keep its contents from her until now.'

'What do we do?' Thane asked.

'We have to find the other children,' Alexia said.

'And we have to go to Naldo,' Elhian said. 'If Telitha or her supporters, whoever they are, planned to kill Hazaka, then she'll have a plan for his battalion as well.'

'Then let's find the children and start packing,' I said.

'Adaliah.' Elhian put a hand on my upper arm. 'Why don't you stay here? Darj and I can go.'

'What?'

'What shall I do?' Thane asked. 'I'm not a warrior like my brother, you know.'

'I don't expect you to fight,' Elhian said. 'Come with us if you like or return to your kingdom.'

'And what? Alexia and I stay here and read poetry while you're gone?' I didn't know whether to feel indignant or offended.

'I just want you and the children to be safe.'

'Elhian, you're smarter than that,' Alexia said, her hand on her hip. 'You know Elryane women don't stay behind.'

'I thought you said you were going to leave your bow in Liane,' Darj said. Alexia gave him a pointed look. Darj rolled his eyes. 'Of course, you brought it. What was I thinking?'

Alexia nodded towards the bed. 'I stored it under there.'

'What about the children?' Elhian asked me. 'We can't leave them here alone or take them to battle. The boys aren't exactly proficient with their wooden swords yet.'

'I think we have a bigger problem to solve first,' Thane said. He was inspecting the door. 'We're locked in.'

'I'm sure we can break it down,' I said.

Thane grabbed the handle and pushed against the door. It didn't move or even rattle. 'I think they've nailed planks over it.'

He and Elhian spent a few minutes ramming their shoulders into it. It didn't budge.

We're locked in.

My heart beat faster. The room suddenly felt small and stuffy and my breaths shallow.

'What's going on?' Jeri asked, tugging on Alexia's sleeve.

She reached for his hand. 'I'm not sure, but we will keep you safe. I promise.'

'How did they get past all the guards?' Darj asked.

'I don't know,' Elhian said, walking towards the only window. It provided us with a view of the south of Tiathi and the front city gates. It was a snowy day, and the grasslands beyond the south wall could be seen through the white haze. Something was there. I studied the view over Elhian's shoulder. We both drew our breaths sharply when we realised what it was.

'It's the Jazmardians,' Elhian said. 'An army of them.'

7
PRISONERS

'Can we climb out the window?' Thane asked, pushing the windowpanes.

I knew it was impossible. We were three stories high, and a stone courtyard greeted us at the bottom.

I struggled to control my breathing. I examined the details of the room, trying to convince myself it was bigger than I thought. This was a battle of the mind I'd taken part in before. I reminded myself that, while the room was a trap, it was not dark or small. It was our best guest room. The four-poster bed was in the middle, and the rug was to the left of it. There was a desk with a comfortable chair, a quill and ink bottle, and a large wardrobe area for hanging clothes and getting changed. Alexia's magenta gown from the ball was hanging at the front. A jug full of water sat on a small table with a plate of fruit, which I had arranged to be sent up to Darj and Alexia. Luckily, they hadn't eaten much of it. The platter would be the only food between the six of us.

I ran my hand over Alexia's gown, trying to keep my mind off the locked door. I studied the sophisticated beadwork that covered the bodice. It was regal and feminine, one of Alexia's best. I wondered if I lived too far away to commission her dressmaker for a new gown. I took it off the hanger to judge the weight of it and was confronted by a small scream. I gasped and fell a step backwards. A young girl had been hiding behind the dress.

'Reyna?'

'I'm so sorry, Your Majesty,' she said, her face white. She lifted her skirt off the ground as she tried to back away from me. 'They were coming this way, and I didn't know what to do. So, I ran to hide in here and . . . and I didn't mean to pry!'

'Reyna, Reyna,' I said, raising my palms. The others watched on. 'It's all right. Where are the children? Are they all right?'

'They were safe in their nursery last time I checked.'

Alexia pressed her lips together.

'Come and sit down,' I said to Reyna.

'Are they attacking?' Darj asked Elhian regarding the Jazmardians. Darj was gradually propping himself up in bed, but his eyes were watery and bloodshot. He rubbed the lump on his head again.

'No,' Elhian said. 'But I can see our guards and soldiers spreading out around the wall. They are getting ready for a Jazmardian attack.'

'If she hasn't attacked already, she only has them there for leverage,' Darj said. 'She will want something in return for leaving Tiathi unharmed.'

'Look,' Thane said, pointing to the door. A white envelope had been pushed under it.

I picked it up and broke the Jazmardian seal. I glanced towards the bottom of the paper first to see if it had come from Telitha as I expected. It had.

'Read it aloud,' Darj said.

'"My request is simple—you will agree to come to the underground cavern at Semanez with me, or I will sack Tiathi with the Jazmardian army. You have until sunset to decide." That's all it says.' I flipped the page over. There was a small symbol etched into the bottom. It was one I'd seen before: a crescent moon and eye with a broken butterfly beside it.

'What is it?' Darj asked.

'Nothing,' I said quickly, scrunching up the paper.

'Semanez . . .' Alexia said. 'But it's destroyed.'

'Well, that's what it says. What underground cavern is she talking about?' I asked Elhian.

'I don't know.'

'Do you have enough men to save Tiathi if they attack?' Darj asked.

Elhian looked out the window again, trying to measure the strength of the Jazmardian army. He was disadvantaged in that the window only allowed him to view one-fourth of the city. 'They could hold them off, I think, but it depends. The Jazmardians may have reinforcements nearby. My officers may be able to send for more soldiers from other towns, but they would need time.'

Darj nodded thoughtfully. Alexia was sitting on the edge of the bed next to him. 'You're very quiet,' he said. 'What are you thinking?'

She hesitated and then said in a soft voice, 'I'm thinking this is the beginning of something I hoped never to experience again.'

The day passed slowly. We spread the fruit evenly between the seven of us and ate it for lunch. By mid-afternoon, I was hungry again. Reyna started telling Jeri a story, desperate for something to do. I felt sick, knowing the other children would be missing us and fretting by now.

Elhian watched the light dimming out the window, his back against one of the walls. 'I think we have to go with them,' he said at length. 'I need to ask her more questions, but if we must travel with her to save our children and our people, then we don't have a choice.'

Darj gave him a consenting nod. Alexia turned away but didn't protest.

'Reyna,' Thane said with a sudden thought. 'She can help us.'

'Me, Your Majesty?' the young girl asked.

'Yes,' Thane said. 'Telitha doesn't know you're with us. When she comes, you could hide again and be left behind. You would be safe.'

Thane was right. She was the key to our survival—why hadn't I seen that?

She blinked at us.

'It means you can help us,' I said. 'Once you're free, you can bring Alexia's bow and arrows and our swords to us. And our horses. If she's taking us to Semanez, they will take us into Targe and re-enter Casmodia through the Gap. Meet us in . . . in Egra, in Targe.'

'Not Egra,' Alexia interrupted gently, but with growing excitement. 'Make it Dawfield.'

Dawfield was a tiny village a day or two short of Egra, the sort of place Telitha would have never even heard about. It would also be a quicker and easier journey for Reyna.

'Dawfield, then. You must leave straight after us. We will escape. We will come and find you and get our things.'

'Is there any paper in here?' Elhian asked. Thane checked the drawer in the desk and found several sheets of it. Elhian sat in the desk chair and dabbed the quill in ink. 'You have to give these instructions to my councillors,' he said to Reyna as he began writing. 'They must protect Tiathi, and Casmodia. If we go and she still attacks, this will tell them what I expect them to do. If they don't attack, the Jazmardians can freeze in the snow.'

He finished off his orders and blew on the ink to hasten its drying. Satisfied that it wouldn't smudge, he folded the paper in half and handed it to Reyna. 'Can you do it?'

She reached for the paper reticently. 'I . . . I . . . ' She took a deep breath. 'I give this to the king's council, I take your weapons to a place called Dawfield in Targe, and you meet me there.'

'Yes, that's right,' I said.

'Can you take a message to my sister, too?' Darj asked Reyna.

'Of course,' Elhian said, rapidly scratching another note. 'You would want her and her family out of the city and safe.'

'It's not just that,' Darj said. 'She lives in the White Isles. She may be able to give us some insight into what is happening there. Ask her to meet us at Dawfield.'

'Have you got that?' Elhian asked Reyna, handing her a second note.

'But . . . but I've never been more than an hour away from Tiathi in all my life. I've never done anything like this. How could I possibly travel to a village in another kingdom? With . . . with weapons?'

I put a hand on her shoulder. 'Adventure knocks on everyone's door at least once. This is your turn. You must find a way.'

'Alexia,' Darj said with a new thought. 'I have a dagger hidden amongst my things. Strap it to your leg. If Telitha doesn't tell us about the children, we'll need to overpower her as soon as we can.'

Alexia searched through Darj's clothes until she found it. It came with a small sheath and belt. Turning away from us, she lifted her dress and adjusted the belt until it fitted around her upper thigh.

'You'd better hide,' Thane said to Reyna, nodding towards the window. 'The sun is almost down.'

There was a thud at the door just as Thane spoke. Reyna gulped and crawled under the bed near Alexia's bow and arrows.

Jeri sat on the bed, and the remaining five of us stood in front of him, facing the door.

There was banging as the planks were removed one by one.

She's going slow to increase our fear.

She's just one woman, I kept telling myself, but I knew that didn't mean anything. Alexia and I were testament to that.

When the door finally opened, Telitha walked in with ten men behind her. They held black crossbows, arrows clicked in place. Alexia reached towards her back as if searching for her bow, just as I had searched for my non-existent sword in the blue stateroom. She dropped her hand again and waited.

'Well? Are you coming?' Telitha asked. She was wearing a long, black gown suitable for a funeral. It made her look severe and unfeeling.

'Where are our children?' Alexia asked.

'Safe. They are coming with us, for now.'

'Do you plan to attack my city?' Elhian asked.

'Not if you obey.'

Elhian held her gaze. 'I need to see your army leaving first.'

8
ROAD TO SEMANEZ

We watched the Jazmardian army fall back from Tiathi. Soldiers escorted us out of the castle and to the snowy forecourt. There we found three sullen servants standing in a cluster with our children. My heart gave way to relief. They appeared to be physically unharmed.

Darj scooped up Nichole, who seemed unconcerned by all that was happening and sat contentedly in her father's arms. Karlen ran clumsily to Elhian and me with tears in his eyes and Jovan on his heels. Eva cried and clung to Alexia. I wondered if she remembered being separated from her mother during the Zalem Crisis and if she were afraid of it happening again. Perhaps it would. We were at the mercy of an unpredictable queen. Alexia did her best to comfort Eva with a hug and kiss, while Elhian and I did the same for our sons.

Our work was undone when Telitha joined us. 'Put them in the carriage,' she commanded.

Surrounded by soldiers, hungry and weaponless, we did as she said. They all cried, except for Jeri, who was trying so hard to be brave. 'We'll see you soon,' Darj said to him, placing a hand on the young boy's head.

We were divided into three carriages. Presumably, Telitha had the first carriage to herself. The children were in the second—we were forbidden to travel with them in what I knew to be another ploy to make us fearful. The only comfort was that Thane was with them. While I didn't know his character fully and wasn't sure of his ability with children, I felt a little better knowing he was there to keep an eye on them.

Darj, Elhian, Alexia, and I were in the final carriage, our hands bound. The door was locked, and the windows were covered with black cloths on the outside. We had no idea where we were or what time it was.

Alexia scratched her nails over the back of her left hand. Red marks began to form until Darj reached over and covered her hands with his, the movement made awkward by their bindings.

Elhian stared at the window as if he were watching the countryside passing by. I concentrated on breathing. I was again confined in a small, dark space, and worse, heading for a cell underground.

'I thought Semanez was completely destroyed after the earthquake at the end of the Northern Invasion,' I said.

Alexia cleared her throat. 'I sent men there to survey the area afterwards, and I believe they set fire to anything that was left and that would burn. That doesn't mean there aren't ruins there or this cavern that she spoke of.'

'So, we're going to a place that is dark and underground and the home of Cades,' I said. 'Cades—the one who murdered his wife and countless other people. Or, to put it another way, where one of the evilest of men lived.'

'Thanks for the summary, Adaliah,' Darj said dryly.

'Why would Telitha take us there?' I asked.

'I don't know,' Alexia said, massaging the bridge of her nose.

'She wouldn't be trying to . . . resurrect the Zalem cult, would she?' I asked.

'How could she?' Elhian asked. 'You destroyed the Dark Orb and the Zalem's Bane.'

'Sometimes, I wonder if there was a darker power that created the orb. Anash's power.'

'Adaliah, please,' Alexia said. 'Not now.'

I opened my mouth to protest but stopped and gave Alexia an apologetic smile.

We stopped several hours later, presumably for a change of horses, but the carriages quickly lurched forward once more. We tried to pass the time with sleep, but it came uneasily. We were often jolted awake when a wheel hit a hole. Telitha had chosen some less-travelled roads, perhaps to make it difficult for us to be tracked. I hoped Reyna had found help. I hoped we were right to trust her or to place so much responsibility on her shoulders. For things to work out the way we wanted them to, we needed her to be right on our tail.

We were well and truly shaken up when the carriage stopped for a second time. The door opened, and I had to squint against the bright sunrays. I hadn't realised how much time had passed.

'You may come out one at a time,' a Jazmardian soldier said to us.

With the door open, I could hear Jovan crying somewhere outside. Nichole was also sobbing, but it was less piercing. I instinctively raised myself off the seat and moved towards the door. The Jazmardian pushed me back and yelled at me in his own tongue. Elhian shouted back behind me, but I wasn't taking in his words. When Jovan cried again, I kicked the Jazmardian right in the centre of his chest.

He fell back on the grass, winded. I stepped out of the carriage after him, but it was only a few seconds before a dozen more soldiers surrounded me with spear tips pointing at my torso. One of them shoved me against the outside of the carriage until my face pressed into the glossy wood. They cut the binds on my hands, forced my arms behind my back, and rebound me so the ropes traveled from my hands to my upper arms.

There were about forty soldiers in total. They must have been waiting for us there, as there'd only been a couple of them when Telitha first imprisoned us in the carriages.

We were in a thick cluster of trees—tall pines with little undergrowth, the sort that grew near Egra, but we hadn't travelled far enough to be near there yet.

My cheek felt hot as I was led back to the others. Thane was on his knees with his hands tied behind him, his face pale and sickly. The children were in a group to the side.

'It's all right,' I called over to Karlen and Jovan as calmly as I could. Their faces were wet with tears, and I felt ill at the thought of what might be to come.

'We will rest here for an hour or two,' Telitha said. 'There is bread. You can eat with your children, but that is all.'

I moved towards the twins, but a hand grabbed my arm. I turned towards the Jazmardian soldier with a rush of anger, but he just nodded towards Telitha.

'Not you,' she said. 'You attacked one of my soldiers. You can wait in the carriage with a slice of bread.'

I shot Elhian a panicked look. He returned one that was filled with helplessness. *No . . . No . . .* I could feel myself losing control. To be separated from my sons when they needed comfort and to be returned to a confined space was enough to drive me mad.

Why did I kick the soldier? How could I be so stupid?

With my hands in such a difficult position, I had to rely on the same Jazmardian soldier to feed me the bread. He started slowly with tiny pieces, making what sounded like lewd remarks as he pressed them into my mouth. I refused to respond or react to any of his sordid looks or touches to my leg, and he grew impatient. After I'd finished half a slice, he shoved the rest into my mouth until I was choking. Then, he left the carriage in a fit of laughter.

I had to spit some of it out in order to manage the mouthful. My eyes were watering. The soldier had left the carriage door open, and the crisp air helped to calm my senses. I narrowed my eyes at the men I could see from my door, my emotions bordering on hatred. But then something wandered into my vision that caught my interest. It was a horse. A horse that looked a lot like my Bagred. I blinked.

He couldn't really be here, could he? But I recognised his tall, strong build and the spotless, glossy, black coat. When he turned his head towards me as if sensing my gaze, his soft, brown eyes confirmed it.

They must have stolen him. He was saddled, but not with my tack. I wondered if they knew who he was and, if so, if they had any idea how obedient he was to my calls. My situation suddenly didn't feel as hopeless. I felt like I had an ally on the outside.

Later, I heard the arrival of new horses for the carriage. After that, it wasn't long before Alexia, Elhian, and Darj were pushed back into the carriage with me, and we were moving again.

'How are Karlen and Jovan?' I asked my husband as he sat next to me.

'As well as can be expected. Jovan didn't eat much.'

'Jeri or Thane will give him more later if he asks for it,' Alexia said. 'They managed to salvage what was left.'

'What are we going to do?' I asked. 'We're getting close to Dawfield, but I don't see how we can . . . '

Alexia lifted her foot and rested it on the edge of her seat.

'Perhaps you could avert your eyes,' she said to Elhian.

He did so with a blush as she pulled her dress up and began to struggle towards the dagger. Hands tied, she managed to get the knife out of its small sheath and to drop it in her lap.

'It's all right now, Elhian,' she said, lowering her leg again. She pinched the dagger between her knees and started to rub her binds against them. It was a clumsy process, but the rope soon frayed.

'Why didn't you do that before?' I asked, amazed. I'd forgotten about the knife.

'We had to be far enough away from Tiathi,' Alexia said, still running her binds up and down the blade. 'Otherwise, they could have easily turned around and ordered the Jazmardian army to attack. Now if we escape, we're near Dawfield, and we have at least a day to get to Tiathi before them or to send word.'

'When did you think of all this?'

'When Darj told me about the dagger.'

'Careful,' Darj said when the blade nicked her wrist. 'I know this road,' he told me. 'If we time our escape right, we should be able to go straight to Dawfield and meet Reyna.'

Alexia concentrated on the last bind, slowing to ensure precision. The rope gave way abruptly, and the dagger fell forward, leaving another cut on the heel of her palm. She disentangled herself from the broken cord pieces and went to work on freeing Darj.

'The carriage doors are still locked,' Elhian said.

Alexia cut the rest of our binds, and we began to discuss our plans in depth.

9
THROUGH THE BLACK WINDOW

We waited several hours for another stop, but nothing seemed to deter Telitha from her purpose.

'We'll be getting close to Dawfield,' Darj said. 'We need to take the alternative plan. It should be dark outside now.'

The alternative plan—also the riskier plan—was up to me. Alexia handed me the dagger. I took it and used the hilt to smash the window. The dark cloth prevented the glass falling outside, so the shards shattered to our feet instead. Some splinters clung to the cloth. I carefully picked them off and dropped them to the floor. We waited to see if anyone had noticed or if the carriage was slowing. It was unlikely they had heard anything over the noise of the wheels and horses, but we had to be sure.

Nothing happened. I used the dagger again to cut through the cloth, pulling it inside. The carriage filled with fresh air, and Darj was proved right. It was dark outside—so dark I knew that the moon was hiding. I couldn't see any stars, either. The night sky was filled with clouds.

The next part was the most dangerous. I slowly leaned out the window to determine where the soldiers were. I saw one following us and pulled my head back into the carriage. After a few more seconds of no response, I looked out again and was able to confirm that there was only the one soldier behind us and only one torch. We had been easy to contain thus far, so they had relaxed their watch. The rest of the soldiers must have been travelling in front. It seemed they hadn't all come with us after the last stop. I turned to examine the door and found the barricade had a lock that I couldn't open without a sophisticated pick, which we didn't have. I sat back down and relayed this information to the others.

'Do you think you can hit him?' Elhian asked, pointing at the dagger.

'No. We're travelling fast, and it's dark. Alexia should do it.'

'Throwing a dagger isn't the same as loosing an arrow,' she said.

'It requires aim and precision, both of which are your areas of expertise, not mine. We only have one opportunity to hit him, and that opportunity is safest in your hands.'

Alexia nodded. 'If I hit him, I will step back immediately so you can get into position.'

'Agreed.'

She took the dagger and put her right arm out the window, feeding the dagger between her thumb and index finger.

'We're going around a bend,' she said when she delayed. 'I can't see him.'

We waited a few more minutes until Alexia confirmed we had straightened again. Her blue eyes narrowed, measuring the speed and distance. Just when I thought she was never going to throw it, she lifted her arm and pitched the dagger into the night.

A subdued cry followed a second later.

She moved out of the way, and I put my leg through the window. I pulled my other one through and leant back against the carriage, my hands resting on the sill and my feet on the step. When I'd agreed to the plan, I didn't think the ground would be so far away and moving at such a terrible pace. How could I launch myself off?

'Go!' Darj urged quietly.

The snow by the road seemed thick, so I pushed myself towards it, trying to land on my side to avoid broken ankles or wrists. I fell into the snow and rolled a few times before coming to a stop on my back. I propped myself up and watched as the carriage drove on, the other soldiers oblivious to what had happened.

I can't believe that worked.

The sight of my loved ones rolling away reminded me to hurry. I carefully stood and patted myself down. My hip, which had taken most of the impact, was throbbing; but otherwise, I had escaped unscathed.

I ran back towards the soldier. He was already a good distance behind. My few seconds of hesitation had put some space between us.

He was still alive. Alexia's aim had landed the dagger about a finger-width below his heart, an impeccable throw under the conditions. However, it meant the dagger had pierced the skin between his ribs and damaged his lung rather than his heart. I took the dagger out and left him there. I couldn't bring myself to speed up his death, even though it was probably the kinder thing to do. I told myself it was because I had no time and concentrated on taking his sword out of its sheath instead. I found a second dagger in his shirt and took that as well.

I searched for the horse he had been riding, hoping it was Bagred, but it was a bay mare I found standing beneath a tree. Sweat had foamed around the saddle, testament to how hard she had been worked.

'I'm sorry,' I said as I swung myself up into the leather seat, sword in hand. 'I just need you to work a little bit longer!'

I dug my heels into her sides and raced to catch up with the carriage.

It was a minute before it was in sight again. The road was hard to see, but the carriage drivers each held a torch that silhouetted their figures. Each driver had a soldier sitting beside him. Three soldiers rode between the first and second carriage, and another three were between the second and third. I counted ten ahead of the first.

Twenty soldiers before Alexia felled the straggler. This would have been so much easier if they had just stopped and we had fought our way out of the carriage like the original plan.

As it was, I had to deal with the driver and soldier riding on our carriage alone and without causing the carriage to crash. They'd chosen me because I was the fastest rider and most agile when it came to climbing out the window.

I drew up behind the carriage and then along the side until I was quite near to the driver. Brief glimpses of light peeked through the trees to my left.

Dawfield. Darj's timing was perfect.

With a close and clear shot available, I threw one of the daggers at the driver. It landed in his back. He lurched forward and dropped the reins.

The soldier sitting next to him must have been asleep. The horses had already begun to slow by the time he realised what had happened. His belated reaction gave me time to circle behind the carriage and come up on his side, but now he was shouting out to the others. Instead of impaling him with my sword as planned, I let him take the reins and slow the horses down properly. I dropped back by the broken window and handed Darj's dagger back to Alexia. By then, all three carriages were slowing, and the mounted soldiers were riding my way.

'There she is!'

The inevitable call sent chills through me, and I wasn't sure if it was adrenaline or fear. I could hear thumping in the carriage and knew Elhian was kicking the door down.

Hurry up, I thought as the soldiers drew closer to me.

I kicked the mare and charged at the nearest one. I ducked his swipe and cut him low on his torso. Another raised his sword to attack me. I blocked his sword with mine, and we engaged in a few quick blows. His thick armour made me conscious of how unprotected I was. I had to rely on skill alone as I read his moves and met them with as much strength as I could gather. I pushed him off his horse, but it took a lot of my energy. I was tired and hungry.

The door of the carriage burst open behind me, and Elhian, Alexia, and Darj escaped.

'Stop them!' Telitha shouted.

Darj stabbed a soldier with his dagger and stole the man's sword. Alexia ran to the second carriage to get to Thane and the children. A mounted soldier drew back his sword to attack Elhian from above. Elhian grabbed the soldier's forearm mid-strike, wrenched him off his horse, and took the sword from him.

It didn't take long for things to change in our favour. We fought and defeated more than half the soldiers in a few minutes. Telitha called out several unfamiliar words, and three soldiers ran back to her. She'd mounted a horse and was ready to flee. One of the three soldiers moved to mount a black horse. Bagred. I brought my fingers to my mouth and let out a shrill whistle. Bagred flicked his back legs up and hit the soldier in the thighs. The man fell back to the ground, screaming.

Good boy.

Telitha jerked her reins, turning her horse away from our battle. She dug her heels into the beast's haunches and sped into the night. I left Darj and Elhian to finish the others and rode after her.

Telitha saw me over her shoulder. 'Get her!' she yelled. 'Get her sword!'

What?

One of the two soldiers accompanying her forced his horse to commit a sharp, uncomfortable turn and charged back at me. I ducked as he thrust his sword in my direction, but he wasn't aiming for me. He cut the strap of my saddle and nicked the horse at the same time. The mare let out a shrill cry and stumbled. The loose saddle slipped. Before I could catch myself, I crashed to the ground for the second time that night.

I spat out snow and only just managed to understand which way was up when the soldier appeared over the top of me. He stomped on my torso with a heavy boot.

I heard myself scream. My hand instinctively moved to cover the damage. My body felt like it was caving inwards, and I could barely breathe. Black spots appeared before my eyes. Between them, I could just distinguish that it was the soldier who had fed me the bread. Another man appeared behind him, drove a dagger into the soldier's shoulder, and pushed him out of the way.

It was Thane.

'Can you stand?' he asked, kneeling beside me.

'No,' I said with a whimper. 'My ribs are broken.'

Thane took my hand, but then he gulped and straightened. A sword point appeared through his stomach.

'No . . . ' I pressed my eyes together, trying to pretend I hadn't seen it. When I opened them, Thane was leaning to his side, white-faced and dying, the stabbed soldier's last act of revenge.

He met my eyes. 'I always loved you, you know,' he whispered, still grasping my hand. 'Even . . . when we were children.' Blood appeared at his lips. 'Tell my brother . . . I'm sorry.'

10
WOLVES

Darj, Elhian, and Alexia hurried to my side. Darj quickly took care of the offending soldier, for good this time. Elhian reached for Thane's limp wrist and felt for a pulse with his fingers, although there was really no need. Thane was covered in blood, and his eyes were opened, unblinking. Elhian shook his head. Alexia placed her hands over her nose and mouth in shock while Elhian removed the sword from Thane's back.

First the King of Jazmarda, now the King of Delya.

Tears rolled down my face. Despite his shy boyishness—or perhaps because of it—I had liked Thane a lot more than I had Hazaka. I couldn't take it in. How would Ren react? He would be king now. They had respected each other, relied on each other.

I was amazed by Thane's last words. I'd never known he'd felt that way. I was touched and embarrassed and sad.

But most of all, I was in pain.

'We have to go after them,' Darj said, his voice edged with emotion.

'Adaliah . . . ' Elhian placed a hand on my right side, gently feeling my ribs. 'Can you tell me which ones hurt the most?'

'No,' I said, more tears stinging in my eyes. 'It's all agony.'

'What about Telitha?' Darj asked. 'One of us should ride after her. She's as responsible for Thane's death as that soldier.'

'Darj, right now, we have to think of Adaliah and the children,' Alexia said. After freeing Thane, Alexia had shut the carriage door and instructed Jeri to keep the younger children safe. They remained inside.

Darj gave her a desperate look. Alexia put a hand on his arm. 'Please.'

'All right . . . ' Elhian said. 'I'll try and . . . ' He put his hand on my left side and his other arm under my knees. 'If I can pick you up, we can at least get you off the road.' He carefully began to lift me.

The movement sent another wave of searing pain through my body. 'I . . . I can't. You'll have to knock me unconscious.'

'I can't do that.'

'Your Majesties!'

I didn't recognise the young voice at first. It was strained and fearful.

'Reyna!' Elhian said.

Reyna? She did it? She found us?

'She's brought our horses,' Elhian told me, 'and there's a boy with her.'

'This is my brother, Finn,' she said, coming over to us. 'I couldn't have done this without him.'

'It-it was my pleasure to help, s-sire,' Finn said. 'We have your horses and your weapons.'

Everyone sounded like they were short of breath. I couldn't speak at all. My ribs were taking all my focus, and I was fighting to stay awake. Then, I heard something on the wind. An animal call in the distance. A howl. My heart raced again, and I couldn't take a breath.

'Was that . . . ?' Finn began.

'Wolves,' Darj said. 'They must have smelt the blood.'

Wolves did not inhabit most of Targe, but Dawfield was close to the Casmodian border. The white mountains there were home to several aggressive wolf packs. They were well-known to attack hunters, who sought them for their pelts. More than one man had died in pursuit of a sellable fur.

They howled again over the top of each other.

'We need to go,' Elhian said. 'We have to get Adaliah off the road.'

The path was littered with dead soldiers. Beyond them, I saw the first wolf stepping out of the trees and onto the roadside. His coat was a grey white, thick for the winter. He was taller and much bigger than a dog. He bared his teeth and snarled at us. Then, five or six more appeared behind him. Their feet padded the ground towards us.

'Alexia!' Darj called.

'Reyna, my bow!'

I heard the footsteps of the young girl as she hurried back to one of the horses.

'Here.' She threw the bow and quiver; Alexia caught them and flung the quiver over her shoulder. The wolves were gaining speed.

'Get in the carriage, both of you!' Elhian shouted.

Finn and Reyna ran to the carriage with the children and shut the door.

By then, the wolves were racing towards us.

'Hurry!' Darj called to Alexia.

She nocked twin arrows on her bow and loosed them. They flew through the air and landed in the sides of the foremost pair of wolves running ahead of the pack. Alexia stood just next to me as she pulled back and shot a third. They were gaining on us. Darj and Elhian stood nearby with swords raised. I shivered, imagining the size of their teeth and thinking they were about to sink into my side.

'Just stay still,' Alexia commanded.

Another arrow whirred past, and another. More sulks and whines.

'There!' Elhian pointed at another one.

Alexia was shooting as fast as she could, her face hard-set with concentration. She downed the one Elhian had indicated, but the next wolf was too close. She didn't have time to shoot it. Instead, she waited until the wolf leaped towards us, pierced its gut with an arrow directly with her hand, and flung it to the ground.

The queen loaded another arrow on her bow and turned on her heel. One last wolf had come up on the other side of us. It launched itself into the air. Alexia ducked towards the ground out of its way but twisted her upper body so she could still target it.

'Lex!' Darj called.

She loosed the arrow as the wolf soared above her. It was a shaky shot but hit its mark mid-air. The wolf yelped and fell to the ground on its side, one of its paws coming to rest on my leg.

'I need to strap up her ribs,' Elhian said as they all bent over me again.

'Here.' Alexia tore off the under-layer of her skirt and passed it to him. He ripped the material into two skinnier pieces.

'Darj,' he said. 'Can you lift her upper body?'

I felt Darj's hands under my shoulder blades. When Elhian was ready, Darj lifted me about a hand-width off the ground. I tried to muffle my pain but was feeling increasingly sick and lightheaded. Elhian wrapped the material around my body, both pieces making it around my torso twice. While the pain didn't stop, my ribs did feel more secure. Elhian tried to lift me for a second time and succeeded. My ribs couldn't move as much, and the pain was a degree or two more bearable.

'Are you all right?' he asked me.

I nodded, forced a smile, and promptly passed out.

I woke the next morning in a bed. Alexia was sitting on the edge beside me, checking the fresh and less rudimentary bandages that had been wrapped around my middle. 'How are you feeling?' she asked as I opened my eyes.

'Better. Not as queasy. Where am I?'

'In Dawfield, in the public tavern.' Alexia grinned at the unsure look on my face. Targian taverns were not known to be places of honour and morality. 'There was nowhere else, and it's quite nice, actually. Although, the people here were a bit shocked to find three sets of monarchs fighting packs of soldiers and wolves on their doorstep, I can tell you. It's certainly given them something to talk about.'

'I can imagine.' I grimaced. 'Thane . . . He saved my life and lost his own.'

Alexia covered my hand with hers, her eyes glassy. 'I know. It's awful. We've already sent a pigeon to Ren. I wish we could have told him in person. He will find out his brother is dead and he the new King of Delya all from a few words scratched into a small note.'

'Two out of five monarchs of the Rhea Lands dead within a few days of each other,' I said quietly.

'Yes,' Alexia said. We both knew it didn't bode well. We didn't need to speak the words.

Everything from my collarbone down felt like it was on fire.

'Elhian says you have two broken ribs,' Alexia said. 'Your skin is showing the bruising already. I'm afraid you won't be able to hold a sword for a week or two.'

My heart sank. I didn't want to go to war, but neither did I want to sit by and do nothing. I'd had to do that during the Zalem Crisis, and it was intolerable. But I also didn't want to be a burden to my friends. 'You should go on without me. Leave me and the children here.'

'We're not going anywhere without you.' Alexia stroked my hair. 'You just have to be careful, that's all.'

I smiled up at her, finding comfort in her touch as always. Alexia filled many roles in my life: a cousin-come-sister, a friend and confidante, a fighting companion, and sometimes even a mother. As she tucked the blankets back in around me and kissed my forehead, everything felt a little better.

'What's that on your arm?'

She had a small bandage wrapped around her elbow. 'That last wolf's claw clipped me on the way down.'

'That was some fine archery,' I said.

'At least Darj now agrees it was worth bringing my bow,' she said, and we shared a laugh.

'Has there been any sign of Telitha?' I asked.

'No. Darj took some of the local men back to the road, and they followed their trail towards the northeast. She'll come after us, but we must still travel north to find Engres and see if he does intend to fight. Then we can think about Telitha. Judging by what we found in her carriage, her intentions aren't peaceful ones.'

'What?'

'There were some notes in her carriage, drawings of the five state crowns of the Rhea Lands.'

'What? Why?'

'I thought they were symbolic of their corresponding kingdoms at first, but Darj and Elhian are convinced they indicate the actual crowns. The drawing seems to imply some sort of ritual, but it's hard to know what. She already has a tick next to Jazmarda's, Casmodia's, and Delya's crowns. I don't know how, but we think she must have taken them.'

'Elhian's crown is locked in our Treasury Room.'

'I know. And as you well know, my crown should be in my Jewel Room, where I hope it is still safe. I imagine she sent someone to get it while we were in Casmodia for the so-called Winter Council. I'm not sure how she intends to get Engres' crown, though.'

I shook my head, amazed. 'Was there anything else?'

'Yes. There was a drawing of the butterfly medallion, the medallion your father melted down to be a piece in your tree-blade. She had a question mark next to it.'

'She doesn't know what we did with it?'

'No. That's the one advantage we have, I think. I don't know what she intends to do with all of these things or what dark power she intends to call on, but if she needs the medallion to do it, we have time on our side.'

'Your crown is likely stolen by now, though.'

'My Jewel Room has a new complex lock on the door. I'm hoping that slows them down.'

I breathed deeply. 'To steal the crowns of five monarchs . . . Why does that feel so violating?'

'A crown represents many things,' Alexia said, 'particularly a monarch's divine right to lead. By stealing our crowns, she is attempting to rob us of our positions. But she obviously doesn't understand us.'

'What do you mean?'

Alexia met my eyes. 'I am more than my crown. We all are.'

I nodded.

'Besides, you and Elhian are here.' She ran her finger over the silver ring that encircled my fourth finger. 'I think it will take her a long time to figure out that you had the medallion reshaped into two wedding rings.'

11
PLANS

I lay there for an hour or so until I couldn't stand the confinement any longer. Alexia helped me down the stairs, and we found the tavern deserted, except for our family and Finn, who was brewing some sort of warm drink for us over the hearth. It was the first time I was able to get a good look at him. He was gangly, about my height, and one or two years older than his little sister. He was slouching his shoulders forward and gazing anxiously at his shoes in the same way I often saw Reyna do. His brown clothes were old and tattered and much too large for him, and he had untamed, thick, brown hair that reminded me a bit of Elhian.

Nichole was running in circles around the chair Darj was sitting on, giggling even as Darj scooped her up and brought her onto the chair with him. Alexia helped me take a seat and then sat beside her husband. Nichole sat upright on Darj's lap, swinging her legs back and forth.

'Reyna is taking care of the other children,' Darj said to me. 'The targarn cleared the room so we could talk.'

'What's . . . what's a targarn?' Finn asked.

'The elder of a small village or town,' Darj said. 'They're responsible for keeping order in a village and report to their local lord or lady. Dawfield's targarn falls under Lord Fenton of Egra's jurisdiction, along with fifteen or so others.'

'Sixteen,' Alexia said. 'Fenton has been in Liane, acting as regent in my absence, though, so a steward is caring for Egra.'

Elhian appeared in the doorway and shook some dirt off his boots before taking a seat beside me.

'Where have you been?' I asked.

He intertwined his fingers with mine. 'Talking to Reyna. She said the Jazmardian soldiers turned east, away from Tiathi. It must be so they can meet Telitha near Semanez.'

'Th-that's right,' Finn said with a nod, handing Elhian a mug. I wondered if he'd always had a stutter or if it was just our presence that made him uneasy.

'The point is Tiathi is safe for now,' Elhian said. 'Alexia?'

'Hmm?'

'What do you know about King Engres?'

'Not a lot,' she said. 'I haven't seen him since I was a child, when Mother was still alive. He was visiting the palace for something.'

'What do you remember?' I asked.

'Just that he seemed old, even then, but I think when you're young, everyone seems old. He was a gentle sort of man, the sort one wouldn't mind having as a grandfather.'

'So, he didn't come across as a tyrant,' Elhian said.

'Not at all, but I was only six at the time. Who am I to say what sort of man he has become since?'

We pondered this quietly.

'I can't believe . . . ' I said. 'I can't believe Hazaka is gone, just like that.' After all that had happened, I hadn't had a chance to feel the weight of his death. 'And Thane.'

'And Thane,' Alexia echoed quietly, sadly.

'I guess now we'll never know what Hazaka was trying to achieve by reinstating the concordat,' Elhian said.

'Whatever it was, he thought it was worth his life,' Alexia said. 'I never thought Hazaka would sacrifice that for anything.'

'Unless Telitha and her friends acted for another reason,' I said.

'But she burned his paperwork,' Alexia said, 'and seemed to enjoy the fire.'

Silence fell over us again. I realised that despite the pain in my ribs, it felt good to be back in control of our situation. We may not have had all the answers, but at least we had our freedom.

I turned to Darj, who was rubbing his chin with his brows furrowed, deep in thought. 'Well, General? I'm sure you've already formulated a plan, so you may as well tell us what it is.'

He gave me a half-hearted smile. 'I think I do know what needs to be done, but I haven't figured out how to manage it yet.'

'Tell us,' Elhian said.

'Someone must return to Liane to get Alexia's crown before they do. Someone must go into the north of Casmodia to find out exactly what Engres is doing and to try and talk him out of an invasion peacefully. And someone needs to take the children to safety. Then there's Thane. We . . . we have to decide whether we will bury him here or . . . ' He held his daughter a little closer.

'You're not going to leave us, are you, Mother?' a small voice asked. Eva peeked around the door before rushing to Alexia.

Alexia pulled her into her lap and kissed the top of her head. 'All will be well, my darling.'

'I don't like the idea of us splitting up, either,' I said.

'I know,' Darj said, 'but I don't know how we can find the time to accomplish all the tasks together. I sent word to Captain Hawl to send us two hundred soldiers to travel with us to Casmodia. They should be here tomorrow. Our northern army is also gathering.'

Captain Hawl had replaced our friend, Raggin, as captain of Chettona, the nearest town with a barracks. Dawfield only had a few guards, and soldiers from Egra would take too long to arrive.

'Captain Xander,' Alexia said with a sudden thought. 'Where is he?'

Darj raised his eyebrows. 'Of course . . . He was transporting new recruits to Chettona for training and picking up horses to take back to Hunt.'

'We must send word immediately and ask Xander to come and see us with Hawl's soldiers,' Alexia said.

'Why?' Elhian asked.

'I know what they're thinking,' I said. 'Xander is a trusted friend. We can ask him to take the children to Liane and to check on Alexia's crown. Am I right?'

Alexia and Darj nodded.

'And we can travel north to face Engres,' Elhian surmised. 'But Alexia, Darj, you don't have to do this. War is not at Targe's door yet.'

'The King of Delya died on my soil,' Alexia said. 'War has already reached us, and Telitha has indicated her intent to dethrone us all. If we have to face her, better we do it together.'

12
BENEATH THE STARS

When I woke the next morning, it was to the sound of a happy and loud group of people coming towards the tavern. I pulled a pillow over my head. Elhian muttered something in his sleep and rolled over.

'Darj! Darj!'

I recognised the trill voice at once. It was Darj's tumultuous sister. I'd forgotten he'd sent a message telling her to meet us in Dawfield. It started to make sense the more I woke up—the mob outside were her children.

They erupted into the tavern, all of them calling out Darj's name. The pillow did nothing to help, so I relented and got up. Elhian could sleep through a military parade marching through the bedroom when he was tired, so he didn't stir as I staggered out of bed and muffled my sounds of pain. I braced my ribs with my arm. Forgetting to change out of my bedclothes, I carefully made my way down the stairs.

'Oh Darj, Darj,' Rosana was saying as I reached the last step. She flung her arms around him. 'When that little girl found us and said you'd been kidnapped—I didn't know what to do!'

'I'm fine,' Darj said, prying himself from her grip. 'Please. Two kings of the Rhea Lands have been assassinated. My wife could be next.'

Rosana was shocked into silence for at least a second. 'Your letter said you wanted information,' she said. 'What can I do to help? What do you need?'

'Sit down,' Darj said, pointing at a chair.

'I'll take the children for a walk,' Franc said with a knowing wink my way. 'Come on, children; let's go.'

'No, you must stay,' Rosana said. 'Tomek, you take them.'

'But I want to listen,' Tomek said.

'You're too young,' Rosana said, pinching his cheek.

'Uncle Darj was already being trained in the army at my age!'

'Go and take your siblings for a walk,' Rosana said firmly. 'Franc, sit here.' She gestured to the seat next to her.

It took a bit of time to wake Elhian and for Darj to find Alexia, who had been outside giving Jeri and Eva a ride on Hazel. Rosana bobbed up and down in her unsure manner when she came into the queen's presence again, but Darj eventually asked her the same question Elhian had asked Alexia: 'What do you know about King Engres?'

'Oh, King Engres,' Rosana said gravely. Franc nodded very seriously. 'He is a good man, I think. Everyone thinks he's a good man ... But ...'

'Since his wife died ...' Franc said.

'Yes, since Queen Isabella died,' Rosana said, 'he seems to have lost touch with the people, and yet the Islanders never say so because they don't wish to hurry his son to the throne.'

'Do you mean Prince Garrow?' Elhian asked. 'I've heard of him but know little about him.'

'As do most people,' Rosana said. 'He's seen about town with a different woman every week and is known to get into fights with ruffians and ... Well, other men his age adore him, want to be him, but most think he is a rogue.'

'A rogue!' Franc said with an authoritative nod of the head.

'Do you have any idea why Engres would want to invade Casmodia?' Darj asked.

Rosana laughed. 'King Engres? Invade Casmodia? He wouldn't have the nerve!'

'He is in the north of my kingdom as we speak,' Elhian said.

Rosana's laugh subsided, and Franc's expression was one of utter confusion. 'Oh, oh that can't be anything to do with King Engres,' Rosana said, recovering quickly and waving her hand dismissively. 'It just can't be. That must be about Prince Garrow and whatever it is between him and Telitha, King Hazaka's wife.'

All four of us sat up a little straighter at this. 'What do you mean?' Alexia asked.

Rosana moved to the edge of her seat, flattered by the queen's interest and attempting to make the most of it. 'Telitha has been visiting often, very often,' she said in the manner of a practiced gossiper. 'It is well-known amongst the Islanders. She is so different from them. She has beautiful, dark skin—'

'Beautiful,' Franc said.

'—and dark brown eyes. The Islanders are all fair with green eyes, so she's very noticeable. She parades around town with Prince Garrow. I tell you, they are on very close terms.'

My thoughts returned to the conversation we heard between Hazaka and Telitha in our castle, each accusing the other of infidelity.

'Were her children with her?' I asked. It didn't have much to do with anything—only my judgement of her character.

'No, we never saw them, did we, Franc?'

'Not at all, dear. That would have been talked of, too.'

Darj had been processing the information in intense silence and now stood up. 'I advise you to find somewhere safe to stay until all this passes over.'

'We would like to help,' Rosana said. 'What can we do? We could be ambassadors to King Engres if you wish. I will tell him I'm related to the Queen of Targe and ask him to leave Casmodia.'

I lowered my head to hide my smile. I could imagine King Engres responding to such a request, if only to escape being harassed.

'I think we will travel on to Egra,' Franc said.

'Egra, dear?' Rosana asked.

'I have never been there, and you have often told me about the beautiful lake. It is safe, is it not?' Franc asked us.

'As far as we know,' Alexia said.

'And it would be too hard to travel back to the White Isles in the snow now, anyway,' Franc said, for once stopping his wife from speaking. 'The children will love the holiday. We must leave tomorrow.' He stood and went outside, presumably to share the news with Tomek and his siblings.

I had never fully appreciated the price Alexia had paid when she'd left Eva behind in Delya during the Zalem Crisis until I had to say goodbye to my own sons two days later. Darj's whirlwind sister and her family had left for Egra as Franc had suggested, and now my emotions swirled like clouds into a storm as we sent our family to safety, too. I could distinguish guilt most of all, followed closely by fear, but somehow I kept both quiet through the self-denial that is required whenever one human being loves another. I spoke to Karlen and Jovan cheerfully to shelter them from my storm, as if they were going on a pleasant journey and would be back on my lap before the day was out. They chattered and cooed while I blinked away the threat of tears. Elhian picked them up and conveyed them to the carriage that Xander was to take them home in.

Home.

Liane had been my home once, but it wasn't anymore. Even now, I had to keep reminding myself of that.

'I am trusting you to be kind to your sisters,' Alexia said to Jeri. She was kneeling before him, cupping his face with her hands. 'Can you do that?'

'Yes, Mother.' There were tears in his voice, but none had fallen.

Alexia enveloped him into her arms. 'You know Captain Xander. He is our friend. He will look after you, and we will return as soon as we can.'

Darj had already settled Nichole into the carriage, and she was babbling to Jovan and Karlen with her sweet, little smile. The three of them seemed as content as they could be. They didn't know how long we were going to be away. Neither did we.

I had asked Reyna to go with them. The boys knew her, and that would make it easier for them. She was as reluctant as the children and had asked if Finn could accompany her instead of going back to Tiathi, which we granted. As Jeri sat beside Jovan, there was only one other seat left, and it was set apart for a princess.

Alexia called for her eldest daughter, but the little girl ran to me to try and hide behind my dress. I wanted to pick her up, but my ribs were throbbing just from the strain of holding my torso upright.

'Eva,' Alexia called again, coming towards us.

'No!' The princess started sobbing loudly. 'Don't leave me, Mother. Don't make me go!'

Her expression didn't change, but the colour fell from Alexia's face. 'It's only for a short time, I promise.'

'Eva, darling,' I said, 'you must do as your mother says.'

'No. No!' Eva gripped the hem of my dress, her knuckles turning white.

Alexia picked her up, and Eva cried into her shoulder. When it came to setting her inside the carriage, Eva rigidly wrapped her legs around Alexia's middle and her arms around her neck. Darj gently pried her off and sat her down next to Nichole.

'I hate you,' Eva yelled back at Alexia. 'I hate you!'

'Do not speak to your mother like that!' Darj said.

Eva's tears became silent ones. She looked sullenly at the carriage floor. Darj whispered something to her and squeezed her hand, but she pulled away.

'We will see you soon, Eva,' Alexia said. 'I promise.'

It seemed to me that Captain Xander was the same as always: steady and reliable. His shoulder-length hair was tied up out of the way. He had ridden almost without stopping after receiving our request for help and had arrived half a day before the two hundred soldiers. We had decided that a hundred of them would travel with him and the children to Liane Palace, keeping them under close guard until we could reunite with them. The other hundred would travel with us into the frozen north.

'We will be at the palace in five days,' Xander said. 'Four, if we don't have bad weather. The roads between here and Chettona are still in good condition despite the recent rains, but I think it is already snowing in Liane. We will stay in a village every night for extra protection.' He was speaking to Alexia and me but receiving little response. 'I will take care of them,' he said, more softly this time, 'as if they were my own.'

'I know,' I said.

Even now, after more than two years, it didn't seem right to see Xander without Raggin. It was like Karlen playing without Jovan, or mountaintops standing without snow, or Alexia's bow being bent back without an arrow. I wondered what he laughed at now that he didn't have Raggin to entertain him.

'Send word to us in Crisock when you arrive in Liane,' I said. 'We will be there in a few days, if the valleys are not impassable.'

'Let me know if you find my crown,' Alexia said, 'and make sure Fenton has every guard at his post until he hears from me.'

'Of course, Your Majesty. Now, with all due respect, I think I should leave before the children become distressed.'

'Thank you,' Alexia said.

'Be careful,' I added compulsively.

Darj joined us as fifty guards rode off in front of the carriage, the others following from behind.

As soon as they were gone, Alexia wrapped her arms around me, the storms within now raining on our cheeks.

We buried Thane in the small graveyard at Dawfield. It was too far for him to be returned to Delya and remain in any sort of honourable condition. That the King of Delya had come to lie in the ground of a small, insignificant village in a kingdom foreign to his own was a sadness that we all felt. There was no regal procession, no Delyan myrrh or anyone to bury him according to the Delyan customs that we knew so little about. Thane had no family members to farewell him—just us and the people of Dawfield. We lit a bowl of oil on a pile of stones in the Targian way, and I spoke about how he had saved my life. It was like someone else was speaking it, as if I were separate from myself, in the way the mind does sometimes to cope. I hadn't told anyone, not even Elhian, what the king had said before he died—that he had cared for me. It seemed too private to share.

Somehow, the people left, the moon rose, and I found myself standing alone at the grave of someone who had died for me.

'Adaliah,' Elhian called, appearing behind me. He gently wrapped an arm around my waist, careful of my ribs.

'There's one thing I know the Delyans do when they're sad,' I said, leaning back against him. 'One thing they do when they're faced with death.'

'What's that?'

'They dance.'

After a pause, Elhian held his hand out to me, and we danced beneath the stars, hoping that good King Thane could see us honouring him from above.

13
QUEENS AT WAR

By the time we stopped to make camp for the second night on the road, now back in Casmodia, I knew we were being watched. I had seen nothing but shadows against a white forest, shapes and movements that could have had a thousand meanings, but for me, there was only one. We were not alone.

'It has to be Telitha,' Alexia said as we discussed it around our campfire. The soldiers had settled across the clearing and were tending to their horses and to their ale.

'Of course,' I said.

'She should stop slinking in the shadows and come out and face us,' Alexia said. She'd been on edge ever since her parting with Eva.

Darj, who was filleting a fish for us, smiled. 'Not every woman is as indomitable as you.'

'Do you think she will go after the children?' Alexia asked with less fierceness in her voice.

'I don't think she was that interested in them,' Elhian said. 'My impression was that they are more of an irritation to her than anything.'

'He's right,' Darj said. 'It's us she wants.'

The next evening, I followed Alexia to a shallow but wide creek, not yet frozen. She crouched and pulled back the loaded arrow in her bow. I lowered myself behind her. She breathed in, ready to loose the shot at an elk standing in the water ahead of us. The fletching was touching her cheek.

'Just . . . a . . . moment . . . ' she said, waiting for the elk to turn.

It lifted its head, droplets of water clinging to his furry chin. Just as it turned the way Alexia wanted, a man stepped out of the reeds on the other side of the creek and threw a dagger at it. The blade landed in its neck. The elk fell into the creek with a short cry, its blood quickly streaming into the water.

Darj moved to retrieve his dagger.

'Darj!' Alexia called, vexed. The two of us crossed the water.

'You were taking too long,' he said.

'I could have shot you!'

'You were aiming at the elk, not me.'

'And I would have got him, thank you very much.' She poked him with her arrow, and he laughed.

'You can have the next one,' he said. 'Come on.'

Alexia shot her arrow. Darj let out a cry of protest as it flew past his shoulder. I thought she was teasing Darj, but it hit something behind him, something that emitted a groan. A splash of water followed.

Alexia didn't move. Her face was white.

I stepped forward to find her fallen prey. It was a man, a Jazmardian. He had been carrying a sword, but it was lying beside him now, unsoiled. He was wearing a Jazmardian red shirt and leather pants, both of which revealed how underfed he was. Apart from the arrow that protruded from his now-unmoving chest, there was nothing notable about him.

'A scout,' Darj said, glancing back at his wife. 'Alexia?'

He stroked her cheek, but it was like she was looking through him. It was the first time I'd seen that particular sort of numbness in her. She was wincing as if a whole army were standing before her, intent on ending her life. It worried me. What if we did go back to battle? Would she be able to cope? Would I? Would we always bear the scars of war?

There must be more hope for our future than that, I said not only to myself but, glancing upwards, to Ru'ach as well.

We rode on through snow-covered pine forests and to the foot of the Casmodian Mountains, often lost in our thoughts as the sun rose and set in a rhythm that failed to bring comfort. I wanted more time to understand Telitha's motives and intentions before we had to face her again, but I was also impatient to get to Crisock in anticipation of the pigeon Xander would send confirming the children had made it safely to Liane. The further north we rode, the greater distance there was between us.

Why didn't I go with them?

I sighed. It was impossible to repair the torn loyalties within.

I knew Alexia was thinking of them, too. Every now and then, she and I would share a glance, silently asking each other if they would be all right. One of us would find the strength to smile, and in that way, we kept reassuring each other without speaking a word.

When we were about a day from Crisock, we reached a small valley swollen with trees and snow. A brook had carved its way along the valley's lowest crease, and it was frozen. Hills gently rolled beyond the valley, shading us from the already-frail sun. A breeze strewed snow through the trees. It dampened our cloaks and slowed our horses. The soldiers who rode before and behind us thinned into a single line as the path narrowed between rocky rises rapidly growing in height. Darj looked around like a hunting dog, sniffing the air for its prey. His hand lingered by his sword, and he rode ever closer to Alexia. I drew near to Elhian, slowly drawing out my sword and laying it across my lap. I scoured the trees for any sign of our enemies. There was none, but we continued on high alert for an hour or two more. The sun was tracking towards noon, and I was just beginning to think that the Jazmardians must not have come through this way when the soldier in front made a sudden call for us to halt.

There were several thuds and clinks of metal against metal. Some of the men fell from their horses and into the snow, arrows protruding from their bodies.

Alexia unslung her bow and shot a Jazmardian archer in a nearby pine tree.

'Find cover!' Darj shouted at the soldiers. With the path too narrow to hurry past the horses and bodies, they dismounted and ducked behind trees and rocks instead.

Telitha darted between two trees, shooting an angry look my way as she made the pass.

'Adaliah!' Elhian was already crouching by a rock.

I slipped down from Bagred. Elhian ran forward to slay a soldier he'd seen behind one of the trees. I spotted another. I forgot about my injury and lifted my sword too quickly. A sharp pain filled my side, and I let out an involuntary cry. The Jazmardian heard the sound and ran at me with a raised sword. I forced myself to hold mine up, but as soon as he brought his blade down against it, I crumpled to the ground. With two broken ribs not yet properly healed, I was no more a warrior than a dove.

'Elhian!' I called. He saw my predicament and threw his sword. It hit my attacker squarely in the chest.

He ran over and stretched out his hand. 'Can you walk?'

I took his hand, and he pulled me up. He kicked down an approaching soldier. The Jazmardian fell by my other side. I realised how cold, hungry, and tired he seemed—not nearly as well-nourished and armoured as the Targian men.

Elhian retrieved his sword and disappeared back into the fighting men. An enemy soldier ran at me from the side. Planting my feet firmly on the ground, I held up my sword at the last moment so that he ran straight into it. Nearby, Alexia loosed several more shots before another volley of arrows rained down on us. More Targian soldiers fell, but I noticed that no arrows landed in the ground near the four of us.

I heard someone coming up behind me. I turned and raised my bloodied sword with a grimace, coming face to face with Telitha herself.

She had a dagger in her hand, which she raised to shoulder height. 'Tell me quickly—where is the Armoured Butterfly? Where did it go after you broke the orb?'

I frowned. That was not a question I had expected. Sweat was beading on my forehead, the pain of my ribs only just bearable. It was not a secret that the butterfly had touched each of our shoulders before disappearing from us forever, but I was not about to offer an answer.

Gritting my teeth, I flicked my sword to disarm her of the dagger. It fell and disappeared into the snow. I kicked her in the side. It had the desired effect of pushing her away from the dagger and into the snow, even wounding her, but I had to suffocate another cry as I wrapped an arm around my middle.

'We will break the butterfly,' Telitha hissed at me from the ground. 'We will break you!'

'Who do you think you are? It's not like you or your Zalems have had any success against us so far!'

Telitha jumped up from the ground and pounced towards me like a cat. Her hands wrapped around my throat. I fell backward, and she came with me into the snow again. I kneed her in the stomach, but Telitha didn't let go. Her eyes were large and wild. I struck my hands down onto her forearms as hard as I could. Her grip weakened. I pushed her off me, picked up my sword, and while she lay on her back in the snow, pointed it at her throat.

'What do you mean, "break" me?'

'You think because you have had victory, you will always have victory. You think that by cleansing the swords and destroying the Dark Orb, you have ended the Zalems. But you have only made us stronger. Your husband killed my father in the Northern Invasion, but it has not stopped me.'

I had no idea who Telitha's father was, and I didn't care. The Jazmardians who joined Cades in that war had fought against us at their own peril.

'But that is like chopping off branches of a tree and expecting it to die,' she said. 'The branches grow back stronger. We are stronger. You have not even come close to the root of the Zalems.'

'I will hack the roots until it is as if the tree never lived.'

Telitha raised her hand to slap me across the face. I grabbed her wrist mid-strike and twisted it slightly.

Telitha grimaced but saw something behind me that made her smile. 'Zarow!' she shouted, the Jazmardian word for 'stop' sounding particularly harsh amongst the white surroundings. She wasn't talking to her men, but the Targians. 'Zarow!'

Her soldiers had encircled us with loaded crossbows.

'Let me go, or your friends will die,' Telitha said.

I glared at her but released her wrist. Telitha crawled backwards before scrambling to her feet and running to her men.

'Surrender!' Darj called to ours. 'Surrender sharply!'

The remaining Targian soldiers, about fifty of them, obediently thrust their swords into the earth and kneeled behind them, a traditional Targian surrender. Alexia alone did not lower her weapon. Her bow was arched back with an arrow firmly nocked in place, and it was aimed at Telitha.

'Put down the bow, Your Majesty,' Telitha said.

Alexia didn't move.

'Ru'ach, protect us,' a soldier said.

Telitha gritted her teeth with more and more displeasure the longer Alexia delayed. Telitha gestured to some of her men. They moved towards us, crunching the snow with each step. One of them put a sword point in my back. I raised my hands, biting my lip as my ribs ached. I refused to give them the satisfaction of making a sound.

'Call off your men,' Alexia said to Telitha, 'or I will shoot you.'

'If that arrow leaves your bow, my soldier will kill the A'zyon Warrior!'

The soldier dug the sword further into my skin, drawing blood. Still, I was silent.

'Call them off!' Alexia yelled.

'You are assuming you will hit your target.'

Her eyes hardened. 'I don't miss.'

I could feel the sword point pressing into my spine. I knew the soldier would never kill me—not now with Elhian standing right beside me—but I kept looking towards my surrendered sword, wishing I could retrieve it.

'I saw you underestimate Adaliah,' Alexia said. 'Only a fool makes the same mistake twice.'

Telitha groaned and waved her hand, muttering a few more words of Jazmardian. Her men lowered their bows.

'Now!' Alexia yelled.

The Targian soldiers stood and threw daggers at Telitha's men. They cut through the air and downed almost all of the Jazmardians at once.

Telitha screamed as her men cried out and died, leaving her with only four. 'Grab her!' she yelled, pointing at me. But Elhian had already slashed the soldier's sword away from my back and pushed him into the mud.

'Surrender!' Darj called again. He didn't mean the Targians this time.

Telitha snarled at him and then at me. 'Your head will one day hang from Iza Tar. I will hack it off myself!'

Iza Tar was a well-known bridge in Etarbelec where the Jazmardians strung up various body parts of their defeated enemies.

'Enough!' Alexia said.

She loosed her arrow at Telitha, just as something hit the side of my head.

14
INTO CRISOCK

When I woke up, I couldn't quite remember if I had really seen the Queen of Targe shoot an arrow at the Queen of Jazmarda in the middle of a Casmodian forest or not.

I opened my eyes and found all three of my friends leaning over me.

'You really need to stop doing this to us,' Darj said weakly.

'What happened?' I tilted my head towards Alexia. 'Did you kill Telitha?'

'She missed,' Darj said.

'Missed?' Somehow the thought of Alexia missing a target concerned me more than the death of the Jazmardian queen.

'I did *not* miss,' Alexia said, rolling her eyes at Darj. 'One of her soldiers stepped in front and died in her place. She got away with the last three.'

'But not before one of them threw a rock at your head,' Elhian said, cupping my face with his hand.

The mention of my head made me aware of the dull ache I could feel throbbing there.

'How did the Targians know to throw the knives?' Elhian asked.

'Surrender sharply,' I said, rolling onto my side before pushing myself up into a sitting position. Every part of me hurt, and I had a strong desire to go to sleep.

'Yes,' Darj said. 'It means give up your swords but take out your knives.'

'Oh,' Elhian said. 'Cleverly done. But I'm really getting the impression Telitha doesn't want us to reach Engres.'

'She seems particularly eager to kill Adaliah,' Alexia said, 'which I find concerning.'

'It worries me a little, too,' I said. Elhian helped me to my feet. I bent over, my head spinning as my body adjusted to the new position.

'We need to keep going,' Darj said.

'What if Telitha has more men waiting for us?' I asked.

The prince-general ran his teeth over his bottom lip. 'Let's just face that when we have to.'

The interchange with Telitha had cost us more than half our men. The forty-two soldiers who had survived buried their friends in the small valley. The only solace—if it could be called that—was that we had caused the Jazmardians more damage than they had us. More than a hundred of them lay dead and covered in a thin blanket of snow by the frozen brook.

How did this happen? How is it that we are at war with the Jazmardians?

'I shot at her,' Alexia said to me as we rode out of the valley towards the plains. She sounded shocked by her own actions.

'Why wouldn't you have?' I asked. 'She is our foremost enemy.'

'Yes, and I guess I thought it was the quickest way to end this, to get back to our children and with less bloodshed overall. But she is the mother of three small, fatherless boys, one of whom is the heir to the Jazmardian throne. I shouldn't have cast that aside so easily.'

'She killed half of our soldiers, all of whom are sons, husbands, and fathers,' I said. 'She personally threatened both of us. You were protecting your loved ones.'

'Yes.' She took a deep breath. 'You're right.'

'And she may still die in the end, by one of our hands.'

Alexia nodded. 'Until then, may she choose a different path.'

We came to Crisock and left the soldiers a short ride outside the town with instructions to set up camp, while the four of us rode into the village in search of Xander's pigeon.

The village of Crisock, only two days' ride north of Tiathi, had benefited from Tiathi's growth. New houses had been built, and there were more shops in the main street than there had been at my last visit—plenty of fish stalls stocked from the local river and farmers selling sacks of wheat, barley, corn, and lentils from the autumn harvest. Livestock—including goats, sheep, chickens, and the occasional dairy cow—added to the general noise of the chattering people. I could smell fresh bread from a bakery and hear a brewer encouraging a group of young men to come and sample his ales. Beyond the food, there were finer products normally only found in larger cities—linen, silk, and even jewellery—all on display at stalls.

We arrived in the middle of the day. 'Make way for the king!' a guard called as we passed him on the main street. The people had not noticed us up until then, or at least had not stopped long enough to recognise who we were. They now turned towards us with curiosity. 'Make way!' the guard called again.

They moved towards the sides of the street, now rapidly clearing our path as their surprise and chatter increased. They bowed and curtsied as we passed.

Elhian rode a horse-length ahead of Alexia, Darj, and me, leading us to the church where the priest maintained the local pigeon coop. We dismounted, and another guard took our horses' reins for us.

'I will deliver them to the blacksmith,' he said. 'He will give them some oats and check their shoes for you.'

'Thank you,' Elhian said.

Darj had already knocked on the arched church door. It moved forward of its own accord, unlocked. We followed him into the nave.

'Forgive me. Forgive me for not being at the door, Your Majesties,' the priest said, rushing towards us from a side room. He was a skinny man, and like most religious servants in the Casmodian kingdom, he wore a simple blue cloak and a pewter pendant around his neck—a small circle with two shepherd crooks in the middle, forming a rough heart shape. The symbol served as a reminder of the most protective and loving Ru'ach and was a common find in the Casmodian church.

He bowed before us. 'I am called Merek. I believe you have come for your pigeon, or rather the note it brought.'

'It arrived, then?' Alexia asked.

'Yes, indeed. It came yesterday with a note bearing the Targian royal seal. I assumed it meant a royal visit shortly. I will get it for you now, of course I will.' He hurried back into his private room. 'I won't be a minute,' he called back to us. 'It was right—ah, here it is!' He reappeared with the small note in hand.

'May I have it?' Darj asked.

'Of course, Your Majesty.' He offered the tiny scroll to Darj.

'I'm only a "highness",' Darj said as his thick thumbs fumbled with the seal.

Merek blushed. 'Of course, of course, I'm so sorry.'

Darj unraveled the parchment and scanned Xander's handwriting. 'The children are safe in Liane Palace,' he said, and Alexia gave a sigh of relief. My own tension dissolved with a laugh, but Darj's smile faded as he read on. 'The Zalems . . . ' He swallowed. 'They have the Targian crown.'

15
THE FLETCHER

Merek left with a promise to get us some food, leaving Alexia, Darj, Elhian, and me to speak privately in his room.

'How . . . how could they have taken my crown?' Alexia asked. We sat at a modest round table, which Merek had rushed to clear of his books and writings. They were now in a clumsy pile on the stone floor.

'I don't know,' Darj said. 'Whoever is behind this either has contacts in the palace or is very clever. What I am most concerned about is what they intend to do with the crowns. We have to meet with Engres and devise a plan to get the crowns back. Elhian, how do we get to Naldo from here?'

Merek had left us with a little but detailed map.

'It's a steep climb from Crisock,' Elhian said, pointing to some mountains. 'The path winds back and forth along the cliffside to the northeast because the snow on the flats is too deep to take horses through. I have heard about another way—still along the mountainside and a less direct route, but a smoother and flatter road, so quicker overall.' He tapped the map at Naldo. 'I haven't travelled it myself.'

'Could we talk to someone who lived in Naldo?' I asked.

'Yes,' Alexia said. 'There must be someone here.'

Merek returned with a tray of nuts and bread and placed it on the table in front of us.

'Merek, are you aware of any one in town who used to live in Naldo?' Darj asked.

'Indeed, I am. There are several, in fact, but only one whose exact whereabouts I know of right now. His name is Wolfgar Sky, and he works at a trade I'm sure you will appreciate, Your Majesty.' Alexia gave him a blank look. 'I mean, he is the town's blacksmith but also a fletcher. A fine craftsman of arrows but a terrible archer. He couldn't hit a wall three steps in front of him.'

'Truly?' Alexia asked with a soft laugh.

'Indeed, but don't tell him I said so. Now, as it is the midday hour, he will be lingering by the well hoping to come across his sweetheart, Josselyn, who comes into town from her father's mill the same time each day. I'll get him for you; of course I will.'

'I think we can afford to let him meet his love first,' Elhian said. 'I don't know about my friends here, but I am starving. Let's eat.'

Merek must not have told Wolfgar whom he would be meeting. The spit that flew out of the middle-aged man's mouth when he walked into the small church room suggested he had no prior warning. He attempted to bow, lost his footing, and ungraciously fell to his knees.

'Come, Wolfgar,' Darj said lightly. 'We need help, not obsequiousness.'

'I don't know what that word means, sire, but I am more than happy to help.' He stood. He was not as tall as Merek, but he was thickset with strong arms formed from years of smithing. He carried with him the distinctive smell of coal dust and molten iron, his arms and face blackened from the work he breathed. His umber eyes, glistening from his recent shock, seemed to be the only clean and bright thing about his otherwise dusty and smudged appearance.

'Sit here.' Darj pointed to the chair we had found for him. Merek stood by the door while Darj waved his hand over the small map. 'What paths are there to Naldo?'

'Naldo? Why do you want to go there? The snow will be heavy and thick now.'

'Let's just say we must get there and in a hurry,' Elhian said. 'Is there more than one way?'

'There are many ways if you know them. But I can't take you.'

'I just want you to point them out on the map,' Elhian said.

Wolfgar chewed on his lip. 'Could I be so bold as to ask for something in return, Your Majesty?' he asked Alexia.

'The Queen of Targe is not here to barter with a fletcher,' Darj said before Alexia could answer. The queen raised an eyebrow at her husband.

'I will give you the directions you want,' Wolfgar said, holding up his palms, 'and ask the priest here to pray for your safe passage. I simply wondered if Her Majesty would do me the honour of testing some of my arrows. I have designed some with the purpose of better penetrating armour.'

'How so?' Alexia asked.

'I wanted to create an arrowhead that can penetrate plate armour without being so heavy that it flies poorly or requires dangerous proximity to the enemy.'

'Were you able to do so?' Alexia leant forward in her chair.

'Yes.' Wolfgar face lit up in the way many artists' do when speaking about their work. 'I drafted the design and now I've created it—a long, dagger-like arrowhead that is refined and strong. I think it works, but I am not a good archer. If the Dauntless Archer could test them and they prove effective, I could go into production and equip soldiers with arrows that don't require them to aim at small, vulnerable parts of the body not always covered by armour, like necks and armpits. They could aim directly at the heart and expect to wound them.'

'The Dauntless Archer?' Alexia asked with a small smile.

'Forgive me,' Wolfgar said, red spots appearing in his cheeks. 'That's the name I've heard you called by sometimes amongst the soldiers. Your skill with the bow is well-known beyond your kingdom.'

Alexia turned to the rest of us. 'Do we have time for me to try these arrows? Please?'

Wolfgar led the four of us to a stone courtyard behind his workshop, where our horses stood with their noses buried in a pile of hay.

'They didn't tell me whose horses they are,' Wolfgar said despairingly. 'Only one of them needed a new shoe—the black one.'

'Bagred.' I patted my treasured horse as we passed.

'I've already fixed it. He was a good patient.'

Wolfgar handed Alexia five of his arrows and directed her to an old set of armour tied up like a scarecrow at the other end of the courtyard. Darj and Elhian were also provided with one, which they examined with prolonged male attention.

'What interested you in developing these arrows?' I asked Wolfgar.

'My brother was an archer. He fought and died in the Northern Invasion. I saw how it happened: a soldier ran at him with a drawn sword. My brother shot at him, but the arrowhead was too weak. It grazed the soldier's breastplate, and my brother was killed.'

'I'm sorry to hear that,' I said, 'but it's a fine thing to use such a tragedy for a greater good. If these arrows work, you may save others from dying as your brother did.'

'That is my hope exactly.'

Alexia loaded an arrow onto her bow, drew back the string, and released. The arrow sped through the air and split effortlessly through the iron helmet of the scarecrow, straight between the eyes, as it were.

'Nice shot,' I said.

'Brilliant!' Wolfgar said.

'They are heavier than my usual arrows,' Alexia said, 'but it is barely noticeable.' She shot another one. It pierced the breastplate at the heart. 'Only a slight correction of aim is needed.'

Wolfgar ran to pick up an old shield that was leaning against the back wall. 'See if you can hit this at a height, to see how the arrows curve upwards.'

Without warning, Wolfgar threw the shield up into the air and stepped back to avoid being hit by it. Alexia loaded and shot another arrow, an excited glint in her eyes. The arrowhead pierced the shield mid-air and came down with a clunk. We clapped.

'You have designed a flawless arrowhead,' Alexia said with an air of amazement. 'Their production will reform archery.'

'It would be helpful to have a blacksmith and fletcher accompany us,' Darj said. 'Are you sure you're not willing to travel with us?'

Wolfgar picked up the shield and took out the arrow. 'Naldo is not a safe place,' he said at length, 'and I fear for those who would travel there.'

'Why?' I asked, glancing at Elhian. 'What do you know about it that we don't?'

He downturned his eyes. 'I dreamt about Naldo—about a royal death.'

'Your Majesties,' Merek said, bursting into the courtyard and startling Bagred, who snorted towards him. 'King Elhian, refugees. You must come and see them.'

The four of us hurried back into Crisock's main street, Wolfgar following. The sight that had panicked Merek was immediately obvious. There was a line of men leading hundreds of people and several farm animals up the road. Snow adorned the people's shoulders, and dirt was smeared across their faces. Most of them were drawn and tired, like they hadn't eaten or slept in several days. A man with a large, white walking stick quickened his steps towards us when he saw Elhian.

'Your Majesty,' he said, bowing.

'Lord Stefan?' Elhian asked.

I gasped. I hadn't recognised him. The weightless, dirt-covered man before us looked nothing like the lord who had danced with his wife so elegantly at the ball in Tiathi. I scanned the people around him and saw his children, but Lady Elena was not amongst them.

'What happened?' Elhian asked.

'The day after we returned home from the ball, Naldo was besieged by the men of the White Isles.' Stefan's eyes were intently directed at the dirt before him, and his voice was stern, like he was trying to bully his emotions into submission. 'Ignallia has been sacked, and King Engres has taken to residing just beyond the walls of Naldo. There is talk of him coming further south before the winter is finished.'

'Ignallia? Sacked?' Elhian asked.

'Where is your wife?' I asked, not quite taking in the news.

'My dear Elena . . .' A sob was the end of him. He crumpled to the ground and raised a hand to his forehead, his mouth open as a heart-wrenching grief overtook him. One of his sons knelt beside him and clung to his arm.

'How did you escape?' Elhian asked the boy quietly.

'The scouts at the outposts told us they were coming to Naldo,' Stefan's son said. 'Officer Lindon told us to collect our things and leave. The White Army attacked as we left, and my mother was . . . was caught in a crossfire of arrows.'

'Were the Jazmardians there?' I asked.

The boy hesitated as he reluctantly recalled the scene. 'Yes. They were fighting as well.'

'Merek, tell the residents of Crisock to open their homes,' Elhian said.

'Come with me!' Merek called out to the people of Naldo. 'Come to the church, and you will be provided with food and water. Come, children.'

The people moved after him.

'There is something you should see,' Stefan said to me, quieting his grief enough to be coherent. He pulled a piece of cloth out of his shirt. 'Some of the men who attacked—not all of them, but quite a few—carried this flag.'

I took a corner of the cloth so it unraveled. It was the same symbol I'd seen before: the eye over a crescent moon, next to a red, broken butterfly.

We returned to the church's side room. The noise of the people from Naldo rose as they tried to make plans and access the bread and water Merek was providing. Wolfgar sat at the small, round table and took a deep breath. 'The quickest way to Naldo is to follow this path and enter a tunnel, here.' He pointed to a steep part of the mountain.

'A tunnel?' I cringed at the thought of close spaces, thick darkness, and dank air.

'Yes. Assuming the snow hasn't become too deep to get inside, you could be in Naldo within three days.'

'Could you forge some of those arrows with personal, gold-tipped, green fletching, like my other arrows?' Alexia asked. 'I will pay you, of course.'

Wolfgar glowed. 'I would be honoured. I can easily add such fletching to a pack of arrows I have already made. And more than that, I will come with you.'

'But I thought you said . . . ' I began.

'I know, but that was before I knew a foreign army had taken my hometown. What is the point of designing better arrows, if not to make a difference in battle? If leading you to Naldo, fletching arrows for the queen, and shoeing horses does anything to keep our enemies at bay, then I will come, and I will help. But . . . ' He paused, looking worried. 'There's something I need to tell you.' All eyes were on him, impatiently waiting for him to continue. 'My brother and I fought with Cades,' he said, cringing. 'I was your enemy once.'

'Are you now?' Elhian asked.

'No,' Wolfgar said solemnly. 'I swore allegiance to you the day my brother died at the Battle of Tiathi. I refused to fight for Cades from that day forward.'

'Good,' Darj said. 'Now let's say goodbye to Merek and go.'

16
THE DESERT HUNTER AND THE COUNCILOR

With Wolfgar's help, our party of forty-two soldiers and four royals found the tunnel before the sun set the next day. The path leading up to it was layered with enough snow to come up to my ankles, but it was passable, and the tunnel's entry was clear. We drew closer and assessed that it was high enough for our horses to travel through but not with us on their backs. We spent the night at the mouth of the tunnel and in the morning, led our horses inside.

Those of us who had brought a torch from Crisock set them on fire as we entered the darkness. The golden light made the inside of the tunnel glow. It was a long underpass—one that would take most of the day to travel through, according to Wolfgar—so there was no light at the other end. Rustic oil lamps were attached to the side of the tunnel at regular intervals. Darj lit them as we passed so the soldiers following could find their way.

I took several deep breaths as I looked back at the sky one last time.

I can do this.

'What's that noise?' Alexia asked, inclining her ear towards the black depths of the tunnel sometime later.

We stopped and listened.

'I can't hear anything,' Darj said.

'There,' Alexia said. There was a whimper, deep in the tunnel.

'It sounds like a wounded man,' Elhian said, frowning. 'Perhaps someone was injured and sought refuge here.'

'Come on.' Darj took off his cloak and draped it over his saddle.

We followed him forward. At first, the noise of the soldiers' chatter echoed around the tunnel walls, but within a few minutes, silence fell over them. The only sound was the crunch of boots and horseshoes on the gravelly ground.

'There it is again,' Alexia said. 'That sound.'

It was louder now.

'Who's there?' Elhian called.

The whimpering stopped.

'Who's there?' Elhian called again.

No answer. Goosebumps rose on my arms.

Darj lit another lamp. A pair of eyes gleamed at us from the darkness. Several other pairs appeared as well. I stood transfixed, both nervous and intrigued.

'Who are you?' Alexia asked quietly, as if to herself. She walked ahead and held her torch up while the rest of us watched. There were men sitting against the walls.

'It's Jazmardian soldiers,' Alexia called back to us.

We caught up with her, and our collective light lit up the tunnel. There were hundreds of them. 'It must be the whole battalion Hazaka posted here,' I said.

Their cheeks were sunken in their dirty faces. A sheen of sweat covered their brows, but they shivered with cold.

'What kind of king treats his subjects like this?' Darj muttered to himself. 'You, there.' He pointed to one who was looking at us intensely. 'Do you understand the common tongue?'

The soldier nodded.

The common tongue was officially called Rheati, a language built on ancient Targian that borrowed words from the older Casmodian and Delyan tribes. The Targians, being the main trader between the two, had once had the primary role of forming and carrying the language between towns, along with their goods. Now the common tongue was spoken easily between the three kingdoms, its precursors all but forgotten except by scholars and sages. The White Isles and Jazmarda, being more remote from the main trade routes, had retained strong ties to their mother tongues, and only a few there could speak Rheati well, hence Darj's question.

'Why are you here?' he asked. 'Why are you all so unwell?'

'Our king sent us to Naldo, but we were given no supplies. No food and no cloaks. We are not used to the winter. He was supposed to send word to us, but none came.'

Darj folded his arms. If Hazaka had been present, he would have received a swift lecture from the prince-general about honourable army management.

'Your king is dead,' Elhian said.

The man straightened. 'Who has the crown?'

Whether he meant the physical crown or the leadership of the kingdom was irrelevant. The answer was the same in both cases.

'Telitha,' I said. 'We believe she intends to reign in her husband's place, perhaps until her eldest son is of age.'

'Jazmarda could be a great kingdom,' the man said, 'but it never had a chance under Hazaka's reign. It certainly will not under hers.'

'What is your name?' Alexia asked.

'Izak Tan of Cazarma. I am a desert hunter, nothing more. We did not wish to come to Casmodia. When we arrived at Naldo, we fought with your people against the White Army until I was forced to retreat. If Hazaka is dead, please, let us go home.'

'You fought with my men?' Elhian asked. 'Why would you do that?'

Izak stood. He was as tall as Darj, with broad shoulders, a serious face, and eyes so brown and wise it was like they had been carved out of an ageless walnut tree. The hair on his head was cut short, and he wore a thick beard that did not yet have any greys. His lips were dry and cracked, and despite his well-defined muscles, he was too thin to be considered healthy.

'My father fought by your side in the Northern Invasion,' he said. 'He returned to the earth fourteen moons ago. At Naldo, I honoured his memory. I know the four of you released Jazmarda of its curse. I know what we owe you.'

Elhian briefly placed his hand on Izak's shoulder in thanks.

'Adaliah?' a familiar voice called.

Someone ambled towards us out of the shadows with a noticeable gait. I recognised the thin and slightly bent-over shape and brought my hands to my mouth. There was no one I could have wished to see more.

'Kadram,' I said as the high councilor from Jazmarda gave me a frail embrace.

'Adaliah,' he whispered over my shoulder. 'Yet again, we meet in the heat of battle.'

'What are you doing here?' Alexia asked with a kind smile as he took her hand and kissed it.

'Intercepting you, of course!' He chuckled. 'Actually, this is a happy chance. I came to meet these men after I heard that Hazaka sent them here to blackmail you. I was fortunate that their captain has more sense and morals than his king.' He nodded towards Izak.

'Hazaka is dead,' I said, 'and so is Thane.'

Kadram cupped my face in his hands. His palms felt leathery and warm. 'I know, my butterfly, I know. There is much I must tell you all. Come, follow me.'

Alexia, Darj, Elhian and I walked with Kadram further into the tunnel. We came to a place where Kadram had spread two or three blankets on the ground. Darj lit the nearest lamp, and we sat cross-legged in a circle.

'I am not able to provide you with a fire in here.' Kadram sighed as if this were one of the more unfortunate facts he had ever been confronted with. 'I wish I had some comfort to bring you all, but in truth, I do not.'

Izak brought us each a cup of water and a plate of bread, which we picked at with our fingers. Izak moved his weight from foot to foot as if unsure where to be.

'Tell us what you know,' Alexia said to Kadram.

'After I heard of Hazaka's death, I came to bring the battalion home. I also wanted to find his eldest son, Mirza, to take him back to Etarbelec, but I believe Telitha may have already sent him and his brothers there alone. As high councilor, I need to determine a regent until Mirza Cazren is aged sixteen and six months.' He took a bite of food. 'I received reports from my informants once I arrived in Naldo. Alexia, have you had any news from your kingdom?'

'Not since Crisock, when Xander confirmed the children had arrived safely in Liane.' Alexia tensed. 'What do you know?'

Kadram prodded the pitiful fire. 'Firstly, I know that Delya has been overcome in its entirety.'

Our mouths dropped. 'What?' Darj asked.

'The Delyan kingdom has been conquered by the Bone Hordes. They are no doubt working for Telitha.'

A stunned silence followed.

The Bone Hordes were collective tribes of savage people living in the desert east beyond Sharlard. They attacked Targe from time to time in small groups. Alexia's father, King Amaz, drove them out from his lands more than once. We knew little about them, not having travelled to their lands, but I had heard they were godless creatures who ate whatever they could get, whether it came from man or beast. They had no king. They had no laws. They knew nothing of the Great Spirit. The Bone Hordes were unpredictable and fierce.

'Have you heard about Ren?' Darj asked. 'Is he safe?'

'Ren escaped to Targe with a small army of Delyans,' Kadram said. 'But Targe has suffered, too. Alexia, Rorinhall has been sacked by the Bone Hordes, and they are making their way through the Hewn Mountains towards Fenellar. They have also taken control of Saltran in Jazmarda, which, as you know, is an important port for trade with the islands and lands in the far south.'

'Rorinhall . . .' Alexia murmured. 'My only seaport.'

'The White Army has drawn us to the north so all this can occur in the south,' Darj said, gritting his teeth.

'What is happening to the people?' Elhian asked.

'Those who do not resist are imprisoned. The others are slaughtered in ways that leave them unrecognisable. Some villages have been entirely wiped out.'

Silence followed again as we tried to take in his words.

'It's happening again,' Alexia said, her voice quiet. Darj put an arm around her.

It was much worse than we had ever imagined. Losing Naldo and Ignallia was one thing, but for the entire kingdom of Delya to be overcome and with invasions taking place in Targe . . .

'What is their plan?' I asked.

'Telitha is creating a new world,' Kadram said, 'and she is using the White Army and the Bone Hordes to achieve it.'

'The crowns . . . ' Darj said. 'That's why they want the crowns. Telitha is going to re-forge them into one, isn't she? She's going to crown herself empress of the Rhea Lands.'

'I do not know what she intends to do.' Kadram raised his hands to the fire. 'She is a complicated woman with a complicated heritage. The truth is I am unsure whether she intends herself or another for power. Her choices have rarely been good.' The light from the lamp flickered across his face. 'There is talk of a shadow, of a darkness that has defied death year upon year. Anash's power is growing stronger, and I believe there is something or someone—other than Telitha—that is calling upon it and feeding it.' He shivered. 'I can feel it in my spirit.'

'Ru'ach will defeat them, whoever they are,' Alexia said.

'Indeed, but regardless of who wielded the sword, Telitha has already successfully arranged the death of the King of Jazmarda *and* the King of Delya,' Kadram said. 'Two out of five monarchs disposed of within days of each other. The threat is not just to our lands.' He gave Elhian and Alexia a pointed look.

'As for you . . . ' He turned to me. 'Those fighting against you are rallying behind the idea of "breaking" the Armoured Butterfly, the symbol of Kest. You are the A'zyon Warrior, but do not forget you are also the Keeper of Kest until Princess Eva turns sixteen. Telitha is inciting hate against you amongst the Jazmardian and Islander soldiers, telling them twisted stories about how you destroyed the Dark Orb, killed Zalems, harmed their cause . . . The stories have reached Hanequin, the scar-face leader of the Bone Hordes army, and he still hates King Amaz from the old days. The word is he wishes to revenge himself upon you, Alexia, perhaps with an attack on Darj. But for now, Telitha is targeting Adaliah above the others, and that can only mean one thing.'

I attempted to ask what, but my mouth had gone dry.

'She and her allies intend to define their victory by killing you,' Kadram said.

17
INTO NALDO

I stepped away from the others and huddled against the tunnel wall, waiting for Izak to rouse the Jazmardians so we could continue our journey to Naldo. The tunnel was bright with the light of all of the torches and lamps, but the air felt thin, the roof low, the darkness heavy. I closed my eyes.

We'll be out of here soon. You can do this.

Until Telitha makes a public display of your death.

'Your Majesty, are you all right?'

Izak squatted in front of me, holding Bagred's reins. My sleepy horse stood behind him. Izak and Elhian had already come to an agreement, the latter promising the Jazmardians food and shelter for the winter if they travelled with us to Naldo. Izak had agreed, and somehow, I felt it wasn't for the food or the shelter.

'I just want to get to the other side,' I said.

'We are ready to go. They are just covering the dead.'

'Are there many dead?'

'About fifteen of my ledzagors.'

'Ledzagor?'

'It means a friend who stands by you even in the face of death.'

I stood and leant against Bagred, the smell and warmth of him helping my mind to settle.

'I do understand, you know,' Izak said.

'What do you mean?'

'I know what it is to fear. My fear is water because I nearly drowned when I was a child. The memories of such things stay with you forever.'

'You live in the driest kingdom of all,' I said.

'It is true that fears are rarely rational.'

'Mine came from being held captive in a tiny underground cell for more than a month. My mind snapped, and I lost my memory.' I rested my forehead against Bagred, old emotions stirring at the reflection.

'Your story is well-known, but I cannot imagine what it was like.'

'People talk about losing their minds, but they don't realise just how crippling it is. When you're that broken, you fear it ever happening again, and you especially fear the thing that caused it to happen.'

'While you fear it, it continues to have power over you. You are the most famous warrior in all the lands, and yet you are letting a tunnel be your master.'

I lifted my head off Bagred. 'And you are a desert hunter afraid of something you rarely see.'

'My father told me you are the bravest girl he ever saw. He would have believed you have what it takes to overcome this fear, and so do I. You are the A'zyon Warrior.' He bowed to me and turned to go. A few paces away, he stopped and looked back at me. 'Cazarma is an oasis, by the way, a place of deep pools. Every day I go out to hunt, I have to wade across them. I fear the water, but it is not my master.'

The rest of the trip through the tunnel felt more bearable, somehow, and quicker. Still, I was deeply relieved to come out at the other end. The wave of fresh air that caressed my face was the most precious gift I could wish for, and as we stepped onto the rocky mountain road outside, my mouth dropped at the sight of something even more beautiful. The entire evening sky was filled with magnificent shades of orange, pink, and red, streaming from a golden sun that possessed the entire expanse.

'A good sign,' Darj said as he mounted Guntar.

'For the weather, anyway,' Kadram said.

Beneath the sky was the fortified village of Naldo, decked in snow and glistening under the sun's fading gaze. Several smoke columns billowed upwards, the only sign that the winter town had been besieged.

All was silent as we travelled the snowy path up to the southern gate the next afternoon. Darj had rightly surmised that the battle would be taking place on the north side, where the White Army had descended into Casmodia.

'Your Majesty!' a soldier called down to Elhian. 'Come inside. The White Army has paused in their advance. Open the gate!'

Soldiers wound the metal structure upwards. Elhian dug his heels into Leuk. Alexia, Darj, and I cantered into the city behind him.

'Sire,' another man said, approaching on foot. He wore the blue tunic of a Casmodian soldier but with gold shoulders.

'Officer Lindon,' Elhian said. 'What's happening?'

'We have managed to negotiate a respite,' Lindon said, bowing as he spoke. 'They stopped attacking at noon and have been collecting their dead. They said they would give us until this evening to do the same. We only just received news from my scout, confirming that Ignallia has been sacked by the White Army.'

Elhian met my eyes, but there was nothing I could say.

'Izak,' he said, 'take your men into the barracks. Lindon will ensure they are fed.'

'Jazmardian men fought by your side once before,' Izak said. 'We have talked about it, and we are prepared to do so again.'

'I'm grateful, truly, but take this opportunity to eat and sleep. We will call on you when the White Army returns.'

'Yes, sire.' Izak began calling out to the Jazmardian soldiers in their own tongue.

'Where is the blacksmith's forge?' Wolfgar asked, appearing behind us. 'I can repair armour, weapons . . . '

'Follow Lindon,' Elhian said. 'He will show you once he has settled the Jazmardians.'

'I will go with them, too,' Kadram said. 'Let me know if you need anything.' He walked away with Wolfgar and the others.

'Engres must have heard that Hazaka is dead and decided to mount the attack without him,' I said.

'Perhaps he always planned to attack, with or without Hazaka,' Alexia said.

'What's your assessment?' Elhian asked Darj.

'Ride out to him,' Darj said with surprising urgency. 'The three of you. Try and negotiate with him. I will stay with Lindon and the Targian soldiers and help Naldo prepare for the next attack.'

'But—' Alexia began.

'We don't have time,' Darj said, briefly clutching her hand. 'Go!'

Elhian rode his horse back towards the gate. Alexia hesitated, her eyes fixed on her husband. 'Go,' he said again, giving her a nod. 'Be safe.'

Alexia turned Hazel. 'When we meet Engres . . . ' She trailed off with a hint of bridled threats. She dug her heels into Hazel, and we sped out of the gate behind Elhian.

The three of us rode as fast as we could through the wintry afternoon, a sliver of sun our only guide. We followed the main Naldo–Ignallia road, the path easy on our horses' feet. Several dead bodies lay in the snow-covered grass. Sleet moved between the trees. I pulled my cloak's fur hood over my head to stop the cold from numbing my ears.

We came to the ridge of a small hill within the hour. We didn't have to search any further for the White Army; they were spread out before us. While it wasn't as big as I was expecting—I had imagined the worst—it was still a startling sight. There were numerous tents and campfires, and the largest one, the royal one, was right in the middle.

Alexia unslung her bow.

'No,' I said, putting a hand on her arm. 'If we are to go in, we must do so peacefully.'

She relented and reluctantly returned her bow to her back.

We rode down the hill towards the camp. The Islanders stirred. At first, there was halted curiosity in their faces. A few of them unsheathed their swords. Then there were calls in a language that sounded brisk. We reached the first line of tents and continued towards the main one, doing our best to ignore the soldiers. They were all on their feet, but not attacking.

Alexia, as resolute as always, did not hesitate to take the lead. She reached the tent, dismounted, and approached the front opening. Elhian and I had to take quick steps to keep up with her.

Two guards stood on either side of the tent opening. 'We are here to see the king,' Alexia said.

'We know,' one of them said in the common tongue. 'He is ready for you. Go in.'

They pulled back the flap, and we stepped inside.

The tent was full of warriors who stopped talking when they saw us. They had golden hair, fairer than I had ever seen. Their eyes were mostly hazel green, bright and inviting. Apart from Franc, it had been many years since I had seen an Islander, and I had never seen so many gathered together. I had to stop myself from staring.

They slowly parted, creating a path to their king. He sat on a large chair at an equally large table. He was as old as everyone had said he was but not yet done with life. He leaned to one side of the chair, as if his body could not quite keep him upright, but otherwise, he seemed to be in good health—not too thin or pale, his face adorned with a bristly white beard, his eyes more grey than green, and muscles still giving his frame the appearance of strength.

Telitha had not stolen his crown yet. The simple gold band that rested on Engres' head didn't proclaim wealth and power but modest authority and steadfastness.

I could easily remember the first time I met King Cades and the fear I had felt in his presence. As we came to the end of this king's table, I didn't feel that fear. Engres Loren had the quality of a venerable grandfather, just as Alexia had said. His expression made me think he was exactly the sort of man who would entertain you with stories of his youth and sneak you desserts out of the kitchen. His eyes weren't hateful when they fell on us. They were sympathetic and sad.

I knew Alexia felt the same way. The agitation went out of her steps. She had intended to berate him; now, she said nothing.

'Queen Alexia,' Engres said, taking her hand and kissing it. 'You are the image of your beautiful mother, Jenethea. Should you ever wonder what she looked like, you need only to consult a mirror.' Engres' command of the common tongue was rustic but clear.

Alexia smiled, but there was an element of sadness there. 'I am touched that you remember her.'

'No one who met Amaz and Jenethea could ever forget them. They were the standard by which all leaders should live.' His soulful eyes turned to me. 'This young lady's reputation has reached every district of the Rhea Lands, even my frozen corner. I heard you escaped Telitha's grip to travel north.' He studied me. I sensed he had more to say, but for now, he held back his words. He indicated the man on his right. 'This is my son and heir, Prince Garrow.'

Up until then, I hadn't paid attention to anyone beyond Engres. I recalled Rosana's account of the crown prince and was very interested to know him, now that he had been pointed out. Garrow stood behind his father with folded arms. He appeared to be about Darj's age, if not a few years older, with shoulder-length, unwashed, blond hair. He seemed disinterested in meeting us and didn't look anyone in the eye. I could imagine him working with Telitha. They shared an air of condescension. I wondered what his father thought of him.

'This is my daughter, Princess Yorella,' Engres said more tenderly, 'the finest spear maiden in the White Isles.'

Yorella gave her father an affectionate glance before bowing her head towards us. Her long, golden hair reached her waist, and her appearance was both innocent and young.

'Now, all of you,' Engres said, raising his voice a little, 'leave us.'

Garrow, Yorella, and the soldiers departed. Once we were all seated and the tent emptied but for the four of us, silence followed. Our main goal had been to meet Engres, and now that we were before him, it seemed that none of us knew what to say. I wished Darj had come with us.

'I have not harmed the people of Ignallia,' Engres offered. 'I charged my son with ensuring their safety in captivity, and I am happy to evacuate them further south if you wish.'

'You have sacked one town and besieged another—and killed my soldiers to do so,' Elhian said. 'Tell me, why are you here?'

'Not for blind greed or selfish pursuits, if that's what you think. In fact, I wish I did not have to be here at all. But I must. I am here for my people.'

'How so?' I asked.

'None of you have visited my home city, Wandryna—or Winterford, as it is known in your tongue—but if you were to do so, you would see the poverty, the overcrowding. It is a great source of shame for me. I am desperate and under enormous pressure to relieve their situation. Casmodia is the nearest kingdom with room to spare. I do not wish to battle nor to make enemies of my neighbours, but I must attend to the needs of my people. When Hazaka didn't send word to his battalion, I made the only decision I could: to press on without him.'

'There must be other ways to fix your problems,' Elhian said. 'Better housing, for one thing. Targe and Casmodia can trade you the materials required at a fair price.'

'And what would I trade for them? Our crops were frozen. There was no harvest this year. The iron and gold mines are depleted; there is not enough money to survey land and install some more. Our main commodity is fish, and that you can well get yourselves.'

'There are other islands, further east, not yet settled . . . ' Alexia began.

'All but impossible to get to when facing the winds and squalls that part of the sea presents.' Engres smoothed out his beard. 'No, this is the only way. By taking my men to battle, I will solve our overcrowding issues, one way or another.'

'You must know we will fight back,' I said.

Engres took a deep breath. 'I know.'

'What do you know about Telitha?' Elhian asked. 'Are you her ally?'

Engres stretched his hands to the corners of the table and folded his fingers around them. The wood creaked. 'I am not her ally. Telitha has her own plans for the future. I do not intend to be part of them.'

'If you continue to invade, I will rally all the armies of Casmodia against you,' Elhian said. 'I will not simply let Ignallia or any other town be taken.'

'And I will bring up the armies of Targe,' Alexia said.

'I can ask for more ships to come from the White Isles. They would be here long before the armies of Targe or Delya could ever reach this far north.' He folded his arms. 'But my heart is not set on war. I do have a compromise in mind.'

'What?' I asked.

'A championship. Tomorrow, at dawn. It was my son's idea, actually. A fight to the death between one of your warriors and one of mine. If mine wins, we will subdue Naldo as planned and continue with our invasion. If yours wins, I will retreat back to the Edeline Sea and sail back to my little island. But I get to pick the warriors.'

'Who do you have in mind?' Alexia asked.

'My son and the A'zyon Warrior.'

18
THE CHAMPIONSHIP

Engres left us alone in the tent to discuss our options.

'Your ribs . . . ' Elhian said. 'Do you think you're strong enough? It's only just over two weeks since they were broken.'

'We don't know Garrow's capabilities apart from what Rosana told us,' Alexia said. 'But then, there is more than Adaliah's life riding on this.'

'It's a fight to the death,' Elhian said heavily, putting his hand over mine, 'and not a clean one. If Adaliah kills the heir to the throne of the White Isles, Engres could well use that as an excuse to continue his invasion. But if he holds to his word . . . '

'What if I were to guard her from the background?' Alexia asked. 'If the championship appears to be going badly, I can shoot Garrow. Not to kill him, just to make him back off. That way, we can guarantee her survival.'

'That's cheating, Alexia,' Elhian said, 'and it could give them cause to continue the invasion.'

'What about Karlen and Jovan?' Alexia asked.

Elhian bristled. 'Do you think they are far from my mind?'

'Can I say something?' I asked, reminding them of my presence. 'I've thought about it as much as I need to, and I say yes.'

'Adaliah—'

'It's not a hard decision,' I said. 'If I do this, and I win, Engres will discontinue his invasion and bring no further harm to us or our people.'

'And if you don't win?' Alexia asked quietly.

'The war will continue, and people will die whether I try and fail or don't try at all. Risking one life to save thousands is not beyond anything we've done before. We have a chance to stop a war, and we need to take it.'

'Aren't you afraid that—' Alexia began.

'Of course I'm afraid,' I said, standing. 'If I waited until I didn't feel fear before I did something, I would still be sitting by Kest River, wondering why I couldn't remember my name. I may wrestle with fear, but I would never let it stop me doing what's right.'

By the time we'd spoken with Engres again and returned to Naldo, the Casmodian soldiers were barricading the gates. I could see Darj's work everywhere. Barrels of thick, black oil were being rolled into place on the walls. Catapults stood in the main square, ready to fling stones over the walls and into our enemy's vanguard. Jazmardian, Targian, and Casmodian soldiers lined the tops of the walls, some with bows, some with swords, many with both. The village was as ready for war as it could be.

'Why did he pick you?' was Darj's first question after we shared with him all that had occurred. 'First the flag and now this. Telitha has targeted you several times, and now they wish to fight you to the death. Why?'

'Presumably because her prowess as a warrior is well-known,' Alexia said. 'If his son defeats her, just think how that will inspire Engres' soldiers.'

'Yes . . . No, it must be more than that.' The concern in Darj's expression became less restrained as he paced the barracks' floor. 'Whoever these people are who are following Telitha, they are rallying behind a flag that represents breaking the butterfly—of killing Adaliah. Notice how they aren't representing her as the A'zyon Warrior but as something fragile. And now, Engres has volunteered you for a championship to the death. He says he's not Telitha's ally but seems to be aware that she has plans. There's something strange about all this.'

'What choice do we have?' Elhian asked. 'If Adaliah wins, she ends this and saves us all.'

'And if she dies?'

'She won't die,' Elhian said. 'I have faith.'

'There's something I should tell you,' I said. 'When Stefan gave us that flag . . . It wasn't the first time I'd seen that symbol.'

The others stared at me.

'Where else?' Elhian asked.

'In Kest once. And it was pinned to a wall in our castle the day after our sons were born, and it was etched into the paper Telitha slipped under the door on the day she captured us.'

'Why didn't you say something?' Darj asked.

'I didn't want to believe the Zalems were still alive, and I didn't want to worry you all. I thought it was just a vain threat.'

'I think it is more of a plan than a threat,' Darj said dryly.

'I've agreed to the championship,' I said. 'Engres has given his word that he will retreat if I win. We have to try.'

'I believe you can do anything, you know,' Elhian said as I later lay down next to him. 'You have achieved far too much already for me to ever doubt it.'

We were in a small room at the back of the barracks, and the bed was the only item of furniture in it. A small fire burned in a hearth, not quite overcoming the chill in the air.

I pulled the blankets up and over my shoulders. 'I know.'

'But Darj's suspicions are usually valid, and I'm afraid of losing you. Be careful. Don't take any risks.'

I stroked his cheek. 'Of course.' I kissed him. He wrapped an arm around me, and our kiss deepened.

The truth was I could barely comprehend the danger that awaited me in the morning. The fear I felt wasn't for my own life. All I could think of was my sons and whether or not I would see them again. I had grown up without a mother; I didn't want them to. Nor did I want Casmodia to become subject to Engres *or* Telitha.

When did I come to care so much about Casmodia?

Elhian kissed me again, and I relaxed into his arms. I knew the answer to my own question.

Since I fell in love with its king.

'You should sleep,' Elhian said, pulling back. 'You need to be fit for the morning.'

'I will,' I said, 'later. Right now, I just want to be with you.'

I woke in the morning when Darj knocked on our door. 'They're here,' he called. His footsteps faded away, and I shook Elhian awake.

Within a few minutes, he had tightly wrapped my ribs with a wide bandage. I checked whether I could still rotate my torso adequately and found I could with minimal pain.

I tied up my hair, and then came the armour. A linen undergarment was first, then a tight-fitting leather cuirass around my torso. I clipped on my leather skirt before pulling on my knee-high leather boots. The vambraces and pauldrons on my arms and shoulders were the last items to be tied into place. Somehow, it all felt heavier than last time.

'I have a gift for you.' Elhian handed me a package wrapped in brown paper.

'What is it?'

'Something I asked Wolfgar to work on before leaving Crisock. He brought the material with him and has been diligently working on it each night, along with arrows for Alexia. He delivered it this morning; I think he was up all night. It's something I hope will remind you of who you are.'

I pulled the paper away and discovered an item of clothing. I held it up. It was a beautiful cape. Three colours sprouted from the shoulder and formed diagonal segments. A purple strip of material was in the middle, with a blue strip on the lower diagonal and a green strip on the top. Gold lines separated the colours and edged the cape. At the shoulder, Wolfgar had sewn in a tiny gold symbol of a butterfly—intact. It was stitched into the purple cloth. *The Armoured Butterfly.*

'The three colours are for your three lands,' Elhian said as he took it from me and clipped it under the pauldron on my left shoulder. 'Green, because you are a Targian lady and warrior. Blue, because you are a Casmodian queen and wife. Purple, because you were born in Kest and are its keeper.' He put a finger under my chin and lifted my gaze. 'The A'zyon Warrior. A woman both beautiful and fearless.'

'I wish that was true,' I whispered.

'It is. May Ru'ach give wings to your courage.'

Elhian let the cape go, and it draped elegantly over my shoulder to just above my hip. 'It's perfect,' I said, running my hand over the fine material.

Elhian kissed my lips and rested his forehead against mine.

'I love you,' he said.

'And I you.'

The men had gathered on a snowy, flat patch of grassland just beyond Naldo's northern gate. The White Army stood to the north, spreading further back than could be seen.

The men had left a circle in the middle, edged with hay bales. Small tents had been pitched on opposite sides of the circle—one with a blue roof, the other with a white one. Bagred was standing near the circle with a Targian soldier.

Elhian walked with me to the blue tent. The Targians, Jazmardians, and Casmodians cheered as I passed through them. I couldn't see Garrow or Engres yet.

I followed Elhian inside the tent, where Alexia and Darj were waiting for me.

'Any advice?' I asked when they said nothing.

'Don't die,' Darj said with a reluctant smile.

I gave a hollow laugh.

Alexia put her hands on my shoulders and kissed my cheek. 'Ru'ach is on your side, and so are we.'

A horn sounded outside, and the cries of the men faded. 'It's time,' Elhian said.

The four of us walked outside. Garrow was at the circle now. He was entirely encased in steel armour, from pointy boots to a white helmet. He nodded at me and slid his visor down over his eyes. His left hand held a steel shield that had the White Isles' ensign on it: an anchor, symbolic of their seamanship. Behind him was his father and another person dressed in black with a shawl over their face. I thought it might have been Princess Yorella, but it was hard to tell.

'That armour will make it difficult to wound him,' Darj said.

'It will also be hard for him to move quickly,' I said. 'Sword fighting is not all about strength and armour. Where are my swords?'

'Are you sure you don't want a shield?' a Casmodian soldier asked.

'I'm sure.'

Targian warriors rarely carried shields. They were taught to fight with a sword in each hand instead. 'Double the attack, halve the need for defence,' my father had told me. Like Darj, I had never fought with a shield and didn't want to start now. Besides, I felt sure my ribs couldn't bear the weight.

Elhian handed me my swords—the one known as the Life Sword, and the other known as the tree-blade. My ribs smarted as I held them up.

Elhian saw me wince but thankfully said nothing.

'Let's go,' I said, trying to sound brave.

Garrow had already stepped into the centre of the circle. The Islanders were chanting his name. Engres watched solemnly from the door of the white tent, his crown on his head.

I stepped over the hay bale. As I lowered my foot into the circle, a clear picture filled my mind: me, holding my sons in our castle in Tiathi. I was in the blue stateroom, and they were sitting on a knee each, listening to their father telling them a story about a deer and a lion who became friends. I could see their smiles, smell their hair, hear their giggling. I ached to be back there, living a safe life. I had long felt that my future held more war, more battles. Now I wondered if the thought of it had somehow caused it to happen. Had I brought this upon myself and my family? Had my choices put all that really mattered at risk? Now, the only hope for the Rhea Lands was for me to kill King Engres' only son.

I lowered my second foot into the circle and returned to the present. I was angry but not with Garrow or the White Army. I was angry with the world for being so war-driven. I wanted the new world I had fought so hard for. Why hadn't it come?

I gave a yell and made the first strike. The men cheered as the championship began. The first few minutes passed uneventfully as Garrow and I evaluated each other's styles. His armour restricted his agility, just as I expected, but he was strong. I had to use all of my might to block his strikes, and each one compounded the pain in my ribs. *This has to be a quick fight*, I decided.

I deflected one of his strikes and went on the offensive, slashing at him several times with both swords until he stumbled backwards. He struck at me again, but I ducked, stepped behind him, and struck him across the back. I knew he couldn't move fast enough to stop me, and I was right. He cried out in pain.

But then he stood and made the first strike back. The blow was harder; he'd thrown all his weight into it. I held up my swords but fell backwards and landed in the snow. He moved to strike me again, but I rolled out of the way, hopped up, and kicked him. He stumbled but quickly recovered. He struck at me again. For the next few minutes, I did nothing but evade his strikes.

Maybe he is the better warrior.

Just as the thought passed through my mind, his next blow disarmed me of my tree-blade. It sank into the snow. I reached down to pick it up, groaning at the pain in my side. Out of the corner of my eye, I saw Garrow raise his foot to kick me. I lowered my body towards the ground to evade him, but I was too late. His foot connected with my ribs. I was airborne, and then I crashed into the ground.

Pain rippled through my body. I flitted in and out of consciousness several times within a few seconds. Alexia called my name. I rolled onto my back in the snow. Garrow leant over me with his sword. Engres was coming towards us.

I wanted to surrender, but this was a fight to the death. Surrendering would not stop Garrow from killing me.

I had one chance to survive. I thrust up my remaining sword towards Garrow, but Engres pushed Garrow out of the way. My sword slid into the king's side. Blood hastened out around the blade, and he fell to his knees and then his side.

My chest tightened as I panicked.

I've killed the king!

Garrow took off his helmet. The men around us were silent.

'You fight well,' he said.

I wanted to speak but couldn't catch my breath.

He's going to kill me.

Garrow kneeled beside Engres. 'I'm sorry, Father.' He kissed Engres' forehead.

Engres ignored his son and reached for my hand. 'Not . . . broken yet.' He gave my hand a faint squeeze before he coughed and died.

I've killed the King of the White Isles.

'I . . . I would have won,' I said, sitting up with a new surge of anger. 'Had he not intervened, I would have killed you. You must retreat!'

'That was my father's promise, not mine.'

The person with a black shawl over their face came into the circle. They laughed. It was a woman, but not the princess. She pulled the shawl away, but I already knew it was Telitha.

I bet this was her idea.

She held a sword, one of the powerful four. The Jazmardian Hope Sword. She must have claimed it from her husband.

'You . . . ' I said. Rosana had been right—they were in partnership.

Garrow took the signet ring from his father's hand while Elhian and Darj ran to me with raised swords.

'How could you?' Darj asked.

Garrow snarled at them. 'My father thought he was here to acquire new land. We are here to further my cause.' He snickered. 'I knew he would not let me die today.'

'What are you going to do?' Darj asked.

'We are taking Casmodia,' Telitha said. 'It is the Supreme Overlord's wish.'

'Who?' I asked from the ground.

Telitha's delight was evident in her wicked grin. 'Mors Zalem.'

I frowned. 'What?'

'The ancient prince from Delya?' Darj asked. 'He died nigh on a thousand years ago!'

Telitha leveled her eyes at him. 'No, he did not. Anash's powers have sustained him all this time—nine hundred and ninety-nine years.'

'That's impossible,' I said. 'No man can live that long.'

'Mors has,' Garrow said, 'and he has commanded us to take you all to him.'

'In Semanez?' Darj asked.

'Yes,' Telitha said.

'You . . . you didn't intend to make yourself empress at all, did you?' I asked. 'This is all to bring him to power. You are the Zalem Servant, like Bylon was.'

Telitha scowled at me. 'I am the new High Zalem. Garrow is the Zalem Servant, as was Cades and Bylon before him.'

Garrow stood and turned to his men. 'She killed our king!' he yelled, holding up Engres' crown.

The crown . . . My breath disappeared again. *They've got all the crowns!*

'She killed my father!'

They are inciting hate against you, Kadram had said. Now, I was seeing it for myself. Swords were unsheathed.

'You cheated!' Darj shouted.

Garrow sniggered, and he raised his foot to kick me once more. An arrow landed in his shoulder. One of Wolfgar's designs, it easily pierced his armour. He yelped and turned around, giving me a clear view of the gold-tipped, green fletching.

'Step away from my cousin,' Alexia said, appearing in my vision. Her bow was already re-drawn, this time with two arrows.

'Not this again,' Telitha said with a groan. 'Garrow, get on with it.'

Garrow raised his sword and called to his men, 'Attack!'

19
THE REGENT

Elhian pulled me to my feet as the White Army charged at us. I could hear Darj yelling instructions, but it was a blur at the back of my mind.

I've killed the King of the White Isles.

A catapult's stone flew through the air above my head and landed amidst the Islanders beyond us. Several more followed.

Darj.

'Here!' Elhian held out the tree-blade.

I grabbed it in time to deflect Garrow's attack. I brought my sword down on the arrow that was sticking out of his shoulder. It bent in two, and Garrow cried out. I pushed him away from me and vomited. His kick to my ribs was still pulsating. Soldiers slid to the ground nearby as Alexia downed them with arrows, protecting me until I could straighten and collect myself.

'I have to secure the gate,' Elhian called to me. 'Get inside as soon as you can!'

'You don't fight fairly,' Garrow said. He pulled Alexia's arrow out of his flesh, making awful, drawn-out groans in the process.

'And this coming from the man who just let his father die?' I wiped my mouth on my sleeve.

'My father has led the White Isles into the ground. It was time for me to claim my inheritance before he lost it.'

Garrow threw the bloodied arrow into the snow. I raised my swords. Casmodian soldiers—with Elhian—stood behind me at the iron gate, ready to prevent the White Army from entering. Archers lined the walls. Alexia was running up a set of stairs to join them.

I was the only one outside the gate. The White Army ran past Garrow and me, charging at the walled town. Many of them carried broken butterfly flags.

'How is Mors alive?' I asked Garrow.

Garrow chuckled. 'Defying death is easy when you make a pact with Anash, the Prince of Death. In a few weeks, Mors will be one thousand years old, and then he will be invincible.'

I brought both swords down against him. He raised his shield and blocked me. I immediately attacked again and splintered his shield. He groaned and threw it away.

Where's Telitha?

The Jazmardian queen had just been at my elbow issuing threats, and now she was nowhere to be seen. My energy almost spent, I struck at Garrow and followed with a high kick, giving it everything I had left.

He sprawled backwards onto the ground.

I whistled for my horse. Bagred stepped over the hay bales and trotted to me. I hopped on one leg a few times before I managed to get my foot into the stirrup and pull myself into the saddle. I dug my heels into his sides. Bagred tossed his head and charged forward.

'Make way!' Elhian yelled to his soldiers. 'Make way!' The Casmodians parted as I rode towards them. The gate was already coming down. I ducked under it, and it plunged into place behind me. Archers were ahead, their bows drawn. I rode to the side. They shot a volley of arrows at the enemy soldiers already pressing against the gate.

I cantered past Darj and the catapults and rode to the barracks, searching for the Jazmardians. I wanted to find Izak and enlist him in an urgent search for Telitha. I hoped the Jazmardian hunter could help me track her down.

There were men everywhere inside the barracks, mostly Izak's neglectfully unequipped Jazmardians hurriedly taking up arms and any armour that could be found. Wolfgar handed out weapons while Officer Lindon—from what I could make out over the general noise—gave instructions for them to follow once they left the barracks.

I couldn't see Izak amongst the crowd, and he was normally easy to spot due to his height. I ran across the main hall and through the side rooms, but there was no sign of him anywhere.

'Adaliah!' Kadram called, seeing me as I came back into the main room. 'Telitha's battalion is here, the Jazmardians she threatened you with at Tiathi. They are just outside the town wall.' He gestured towards a small door behind me. 'That way!'

I turned and ran.

Outside, on the other side of the barracks, the battalion filled the road for as far as I could see. Izak stood ahead of their frontline, and before him was the Queen of Jazmarda.

'You must fight for your kingdom and make these men do so,' she said. Her black hair was spun into a tight, practical bun with every strand drawn back from her wide forehead. 'As your queen, I command it!' She thrust the Jazmardian sword at Izak.

'These men are true, Jazmardian men!' he shouted, and the soldiers behind him raised their weapons into the air in agreement. 'They have agreed to fight by my side.'

'They would not be so quick to abandon their loyalties to their queen!'

'You have not fed or paid them for months. Do you truly think that earns loyalty? Your regency is not confirmed by the court. You cannot demand our allegiance, and we will not war against a king who has saved our lives and who offers us the basic kindnesses you continue to neglect.'

'I do demand allegiance, from all of you. Get out there and fight for me!'

I stepped closer. Izak caught sight of me and straightened. 'We will fight, but not for you. Ledzagors!' he called to his kinsmen. 'Do not draw your weapons against our Casmodian friends.'

The men sheathed their swords. Telitha ground her teeth like she was considering spitting poison at them and slowly turned to see what had caught his attention. Her round lips became taut in a sour smile when she realised it was me. 'The problem with you and your cousin is I cannot decide which one I hate the most.'

'How did you get here?' I asked.

'I rode through the gate, right past your oblivious husband and straight through town. He is an embarrassment to his heritage.'

A loud crash sounded behind me, and the barracks shuddered. A hole gaped in the snow-covered roof.

'Oh.' Telitha rocked forward onto the tips of her toes and back again with her hands clasped behind her back. She smirked. 'It seems our artillery has arrived.'

'Adaliah, Izak,' Kadram said, bursting out of the barracks with a red face. 'We have to get everyone out of Naldo. The town is coming down.' He saw Telitha and paled.

Telitha's insincere smile grew. 'Kadram. How delightful to see you again.' She raised the Jazmardian sword at him. 'You have the authority to make me regent. Do so now.'

Kadram scoffed. 'I may have the authority, but I do not have the inclination or intention.'

'I am the widow of the king, and Mirza is not of age!'

Kadram moved in front of me. 'I may have done it once, but now I would not crown you if all the Jazmardians in the world were dead and we were the only two left alive.'

Telitha's nose twitched with irritation. 'How dare you. I am of noble blood—'

'I dare because I will not let evil reign while I draw breath, no matter who you are.'

Telitha pulled a wooden instrument out of her cloak—a pipe of some sort. She brought it to her mouth and blew into it. A dart shot out the end. I pushed Kadram out of the way. The dart landed firmly in my shoulder, just above my right armpit. I bent forward with a cry and ripped it out.

Kadram snatched it from my hand and sniffed it. His face fell. 'Oh Adaliah . . . ' He grasped my upper arms. 'It is Dragon's Breath.'

There was a collective gasp from the Jazmardian soldiers. I teetered. *Dragon's Breath?*

I clutched at my heart.

I'll be dead within seconds.

My mind filled with the people I loved. Elhian, Alexia, Darj . . . My sons. I wasn't ready to leave them, and now I wouldn't get to say goodbye. They would grow up without a mother, as I had. Elhian and I still had so much to do together; now he would have to do it alone.

Telitha snickered uneasily. 'A fitting end for a murderer.'

I gulped.

A clear picture of Engres dying filled my mind. Telitha was right—I had murdered him.

I felt like I was going to vomit again.

Izak struck at Telitha with his sword. She raised the Jazmardian sword to counter him, but not quickly or strongly enough. It fell from her hand.

Izak snatched it up.

Telitha paused with an angry look before fleeing from us. I wanted to follow. I fell to my knees instead. Kadram caught me under one arm, and Izak rushed to grab the other. The Jazmardian men watched on with great concern.

'What can I do?' Izak asked as he and Kadram helped me lie down on the wet and muddy ground.

'Get Elhian,' Kadram said. His eyes filled with tears.

'There must be a way to save her,' Izak said. 'You and Lezan always know the remedy.'

'Lezan . . . ' Kadram muttered. 'How sad that she should die of poison, just as he did.'

'She is not going to die,' Izak said. 'She cannot!'

I gulped.

'It is Dragon's Breath,' Kadram said solemnly. 'Now please, get her husband—and the queen.'

The barracks trembled again as another stone catapulted into its side behind us. Izak ran.

'I am so sorry, Adaliah,' Kadram said, tears running down his cheeks. 'You should have let me take it. I am old and have lived a full life. It was me she wished dead just now.'

'Kadram,' I said. 'I don't feel any different.'

Kadram frowned as he took in my words and then my appearance. Now that the initial shock was subsiding, I realised I didn't feel sick in any way. I wasn't shuddering or frothing or waning. Apart from a fast heartbeat, I felt perfectly normal. Perplexed, Kadram pulled away my armour so he could see my shoulder. There was only a tiny prick of blood there—no redness, swelling or purulence.

'Impossible,' Kadram said.

I sat back up. 'Hazaka was almost dead by now. I feel nothing.'

'It seems . . . I do not know how it is possible, but it seems you are immune.'

I stood, and Kadram shed several more tears, this time from relief.

'Adaliah!' Elhian sprinted out of the barracks and towards us with Alexia close on his heels. Their eyes were wide with terror, and both their mouths dropped in confusion when they saw me standing as if nothing had happened. Izak, who had followed them back, smiled so widely at the sight of me that his white teeth seemed to take up most of his face.

Elhian and Alexia both encircled me in their arms. 'I thought . . .' Elhian began. They drew back, and Elhian squeezed both of my hands in his, closing his eyes and shuddering. 'I thought it was the end.'

'How are you still alive?' Alexia asked breathlessly.

'I don't know.'

'It appears she is immune to Dragon's Breath,' Kadram said. 'How or why, I cannot tell you, but she saved my life.'

'You are a miracle,' Izak said.

Alexia kissed my cheek with a small sob.

Another hole appeared in the roof of the barracks, reminding us all of the battle that was still taking place on the other side.

'Izak,' Kadram said. 'This battle is not going well. Even with the extra Jazmardians fighting for us, we will not have victory here this day, and there is something we must do while we still have time. Take my hand.'

The desert hunter stepped forward and awkwardly complied with his spare hand. The other was still holding the Jazmardian sword.

'You must be regent.'

'Me?' Izak asked with alarm, trying to retract his hand. 'I hunt dinner for my village. I am not royalty, nor do I have any notion of how to run a kingdom.'

'I have just seen how these Jazmardian men follow and respect you. You are the one to lead Jazmarda and to teach King Mirza the ways of the kings of old. As monarchs, do either of you have any objections?' he asked Elhian and Alexia.

'No,' they said.

'But—' Izak began, but Kadram cut him off.

'There is no time. Adaliah, you, Elhian, and Alexia stand as witnesses. Izak, you must repeat after me. I swear I will act faithfully as regent of Jazmarda until the king is of age.'

Izak Tan repeated the words in a quiet, unsure voice.

'I will bring Jazmarda hope and not despair and govern the people in fairness and truth. I will do my utmost to preserve the wellbeing of the people and to be a faithful father and guardian over King Mirza Cazren and his brothers.'

Kadram's delivery of the oath was punctuated with screams and rumbles within the town. Izak echoed the words with growing speed and conviction.

'The breath of Holormaza help me.'

'The breath of Holormaza help me,' Izak finished, referencing Ru'ach by the Great Spirit's Jazmardian name. He touched the side of his hand to his forehead and nose in the way Jazmardians do when making solemn promises. 'I will do all I can to restore the dignity of my kingdom.'

'You must go to Jazmarda and gather a greater army to bring back to Liane,' Kadram said.

'Liane?' Alexia asked.

'From there, we can direct them wherever needed. We must work to stop the Bone Hordes from coming any further north. Can you do it?' Kadram asked Izak.

Izak gulped and nodded.

'That will give you authority.' Kadram pointed to the Jazmardian Hope Sword Izak had taken from Telitha. 'Now, take whichever of your men you please and go.'

20

THE SUPREME OVERLORD

Catapults perforated the walls from outside the village. The White Army had breached the gates, and the battle was now in the streets. Stones peppered through roofs, and flames licked at doors, seeking entry into empty homes. Our catapults were either on fire or unmanned. Izak directed the majority of his battalion and the Jazmardians he had just redeemed from Telitha to stay with and support the Casmodian army. He and an elected few fled Naldo and began their journey to their red kingdom. I wondered fleetingly how Izak's kinsmen would receive him.

'What happened?' Darj called to us.

'I'll explain later,' Alexia said as she shot an Islander.

I took up my sword and rejoined the fight, but I took several blows and inflicted few in return. Apart from my ribs, I still felt well in my body, but in my mind, a word was growing like a suffocating weed.

Murderer.

I tried to keep it out, tried to fight against it while holding my ground against our enemies.

We fought until nightfall. I'd like to think our stand was valiant, but in review, we stayed too long, lost too many. Naldo fell. It was Elhian who made the decision to surrender. By then, at least half our men had died. A fatigued but resolute Darj and a small group of warriors held off the White Army in the town centre while the rest of us rounded the allied soldiers and Wolfgar out of the southern gate.

They escaped into the snowy night. I called Kadram and asked him to go after them.

'I will see you soon,' he said, briefly grasping my hand.

'I hope so.'

I watched him go, and then the gate unexpectedly slammed to the ground, almost landing on my foot. The men holding the chains in place had been slayed; Telitha, Garrow, and their soldiers had surrounded us with crossbows. Flames gave the night sky an orange glow, a hot reminder of our defeat.

And we were prisoners once more.

I was silent as they bound my hands. Three of Telitha's men shepherded Darj, Elhian, and me to the stables—one of the only buildings still intact. Telitha tied Alexia's hands behind her back and brought her over to us. Alexia's face was thunderous as Telitha prodded her in the back with a stick and laughed. When she did it a second time, Alexia spat in her face. Telitha furiously slapped her cheek in turn. My cousin tumbled to the ground, her bound hands unable to break her fall.

'Alexia!'

It was hard to tell if Darj's call was one of concern or reprimand.

One of Telitha's men hauled Alexia to her feet again and brought her to my side. She attempted to give me a reassuring smile, but her lips and cheek were smeared with blood, and her eyes still held a livid glint.

Telitha appeared in my face. 'How did you do it?' She spoke lowly, dangerously, but I detected a hint of relief there, which I found confusing. She seemed determined to kill me yet comforted to know she hadn't. 'How did you defy death in such a way?'

I didn't answer. I didn't know.

Coming up behind her were two Islanders carrying the body of an old man. My stomach lurched when I realised it was Engres. He was now more rigid and whiter than ever, his clothes covered in blood.

Telitha saw something in my face that pleased her.

'Yes, gaze upon the old man you murdered. Does it bring you satisfaction and pleasure? To be the murderer of a king? No?' She licked her lips. 'Do you know who he reminded me of?' She put a finger under my chin and tilted it up. 'Your father.'

Princess Yorella ran to Engres' body, weeping. I remembered my own father's death, and something inside me silenced.

Our weapons were confiscated and locked in a large, wooden box. One of Telitha's men led Leuk, Guntar, Hazel, and Bagred away. 'These are good strong horses,' I heard him say. 'They'll do well in battle for us.'

I frowned as Bagred's tail disappeared around a corner, away from me once more.

He will not fight for you.

Garrow and Telitha took us to the White Army's camp and pushed us into a small, leaky tent with a few furs thrown on the ground. I stood there staring at the floor, numb and exhausted. My arms ached, and my ribs throbbed from Garrow's kick. Elhian spoke gently to me, directing me to a patch of furs and helping me to lie down. I couldn't remember resting my head, just waking up several hours later with my back muscles aching and my heart heavy. It was still dark outside, but I could see the shadows of at least five soldiers spaced around our tent as guards.

Darj slept a few steps away from me, and Alexia and Elhian were whispering. I lay on my back and listened.

'How do you think she survived?' Elhian asked.

'I don't know. I'm just deeply thankful to Ru'ach that she did.'

'As am I.' A pause. 'Alexia, do you ever wish you had a different life?'

'Of course,' Alexia said with no change in her tone. 'Why?'

'Sometimes, I wonder if I'm fighting the best fight I can.'

'Losing one battle doesn't make you a failure. We were at a disadvantage from the start—greatly outnumbered and the town already besieged before we arrived. It was a success to get most of the people out and away safely.'

'We owe thanks to Darj for that,' Elhian said. 'You know, by the time you were my age, you had already reclaimed all of Targe from Cades.'

'Before that, I had lost all of Targe—everything my father had bequeathed me—and I only regained it with the help of you three. You were the one who saved my daughter from Cades' clutches, remember?' Alexia tilted her head. 'What's really troubling you?'

He took a deep breath and held it for a few seconds before expelling it. 'I'm worried I don't have what it takes.'

'What? To do what?'

'To do whatever a king is meant to do.'

'I think we're here to bring peace and prosperity to our people and to keep them safe. Don't you? That's what my father taught me.'

'There are times when I envy your clarity and confidence.'

'Elhian, I am making things up as I go most of the time. It's hard. You and I are responsible for so many lives. We're constantly being judged by all who live and work for us and threatened by those who would come against us. We are held accountable for every decision, and sometimes, I make the wrong ones, just as you will. But you know what?'

'What?'

'Every king and queen before us made wrong decisions, too. They lost battles. They hurt people they cared about. People died in their name.

We won't always make the right decisions; we just do our best to rule as wisely and as fairly as possible. Holding ourselves to an impossible standard isn't going to help anyone. Sometimes, this is hard because you and I . . . We were born into this. Our lives were chosen for us. But I have to believe that if Ru'ach brought me here to be the daughter of a king and to take up his sceptre, then he must have given me what it takes, and I just have to find it. The same is true for you. I believe in you. We all do.'

Elhian rubbed his face in his hands. I knew what the gesture meant. He was exhausted. But he did smile a little. 'You remind me of King Amaz when you talk like that,' he said wistfully. 'What I would have given to have him as my father.'

'You may consider his daughter your sister, if you wish,' Alexia said.

'I already do,' he said, and they both smiled. 'Adaliah seems so devastated by Engres' death,' Elhian added.

'I know,' Alexia said, more quietly. 'But we will help her through this. We will help each other through this.'

I still didn't feel up to talking when soldiers herded us from Naldo, into a carriage, and towards Semanez for our meeting with Mors. I alternated between torment and shame. Why had Engres' death stolen my voice when I had seen so many terrible and dark things before? My own father was killed before me. So were Ethaniel and Lezan and Zavad and Hazaka and Thane. I had killed many, many soldiers in battle. Death and I were neither friends nor strangers. I knew my silence was hurting my loved ones, but there were no words for how I felt. I was overwhelmed by guilt and haunted by Telitha's new word for me.

Murderer.

I hadn't been to Semanez since Alexia, Darj, and I released Targian soldiers there with young Zavad's assistance in the Northern Invasion. I had no desire to visit it again. It was Cades' foul residence, and I wanted no memory of him.

Hours passed with a sharp, lonely pain from all the things I could not say. The suppressed emotions seemed to swell between my stomach and heart.

'Have you come up with a plan to save us yet?' Alexia asked Darj as we rolled past snow-covered trees. The windows were not covered with cloths this time.

'No. Have you?'

'You're the general.'

'You're the queen.'

'Yes, but I delegated this job to you.'

'Being your husband already takes up all of my time.'

'Are you suggesting I'm high-maintenance?'

Darj scoffed. 'Does the sun rise in the east?'

Alexia leveled her gaze at him and laughed. The light, lovely sound was unexpected. Elhian and I looked at each other, and then we all laughed. I don't think any of us knew why exactly, given our dire situation; but just for a moment, the darkness and tension eased. Alexia moved towards Darj's face and kissed him. I pressed into Elhian's side, wishing I could take his hand or wipe away a tear.

'I'm so sorry,' I said with a sob. Now I wasn't sure if I was laughing or crying.

'She speaks!' Darj said.

'Oh, Adaliah,' Elhian said, kissing the top of my head.

I rested my head on his shoulder. 'Engres' death . . . It is burnt on my mind.'

'Garrow arranged that, not you,' Darj said firmly. 'You do realise he pulled Engres into the path of your sword, don't you?'

'What?' I had not realised that at all; I'd been so focused on saving myself. But now, I could see it. Engres had come to help his son, and Garrow had pulled him in front like a shield. That's why it happened so fast.

'Don't let that woman get inside your head,' Darj added masterfully.

I gave him a grateful smile. 'I'm so thankful to have you three with me.'

'You are our A'zyon Warrior,' Elhian said, 'and we love you and will help you.'

The despair I'd been feeling faded, like a black bird flying off into the distant sky. And the next thing I knew, I could breathe again.

It took us more than a week to reach the ruins of Semanez in the snow. I leaned against the carriage window—Telitha had not covered them in cloth this time—and saw what used to be the seat of the Casmodian monarchs: the ruins of Cades' castle, which had been set alight and left to burn at the time of the Northern Invasion. I had never seen it after the fire. It stood on the mountain still, but the top east corner had fallen away. The remaining stonework was black except where it was dusted in snow. It seemed strange that they were bringing us here, now. It was a reminder to me of what the Targians could achieve, of what we *had* achieved.

They drove us to the ruined castle forecourt. Telitha and Garrow escorted us inside the building. Elhian quietly took in the ravaged surroundings, walking in the steps of his childhood.

We were led down a set of spiral stairs into a basement, where they opened a stone door that had perfectly blended in with the rest of the wall. Elhian uttered a sound of surprise—even he had not known this was there. After that, we continued to walk down what felt like a thousand steps, the stone walls around us turning into raw, dirt ones.

I can do this.

I was determined not to be overcome by the cramped space. Thankfully, I didn't have to worry long. The stairs stopped, the tunnel ended, and the next thing I knew, we were standing in an enormous underground cavern. There was a thin layer of water across the ground like glass. It held the sparkling reflection of the five large candelabras dangling from the rocky ceiling. Something else hung from the ceiling—a large crescent moon, with a skull affixed in the centre of it. I shivered.

Garrow forced Darj, Elhian, Alexia, and me to our knees in a row, facing the back of the cavern where there appeared to be an iron table. The light was dull, so at first, my eyes didn't understand what they were seeing. The gold and silver shapes eventually started to make sense. The five crowns of the Rhea Lands sat on the table. Alexia's and Elhian's crowns—both in reach. The others noticed this, too.

Should I run up and grab them?

My hands are bound, I reminded myself.

I had spent a lot of time imagining what Mors would be like, but there was simply no precedent for what to expect when meeting a man who was said to be nine hundred and ninety-nine years old. Would he be old and deathly? Or surprisingly youthful and attractive, as the High Zalem in the Zalem Crisis had been? He had motivated so many men to evil, including Elhian's father. Ultimately, it was he who was responsible for the wars that had plagued us over the last six years. He could be blamed for the deaths of our loved ones and for the evil our enemies had performed. Anger stirred within me at the thought.

Garrow and Telitha stood behind Alexia and me.

'Adaliah Clair Edangard,' a voice said. 'There have been many deaths I have wished for, longed for, but none so much as yours.'

A figure hobbled towards us. The creature wore a black cloak that had successfully hidden him against the bleak walls. Taking one agonising step at a time, he eventually came into enough light for me to see his face.

He was vilely ugly. Scrawny and short, he had no hair on his body. His nose was long and pointed and his forehead burdened with innumerable wrinkles. Long slits were in the place of eyes and the irises beneath them appeared to be almost white. He carried a black stick with him that he tapped on the ground ahead of each step. His nails were so long, they doubled the length of his hands and made them look like claws.

A part of me wanted to laugh. This was the pathetic creature who had caused us so much trouble? This small, boney mortal? He did look old, the oldest man I had ever seen. But not nine hundred and ninety-nine years old. Something corrupt had preserved him all this time.

Behind him was another man standing with a large book in his hand, making various notes with a quill adorned with an excessively long raven feather. He was bald, too, but normally formed—taller than Mors, but shorter and rounder than the rest of us. I thought there was something vaguely familiar about him, and then I saw the scar on his chin. I caught the moment Alexia saw him and knew she had recognised him, as had Elhian on my left. His expression was one of disgust.

'Cordale,' he said.

I remembered the two small encounters I'd had with this man previously. First, the night Alexia had killed the High Zalem. When I had heard Sirvan talking about Darj, it was Cordale he had been speaking to. Second, when I went after Alexia to bring her the cure and found her in the Zalem tent, Cordale had been there, too.

And he had been there when they beat Elhian in Sharlard.

Bylon's secretary, the one in charge of non-combatant matters.

He busily scratched away in his book as if we weren't there.

'Which one shot you?' Mors asked Garrow. His voice was clear and even, and he spoke slowly, deliberately.

Garrow put a boot in Alexia's back and kicked her forward.

'Don't touch her!' Darj said, struggling towards his wife. Garrow grabbed Alexia and dragged her forward, away from Darj.

Telitha pressed a sword point into the back of Darj's neck. 'She took a shot at me as well,' she told Mors with bitter delight.

'Loosen her binds,' Mors said.

Garrow thrust a knife against the ropes around Alexia's hands, cutting them roughly and purposefully nicking her wrists. She didn't flinch.

'Extend her arm,' Mors said.

'No!' I imagined he was going to cut it off.

Telitha hit me with something on the side of my head. I fell to my side, my vision blurring.

Garrow stretched out Alexia's arm on the ground, his hand around her wrist. She didn't have time to be terrified. Garrow removed his hand; Mors lifted his heavy boot and brought it down on her fingers, crushing them. They cracked. Alexia cried out behind her teeth.

Darj's and Elhian's shouts echoed around the cave until they, too, were struck across their heads.

'She will never shoot a bow again,' Mors said.

'No,' Darj said, struggling against his binds. 'Alexia!'

Shaking from the shock of it, the queen stayed huddled against the ground and covered her disfigured fingers with her other hand.

'Three kings of the Rhea Lands have been killed,' Mors said. 'What do you think the next part of my plan is?' He turned his face towards Alexia and Elhian before calmly walking back towards the iron table and pulling a black cloth off something. It was a large cauldron on hot coals, full of molten liquid.

'It is time to forge one crown,' he said. 'The combined powers of state will give me unrivalled supremacy, but there is something even greater I need for it to work.' He licked his lips. 'The Medallion of Courage. Where is it?'

'Gone,' I said quickly. Too quickly.

Cordale scratched more notes in his book, staring intently at the pages. Mors picked up Engres' crown and discarded it into the cauldron like a butcher throwing away offcuts.

'Tell me.' He dangled Thane's crown over the mounting flames. 'Now.'

'Prince Bagred melted it down years ago,' Elhian said.

Mors dropped the Delyan crown into the boiling pot. 'Into a small arrow in his sword, which is now no longer there.'

The two discarded crowns shrank and melted away by the time Mors clawed at the Jazmardian one. 'Adaliah, do you know what you did when you thought you destroyed the darkness in the four swords? You released their darkness, Anash's darkness, back to me.'

Hazaka's crown fell into the cauldron with a gentle plop, like an apple falling from a tree. 'And do you know what happened when you broke the Dark Orb?'

I felt myself shrinking.

'I grew stronger.' He tapped his stick against the cauldron. 'I created them with Anash's power. Destroying them only returned their power back to me.'

The three crowns clung to each other in a golden mess. Now, Elhian's was in Mors' hands.

'Adaliah stopped their dark powers from being used against us,' Darj said.

'No, her actions merely delayed your defeat.'

Elhian peered at his crown in Mors' claws, sweat forming on his forehead. He gulped as Mors dropped it into the melting pot along with the others.

'It brought us to you,' Darj said, 'the lethal root of it all. Almost all of your protectors are—'

Garrow struck Darj across the face. Darj made no sound but bared his teeth at Garrow with restrained ferocity.

'This one is said to be the most beautiful of them all,' Mors said, using both hands to lift the Targian crown high into the air as if it were a sacrificial offering to a formless god. He glided his fingers over the twelve stars, seeing them with his hand.

Alexia hadn't moved. It was like she was no longer in the cavern. She paid no heed to what Mors was doing and didn't react when Garrow retied her crippled hand behind her back with her other.

Mors flung the majestic crown into the cauldron with the others. I wanted to cry, not just for what it meant for the kingdom, but also for the queen. It had been her father's crown and his father's crown and so on for many generations. It was a symbol of Targe. With no other ruling queens before her, Alexia had been the first woman to wear it. Now, it was dribbling in a pitiful pot. The queen stared numbly at the floor.

'The Medallion of Courage?' Mors asked, turning to Elhian and me. We said nothing. Cordale gave an almost indecipherable nod towards Telitha, who seized my hand like a cat and ripped off my wedding ring, taking a chunk of skin with it.

How did they know?

Garrow made the same move on Elhian, but Elhian ducked out of the way. Garrow grabbed his upper arm; Elhian bit his hand. Now incensed, Garrow raised the knife he had used on Alexia and tried to stab Elhian. Elhian moved away again, but the knife sliced off a piece of his earlobe. Blood ran down his jawline and neck. With Elhian distracted, Garrow took his ring.

Garrow and Telitha placed the two rings onto Mors' open palm. Mors tossed them together across his leathery white skin like he was shuffling a pair of dice. He clenched his fingers and moved his hand above the cauldron. Then, he let them drop into the fire.

21

A LETTER

'Why are you doing this?' Elhian asked as the mass of metals in the cauldron puffed and coughed. Gold sparks spat upwards.

'Why does anyone do anything?' Mors answered coolly. 'Why does anyone do anything if not to gain power? It all comes back to the one question that haunts us all, and power is the answer to that question and everything else. I have lived a long time and experienced many things. I believe that all fears come back to one. Sometimes, it is buried so deeply behind other fears, we hardly know it is there, let alone name it. But there is a question, a doubt, a fear that haunts us all. What if I'm not worthy?'

The cauldron bubbled.

'The four of you are the most well-known and influential people in all the Rhea Lands,' Mors said. 'And yet, what I have before me is a king who, despite defeating his father against all odds, still questions whether what he did was right, still questions whether he is the best person for the job, still asks himself, "What if I'm not worthy?"' Mors stepped towards Alexia. 'Beyond his southern border is his ally, a strong and beautiful woman renowned for raising her kingdom up out of the ashes, bringing prosperity and stability. She is one of my own descendants.'

He paused, giving us time to remember that through her mother, Alexia was said to have descended from the Zalems—from Mors himself. That was why they had hunted her in the Zalem Crisis. Did

Mors intend to draw her over to his side again, as Sirvan and Bylon had wanted? Is that why he hadn't killed her?

'No,' he said, as if reading my mind. 'She was offered all power and helpfully assisted in the assassination of the one High Zalem who ever betrayed me. He sought power from Anash to replace me as Supreme Overlord. He had to die, and who better to replace him than one of my own descendants?' He took a deep, weary breath. 'But twenty-eight generations allow for much change.' He turned his face towards Alexia. 'This worshipper of Ru'ach'—he spoke the name like he was coughing up something unpleasant—'made her choice to stand against me, and yet at night, she still wanders the gallery of portraits in her palace, stares at the kings and queens of old, sits by her daughter's bed and asks herself, "What if I'm not worthy?"'

'Her husband is even more interesting.' Mors pointed his stick towards Darj. 'Born the son of a scribe with a name no one beyond his village had even heard of, this boy joined the army and swiftly moved through the ranks until he became commander-in-chief of all the soldiers in Targe. He is the most powerful man in the kingdom, married to the most influential monarch, and yet he looks at his wife and child and constantly torments himself with that same ancient question. "What if I'm not worthy?"'

Mors' worn boots appeared in front of me. I kept my eyes fixed on Elhian, wishing I could go to him and stop his ear bleeding. 'And then there is this girl, seemingly the most unremarkable one of them all. The A'zyon Warrior is no stranger to fear. This girl knows what it is to lose herself, including her memory, and yet she has made sacrifices, fought wars, and defeated evil in many forms. But every time she is called to face a new enemy, a new fear, every time she stands before the ones she is to save, she doubts herself, asks herself, "What if I'm not worthy?"

'Over and over and over, everyone asks the same question,' Mors said, 'and power is the answer we seek. Power is the answer to fear. That is why we cling to it.'

'Power is merely a distraction from fear,' Darj said. 'You say the four of us are powerful and that we are still asking that question. How, then, does one cancel out the other?'

'That is true,' Mors said, returning to the cauldron.

'All you are saying is that we're afraid of letting each other down,' I said, 'and that comes from love. Love serves, but power is just a means for one person to impose their will upon another.'

Mors nodded. 'That is undeniably true. It is what makes power so enticing.'

'How did you get our crowns?' Elhian asked.

'They were stolen by one of my servants, long before you realised they were missing. With my thousandth birthday drawing near, I need them.' He added, under his breath, 'I need all the power I can get.'

'What will happen exactly, when you turn a thousand?' I asked.

'Oh, that is the best part,' he said, pausing to lick his lips. Cordale scratched furiously in his book, and Mors clicked his fingers.

All at once, our eyes were forced shut, and a vision appeared in our minds. In it, thousands of people knelt before Mors in the palace forecourt at Liane. Only, it wasn't the forecourt we knew. It was covered in listless, black leaves. The sky was tumultuous with storms and wind. Dead, twisted vines choked the palace's facade. The people had empty expressions, as if they had no sense of what they were doing, and they were chanting something dark and deep whilst bowing to Mors.

'When the sun sets upon my birthday,' he said, his voice bringing us back from the vision, 'when I have the victory I have long fought for, I will gain the power to bind every follower of Ru'ach to me as servants unto death, as servants of Anash.' Mors reached his hand out towards us and closed his fingers into a fist, as if he were snatching something. 'I will draw them to me, and they will serve me as a god.'

'We will lose our freewill,' I whispered.

'Isn't that the ultimate goal of power?' Mors asked. 'To control other people's wills, and to never again be at risk of being controlled?'

I cringed to imagine a world wherein Elhian and I and Darj and Alexia served Mors. No longer followers of all that is good, no longer able to determine our own thoughts and desires, but enslaved to darkness, to Mors. Our people, our children forced to worship him as they had once worshipped Ru'ach. No longer free. No longer us.

'You're going to make us Ghosts,' Alexia said. 'Like Bylon, Odavan, and Sirvan wanted.'

Mors reached his hand into the burning cauldron. I winced, but he didn't scream as I expected. Nor did the melted metals seem to burn him. Instead, he pulled out a new crown, one that had formed entirely of its own accord within the flames. It was a tall, sharp combination of the five crowns, large and imposing. Ten ugly, metal horns had risen around the circle.

'Yes,' Mors said to Alexia, 'but this time, I will only need to place your hand upon this crown. There won't be a bane, and so there also won't be a cure.'

With a self-satisfied smirk, he planted the crown on his head.

Cordale closed his book. He, Garrow, and Telitha dropped to their knees, the latter with tears in her eyes. 'Long live Emperor Mors,' she said. 'The Supreme Overlord.'

Mors began to change. The crown melted into his forehead, becoming a part of his flesh, a part of him. Thick, brown hair grew across his head, his wrinkles merging into one. He looked younger. The white in his irises faded, making way for a dark brown colour. I knew at once he could see again. With a yellow glint flashing across his eyes, Mors bent his knees and lowered himself towards the ground with an open palm. It was then I saw red scales forming across both palms and spreading rapidly up his arms to his shoulders like he was becoming part reptilian. His fingernails turned into long, sharp talons. He touched the thin layer of water with his fingers, and it changed colour.

Alexia took in a sharp breath. Elhian blanched. Darj glared savagely at Mors. I struggled against my binds, trying to get to my feet and out of the blood that now covered the cavern floor.

Garrow took us from the cavern, through a short, damp tunnel, and into a heavy-feeling, black room with only a small, high shaft letting in light and air. There were five cells in the room, several tables, and a wall covered in tools. Garrow pushed us into a cell each, locked the doors, and walked out.

'What are they doing?' Elhian asked from the cell to my left. He had ripped a piece of cloth from his clothes and was holding it to his ear. 'Why haven't they killed us or enslaved us to the crown?'

'We must still be of value to them,' Darj said from the cell to my right.

'How did he turn the water into blood?' I asked.

'He is a master of the dark arts,' Elhian said. 'Did you see those scales?'

'Yes.'

Darj leant through the bars to Alexia, who was imprisoned on his other side. 'Give me your hand.' She was nursing it against her chest. 'Come on,' Darj said soothingly. 'You know I have to put them back into place, or what Mors said will be true—you will no longer be an archer. Don't you want to defy him?'

Alexia grimaced. She took a step towards him and tentatively reached her hand through the bars. Darj wrapped his fingers around hers and placed his other hand on her shoulder to keep her steady. 'Are you ready?' he asked.

'Do what you must.' She bit her lip.

Darj crunched her hand with his, forcing the bones back into place. Alexia didn't cry out, but she bit her lip so hard, it bled. She swayed; Darj's hand kept her upright. She rested her forehead against his with a shudder.

The air coming in through the shaft was icy, and snowflakes wafted down towards us. Time passed, and the light from the shaft slowly moved to the wall across from us. A symbol was drawn across the black stones in white chalk. I had just recognised it as the broken butterfly when Telitha appeared.

Alexia groaned, no longer capable of hiding her dislike for the Jazmardian queen. She and Darj shared a significant look, and Darj gave her a slight nod.

'What's this?' Telitha asked. 'The Queen of Targe is not known to be ungracious.' She strutted towards Alexia's cell. 'I know how pleased you are to see me. Besides, I have wonderful news. We have just heard that Fenellar has fallen. Your green city is now controlled by the Bone Hordes.'

None of us responded.

'They will be on their way to Liane soon,' Telitha said with a note of glee. 'They will secure your palace for Emperor Mors.'

Alexia raised an eyebrow. 'Liane? Why is everyone so interested in my city?'

'It is merely its central location in the Rhea Lands that is desired, not any connection with you. But what makes it particularly delightful is that your children are all there. Unprotected. We will kill the youngest one first,' she said with a sneer towards Darj. 'She is only the child of a commoner, after all.'

Alexia's good hand flew up through the bars and around Telitha's throat. Telitha gasped. She dug her nails into Alexia's wrists until she let go. Telitha stumbled backwards, eyeing Alexia like she was a dangerous animal. Alexia's expression was unapologetic.

'Mors will turn a thousand in less than two months,' Telitha said. 'He will become immortal, and the world you saw will become your reality! He will force your hand upon the crown, and you will serve him unto death.'

'Why has he made himself known now, then, when he is still vulnerable?' Alexia asked.

'There is something—or should I say, *someone*—he must deal with before his birthday.' She glared at me.

'Why hasn't he killed us already?' I asked.

'Oh, you will die, dear one, you will die. But as for your friends here . . . Why would we kill them when they could serve Mors as Ghosts instead? That will be much more satisfying.'

'You killed your own husband to bring such a man to power?' Elhian asked.

'Husband?' She scoffed. 'I only married Hazaka to bring me closer to the crown. He was an unfaithful leech who deserved to die. It was Mors who gave me hope and a purpose. I am proud to serve him. Now, the crown has been reformed into a better one, imbued with all the evil power you cast out of the swords and the orb. That is why we will always survive. Whenever you think you have conquered our power, you have actually just released it back to us.'

'We will destroy the crown,' I said. 'We will destroy Mors, and we will destroy you. This world of his will not come to pass.'

Telitha took a step towards me. 'The crown can only be destroyed by the Supreme Overlord or one empowered as his High Zalem—me. Anyone else who tries to do so will die. It is like being one of the Ordained, only better. And who is here to give you another Jazmardian blessing that you might kill me?'

'Why are you afraid of my arrow, then?' Alexia asked.

Telitha glowered at her. 'I am afraid of nothing.' She turned on her heel and left the room.

'You really need to stop letting her get to you,' I said to Alexia once we could no longer hear Telitha's footsteps.

'I know, I know,' Alexia said with a sigh, now calm again, 'but she's so provoking. Did you get the keys?' she asked Darj.

Darj held up the ring of keys he had stolen from Telitha's belt while she'd been in Alexia's grip. Alexia smiled.

'You'd better hurry,' Elhian said to Darj, dropping the cloth away from his ear. 'It won't take her long to realise the keys are missing.' His ear had stopped bleeding, but there was a chunk gone. It gave him an untamed look, like a picture of a sailor from the Edeline Sea I'd seen once.

Darj fiddled with the keys and tried one in the lock to his cell. The door clicked open, and he proceeded to let me out, followed by Elhian.

'You would free me last, of course,' Alexia said wryly when Darj opened her cell.

He stood in the doorway with his hand on his hip. 'I have heard tales of men with mild-mannered wives,' he said.

Elhian laughed. 'I've heard tales of faeries and dragons, too.'

'What?' I asked.

Elhian shrugged, his mouth open innocently. 'What?'

There were two doors in the room. Elhian shoved a table up against the door Telitha had come in. Darj tried the various keys on the other door while I studied the tools that were hanging up on the walls. There was an odd mixture of straight and curved knives, chisels, shears, and manacles. Some of them had faint, red-black stains on them.

'I . . . I think this was a torture room,' I said.

'Probably one of my father's favourite,' Elhian said, jamming the table up under the doorknob.

I studied the chalk symbol of the broken butterfly. I didn't want to admit it, but I found it unnerving each time I saw it. I checked over a table covered in bits and pieces, found a lump of chalk, and scribbled over the top of the butterfly.

'I think I can hear someone coming,' Elhian said, pressing his good ear against the door he had just blocked.

Darj put the keys down and kicked in his door. Once was enough— it burst open. Darj led the way into the passage beyond, and we followed. I checked my writing on the wall as we left.

Not broken yet.

We passed through the silent and ghostly castle, Elhian leading us out. Several paths were blocked by rubble. Parts of the castle were significantly damaged by the rain and snow that had come in through the sky ceiling. Darj's leg slipped through a section of rotting floor, and we all had to help pull him out.

Eventually we reached a small library, which Elhian said his mother often used to write letters. The room was intact but dirty. I took note of a red sofa, several bookshelves, a desk, and a dusty fireplace.

'I'm sure there's another door in here that leads to a path out,' Elhian said.

Darj peered at the walls with his hands on his hips. Elhian moved a bookshelf across the door we had come in by, blocking it from any followers.

'This feels like a false wall,' Darj said, pressing his body against some stones on the other side of the room.

'Yes,' Elhian said. 'I think it is.'

They sought a latch or lever to open it.

'Actually, I think the lock for this door broke years ago,' Elhian said. 'It used to connect to that button up there.' He pointed to a stone brick that jutted out more than the others.

He and Darj dragged a table over to try and reach it, but it wasn't high enough. Darj squatted so Elhian could stand on his shoulders.

'Adaliah,' Alexia said, 'come and see this.'

She was kneeling next to a wooden box, the one our things had been stored in back at Naldo. It had an open padlock holding it shut, which Alexia easily removed. I helped her with the heavy lid. Inside, we found our swords and her bow.

'Telitha must be using this room,' I said uneasily as Alexia lifted her bow with her good hand. 'Why else would they be here?'

Neither of us had an answer, so we proceeded to remove the swords—my Life Sword and tree-blade, Elhian's Faith Sword, and Darj's two swords. Underneath were a few items of leather armour not belonging to us: several sets of boots, pants, and cuirasses.

'I know it's unladylike, but perhaps we should take the pants,' I said. 'It would be warmer than what we have on.' I was still wearing my leather armour and cape from the championship, including my leather skirt. It allowed for easy movement and a feminine look, but not warmth. Alexia was wearing a long-sleeved dress that was simple but impractical. The bottom half of it was stained from Mors' blood trick. Alexia agreed to the suggestion with a nod, and we proceeded to put on the pants. Alexia took a pair of boots and claimed one of the cuirasses. I used a sword to help her trim her dress so that it fell to her hips instead of her ankles, a makeshift undershirt that she tucked into her pants. Elhian and Darj kept trying to come up with ideas to reach the button, while Alexia and I sat on the sofa.

I took her sore hand into mine. It was red and swollen. 'It will heal properly, in time.'

'I hope so.' She leant her head back.

Darj and Elhian piled several items of furniture on top of each other in a rather precarious manner.

'Do you think we will be able to get out of here?' I asked.

'I'm sure we can,' Alexia said.

'What do you mean?'

'I could shoot the button with an arrow.'

'Why haven't you already? Oh, your hand!'

'I think it'll be less swollen if I can rest it. We're all tired. They don't know we're missing yet. We should take the opportunity to sleep. Besides . . .' She glanced towards Darj again, who had just slipped off their tower of furniture. 'I want to see how long it takes those two to come to the same realisation.' We chuckled. Elhian and Darj eyed us suspiciously.

Eventually, they gave up on their quest and agreed to rest before considering other options. The others fell asleep swiftly, Alexia lying in Darj's arms on the sofa, but I remained awake. I got up and opened the drawers in the desk. The first one contained an old, dried-out inkpot and an unwashed, rusty quill. The second contained a wad of paper, which had browned over time.

The third one harboured a single letter in an envelope. The outside was addressed to 'Her Majesty Queen Brielle Edangard'—Elhian's mother. I pulled the frail letter out and gasped when I saw the name of the sender. The beautiful handwriting was that of Princess Cassondra Elryane—*my* mother. I made a quick calculation from the date in the top corner and concluded that it was written when I was one-and-a-half years old. She would have been pregnant with my brother by then, just a few months away from their deaths. I felt both amazed and nostalgic.

The letter described my mother's agreement to one day introduce me to Elhian.

My daughter is beautiful, good-natured, and strong, and I love her dearly. If she were to form an attachment to your son, we would have no objection and would indeed be happy, even if they only chose to become good friends. Allies are hard to come by in this current world, as you well know.

I had no memories of my mother. To see something of how she thought of me was surreal. I clutched the letter in my hands, wanting to retain its words in my heart forever.

Somehow it was reassuring to know our mothers had blessed mine and Elhian's union long before we knew each other. But there was something else my mother had written, and when I got to the end of it, I was so stunned I went several moments without breathing.

I have completed the inquiries you requested. Given that we live much closer to Etarbelec than yourself, the information has come back surprisingly quickly. It is not good news, Brielle. In fact, it is just as you feared. The mother to the child is a Jazmardian 'damzalla'—what we would call a lady. She is married, but her husband has given her no children. She brought forth a daughter to Cades just five weeks after your princeling was born. Her husband must know she can't be his, but he hasn't abandoned them. The damzalla named her daughter Telitha.

I am so sorry, dear Brielle, to further crush your spirit.

I dropped the letter.

'You killed my father in the Northern Invasion,' she'd said to Elhian that day.

Telitha is Cades' daughter.

22
THE WHITE PRINCESS' PLEA

Once the shock had passed, I put the letter in my pocket and lay down to try and sleep. I was successful, but not for long. I woke just after dawn to a loud thud and jumped up. Another thud followed.

'Break it down.'

I recognised the cold voice on the other side of the door. It was Telitha.

Cades' daughter, I realised all over again. The traits between them were not so different, now that I considered it. It was strange to think she was related to Elhian, who I knew to be kind, strong, and merciful—everything Telitha was not.

I nudged him. He blinked, his chipped ear still swollen and caked in blood. I shook Alexia and Darj awake.

'Time for us to get out,' I said to Alexia, nodding towards her bow.

Darj looked about urgently, trying to come up with a solution. The door shook as Telitha's soldiers assaulted it with kicks.

'Alexia,' Elhian said with a sudden thought. 'You could shoot the button!'

Alexia, who had already picked up her bow, smiled at him. 'You are so smart.'

Elhian narrowed his eyes like he knew he was being teased but wasn't sure how or why. His questioning look to Darj was met with a slight shake of the head and upturned palms.

Alexia loaded her bow with an arrow. She grimaced as her sore right hand pulled back on the string. She aimed and let the arrow fly.

It hit the wall, a stone away from the button.

'You missed,' I said with horror. 'You missed!'

'You don't miss!' Elhian said, glancing towards the bookshelf at the door. A few books fell to the floor after another thud.

Darj's mouth was open. 'What happened?' he asked.

'What hap—you do remember four of my fingers were dislocated and fractured yesterday, don't you?' Alexia picked up the arrow. This time, she groaned as she forced her hand to do what she wanted it to. With a cry of pain, she released the arrow and hit the button. The false wall immediately moved aside.

'Go!' Darj said.

Alexia collected the arrow for a second time and ran into the passage with me on her heels. Darj and Elhian followed. I heard the bookshelf fall to the ground as Telitha's men broke through behind us.

'That way!' Elhian pointed to a path that veered to the right.

We ran as quickly as we could through burnt and broken hallways with crumbling walls, careful where we placed our steps lest we fell through the floor as Darj had almost done the day before. We came out on top of one of the castle walls where snow was falling. We had lost our followers but could hear lots of shouting back inside. We ran down the exterior stairs of the wall to the frozen ground.

'Adaliah,' a voice called.

Crouched amongst some trees were three people I immediately recognised. One was Wolfgar the blacksmith and fletcher. One was Kadram. The other was Yorella, Princess of the White Isles.

The four of us crossed a white road to meet them. We were now outside the city entirely, at the back of the castle and in the shadow of one of the mountains. We moved further away from the castle wall and into the forest.

'We were coming to rescue you,' Wolfgar said.

'Why are you here?' I asked Yorella.

She looked younger than I remembered. Her long, blonde hair was draped across her shoulders and shimmering, captor of several snowflakes that added to her look of purity. 'I came to help.' Her sage eyes were earnest. 'My brother has strayed far from the Islander way.'

'I killed your father.' It came out compulsively. 'I'm so sorry.'

'No, my brother arranged that. He is . . . vile.' I met her eyes and sensed what she meant. Most importantly, she seemed genuine. 'Without my father to restrain him, he is also dangerous.'

'We need a plan,' Alexia said.

'Well, we have half a plan,' Kadram said, 'but more on that later. Come with us and get to camp first.'

We followed Kadram, Wolfgar, and Yorella for most of the day along a path so thin, it was like a piece of string fastened to the side of the mountain. Wolfgar struggled with the steep steps and thinning air the most, but it was hard on all of us. The cold was the greatest problem, as none of us had the fur coats generally needed for such weather and altitude. I tried to walk faster to maintain my body heat, but I was losing warmth so fast, my muscles were cramping and refusing to move the way I wanted.

Around a bend in the mountain, towards the east, there was an unexpected, treeless plateau. Across the plateau was an army of tents. Smoke rose from campfires, the woody smell familiar and comforting. Numerous soldiers sat around them, some of them roasting meat for their dinner, others sharpening their blades. Some noticed our arrival, stood, and bowed their heads to us. A soldier talking to a man with shoulder-length, black hair pointed at us, and the man—our friend Xander—turned around.

'Your Majesties,' he called. He walked towards us with high, fur-edged boots that left deep imprints in the thick snow. His hair was dampened from the snow, and he had smears of dirt on his arms and chin. He almost always wore a serious expression, as if he were intently and carefully studying everything around him. Such a look framed his face now.

'Captain,' Darj said, 'where did you get these men?'

'They are our soldiers from Chettona, Hunt, and some smaller villages; about two thousand men,' Xander said. 'I brought them here to rescue you, although clearly, that isn't needed. But they can also fight if it comes to that.'

'It may well come to that,' Darj said.

Xander patted the prince-general's shoulder. 'Come inside and talk.' He turned to Alexia. 'Your Majesty, I took the liberty of bringing your royal tent with me from Liane. The men have set it up, and it is warm and comfortable.'

'Oh Xander,' Alexia said with great relief, 'don't tell the others, but you are my favourite captain.'

Xander grinned as he took us to the large tent, where a fire happily crackled in a small pit inside. The floor was otherwise covered with rugs. A bed was made up for Alexia and Darj to one side, with another for Elhian and me on the other side. The warmth thawed my frosted fingers, and I felt deeply grateful. Xander gave us each a blanket. I put mine over my shoulders and pulled it in closely.

'Make yourselves comfortable,' he said. 'I've sent one of the men for food.'

The four of us, plus Yorella, Kadram, and Wolfgar, gathered in a circle around the fire. I hovered my hands above the flames as closely as I dared.

'After we left Naldo,' Kadram said, launching straight into the story, 'Princess Yorella joined me within the hour.' His eyes sparkled at her.

'I knew the time had come for me to leave my brother's hold,' Yorella said. She was trying to be brave, but her grief wasn't far below the trembling lips and watery eyes. I looked away, my guilt at her father's death and the consequential responsibility it had thrown on this young girl still raw.

'The soldiers who escaped with me helped me retrieve your horses one night while the Islanders were sleeping,' Kadram said. 'They assisted me in tracking you all from a distance, from Naldo to Semanez. We didn't have enough numbers to challenge the Islanders openly, but not one of us wanted to return home or go to Targe without you.'

'I left Liane the day after I delivered the children,' Xander said. 'I felt certain you would need support, so I called these men to arms and followed your trail to Crisock. We cut across the back of Naldo, where I found Kadram.'

'What about our children?' Alexia asked.

'They are being well cared for,' Xander said. 'Lord Fenton is still residing in Liane Palace. He has sent a good portion of the Targian army south to try and stop the Bone Hordes from coming any further north. He thinks they will meet in battle near Levanna.'

'I am grateful for his help,' Alexia said.

'Here,' Xander said. 'I brought this for you.'

He took out a piece of paper from his shirt pocket and unfolded it. It was a collage of drawings and writings from the five children we had sent to safety. There were prints of my twins' hands and feet in blue paint. Running my hand over them felt surreal. Little Nichole's prints were there in green. Jeri had written a short note on the top left corner: 'Please come home as soon as you can. I am worried about you.' Next to his words were Eva's. The writing was unpolished and large but clear: 'I love you, I love you, I love you.'

The following days brought bad weather that forced us to rest. The falling snow and wind cleared at dusk on the third day, after which I found Alexia standing outside in the cold, gazing up at the glistening sky. The stars were particularly clear and numerous, like sugar spread across a black canvas. I was still getting used to seeing Alexia in pants. She had tied her hair up in a ponytail, giving her a practical look that was far from the queen who graced the ballroom in elegant gowns. I linked my arm through hers.

'Do you think we're letting our children down?' she asked.

'No.'

Alexia seemed puzzled by my quick response.

'I miss them,' I said. 'I worry about them more than I can say, and of course I hate that we have to be separated. But ultimately, we are doing this for them, to secure their future. If we don't fight, if we were to return home and let Mors win . . . You saw the world he desires, the world he is striving for. You saw what he wants to do to your palace and our people. Letting such a world become a reality for our children, letting them become Ghosts . . . *That* would be letting them down.'

'Do you mean to say we must put duty ahead of family?' she asked with a faint smile.

I hesitated. 'In this instance, I think protecting our people and our family can be achieved at the same time.'

'Yes.' Alexia turned her face back towards the stars. 'I worry the most about Eva. She's always been more sensitive. I know it probably sounds strange, but sometimes I think it's because my pregnancy with her was so fraught with fear and stress—the darkest days in my life. My time carrying Jeri and Nichole was characterised by love and happiness, and the two of them are much more settled in everyday life. When Eva said those things to me in Dawfield . . . ' Alexia brought a hand to her face as a tear appeared. 'I can't help but feel like I'm letting her down.'

'Not for the first time, you take on too much.' I hugged her, rubbing her back. 'It is hard for a warrior queen to keep her children safe, but your love for them will be what saves them. Hope marked your pregnancy with Eva more than anything else. This is not your fault. This is evil's fault. Stop trying to take responsibility for everything and everyone. We are doing this for them. That is love, not neglect.'

She nodded. 'I am afraid of losing Darj, too. I saw him in my vision, the one Mors forced on us. I saw him dying in my arms, just as Ethaniel did. I can't go through that again. There have been times, even before that, when the mere thought of his death paralyses me.'

'Oh, Alexia,' I said, hugging her again. 'Darj is the strongest warrior I know. You must have faith in him and not give heed to Mors' attempts to scare you.'

'I know.' She wiped away the rogue tear that had fallen on her cheek. 'Now, is what Mors said about you true?'

'What do you mean?'

'Do you question your ability to conquer fear, even now?'

I shrugged uncomfortably. 'Is it true you feel unworthy next to your ancestors?'

'Well, perhaps,' she said. 'But you have achieved too much to let such fear be a part of your life. Don't you know how much we owe you? How much we admire you?'

I shrugged again, embarrassed. 'Sometimes I think all of you admire the idea of me—the idea of the A'zyon Warrior.'

'No.' She clasped my upper arms. 'It wasn't an idea that defeated Jag or destroyed the Dark Orb, or that brought me back from the depths of darkness when I may have otherwise died or been driven into madness. It was this woman right in front of me, and I am so glad she is here with me now.'

'You were there for me, and I'll always be there for you, remember?'

The quote of her childhood promise to me brought a smile back to her face. 'Always.'

'Kadram, tell us more about your half-a-plan,' Darj was saying when Alexia and I found them standing at the edge of the plateau, facing the ruins of Semanez. There were a few lights visible in the old castle, but otherwise it was a ghostly sight made all the more eerie by the white moonbeams accentuating the dark shadows and crumbling houses.

Beyond the city walls, there was the faint indication of fires—the campfires of the Islanders who had followed us from Naldo. They would all be talking of our escape by now.

'The Islanders will continue to conquer Casmodia in the north,' Kadram said, 'while Fenton is fighting the Bone Hordes in the south of Targe.' He drew a rough map in the snow. 'Mors is at the centre of it all. Now, I have been thinking. Yorella has a claim to the crown of the White Isles. We need her to convince the Islanders to stop attacking. We need her to take charge of them.'

'But for her to truly have a claim to the crown, we must remove Garrow from the royal line,' I said, 'and soon.'

'Yes,' Kadram said. 'That is certain.'

'Mors will turn a thousand soon,' Elhian said, 'and that will somehow make him more powerful.'

'We have to act quickly,' Darj said. 'In the morning, let's take our men down to the White Army and see if Yorella can convince them to abandon their loyalty to Garrow, as Izak did with the Jazmardians.'

'It's a large burden to place on the shoulders of a young girl,' Alexia said.

'You and Adaliah were burdened with more at her age,' Kadram said, 'and were victorious.'

Alexia seemed unsure. 'What if she doesn't succeed?' she asked evenly. 'We can ride out there with her, but if it comes to battle, I don't think we have enough men to face them and win, and . . . ' She raised her sore hand, which Elhian had bandaged to stabilise her tender fingers. 'Shooting a single arrow is one thing, but battle requires me to shoot several hundred—not something I can do right now. I will be a millstone if I ride to the front with you. A lame horse.'

'We have to stand together,' Kadram said. 'Otherwise, we will appear weak. The four of you must face the White Army with Yorella together.'

'And pray to Ru'ach for a miracle,' Darj added solemnly. 'Otherwise, a safe retreat is the best we can hope for.'

I hadn't told Elhian that Telitha was Cades' daughter. As I tried and failed to sleep that night, I wondered what good it would do. Would it have any impact on anything? As Cades' child, she was a potential threat to the Casmodian throne, but she had never indicated she was interested in ruling. As a younger, illegitimate child, any claim she made would be a tenuous one.

Not telling him didn't sit well with me either. We had long ago promised that no secrets would ever come between us. Didn't that have to override everything else? But I also didn't want to breathe life into the pain his father had already caused him by telling him Cades' lust had brought forth our current enemy. It was such an insult to Elhian—and to his mother.

Still unsure and tormented with the knowledge, I decided not to say anything until after we had confronted the White Army. I turned over and tried to sleep.

'Adaliah, get up,' Darj said, touching my shoulder at dawn. He did the same to Elhian next to me. 'Come. We need to go.'

Within the hour, our soldiers—a mixture of Casmodians, Jazmardians, Targians, and one White Isle princess—travelled down the mountain towards Semanez. Darj, Elhian, Alexia, and I had been reunited with our horses, and we led them along the fragile mountainside track. Riding them along such a path was impossible, especially when the wind picked up and snow squalled around us.

Before reaching the city, Elhian took us down a path that led us away from Cades' castle. We trekked through a sparse pine forest, circling the ruined city towards the White Army. A scout had reported that they were still stationed at the western gate.

Yorella had agreed to try and convince the men to follow her, but her face was paler than normal. At sixteen, I was inclined to think Alexia was right—this was a lot of responsibility to place on her shoulders. But Kadram was also right: I'd only been seventeen when I defeated Jag at Kest River.

Age is not the only measure of a leader.

Our men marched towards our destination until the front line stepped out of the forest and in sight of the White Army. I mounted Bagred and pulled Yorella up behind me. Leaving our soldiers in position at the trees' edge, we rode towards the White Army alone.

They had already seen us. Perhaps they had known we were coming all along. They weren't lazing about in their tents. They were up, armed, and ready for battle.

I hadn't let myself think too much about the chances of this plan turning to combat. We were outnumbered, so if battle ensued, we would most likely have to retreat and hope to make it to Targe, as Darj and Alexia had warned. I kept telling myself Yorella could convince them. If we could make an ally out of the White Army, we could storm the castle in Semanez and defeat Mors well before he had his birthday and increased in power. It could all be over by nightfall. I imagined us riding victoriously towards Liane the next day to reunite with our children.

I didn't want to think about the alternative.

The Islanders called to each other in their own language.

'They are preparing to attack,' Yorella whispered in my ear.

With an angry impulse, I dug my heels into Bagred and cantered towards them. Elhian, Alexia, and Darj called out to me, but their voices were hard to hear over the wind.

I rode right up to the Islanders' frontline. Surprise hummed across the army when I turned Bagred and they saw Yorella. She was breathing quickly, puffs of white air shooting out of her mouth.

'How dare you kidnap the Princess of the White Isles?' one of the bulkier men yelled. 'Princess Yorella, say the word, and we will kill your captors!' The men jabbed their weapons into the sky. One of them aimed a spear at me; I scowled at him.

Yorella slipped off Bagred's back and stood in the snow, her green eyes wide and pleading.

'She killed our king!' one of them called.

'No,' Yorella said. 'No, you don't understand . . . Garrow—he arranged that. These people . . . They are our friends. I went to them willingly.' Her voice was feeble against the wind. The men looked at her like she was a rabbit and they the foxes. 'I am still your princess . . . And I . . . I command you to . . . to drop your weapons.'

No one moved. The wind whistled around us. I shivered.

'Sister!' a voice called. The men parted, and Garrow walked towards us. His blond hair was grittier and oilier than before. 'I've been so worried about you. Come here.' He held his hand out to her and glared hatefully at me. 'Come here now and I will let your "friends" ride away unharmed.'

'Please, don't fight them,' Yorella said, a little more loudly this time. 'I want us to return to our families and homeland in peace.'

I studied the faces of the men ahead of me. Some of them seemed to be listening to her, but not one of them moved. They would not defy Garrow. He was their king now.

'Get back on the horse,' I whispered sharply to the princess. If they decided to attack, I wanted a quick escape.

She gave me the slightest shake of her head. 'My father never wanted it to come to this,' she said to the Islanders, more confidently this time. 'He would never have aligned with the Zalems. By fighting with Garrow, you are aligning yourself with them, with evil, with Anash. You know what the Zalems have done to Targe and Casmodia in the past and how they have conquered Delya now. Do you want them to defile and defeat the White Isles, too?'

Garrow stepped forward with his hand outstretched like he was planning to clamp it over her mouth. But then a strange thing happened. One of the Islander soldiers threw Yorella his spear. She caught it, and using it like a staff, she delivered a perfect blow to the side of Garrow's head before he could touch her. It was hard enough to force him down without rendering him unconscious. But now he was mad.

'All of you who would stand with me, fight now!' he yelled.

'All of you who believe in the true Islander way, come and fight by me!' the princess called.

There followed another tense moment as the soldiers considered their options. Several of them defied Garrow by walking to our side. Some of them had friends who grabbed their shoulders, but most shook them off and kept walking towards the princess. More and more followed. There were arguments. Garrow was yelling at his betrayers, but they didn't listen.

About a third of them formed a battalion by us. Yorella gave me a happy look.

I tried to return it, but I knew the truth.

She hadn't won over the entire army.

We were going to battle.

23
THE BATTLE OF SEMANEZ

Some moments like this blur in my mind—not from the decay of time, but from the dreamlike chaos of it all. One minute, the two armies faced each other, unmoving, negotiating. The next, we were fighting. I don't remember how it came about. We had wanted to avoid battle. No one gave the call to fight, at least not that I heard. But before I knew it, my sword was bloodied, and the allied army was charging at the Islanders with unsheathed blades.

I worried for Alexia, whose hand made it impossible to fight, but when I saw her riding towards Semanez itself, I became even more anxious. She couldn't remain in the battle as an archer with a wounded hand, but surely she hadn't decided to go and find Mors herself?

I sighed. *Nothing would surprise me.*

Yorella proved to live up to her father's word as the finest spear maiden. She wielded her weapon almost effortlessly, even though it must have been heavy and tiring to bear. Garrow also used a spear, but he appeared to enjoy the killing.

The two armies meshed together. Bodies fell to the ground. Darj landed a mighty kick in an Islander's chest, and the man went flying backwards into the snow. I shattered an Islander's spear with my sword and impaled him.

Time passed. I remained on Bagred for as long as I could, but as I reached down to slay a man to my right, another pushed me off my horse from the left. My ribs smarted when I hit the ground. I rolled over and swiped my sword at the leg of the man who had pushed me. He jumped with pain and stumbled away.

Elhian pulled me to my feet. Blood was trickling down his neck again. Someone had upset the wound on his ear. He looked wild and desperate.

'Where's Alexia?' I asked.

'I don't know.' He ran his sword into a soldier who had come up behind him and pushed him to the ground. 'She rode towards Semanez.'

'I know. I haven't seen her since.'

The battle wasn't going as badly as I'd expected. I could see our men holding their own, possibly because Darj and Elhian were doing the work of ten men each. Yet both sides were suffering significant casualties. We battled on, and the sun's descent soon flooded the sky with orange.

'Get her!' a shrill voice yelled.

Alexia was riding towards us, her empty bow in her right hand. Telitha chased her on foot.

'Stop her!' Telitha yelled again.

As Alexia came closer, I realised she was clinging to her reins as if they alone were responsible for keeping her alive.

What's happened?

A loud and awful screech pierced my ears. It seemed to come from within Semanez. The men on the field stopped. There was another screech, followed by the thud of heavy hooves.

Elhian and Darj rode to me, Elhian leading Bagred beside him. I mounted my horse, reached across to Elhian's arm and dug my nails into him, fearful but not quite sure why until Mors came galloping out on the field. He was carrying a burning torch and riding a magnificent beast—a great, silver horse with feathering around her ankles and a broad back. She was at least two hands taller than Bagred. Mors opened his mouth as if to shout, but he did not make a sound. He raised the torch in front of his face, and when he exhaled, a rush of flames burst forth.

The men on both sides fled amongst the trees. There was screaming and chaos on every side. Telitha laughed hysterically as Mors charged towards Alexia. There wasn't time for any of us to react or help. He drove his horse directly into Hazel, sending both the mare and her mistress to the icy ground. Hazel struggled to her feet, but Alexia lay unmoving.

We ran for her, but Mors shot a fiery breath towards us. It was green in colour and hot and smoky. Elhian drew in a lungful of the smoke and coughed so violently, he dropped to his knees. Strangely, it seemed to have little effect on me. Mors swerved towards the fleeing men and caught up to them within a matter of moments. He breathed fire towards their backs. The soldiers screamed as they were scorched. Some of them were wreathed in flames, flailing their arms. One of them ran past me, bumping me in his terror and causing me to lose my grip on my Life Sword. It fell to the ground.

Mors slowed and slumped in his saddle like he couldn't support his own body weight. Somehow, the fire breathing had weakened him.

'Adaliah, your sword!' Yorella shouted at me.

Garrow snatched the Life Sword and sprinted away. I threw my tree-blade after him. It flew through the air but landed short of its target. I stood on the spot, briefly unsure what to do. Alexia was only just standing, dusting herself down. To go after Garrow was to abandon everyone else. To let him go was to relinquish my sword. What that might mean, I couldn't imagine.

He cannot wield it for bad. There is no power he can gain from it.

With that thought in mind, I picked up the tree-blade and returned to the battle on Bagred. It was almost completely nighttime now. I rode for Mors.

He was sitting up straight again, the ugly crown still sunken into his head. 'Where is the Armoured Butterfly?' he asked me with a glare.

There had been two. The original one shattered after I cleansed the swords, and the spare was once kept in Alexia's Targian Orb. It flew away after I destroyed the Dark Orb. It hadn't been seen since.

'Do you think it will give you more power?' I asked.

Mors' dark brown eyes peered into mine. 'In a way.'

'The Armoured Butterfly only serves the Keeper of Kest. Until Princess Eva turns sixteen, that is me.'

Mors chuckled. 'I don't want it to serve me. I want to destroy it.'

'Why? The Armoured Butterfly is no threat to anyone. Its main function is to carry messages. Are you so frail that you see it as a threat to you?'

Darj rode up next to me, presumably to help. Before he could speak, Mors raised the torch to his mouth and directed a breath of fire towards us. Thankfully, it was a short streak that failed to cause harm. Mors sneered and rode after our men once more, sending scorching flames their way. Darj uttered his least favourite word: 'Retreat!'

I rode through the men, yelling the word over and over until I was sure they had the message. They ran for the forest, Alexia leading them. I imagined she was injured from Mors' attack, but obviously not to the point of incapacitating her in any serious way.

The Islanders chased us. I focused on them—a problem I could assist with solving—and rode alone through the gap that was growing between the two armies. I used the tree-blade to slay those who were hounding our soldiers. Elhian joined me, having ridden in from the other side, and together we gave our men the chance to escape. Using the torch, Mors continued to spit out green fire that melted snow and set trees aflame. More of our men burned. Mors' iron-like talons eviscerated many others. The only thing that saved us was that once again, his strength waned. He sank forward in his saddle before sliding to the ground. This didn't seem to matter to his men. They cheered so hard at their victory that it was a relief to enter the snowy forest and ride away from Semanez forever.

24
RETURN TO TARGE

We reached the Targian border at midnight, frozen and numb—and not just from the winter. Few words were exchanged amongst any of us until we finally conceded that Mors was not hunting us down and made camp.

Elhian and I attempted to sleep the rest of the night in a flimsily constructed tent one of the men brought with them, but it was useless. How does anyone sleep after being confronted by a fire-breathing man? And why had Garrow wanted my sword so badly that he had run away with it and abandoned the battle he and Telitha had incited? I told myself over and over that there was nothing he could do with it, but the dread in the bottom of my stomach refused to leave.

After tossing and turning for two or three hours, Elhian and I gave up and stepped outside to a dawn just blushing on the horizon. We saw Darj and Alexia already in conference with Kadram and stumbled over to them. I knew at once that Darj had not slept. The brims of his eyes were red, and dark blemishes had bloomed beneath them.

'Tell them,' he said to Alexia.

'When I went after Mors,' she said in a low voice, 'I shot him. I shot him right in the heart with one of Wolfgar's arrows.' She placed her hand over her own heart to emphasise her point. 'Any other man would have died instantly, but he didn't. Instead, he screeched and breathed fire at me.' Her voice was on the edge of breaking from the shock of it all.

'But . . . ' I took a deep breath. 'Telitha said he wouldn't be invincible until he turned a thousand, and that is weeks away.'

'There must be a way to kill him now,' Kadram said. 'If life has taught me anything, it is that there is always a way.'

'Did you see his horse?' Darj asked. 'It was Brzina, the fabled Targian horse renowned for her speed and strength.'

I remembered Darj speaking about her in our stables. 'She is no longer a fable,' I said. 'She's terrifying.'

'I propose we go south, to Levanna,' Darj said. 'We don't have enough men to face Mors again here, but at Levanna, we can meet our southern army and try and stop the Bone Hordes from coming any closer to Liane. That is, if Elhian is agreeable to the idea.'

I knew what he meant. To go to Levanna in the south of Targe was to abandon Casmodia. The Casmodian army would defend Tiathi and the southwest corner, but the rest of the kingdom would belong to the Zalems.

'I think that Mors, Garrow, and Telitha will follow us with their soldiers to Targe,' Elhian said. 'If you're worried about Casmodia, don't be. The threat will come with us.'

'Are we unnecessarily risking Targe?' Alexia asked Darj. 'Or Casmodia?'

'I don't know,' Darj said, running a hand through his hair. 'What I do know is that both kingdoms are already greatly at risk. Both have been invaded. We have no advantages in fighting them here, in our current position, but I think we will have a chance if we can regroup in Levanna.'

'Can we stop at Liane on the way?' Alexia asked. 'We should talk to Lord Fenton to find out what information he has, and we could see the children.'

Darj reached for her hand. 'Of course.'

For fifteen days, we rode deeper into Targe with Kadram, Princess Yorella, and our army. There was no sign of Mors, but we feared he would come upon us at any moment. During that time, I pondered the gravity of our situation. Never before had history seen three monarchs dead in such a short time, and yet Mors was still alive and incredibly powerful.

Soon after we passed near Amathea's Knoll and into the rolling plains I had once called home, the four of us said goodbye to the rest of our followers, except twenty men charged with escorting us to Liane. Kadram, Xander, and Yorella agreed to ride with the rest of the soldiers directly to Levanna and to make preparations to defend the town. We planned to join them no more than a week later, leaving us with a very short time to visit Fenton and our children.

It was with relief that Liane came into view on the sixteenth morning. The four of us were tired, cold, and irritable. We knew and loved each other well and coped with travel better than most people. But by the last few days, Elhian and Darj were chipping at each other's sense of direction—'Are you sure we're going the right way?' Alexia and Darj got snappy over who should hunt dinner with her bow and arrows, and I received a lecture from all three for losing concentration and making too much noise as we rode through a forest. It had also been a long time since any of us had bathed. The rivers were either frozen or too cold, and we had avoided villages for fear of Mors hearing word of our location. We all smelt like the wild.

Having travelled together many times, we knew each other's peculiarities well. Darj, for example, was unable to pass by trickling streams without them having a swift impact on his bladder. It was such a hindrance that we did our best to avoid them, even when it meant riding further than we otherwise would. Elhian hated sleeping with anything on his feet and left them hanging out of the blankets, claiming that his calloused feet were impervious to the snow. His feet stank so badly from being unwashed and confined in leather boots all day that Alexia refused to sleep downwind of him. The queen herself had the habit of piously claiming that she didn't need anything to eat every time the rest of us stopped to cook something, only to complain an hour later, once we had resumed our travels, that she was starving. Apart from my slip with making too much noise, I, of course, never did anything to irritate anyone.

We talked on and off about our situation and what to do, but so much of that depended on what we would find at Liane and then Levanna. As we rode through the north gate of the great Targian city, it was clear it was not under siege—something I had feared—but it was hushed. We saw few people about until we came into the forecourt of the palace. There we were surprised with the sight of hundreds of men, women, and children, all in torn or thinning clothes. Most were shivering from the cold with bloodshot eyes. Piles of thin blankets lay on the cobbled ground where they had tried to make beds for themselves.

Several Targian soldiers were spread around the edge of them. They had been sitting and talking to their friends but jumped to their feet upon our arrival. The refugees were quiet before they noticed our presence, and once they saw the queen, they knelt and bowed their heads to her. Silence gave way to all but the wintry breeze in the trees.

'Where have you come from?' Alexia asked with great concern.

'Your Majesty,' one young man said, not lifting his head, 'we have come from the south—some from Bymoor, some from Rorinhall, some from Fenellar, many from small towns in between. Our homes were overtaken by the Bone Hordes, and many of our loved ones were killed. We fled north and knew not what to do, so we came here seeking help.'

'How long have you been making these stones your home?' I asked.

'Nearly seven days now,' the same man said. A gust of snow blew across the forecourt.

One of our soldier escorts led our horses away, while Alexia's head servant opened the large front doors of the palace and greeted us with a bow.

Alexia walked through the people towards him with Darj, Elhian, and me following. 'Master Rowan,' she said. 'Why have these people not been given proper shelter in my absence? Where is Lord Fenton?'

'He is travelling towards Fenellar, Your Majesty, and requested all of the southern Targian captains to bring their men there. I believe it is to try and free the great green city. He left before these people arrived.'

None of us were sure what to say about this. To have left Liane unprotected apart from the few soldiers in the forecourt was concerning and a large risk for a regent to take. But then his idea to stop the Bone Hordes from coming any further north was the same as ours.

'They should have been cared for, nonetheless,' Alexia said. 'These people are victims of war.'

'We have been providing them with a meal a day, Your Majesty,' Master Rowan said, sounding affronted. 'Beyond that, we did not like to make pronouncements on the use of your provisions without you or anyone else of authority being here.'

'Tell the servants they may use as much of my provisions as they need to feed these people regularly,' Alexia said. 'Prince Darj or I will speak to the soldiers and have them arrange shelter before the day is out, as you should have done.' She turned back to the people, who had been watching in prolonged silence. 'You will not spend another night under the stars,' she said to them. 'I will take care of you until we can give you a safe home to return to.'

'Thank you, Your Majesty,' the young man said, and the rest of the people echoed the sentiment.

'Are our children safe?' I asked Master Rowan.

'They are in perfect health,' he said and stepped aside to make way for us.

There was something instantly comforting about Alexia's palace. It was just as grand and warm and inviting as ever, as if nothing dark was looming beyond its walls. It was not yet touched by Mors, not yet encased in gloom. I no longer felt as fearful for our children. In this environment, they would know nothing of fire-breathing monsters and the foreboding times to come. We had done the right thing.

Reyna brought our twins down the stairs first. Their little feet raced clumsily towards us as they cried and called out to us. Elhian and I each scooped one up into our arms. I wondered briefly if reuniting with them now was going to make our second goodbye all the more painful, more traumatic. But I pushed the thought away. I had a few days to spend with my sons when not long ago I had wondered if I would ever see them again. The rest I could face later.

A maid carried Nichole down, but Jeri and Eva, who were running at full speed towards their parents, overtook her. Eva's little arms wrapped around her mother's neck. 'I'm sorry, Mother,' she said. Alexia gently rubbed her back and brushed away the tears on her daughter's cheeks.

The next morning, before the children had risen, I found the queen on her knees in the private royal chapel. The sun shone through the stained-glass windows at the front of the chapel, filling the room with streams of green and gold. Candles burned near the altar. The air was cold; the queen had opened one of the windows.

'What are you doing?' I asked, hugging myself as I walked to her.

She tucked a loose strand of dark hair behind her ear. 'Connecting with Ru'ach and trying to understand Hazaka.'

'No wonder you came to the chapel for inspiration.'

'The Cazinian Concordat he wanted us to sign . . . It didn't include the White Isles. He must have known Garrow and Telitha were in partnership together.'

'I suspect he found out everything—that Garrow and Telitha were planning to assist Mors to power. He was seeking to take advantage of the situation by sending his battalion to Naldo and trying to blackmail Elhian into better access to resources, to make Jazmarda stronger.'

'But why didn't he take Telitha's side? Why didn't he join his wife?'

'If he had, his own kingdom and people would have been lost to Mors. Perhaps he was a better man than we gave him credence for.'

Alexia grimaced uncertainly. 'Do you remember the Cazinian Papers? They talk about a dragon gaining power. I always thought it was Cades and that once we had defeated him, we were safe. I never suspected it could mean something more—a fire-breathing man, for instance.'

I blew up my cheeks, unsure what she was getting at.

'You're right,' she said at length, even though I hadn't said anything further. 'He must have wanted us to sign the concordat so we could stand against Mors and the Bone Hordes together.' She rubbed her arms against the cold. 'It just seems unusually brave of him to defy his wife, especially when she held all the power.'

A purple light flickered through the stained-glass window. Somewhere in the back of my mind I knew what it was, but I couldn't make sense of it straight away. The light grew stronger until the room was glowing with it.

'The Armoured Butterfly,' Alexia said as it fluttered down onto the windowsill in front of us.

It carried a small letter addressed to the Keeper of Kest.

I regarded it with wonder. Although it was the main function of the Armoured Butterfly to deliver messages, I had never personally received one. My father did many times, but after Eva's birth and the end of the power of the four swords, it hadn't fulfilled its original purpose. Until now.

'Well, open it,' Alexia said.

I carefully pried the letter away from the butterfly. My awkward position as a transitional Keeper only—that is, as a steward of the position until Princess Eva's sixteenth birthday—meant that I was no longer one of the Ordained. The butterfly still served me and only me, but if I touched it, it would already burn my hand and almost kill me.

I broke the seal and read the letter aloud:

> There is a prophecy that begins in the common tongue, 'once the four swords are river cleansed'. I cannot recall the rest but feel sure you should read it. If I had the Cazinian Papers in my possession, perhaps I could have provided it to you in full.
>
> —*King Hazaka Cazren*

'Hazaka?' I asked.

'He never did come to terms with me having the Cazinian Papers,' Alexia said, not quite hiding her amusement at the fact.

I flipped the piece of paper over and saw the seal of the Jazmardian monarchy imprinted on the back: an encircled king sitting on his throne with a sword across his lap. The seal of King Hazaka. It was disconcerting to receive a letter from a murdered king, let alone one I had not particularly liked.

I showed Alexia the seal, wanting confirmation that it was indeed his and hadn't been forged. She confirmed with a nod it was authentic, having seen it many times in their correspondence. Below the seal was the Kestian stamp—a butterfly—showing that the message had come by Captain Darack Symes at the Keep.

'Hazaka must have arranged for its delivery there so the Armoured Butterfly could bring it to us, wherever we were,' I said.

'Look at the date,' Alexia said, pointing to the mark at the top. 'It's the same date as the Winter Council. He sent it the day before he died.'

She led me out of the chapel and through the palace corridors until we reached the grand library. Alexia collected some keys on the way and asked one of her servants to bring us a jug of honeycomb, a warm Targian drink perfect for winter days. Even though it had snowed heavily overnight, the sun now flooded in through the library's tall windows, making it bright and inviting. Grand vases filled with tall, leafy plants sat in almost every corner, a new addition. We found Jeri standing by one with Reyna, the two looking through some books together.

'What are you doing, Mother?' Jeri asked when he saw us, handing his book to Reyna and running over. Reyna curtsied and left.

Alexia leant down to her son. 'Have you ever seen the Cazinian Papers?' she asked.

He shook his head, his eyes widening. 'Can I?'

Alexia peered at him very seriously. 'What do you think, Aunt Adaliah?' she asked.

'Oh, I think we can trust him,' I said, winking at him.

Jeri's face lit up. Alexia smiled and took his hand, and the three of us walked through the books in the direction of the queen's Secret Room. A few rows before the hidden door, we stopped at two shelves locked under a glass panel. Underneath were wads of loose sheets, which had browned and crumbled over time.

'These are a thousand years old,' Alexia told her son. 'We must handle them very carefully. Are your hands clean?' He upturned his palms for inspection. 'Very good.'

She unlocked the panels with the keys. She and I gathered all the papers as carefully as we could and took them to a large table near a window. We spread the papers out. The servant with the honeycomb arrived and set it on a smaller table beside us. Luckily for Jeri, it was a breakfast version with no brandy in it, and he shared a glass with us.

'We are looking for a poem in the common tongue,' Alexia told him. 'See this?' She held up a piece of paper covered in strange symbols drawn with thick lines. 'This is how the Jazmardians write. If you find any sheets of paper with that on it, carefully put them to the side.'

'The one we want may be small,' I said, 'so we have to look very hard.'

The three of us spent about an hour sifting through the papers, Jeri creating an immaculate pile beside him after he examined each page with wonder. 'Who's this, Mother?' He held up a portrait of an old man, drawn with inky black lines. The man looked impressive but peaceful at the same time.

'You know him,' Alexia said. 'It's the famous targarn, Jeri, for whom you were named. Don't you remember his story?'

'A little,' Jeri said. 'What did he do?'

'He lived many years ago to the southeast, near where Jeriton is now,' Alexia said. 'There, wild tribes—precursors to the Bone Hordes, I believe—roamed through the lands, raiding and burning Targian farmlands. Jeri was a young, humble stable hand working in a small farming village. Wild warriors came one day and set houses alight and rounded the villagers into the town square. It looked like they would all be killed. Jeri had hidden behind some hay in the stables. He could have escaped and saved himself, but when he heard the villagers crying out, he took hold of a pitchfork and confronted the warriors. They laughed at him, taunted him—what could a stable hand do against twenty men? Jeri threw the pitchfork at their leader. It landed in his forehead, and he fell down dead.'

'What did the others do?' Jeri asked.

'Well, the villagers realised they did not have to submit to these men, and they, too, fought back, using whatever they could put their hands on. Within just a few minutes, all twenty of the warriors were dead, and the village was saved. Jeri's courage had inspired them. He became the targarn and ruled fairly and wisely until his death. He is a reminder to us that *anyone* who chooses selfless, moral courage when they could flee can turn the tides of battle, can make a difference in the lives of others. That is why you bear his name. One day, you will be a fair and wise ruler who makes a difference to others, too.'

Jeri's wide eyes suggested he was a little daunted by this prospect.

'Sometimes, we can call things into fruition simply by speaking it,' I said. 'They called me the A'zyon Warrior long before I felt remotely fearless.'

Jeri smiled at me, and we returned to sifting through the papers.

'Is this it, Aunt Adaliah?' Jeri asked later, once we had finished the last of the honeycomb. He held up a particularly small piece of paper for me to inspect. 'It speaks of a sword and crown.'

I took it and read it aloud:

> *Once the four swords are river cleansed,*
> *And the blessing's made her immune,*
> *The sword of life and not of death*
> *Will save the Rhea Lands from doom.*

> *But a greater weapon was forged*
> *When her light made the shadow flee;*
> *Now blessed to split the hateful crown,*
> *May love's sacrifice set them free.*

> *But break the purple butterfly,*
> *And this will leave them all to die.*

'That's it!' Alexia said, hugging him with an arm around his shoulders. Jeri beamed.

I read the poem again. 'The blessing . . . Taking the Jazmardian Blessing and adhering to it until it fulfilled its purpose must have been what made me immune to Dragon's Breath, the source of death in the Zalem's Bane.'

'Yes,' Alexia said, taking the page to read herself.

'Mors said he wanted to destroy the butterfly,' I said. 'It must be offering us some sort of protection. He must need to break it before he can harm us or turn us into Ghosts.' I turned to Alexia for help with my thought process, but she was studying the poem and not paying any attention to me.

'The sword of life . . . save the Rhea Lands . . . ' Her eyes were alight and focused. 'That's why Garrow took your sword. That's why I couldn't kill Mors with an arrow!'

I took her meaning. 'Only the Life Sword can defeat him. But . . . ' I groaned. 'Garrow has it.'

'Yes, but the point is Mors can be defeated, and we know how.'

I pondered the second verse. 'A greater weapon . . . '

'Maybe that's your bow, Mother!' Jeri said.

Alexia chuckled at his enthusiasm. 'No, darling, I think the Life Sword must have become greater, somehow, after Aunt Adaliah destroyed the Dark Orb. And with this additional strength,' she said to me, 'it seems you have the power and the blessing to destroy the crown, despite what Telitha said. Perhaps the blessing is still with you. Perhaps you can defeat her, even if she is a High Zalem.'

'How strange that Cazine wrote this in the common tongue when the rest of her writings are in Jazmardian,' I said. 'And how strange that we should receive Hazaka's note leading us to this now, just when we had been talking about him and questioning his character.'

'Perhaps Ru'ach wants us to trust him,' Alexia said.

'Yes . . . '

But how can I possibly defeat both Mors and Telitha?

25
LEVANNA

Alexia took the Armoured Butterfly to my guest room for safe keeping. We shared the note with Darj and Elhian, and our discussion ran in circles. The means of defeating Mors and destroying the crown was with Garrow, and we still had no idea where he was. Scouts had reported that his part of the White Army had been sighted somewhere near Gristern in the east of Targe, presumably on their way to join with the Bone Hordes at Fenellar in the south, but that didn't mean the new Islander king was with them.

Elhian had been right that the enemy left Casmodia and pursued us to Targe. In a way, this was comforting. At least we knew the Islanders were not ravaging Casmodia in our absence. Elhian took the opportunity to send a note to his head officer in Tiathi, requesting that he send soldiers to the north of Casmodia, to try and free Naldo and Ignallia. If they succeeded, Elhian's further instructions were to protect the border at the Edeline Sea to ensure no further boats full of warring Islanders could set foot into his kingdom. Somehow, this gave us all confidence. We had an element of control in one area, if nothing else.

Elhian also asked for a five-thousand-strong battalion of Casmodian riders to come to Liane, ready to go wherever war came. It would take some time for them to arrive, but it was a comfort to know they would soon be on their way.

Without Fenton to talk to and with news of the White Army moving south, we spent two days less in Liane than planned. We tried to make the most of the four days we did have. We saw to the refugees and ensured they were well-fed and warm. We bathed, ate hot meals, and cuddled and reassured our children at every opportunity. Alexia sent scouts to find out how Fenton was faring at Fenellar and if he had managed to save it. If not, her message was for him to retreat and join us in our stand at Levanna. Like the rest of us, the queen was determined to stop the Bone Hordes from getting any closer to her capital city in the north.

I had come to realise on the second day that Reyna was somehow more assured. She looked us in the eye now and no longer fled from our presence. I wondered if her brother, Finn, whom the children adored, had helped her with this and grown as well. He stuttered less.

It made it easier to say goodbye to the children for a second time, but not by much. When I had first said goodbye to Karlen and Jovan in Dawfield, I hadn't known my sword must be the one to defeat Mors. Now, I was even less certain of seeing them again. But I didn't cry. I just thanked Ru'ach for them and rode out of Liane without looking back. It was like grief was following me and would swallow me whole if I did. I would spend the next few days running from it.

Levanna—the birthplace of Darj and of Alexia's first husband, Ethaniel—is to the southwest of Liane, not far from Kest. A few days' ride from the capital city, Levanna was then a small but pretty town, with a clear brook running through the middle of it. The brook was bordered with small, tidy cottages, each with their own gardens that were bare for the winter but which I could imagine to be full of colour and fragrances in the spring. Levanna was known in particular for tulips. In ancient times, the people there used tulips for trade, giving rise to the name 'tules' for Targe's most common coins.

Almost all of the cottages had smoke pouring out of their chimneys, giving the air the pleasant scent of charred wood. Several footbridges crossed the brook, painted green and weathered in places. Like most Targian towns, Levanna was protected with stone walls and had a grand lord's manor in the centre of it. From the village, we could find out how far Mors' reach had spread throughout Targe and hopefully stop him from bringing war to Liane.

When we arrived, we found the soldiers we had entrusted to Xander, Kadram, and Yorella encamped to the north of the town, just outside the walls.

'More and more northern Targian soldiers are arriving every day,' Xander said when we met him on the steps of the lord's manor. 'They are waiting for your command, Your Majesty.'

'Very good,' Alexia said, but she drew quiet as we entered the regal house.

'What is it?' I asked when no one else could hear.

'This is where Ethaniel grew up,' she said to me.

The memories of the past surrounded her, surrounded us all. Darj had grown up in the shadow of this house, too, as his father Naythan had been scribe to Ethaniel's father, Lord Benne. I studied the general's face as he walked beside me. Both his parents and his younger sister had died in Levanna. Did the memories trouble him, too? It was hard to tell by his expression alone. As usual, it gave almost nothing away.

Ethaniel's cousin, a man by the name of Jordanas, was now Lord of Levanna. We heard from one of the members of his household staff that Jordanas and his local captain had taken a battalion of soldiers to help Lord Fenton fight the Bone Hordes at Fenellar.

Alexia and I found Kadram in the manor and showed him the note the Armoured Butterfly had led us to. He read it over and over, pondering it for some time. 'I thought someone must have translated this at first, but I feel certain this is Queen Cazine's handwriting. I have read many of her prophecies, many of her letters. I have studied her writings like some study the stars, but never before have I seen her write something in the common tongue, a tongue that was only just starting to be spoken at the time and not in Jazmarda.'

'Do you think our interpretation is right? That the Armoured Butterfly is protecting us?' I asked.

'Yes, I think that is certain,' he met my eyes, 'and that you must defeat Mors with the Life Sword.'

'Why me, though?'

'I saw the fire he breathed,' Kadram said, 'and the poisonous smoke that followed. I believe he is inhaling Dragon's Breath—a mild form, perhaps, but enough to make his breath deadly. And you, my butterfly, are the only one with immunity to it.'

I opened my mouth but could not find the words I wanted.

'As for the "greater weapon",' Kadram went on, perplexed. 'In truth, I am not sure what that verse means. Perhaps you are right, Alexia. Perhaps destroying the Dark Orb made the sword stronger, somehow. Strong enough to destroy a monster. Overall, there is only one explanation that makes sense.' Kadram folded the note in half and pressed it under his nose as if smelling it. 'Cazine must have foreseen you in the future, Adaliah. She must have known that you would be the one to face Mors and Telitha.' He held the note out for me to take. 'She wrote this for you and no one else. That is why it is not in Jazmardian.'

I slipped the note back into my pocket.

'And Hazaka?' Alexia asked.

'He must have discovered Telitha's plans and decided to try and stop her. He knew you were the key, Adaliah. Perhaps he was not quite as self-serving as we thought.'

The next morning started with a visit to Wolfgar, who had travelled with our men all the way from Casmodia. With permission, he had taken over one of the blacksmiths in Levanna. I found him attending to several packs of his new arrows. Amidst them was a set of about fifty more arrows for the queen, with gold-tipped, green fletching.

'Have you found out where Telitha is?' Wolfgar asked.

'No. There has been no word from the scouts yet.'

'She hates you and your cousin,' Wolfgar said, 'that's no secret. I heard the general talking about what Garrow might do with the sword, but I've been thinking. If I was them . . . if I was Telitha . . . I think she has it and intends to use it against you.'

'What do you mean?'

'She must know the sword is the only way to defeat Mors. Wouldn't it glorify their victory if they used that very sword on you? She is probably fantasising about killing you with it as we speak.'

Before I could process this properly, I heard a great screech. I tensed, knowing I had only ever heard that sound once before. Mors was nearby. I ran towards the closest wall and sprinted up a set of stairs. I couldn't see anything but fields dressed in snow. I ran around the wall to the southern side. There was another screech followed by shouting and screams.

A large army of our men was riding towards Levanna.

'It's Ren and Fenton's men,' I said to Elhian as he arrived beside me. 'The Delyans and the rest of the southern Targian army. They have come from Fenellar.'

Mors and his soldiers, whom we recognised as Islanders—Garrow's Islanders—hounded them from behind. Riding Brzina, Mors dug his talons into one of our men and threw him across the field.

Yorella and Alexia came to the top of the wall, the latter grasping her bow. A hundred or so archers followed her and spread out along the wall.

'Nock your arrows!' Alexia called.

'Wait!' Wolfgar had shouldered two large baskets of his special arrows and was lumbering up the stairs with them. 'Take these.'

There was turmoil as the archers hurried to grab their share.

'You're taking too many!' one cried.

'Give me more!'

'No, I need these!'

'Archers!' Alexia shouted over them.

They flashed guilty looks at their queen and quietly turned towards Mors and his men. The enemy was still too far away. They couldn't shoot without risking the lives of our men.

We waited. Mors screeched. Yorella's face filled with childlike fear.

Our men rode closer. Their horses' hooves battered the snow-covered earth. Prince Ren led them, Lord Fenton at his side. Darj and Elhian ran downstairs to arrange for the gate to open.

Mors brought Brzina up alongside our men. Alexia jumped up on the edge of the wall, nothing between her and a fatal fall. She drew back an arrow and let it fly. Everyone held their breath as the arrow glided through the air.

It lodged in Mors' chest.

Mors screeched, took a spear from one of his nearby followers, and thrust it through the air, directly towards the queen. She froze. There was that numb, distant look in her eye again. I pulled her off the wall's edge just in time, the two of us falling onto the stones. She groaned as she landed awkwardly on her back. I wasn't feeling sympathetic. This was not the first time she'd deliberately antagonised him.

'Do you want to die?' I asked. 'He could burn you alive!'

Alexia stared at me like I was speaking a foreign language.

The other archers loosed their shots at Mors. He emitted a noise that sounded like pain and gave a loud call that caused his soldiers to melt away from Levanna and retreat into the distance. While the archers had staved off Mors' attack, I knew it wouldn't be enough. My sword was the only way to defeat him properly, and we still didn't have it.

Annoyed as I was with Alexia, her distraction had allowed our men to reach Levanna without any further casualties. They poured into town, and the gate shut behind them.

Alexia and I ran down the stairs to meet with our friends. Ren was in the midst of his men, and it took a few minutes to get to him. There was no happiness in his eyes when he saw us.

'How are you?' I asked feebly.

'My brother is dead, I have lost my kingdom, and I've just been attacked by a man who can breathe fire and who has the scales and talons of a dragon. How do you think I am?' He wiped his arm across his brow. 'Excuse me.' He gave a curt nod and walked briskly for the small barracks. Alexia and I stared after him.

'Forgive him,' Lord Fenton said, arriving at our side. 'He has taken his brother's death and his sudden rise to the throne very hard.'

Apart from a red and sweaty face, Lord Fenton was mostly unchanged since I'd last seen him: polite, deferent, unremarkable in his appearance. A little grey had gathered around his ears, but otherwise he was the same dry, Targian bachelor I'd always known.

'I am relieved to see you safely back in your kingdom and to be discharged of my regency duties, my queen,' he said.

'I am sorry it extended as long as it did,' Alexia said.

'I am sorry it resulted in us losing the south of Targe. We were taken completely unaware.'

'I know,' Alexia said. 'How did you come to be at Fenellar?'

'I discovered that Prince—I'm sorry—that King Ren was coming up from the south, fleeing his kingdom. We agreed to try and free Fenellar together, as we thought we could begin to push the Bone Hordes back south again if we achieved that.' A mild blush filled his cheeks. 'I had hoped to solve all that before you returned.'

'A little ambitious,' Alexia said, 'but the sentiment is appreciated.'

'You didn't succeed, I gather,' I said.

Lord Fenton bristled. 'No. They have made Fenellar a stronghold. We could not breach it. This brings me to a concern I wish to raise with Your Majesty.'

'What?' she asked.

'The prince-general. With him abroad and unexpectedly unaccounted for, we had no one to oversee the military plans and to give the appropriate level of approval. The captains found it difficult to work together and argued over who had the authority to make decisions.'

'What are you saying?' Alexia asked.

Lord Fenton took a deep breath. 'Perhaps Darj should relinquish his role as general—'

'When I delegated the regency to you, that included the authority to make military decisions.'

'I am not a military expert.'

'Nor am I. That is why the court is full of advisors.'

'Ah, yes, but you married the one we needed the most. Darj cannot fulfill his role in the war room if he is also required in the bedroom.' Fenton laughed and only stopped when he realised Alexia's face was reddening.

Lord Fenton had once imagined himself as a suitor to the queen and was generally a friend to her, but as she walked away from him, biting her tongue, I knew that friendship would be tested.

'Well,' Fenton said, waving a dismissive hand after her. 'Can you believe that?'

'Fenton,' I said, 'she is the sovereign of this kingdom, and she endures enough criticism about her relationship with Darj as it is. I'm sure you don't need me to tell you that was inappropriate, particularly at a time like this. Now, feed your men and get them to rest while they can.'

26
THE BONE HORDES

I found Darj down a quiet lane the next morning, having somehow escaped the throng of Targian and Delyan soldiers that were permeating every corner of Levanna. He stood alone before a dilapidated cottage, his hands clasped behind his back and his feet a step apart like a foot soldier. He saw me coming and gave me a wisp of a smile before returning his focus to the cottage.

The cottage's roof had a hole in it, and the entire building needed recladding. It was on a lean. Weeds had overcome the garden, and one of the windows was broken.

'This was your home,' I said.

Darj cleared his throat. 'Yes. This is where Sirvan killed my father, my mother died of a fever, and my younger sister took her own life. This is what I come from.'

I linked my arm through his. 'There's nothing to be ashamed of.'

'No, I'm not ashamed. I'm disappointed.'

'What do you mean?'

He stepped forward and rested his hands on the irregular front fence, his back to me. 'I let them down.'

'Darj—'

'Why do you think I had so much trouble facing my sister? How could I face her when I failed to keep our parents and younger sister safe—when I failed her? Just like I failed Alexia when Jeri was . . . when we thought he'd died.' He took a deep breath. 'I don't deserve her.'

I put my hand over his. 'Darj . . . '

'I keep thinking about the time we faced the Zalems, when I sent you off to kill her if necessary, and that great light filled the sky. I should have had more faith in her, but I thought she was dead.'

'But she's not dead. She's here with us, as fiery and passionate as ever. In fact, she's in fine form. She just had an altercation with Fenton. About you, no less.'

'I suppose the court still thinks I'm not good enough for her.'

'I don't understand you at all. You have no qualms riding out against an army, and yet you crumble in front of a few lords and ladies. What's Lord Fenton compared to Cades or Jag or Sirvan? What does their opinion matter when the queen has chosen you? Besides,' I went on before he could answer, 'you've got to stop questioning your marriage. It's too late for that. What could you do about it? Abandon her? Live separate lives? Forget the child she gave you? Stay in this house by yourself, surrounded by your terrible memories? What would the court make of that? Both of you would be miserable, not to mention the disastrous ramifications it would have on the crown and your daughter. You promised to love and care for each other forever. It's simply too late to care what the court thinks.'

Darj stared at me with high eyebrows and an open mouth, as if I were the spirit of all wisdom. 'You're right,' he said, blinking.

'I'm always right,' I said airily.

He laughed. 'Thank you. That was the truth I needed.'

'You're welcome.'

I turned to go, but he stopped me with a hand on my shoulder. 'This question about you doubting yourself . . . '

I stiffened. 'What about it?'

'Don't you see, Adaliah? Everything you have done so far has prepared you for this. You must have faith that the reason this task has come to you is because you are the one, the only one, who has exactly what it takes to complete it.'

'But I'm so tired, Darj,' I whispered. 'How can I alone stop Mors from transforming our world into a twisted one of his own making?'

'Borrow our strength,' he said. 'We may not be able to do your task for you, but we are here for you always. You need never be alone.'

I hugged him. I couldn't put how I felt into words, but I knew Darj would understand. In many ways, he was the big brother I'd never had.

'By the way,' I said, stepping back. 'You have never let any one of us down, so stop agonising over that, too. Your parents would be so proud of all you've become. With every year that passes, I only grow in pride for you, too. Rosana clearly loves you and wants to know you again. We all owe you a great deal.'

He squeezed my upper arm, smiling.

'Sire?'

A Targian soldier came up behind us.

'Yes?' Darj asked.

'The Bone Hordes are here.'

Darj and I returned to the top of the wall. The Bone Hordes steadily approached in the far distance. I'd heard many stories about them but had never seen them for myself. There were thousands of them—tens of thousands. Their various tribes had united against us, but I refused to be daunted. We had always been outnumbered, and we had always won in the end. Victory was not assured now—we had never fought a dragon-man before, and so far, we'd had one defeat after another—but the size of the army alone was no longer enough for me to concede defeat. The hordes wore primitive furs and skins, and they weren't mounted except for one man at the front.

'That will be Hanequin,' Darj said. He was much too far away for me to see if he had the scars Kadram had described, but I believed Darj nonetheless. 'Mors must have stood the Islanders down to recover,' he said. 'He has sent these men to fight us instead.'

'What do you know about Hanequin?' I asked.

'I'm told he behaves more like an animal than a man. He raided Targe numerous times in Amaz's years as king, but Amaz fought him off and forced him to sign a treaty that allowed for any Bone Horde that stepped onto Targian land to be hanged without a trial. Hanequin hated him for it. He will relish the chance to walk all over Targe now, but he is certainly deluding himself if he thinks I'll allow him to avenge himself upon my wife—through me or otherwise.'

'What do we do?' I asked.

'Elhian's and Izak's armies won't arrive for at least another fortnight, by the time they gather and travel,' Darj said. 'We need to buy them time and stop the Bone Hordes from getting any further north. Every soldier here must ready themselves. It's time to fight.'

'Yorella and her men will join us,' I said.

'For which I am very thankful,' Darj said.

'Darj,' I said, stopping him before he could walk away. 'I know what I must do.'

'What are you talking about?'

'They want to destroy the Armoured Butterfly so that we are no longer protected. You know we brought it with us. I need to use it to draw them out. Then I can fight them and get my sword back from Telitha.'

'Do you think she has your sword?' Darj asked.

'Yes. It's something Wolfgar said: that she would want to kill me with it. I think he's right. I think Garrow stole it to give it to her.'

Darj wanted to discuss it with Elhian and Alexia. Once we found them in the manor house, I repeated the same thoughts to them.

'What are you planning to do, exactly?' Elhian asked. His thick, brown hair was getting long and a little wild. He pushed it back from his forehead.

'Telitha and Mors will not be far away. I need you or Alexia to release the Armoured Butterfly, since I can't touch it. Telitha will see me, she will see it, and she will come for me. I will fight her and take back my sword.'

I braced myself for their flood of advice and list of worries, but the three of them didn't say anything. Elhian squeezed my hand. 'All right,' he said. 'We are behind you.'

As I rode Bagred to the closed gate just before dawn the next day, my cape unmoving on my shoulder, the tree-blade in my hand, and an army of men behind me, I felt afraid. I tried to remember what Darj had said to me, but shadowy thoughts were already returning to my mind like a constricting, thorny vine.

You can't do this. You're going to fail.

Alexia was on the wall above me, her quiver full and her bow in hand. A few weeks on, her fingers were well enough to be of more use but hadn't completely returned to their full strength. And yet, there was no stopping her.

Darj rode towards me through the men. The soldiers dipped their heads and put their hands on their chests in deference to him. He reached my side and turned to address them. 'Whatever happens today, they must not take Levanna! This must stop here!'

The men were quiet. Perhaps they were afraid as well. Many had lost their homes, and the Delyans had lost their entire kingdom and their king. Ren, who still had not spoken to us, stood with his men near the back of the town. They knew what the enemy was capable of. They knew we could fail.

But Darj was not about to let them give up. 'We have fought the enemies of Ru'ach before,' he said. 'We have fought hard, and we have ultimately found victory every time. We must stand firm and give the A'zyon Warrior the time and opportunity she needs to get her sword back. We fight for her, but we also fight for salvation from the darkness that threatens us all. Today, we are the defenders of light and life, the guardians of the world Ru'ach gave us!' Darj raised his sword above his head. 'He is with us! Arjla divala!' The men responded by mirroring the gesture and shouting. It was a formidable sound.

If only the full armies of each kingdom were here.

I felt confident the Casmodians would be marching to us from the north. Hopefully, Izak Tan had organised the Jazmardian soldiers in the west and was marching towards our lands, too.

The gate opened. I moved Bagred forward and could hear the roar of the horses' hooves following me out onto the frozen grass. The white plains spread out before me, glistening in the sunlight. Soldiers rode to my left and right, forming a long line. Many more were behind.

The Bone Hordes marched towards us. Their leader, Hanequin, raised his arm into the air and spoke instructions in a harsh and fragmented language. His men broke into a slow run, their heavy feet pounding and shaking the ground. I raised my sword, scanning the enemy's lines for the woman I wanted. Cades' daughter. I couldn't see her anywhere.

She won't be in the charge, I realised, *not amongst the common soldiers.* I swallowed. *With Ru'ach we stand.*

Darj sounded the horn. I kicked my heels into Bagred, and together, we galloped into battle.

The first few minutes were carnage. Men from both sides fell. I killed a man who had a grotesque bone-piercing straight through his nose. The Bone Hordes fought like animals of the wild—scratching and biting us, flicking dirt into our men's eyes, and impaling soldiers without a fight whenever they could. Some of our soldiers rode them down on their horses. Yorella speared one through the middle while Ren fought another with his daggers. Arrows flew over our heads, the archers led by the queen back on the wall. One landed in the chest of a man directly in front of me, and he screamed loudly.

Hanequin, a thickset man who reminded me of a bear, used a long, bone-spiked mace to strike down several Rhea soldiers at once. The men stopped attacking him, no longer sure how to do so without being struck.

I gave an expressive wave back towards Levanna, hoping Alexia would see me. We had decided she was the best one to release the Armoured Butterfly, as she wouldn't be in the heat of battle like Elhian. If harm came to him and he couldn't release the butterfly, our plan would be at an end.

Nothing happened at first. I continued to slay soldiers, keeping a vigilant eye out for Mors and Telitha. Hanequin saw me and shouted, a deep and angry frown carved into his gristly face.

I waved again. *Come on, Alexia.*

Her archers shot arrows in volleys that flew over our heads and into the hordes, flattening tens of them at a time. I had no way to tell if Alexia had seen my wave or not.

Hanequin swiped his mace across three soldiers, instantly killing them. Yorella threw her spear at him; he flung it out of the way with his mace and stepped towards her, preparing to strike. I ran, leapt at Yorella, and pushed her out of the way. Hanequin's mace flew just above our heads.

'Go,' I told Yorella. Before Hanequin could strike at us again, she grabbed her spear and ran back at the Bone Hordes.

Hanequin took a step towards me, his gait long and crablike. A grimace showed a row of chipped and yellow teeth. 'You will not destroy the crown!' he shouted at me. 'You will not touch the High Zalem!'

'I will do whatever I have to,' I said.

He came closer. 'Who are you?' he yelled, spit spraying from his mouth. 'Amaz's daughter?'

'No. But I am his niece.'

His soldiers stepped out of his way as he walked faster and faster towards me, so heavy-footed I could feel the vibrations coming through the soil.

My eyes fixed on his mace and its spikes. I had never battled anyone with such a weapon before. One blow and I would be a bloodied mess.

Bagred tossed his head. I slipped off the saddle—the mace could easily wound my horse, and I wasn't prepared to risk that.

I spread my feet apart on the damp ground and held myself lowly, ready to escape the next strike. It came, and I scrambled to the left, successfully ducking the blow but losing my footing and gaining an icy wet stain up my pant leg. Some of the hordes laughed.

Hanequin swatted the mace after me like he was trying to get rid of an irksome fly. I kept scaling out of the way, unable to find an opportunity to retaliate until he swung too hard and lost his footing. He stumbled, showing me his back, which I promptly slashed with my sword. It was an unfair attack, but I was desperate. He let out a loud and long yell, and when he turned back to me, his face was empurpled. He started calling to his men; those nearby turned and ran at me. I slashed down the first one, but they quickly surrounded me on every side. I ducked a sword strike from behind, but only just escaped its sting. I impaled one man, and then another, but a third managed to flick his rudimentary sword point across my arm. Another pushed me to the ground.

Before I could turn myself over, a great horseman charged into the hordes and dispersed them away from me. It was Guntar and the prince-general. Elhian followed on Leuk. He and Darj fought fiercely against the men about me, giving me the chance I needed to get back to my feet. Hanequin yelled rapidly in his own language, pointing his mace at Darj. The colour in his face deepened as he went on without taking a breath.

'Who are you?' he finally managed to spit out in the common tongue.

But Darj was too busy fighting to hear him, Elhian at his side. Hanequin opened his mouth to ask the question again, but his anger shifted to curiosity as he pointed to something over my shoulder, calling his men to look, too.

Something light landed on my leather pauldron. It was the Armoured Butterfly, shining brightly and fluttering its wings.

27
BROKEN

The butterfly rested there for just a second before flying away to the west. A sea of nonplussed faces was before me. The Bone Hordes didn't know what to make of this.

'Follow it, Adaliah!' Elhian yelled.

I ducked another blow from Hanequin. Darj and Elhian kept the throng of men from reaching me as I ran for my horse and rode after the butterfly. I still hadn't seen Telitha or Mors. The battle was going neither badly nor well at that point, but when I glanced back at the battlefield behind me and saw how many had been slaughtered, my heart sank. There were still thousands of Bone Hordes coming against our men. Could our men protect Levanna? Even if they could, how many would survive? Would Darj and Elhian get away safely?

I couldn't think about it. If Telitha were nearby, she would not miss this chance to strip me and the other three of our protection. I had to keep the butterfly in my line of vision, even if it meant leaving the battle to my loved ones. I didn't look back again.

I was out of sight of Levanna and the fighting men before long. The sounds of battle faded behind me. Bagred was soon breathing hard. I didn't know where we were going, and at that point, I didn't care. I just wanted my sword back. I just wanted it to be over.

The sun slowly moved across the sky until it began to dip in the afternoon. Despite the hours that had passed, I was surprised when I came over a rise and found myself on the edge of Kest. I rode through the foot of the hills that separated Kest from the rest of the world, and suddenly the wide, ever-flowing river was ahead of me.

'We have to foul the water,' I heard a voice say, 'or they may take the chance to use its redemptive powers against us.'

Mors and Telitha were mounted on their horses in the middle of the river, further upstream. The latter held a torch in her hand, and my sword lay across her lap, just as Wolfgar had guessed. I was interested to see they hadn't destroyed it. In the brief moment I used to take all this in, I lost track of the Armoured Butterfly.

The valley was more open there, filled with swampy, frosted grass rather than dense trees. I pressed Bagred forward into the river, and Mors dismounted and landed in the water. Red liquid pooled out from under his feet until the entire river flowed with blood. Bagred tossed his head back, panicking as it lapped at his ankles. The snow at the river's edges turned from white to scarlet as fish floated to the top and the frozen grass along the edge withered.

Mors took the torch from Telitha and used it to breathe green fire out of his mouth. The flames touched the water, and the entire surface of the river caught fire.

I pulled on Bagred's reins, dragging him away from the flames and to the sludgy snowbanks on the side. We made it just in time, the fire reaching the edge of the river just as we escaped it. Bagred whinnied, and Mors and Telitha's faces snapped towards us.

'The Bone Hordes will be storming Levanna by now,' Telitha called out to me. She dismounted and walked across the river, wearing steel armour over chainmail. Only her forearms were bare. The flames licked about her, but she remained unharmed. Mors breathed angrily, black smoke shooting out of his nostrils.

I hesitated. The truth was, I didn't know what to do. I wasn't afraid of death. The Armoured Butterfly still had the power to protect me. But how could I defeat both Mors and Telitha at once? Thoughts of our soldiers on the battlefield were ever present in my mind, too. The longer I delayed, the more of them would die. Darj, Alexia, Elhian—they were all risking their lives to give me time.

The Armoured Butterfly reappeared amongst some trees on my side of the river. Telitha saw it as well. She pointed and yelled at Mors.

'Yah!' I shouted at Bagred, urging him towards it.

Brzina whinnied again as Mors remounted and dug his heels into her. I knew he was coming for us, but I kept riding forward, desperate to get to the butterfly before he or Telitha did.

Mors rode up beside me, and I felt a talon dig into my side. Mors tore me from my horse, and I fell to the ground, blood wetting my clothes. It hurt so badly, I thought I had been disemboweled and frantically tried to cover the wound with my hand.

Telitha and Mors dismounted and walked up behind me. I wiped my sleeve across my sweaty cheeks. I stood, determined to face them, my hand still clutching my sliced side.

My courage perished when I saw what Mors held in his hand.

The Armoured Butterfly. He caught it.

I didn't know how it could be destroyed, but judging by the excitement in their eyes, they did.

'When you fulfilled the Jazmardian Blessing,' Mors said, 'you received immunity against Dragon's Breath, the very thing that sustains me. And when the butterfly touched each of you before disappearing, it gave all four of you protection from me, from Anash. It was your noble sacrifices that allowed it.' He said the word 'noble' as if it were blasphemous.

I turned my mind back to that scene. After I'd cut the Dark Orb in two, the butterfly had touched Darj's, Alexia's, Elhian's and my shoulders and then simply flown away. It had not felt like a particularly auspicious moment. I hadn't seen the butterfly since, and I'd never known what gift it had bestowed upon us. It was like it had anointed us in some way.

'If I or any other directed or empowered by me were to try and kill you or the others or try and destroy your filthy Life Sword, the act would see me dead,' Mors said.

That's why Telitha was relieved when I didn't die from the dart, I thought. Hanequin, on the other hand, definitely hadn't been overly concerned about preserving my life to save Mors'.

'But none of that will be a problem,' Mors said, 'once we destroy this butterfly.' It sat unmoving on his palm.

The butterfly was an object of the Ordained. Since Eva's birth, I was no longer ordained. The butterfly would cause me serious damage if I touched it. Mors was not one of the Ordained either. So why could he touch it? Was his supremacy so great that he had overpowered it?

'Do you know why I have been trying so hard to kill you?' he asked. 'Why I have appeared before my thousandth birthday, still vulnerable, to personally stop you?'

'Because I am a threat.'

'They call you the A'zyon Warrior,' he said, 'but you are also the Keeper of Kest. And what is the Keeper's choice? Indulge me.'

'Life and death,' I said uneasily.

'Yes. Exactly.' He stepped towards me. 'When you cleansed the swords, you chose life. In order for me to become invincible on my birthday, I must defeat life.' He thrust a finger towards me. 'I must defeat you. I hoped others would do it for me, but they failed. Then this awful butterfly stepped in, giving you Ru'ach's protection from my hand. But not for much longer.' The butterfly didn't move from his hand. His use of Anash's power had completely disabled it. Mors raised his fingers, preparing to crush it.

'No!'

I had thought the word in my mind, but it was another voice that had spoken it aloud. Kadram rode towards us. He came to a stop by my side, dismounted, and unsheathed a sword. Telitha ran at Kadram with mine. 'You should have made me regent when you had the chance,' she said, bringing my sword down against him.

'I have chosen better,' Kadram said. He raised his blade to block her strike, the swords clanging as they met.

'I can kill Izak!' Telitha said.

'He is our kinsman and one of your people!'

'He is no kinsman of mine!'

'Stop this!' Kadram yelled. He pushed hard against Telitha's sword and forced her away from him. 'Stop this now!' He struck at her again, making her take a step back. 'Do you not understand?' he asked, his voice now pleading. 'You do not have to be like him. We do not have to do this. It is not too late to make amends.'

'I have made my choice—'

'It is not too late to choose something different. Is that not what I have been telling you your whole life?'

What?

They stared at each other in silence. After a few moments, Kadram turned towards me, his eyes sweeping over my confused face. 'Telitha is the daughter of my late wife, Ida,' he said softly.

My mother's letter came to mind: *her husband must know she can't be his, but he hasn't abandoned them.*

'I never knew you were once married,' I said, bewildered.

'He drove my mother to the grave,' Telitha said coldly.

'Not I,' Kadram said. 'Cades forced her to lay with him when he visited Etarbelec, simply because he was drunk and she was beautiful. I caught him as he was leaving, too late to prevent what had happened. I could never father children, you see, because of a disease I had as a child.'

'I would have never known Cades was my father if not for your mother,' Telitha told me with bitter delight. 'Cordale found her letter to Queen Brielle when he sifted through the ruins at Semanez after Cades' demise. It was safe in the library, untouched by Targian flames. Thanks to Cassondra, Mors sought me out and gave me the purpose I had long been searching for.'

'You showed signs of being Cades' daughter long before that,' Kadram said. 'But you could have chosen a different path, as did Elhian.'

Mors took long strides towards Kadram with the butterfly. 'She has made her choice, and it will bring her the great power and glory you never could.'

'He is using you as a means to bring *him* power, Telitha,' Kadram said.

Mors blew on the butterfly, forcing it to fly a few steps ahead of him. He raised the torch to his mouth. His shoulders heaved as he took a deep breath, preparing to engulf it in thick, poisonous flames.

'No!' Kadram shouted again.

He intuitively reached for the butterfly and drew it close against his chest.

I opened my mouth to protest but could not form the words.

Mors' breath engulfed him.

Kadram met my eyes, wreathed in poisonous flames. He fell backwards onto the ground, the butterfly still trapped tightly in his fist.

Someone shouted, and I didn't realise until later it was me. I ran towards him, my stride long and unsteady. I rolled him over, throwing snow onto the flames until they had all dissipated. Then, I knelt in the grass beside him and grasped at his wrist, trying to find a pulse. He was badly burnt, and if he wasn't dead, he would be in excruciating pain. I shook him and sobbed. *No, no, no.*

'Kadram . . . '

He blinked. 'Remember . . . you were first . . . the Keeper of Kest.'

I brought his hand to my lips. 'No, I can't do this without you. Please, I can't lose you, too.'

Kadram touched my cheek with his burnt hand. Then, it fell away from my face.

'No!'

I could feel myself losing control.

This man had saved me at Kest River when I had been near death . . . *Perhaps if I can drag him to the river, I can save him, too.* I jumped up and grabbed his arm, pulling him towards the river and forgetting all about Mors and Telitha, who smiled as they watched me clamber. I reached the edge of the water and remembered with a sinking heart that, while the river had once been a source of life that had saved me, Mors had poisoned it with death. The flames would only damage Kadram's body further, not heal him.

I couldn't save him. Mors had made it impossible.

'No . . .' I sobbed again. I pried at the hand he had sheltered the Armoured Butterfly in, thinking, praying, hoping he had at least saved that. His fingers were charred—not one of the Ordained, the butterfly had burned him, too. They fell away easily. Inside was a pile of black ash where the butterfly had been. The breeze scattered the ashes across Kadram's chest.

The Armoured Butterfly was gone.

And Kadram had died for nothing.

28
SEPARATED

The ashes of the Armoured Butterfly blew into the river. I turned my back on my enemies and knelt on the ground. In that moment, I didn't care if they beheaded me and strung up my remains on Iza Tar, as Telitha had threatened. The Armoured Butterfly was gone. Kadram was dead. So were three kings. It was hopeless. Darkness weighed on me like a fortress bearing down on rotting foundations. My cape fluttered meaninglessly around my shoulders.

'Adaliah!'

It was my cousin's voice.

She, Darj, and Elhian were riding towards me. I was glad to see them at first, but then I saw Garrow following them at a distance. My heart sank further into despair.

'Oh, no,' Alexia said as she came into view of Kadram's body.

'How nice of you to join us,' Telitha said. 'Now that we can kill you all, that is.'

Elhian dismounted beside me and placed a hand on my shoulder. His other held a bloodied blade. 'What do you mean?' he asked her.

Telitha struck at him with a sword, my sword, but Elhian deflected the blow easily. Telitha smirked at him. 'I mean the Armoured Butterfly is destroyed, and I am free to kill the murderer of my father.'

Mors is the murderer of your father, I thought. *The father who mattered.*

They engaged in a heated sword fight. It was the first time I had really seen her wield the sword. I had to admit, for someone who had spoken against directly engaging in battle, her skill matched his.

Alexia drew an arrow and aimed it at Telitha. Just as she was about to loose it, Garrow rode up behind her and knocked her off Hazel with a blow to the head.

'Is it done, Supreme Overlord?' Garrow asked with a lustful tone. 'Is the barrier to killing them destroyed?'

'It is,' Mors said, with even more delight. 'You may kill one of them.' He rubbed his hands together, anticipating the entertainment. I leveled my eyes at him but didn't move.

'Adaliah, *get up!*' Darj said.

His tone was so forceful, even angry, that I broke out of my trance, forgot about my worries and the pain in my side, and did as he said.

Elhian grunted as he thrust his sword towards Telitha again. Darj helped Alexia to her feet. She pressed a hand to her bleeding head, dazed.

'Who should I pick?' Garrow hungrily considered us all as if he were a crocodile and we were his prey.

It didn't take him long to decide. He attacked me. All at once, I transformed. Seconds before I had invited death; now, I was so angry that I confronted Garrow with every part of my being, striking my tree-blade against him again and again until he was forced into the edge of the still-flickering river.

I should have killed you in the championship, I thought to myself, and then I remembered Engres' death and felt angry all over again. He lost his balance; I landed a kick to his arm that forced him to lower his sword. 'How dare you!' I shouted, thinking of his part in bringing Mors to power.

Elhian struck a blow that caused Telitha to loosen her grip on the Life Sword. It fell into the river, beneath the flames. I pushed Garrow away and plunged my hand into the water to grab it. I shrieked as the flames licked about my wrist but didn't let go until I had raised the sword up and out of the river.

I faced Mors, holding up the Life Sword with both hands. 'Enough!' I shouted. 'No more of your selfish, evil acts! I've had enough of you persecuting me and my people!' I thrust the Life Sword towards him. 'I have certainly had enough of you arrogantly thinking that we will submit to you just because you are powerful. I am not going to give up, Mors, not this day nor any other.'

He tensed and peered at Telitha and then at Garrow. Both waited to see what he would do. He considered my sword. Then, he raised the torch to his mouth and sent forth an enormous rush of flames, forcing us all back and giving him the opportunity to reach Brzina and ride away.

Telitha gasped as she watched him go. I took advantage of her surprise and pushed her to the ground. She and Garrow stared after Mors, who was already far in the distance. Neither of them uttered a word. It seemed that no matter what he did, neither of his servants would speak against him.

Telitha rose to her feet, but Elhian pushed her back down and pointed his sword at her. His face was red, and he was puffing.

'We have to get back,' Telitha said from the ground.

Garrow gave a small nod. Then, with a quick and powerful move, he struck me with his forearm and fist across my back, forcing me forward. Winded, I dropped the Life Sword.

It clanged on the ground and broke in two.

Elhian brought down his sword against Telitha, but she rolled out of the way. 'You can't kill me,' she said. 'I am the High Zalem, remember?' She lunged for and seized the part of the Life Sword that was nearest to her—the blade without the hilt. She gave a wild laugh, made a run for her horse, and rode after Mors. Elhian took a dagger from his boot and threw it after her. It landed in her shoulder, but she gave no cry of pain. Without stopping, she ripped it out and dug her heels into her horse.

Only I can kill her.

But I didn't have time for that now. 'Get the blade!' I yelled at Darj and Elhian as I blocked Garrow's next strike with my tree-blade. They ran to Leuk and Guntar, launched themselves into the saddles, and raced after Telitha and Mors.

I pushed at Garrow, forcing him to step back from me.

'What happened to the sword?' Alexia asked him, the three of us the only ones remaining. The queen still held a hand to her head.

'It is said Ru'ach was born of this river, that he gave it life,' Garrow said. 'But now, Mors has invited Anash to become the soul of it. Anything not of Anash that touches it becomes brittle and dies because he is the true Great Spirit.'

'Ru'ach is the only Great Spirit,' I said, 'and he is much stronger. Otherwise, why was Mors so afraid of my sword?'

Garrow scoffed as if I'd deeply offended him. 'The Supreme Overlord is never afraid. May death come upon you for suggesting it. In just sixteen days, he will be invincible.'

I caught my breath. *In just sixteen days, our world may be lost forever.*

I moved to strike him again, but Garrow coolly grabbed Alexia's arm and drew her in front of him, causing me to stop my attack mid-motion. Alexia's head wound wasn't bleeding as much now, but her eyes were dull. It was clear she was not up for a fight. Garrow pulled a knife out of his belt and held it at her throat.

'I am the one with the power now,' he said. 'That gives me the right to . . . How did you phrase it? "Impose my will on others".' He sneered. 'Put the sword and cape down.'

I didn't respond straight away. Garrow pressed the knife further into Alexia's skin. Recollecting myself, I let the tree-blade fall into the bloodied snow at my feet and unclipped my cape. It fluttered to the ground. Alexia silently mouthed the word 'sorry' to me.

Garrow made us sit down while he took all of our weapons and tied them to Bagred and Hazel, except for the hilt of the Life Sword, which he balanced in the sheath by his hip.

I didn't want to think about what he intended to do with us now. Alexia and I huddled closely together.

He is playing with us.

Garrow slapped Hazel's hindquarters, and she cantered into the trees, taking Alexia's bow and arrows with her. He stepped towards Bagred and raised his hand but stopped as something else distracted him.

'Your Majesty,' an Islander soldier called breathlessly. He and another soldier had appeared further up the river on foot. 'Mors sent us to tell you to return to your cave.'

Garrow sighed with a frown but quickly caught himself. 'I'll ride ahead,' he said. 'Bring these two after me.'

He climbed onto his horse and rode on to answer his master's call, taking the hilt and leaving us unarmed and alone in a frozen valley.

29
IN PURSUIT

The two soldiers who stayed behind at Garrow's behest shared licentious grins as they walked towards us. This did not impress my cousin or me. Impatient, jaded, and mostly running on heightened emotions, I waited until they were close, then stood and drove my fist into the first one's jaw. He fell backwards to the ground, and I took care of the second one with a similar strike. They both lay in the snow, senseless.

'Thank you,' Alexia said.

'You're welcome.'

She took a deep breath. 'I can't believe the sword broke now.' She scrambled unsteadily to her feet. 'If we are to have any chance of . . . of destroying Mors, we need it.'

'I know,' I said, putting a hand on her shoulder to keep her balanced. 'But where are we going?'

'Garrow is headed to Sapphires Hold. I'll explain on the way.'

Sapphires Hold was a small mining village on the border of Kest and Targe, tucked away on the edge of the Hewn Mountains, southwest of Levanna.

Alexia seemed so thin and fragile standing before me with blood through her hair, but her face was ever determined. I gave a reluctant nod.

The queen cupped her mouth with her hands and uttered the bird cry Elhian had taught her as a call for Hazel. We kept our eyes on the tree line, waiting to see if she would answer. *Nothing.* Alexia tried again.

This time, there was a grunt, and the beautiful mare trotted back out of the trees towards her mistress.

Bagred snorted as I pushed him up hills covered in deep snow and through forests so dark and thick with trees, my legs continually scraped against them until there were holes in my pants. The moonlight filtered through the trees, turning them into hushed silhouettes. When Hazel stumbled over a log hidden in the snow, causing a weary Alexia to lose her stirrups and then her seat, we had no choice but to stop.

I slipped off Bagred's back and took Hazel's reins. 'Hop down.'

Alexia's feet hit the ground, but her legs were uncooperative. She fell onto her side. 'We have to get your sword,' she said, her voice light and airy.

'What?'

'We have to fix the sword. The only thing that can defeat Mors is your sword. That's why they want it destroyed.'

'Yes, but we already knew that.' I knelt in front of her and gently pulled her into a sitting position.

'Garrow has been setting it up for ages,' she said. 'Hanequin bragged to Darj about it on the battlefield, just after you left. Garrow enslaved several Casmodians when he and Engres sacked Ignallia. Garrow had them brought here. He has them in a mine digging up gold to fund his invasion, to pay Hanequin and the Bone Hordes for their service. It's the one near Sapphires Hold.'

'That's why Hanequin doesn't care if he kills me and Mors dies,' I said to myself more than to her. 'He's just in it for the money. If they were so concerned about me dying before the butterfly was broken, they shouldn't have left him unattended on the battlefield.'

'Yes,' Alexia said. 'Mercenaries have no loyalty. Now, Garrow will wait for Mors and Telitha at Sapphires Hold. The two pieces of the sword have to be together before Mors can truly destroy it as he did the butterfly. That's why they hate you—because you took the evil out of the swords—and if you hadn't, they wouldn't need to destroy it, and this would be a whole lot easier for them, but now they're so afraid that the greater weapon will "divide the crown" before Mors conquers the Rhea Lands—'

'You're going to faint if you don't take a breath.'

Alexia inhaled deeply and slowly let the air out. 'I'm sorry. It's just that we're talking about defeating a man who behaves like a dragon, and I'm still unaccustomed to such conversations.'

I smiled. 'So, you're saying that we have to get the hilt from Garrow before Telitha returns with the blade and before Mors destroys the only weapon I can use to kill him and destroy his crown.'

'Exactly.'

'One more question,' I said. 'Why did you come after me, and how did the battle finish at Levanna?'

'That's two questions.'

'I know. I cheated.'

'We came almost directly after you when we saw the Armoured Butterfly leading you off the battlefield. Did you really think we would let you go alone?'

I squeezed her hand. 'I am so grateful to you all.'

'As for the battle, the numbers of the Bone Hordes seemed endless. Darj gave orders to bring the men closer to the town and to make Levanna as secure as possible. He locked all the gates, put more men up on the wall as archers, and arranged for several soldiers to evacuate the people through the tunnel.'

'What tunnel?'

'Lord Benne built a tunnel leading out of the village for just such an occasion. My father consented to its development but ordered that it be kept secret, lest an enemy use it to advance an attack. Once the people were through it and safe, Kadram rode after you, and we followed as quickly as we could. We didn't want you facing Mors and Telitha alone.'

I thought about all of this silently for a moment or two. 'You need to rest,' I said. She seemed a bit hysterical to me.

Alexia closed her eyes. 'Honestly, can you believe we are fighting a man who can set his breath alight? A man who could burn up the Armoured Butterfly?'

I shook my head. 'Sometimes—no, often—I wish life was a little less surprising.' I took her hand, the one Mors had crushed. The evidence of his brutality was still visible in her bruised and stiff knuckles. 'Even if we manage to reclaim and remake the sword, how am I ever going to defeat him?'

'I . . . have no idea.' She sighed and then said in a soft voice, 'I don't want to be a Ghost, Adaliah.'

'That is not going to happen.'

'I've been in that darkness before. I can't go back.' She shuddered. 'I wish Kadram were here to tell us what to do.'

Kadram. He had told me I would have to defeat Mors, but that was all. No details. No further instructions. No clue as to how to make it possible. I covered my face with my hands and began to cry.

Kadram is dead.

Alexia put an arm around me and drew me into her shoulder. She kissed the top of my head, but she was crying, too. Kadram had been a friend to all of us. Even when faced with impossible tasks, he had always helped me to find a way. He was the one who had saved me at the end of the Northern Invasion, the one who had told me what to do with the swords. He saved me again when Alexia shot me in Hunt whilst under the power of the Zalems. I owed so much to him.

And now he was gone.

I told Alexia what I had found out about Kadram's connection to Telitha without mentioning Cades was her father. I needed to tell that to my husband first.

'It must have caused him much harm and shame,' Alexia said softly, 'to know his wife was violated and to see their daughter turn to evil. No wonder he never spoke of it. And she just let him die, without a moment's regret. The hate that fills her must be an unbearable torment.' She said this sadly, as if she pitied her.

'He died trying to protect the butterfly,' I said, 'but Mors still destroyed it.'

'No, he didn't,' Alexia said gently. I tilted my head back so I could see her face. She smiled at me through her tears. 'The butterfly is a symbol of Kest. You. And you're still here, dear cousin. You are not broken yet.'

I wanted to light a fire but didn't want to give our location away. Alexia, as resolute as always, convinced me that the best thing to do was to help her back onto Hazel so we could keep following Garrow's tracks into the night. I dried my tears and did as she said. At first it was easy— the horse prints were clear in the snow and visible in the moonlight.

But then we reached a tributary, a small, frozen creek that eventually ran into Kest River. The horse prints stopped at the edge of it.

Alexia was shivering so much, she could barely remain upright in the saddle.

'That's it,' I said, 'I'm going to light a fire.'

I dismounted and searched for wood. After finding a few scrappy, damp branches, I got the flint out of her saddlebag and spent a small while trying to get them to light. At last, I was successful and held my hands up to the pitiful flames. Having Bagred and Hazel with us meant we had a few supplies and something to eat. Alexia unrolled a fur skin under a large tree and lay down by the fire. I wanted to talk more, but almost as soon as she rested her head, she was asleep.

Sleep was not so kind to me. I was intimidated by the idea of defeating Mors and still reeling over Kadram's death. I kept thinking how Mors could ride to Liane on his great, silver beast and scorch our children at any time. I shuddered and turned to the night sky.

Please protect them, Ru'ach.

There were so many times over the wars with Cades and the Zalems when I was awfully tempted to melt into nothing and give up. I fantasised sometimes about riding to the coast and sailing away to new lands in a ship. I thought of the story Alexia had told Jeri about his namesake, how he had shown courage when he could have fled. His choice had saved lives, but why did such choices have to be made so continuously? I knew that people would talk about the flashes of heroism, but not many would know about the quiet times alone in the wilderness, when we had no idea how to defeat the enemy or where to find the strength to stand against them. Few stories told of the fears and sense of hopelessness that arise when all else is silent. I was separated now not only from my children but also from the man I loved. I had sent him and Darj to chase Cades' unhinged daughter. I was frozen and physically exhausted from a day of fighting. I would never give up, of course, no matter how tempting the thought was. But not for the first time, I doubted whether we could do this, whether I could come through for those who were relying on me.

What if I let them down?

30
SAPPHIRES HOLD

I finally fell asleep leaning against a tree, Bagred standing beside me. Alexia hadn't moved since she had first laid down. I woke briefly before dawn, saw an Islander pounce on Alexia, heard Hazel whinny, and blacked out.

When I woke the second time, it was with a thumping headache. I felt so cold and light that I thought I was naked. I was wearing my undergarments and nothing else. Alexia was a few steps away, lying on her back with her leg tucked awkwardly beneath her. She was in her undergarments as well, including the severed shift we had shortened to be a long shirt. There was no sign of our clothes.

Please don't be dead; please don't be dead. I crawled over to her, noticing other things. One, the fire was out. Two, Bagred and Hazel— and thereby our supplies—were missing. Three, the sun was thankfully quite warm. Four, both of us had blue feet. Five, if we didn't get clothes, food, or shelter soon, we would freeze to death.

With that thought in mind, I put my hand on Alexia's shoulder and gave her a gentle shake. She groaned, and I sighed with relief. 'Can . . . can you hear me?' I asked.

She opened her eyes, saw me, and sat up somewhat quickly. 'Are you all right?' she asked, placing a cold hand on my cheek. 'Your face is covered in blood, and your lips are blue.'

'I'm a bit c-cold.'

'Did you see who did this?' she asked.

'I think it was those Islanders I felled before. I should have killed them properly. They've robbed us.'

Alexia lifted her hand. 'Not entirely.' Her signet ring remained on her finger. 'Why didn't they kill us? The butterfly isn't protecting us anymore.'

'I don't know,' I said.

Alexia took in our surroundings.

'Do you know where we are?' I asked.

'Yes. We're not far from Sapphires Hold.' She stood up. 'We'd better move.'

'We have no horses.'

'On foot, then.'

It helped that there was no wind and the sun remained warm. Our bare feet suffered the most as they padded the frozen ground, but our eyes were also pained. The sun's reflection on the white surroundings was blinding. We dug up some mud and pasted it onto the skin around our eyes. It seemed to help, even if we did look more primitive than ever.

We stumbled upon a path and followed it in a slow run, trying to keep our body heat up and our blood moving. We came to a dead body lying in a ditch to the side of the road, one of the Islanders Garrow had left us with the day before. Upon closer inspection, I found several cuts and bruises on his chest, most resembling the shape of horseshoes. Another one was further off the road and in the same condition.

I understood at once. 'Bagred, Hazel . . . They didn't abandon us. They chased these men away and trampled them! That's why they didn't get a chance to finish us off or take us to Garrow.'

'Where have they gone now?' Alexia asked with an air of amazement.

'I don't know.' I studied the wilderness about us while Alexia called for her horse again. There was no sign of her or Bagred, but I saw smoke rising above the trees.

A town.

Alexia and I hurried towards the plume. The path became a road, and we passed a small cottage and then another one. We saw a woman in a thinning fur coat, who stopped and looked at us like she was faced with two prison escapees. She dropped a few of the logs she had been carrying and rushed back to her house.

'I know we haven't had a bath in a while, but I hardly think that's fair,' Alexia said.

I looked at her. In addition to her muddied eyes, her shirt barely reached the middle of her thighs. There were cuts and bruises visible all over us, and we both looked like we had been purposely rolling in dirt and blood.

'I've seen more attractive wild bats,' I said.

'Those bats haven't been through what we've been through.'

Next, we came across a man covered in dust. He was carrying a pick over his shoulder. He put his head down and walked faster when he saw us, but I stood in his way. 'We need your help.'

'I don't associate with women such as you,' he said.

I put one hand on my hip and gestured towards Alexia with the other. 'For your information, this woman is—'

'Lost and tired,' Alexia cut in, giving me a significant look. 'Our husbands went hunting, and we heard they may be in trouble because of some rogues in the area. We came to find them, but we were robbed on the way. I promise, we are respectable women.'

The miner looked from one of us to the other. Then, he burst out laughing. 'Good one.'

'It's true,' I said crossly.

He continued to laugh.

I was in no mood to be mocked. I grabbed his spare hand, stepped behind him, and locked his arm up against his back. 'It's true,' I said.

The miner gulped and dropped his pick. 'Forgive me.' He fell to a knee. 'What can I do to help?'

'Where are we?' I asked.

'Sapphires Hold,' he said. 'I work in one of the mines.'

'Have you seen anyone suspicious in these parts lately?' I asked.

The miner shook his head. 'There's been talk that there are mysterious folk coming and going from the lost mine further down the river,' he said. 'Chimeric Cave, it's called.'

By this time, we had attracted the attention of several other residents of Sapphires Hold. They gathered around us.

'What have you caught here, Bobban?' one of the men asked. 'Or should I say, what has caught you?' There were a few chuckles among the villagers.

'Let me go,' Bobban said resignedly. 'I'll take you to my house.'

We followed him to his small cottage by a frozen creek, which in the daylight was a bright icy blue. Inside, Bobban's wife was stacking logs onto the fire. She was the woman we had seen earlier. She seemed even more uncomfortable about us, now that we were in her home. She glared at her husband, and he kept shuffling away from her as if meeting her eyes would cause him to burst into flames.

'I hope we're not intruding,' Alexia said to her, as we clearly were.

'It's two respectable women searching for their husbands,' Bobban said. His tone suggested he was still unconvinced but too nervous to challenge us any further. I hadn't planned to intimidate him; I was just so tired and cold. His wife said nothing.

'We're only seeking to refresh ourselves, and then we will be on our way to Chimeric Cave,' I said, hoping to sound calm and reassuring. The woman still didn't move.

Bobban gave us two bowls of warm water, which we gratefully used to clean ourselves. I cleared the blood out of my hair where one of the Islanders had knocked me down the night before and washed out the claw-like wound where Mors had grabbed me. I knew then it would leave a scar. Still, the warmth from the water and fire brought life back to my fingers. Bobban's wife eventually conceded to make us toast with a pumpkin butter spread while Bobban left to source clothes for us. He returned with two thin, common dresses and two pairs of fur boots.

'This is all we have to spare.' He studied us with a contemplative frown as we dried our faces. Now that we weren't covered in filth, we looked more like ourselves—wounded, exhausted, and thin, but Adaliah and Alexia, nevertheless.

I pulled one of the dresses on and tied up a pair of fur boots over my blue feet. The clothes still weren't warm enough to endure prolonged time out in the winter, but they were better. And according to Bobban, Chimeric Cave wasn't too far away—just a few hours' walk. Alexia and I stood with our backs to the fire, thawing ourselves and eating the toast before preparing to go. We thanked them both for their kindness and headed towards the door.

'Wait,' Bobban said. 'Have this.' He held out a fur blanket. 'The winter is particularly bitter this year. You may need it.'

Alexia reached out to take it; Bobban saw the signet ring on her finger. A miner at the foot of the Hewn Mountains was unlikely to have ever seen one before, but I could tell he knew it was important in some way. 'There is something familiar about you both,' he said, 'but I just can't place it in my mind. What are your names? Perhaps I know your parents.'

The queen held the folded blanket in her arms. 'This is my cousin,' she said quietly. 'Her father's name was Bagred, and mine was Amaz.'

It wasn't until we slipped out the door and glanced back that Bobban's mouth dropped open.

We followed the creek south, just as Bobban had told us. There was still no sign of Bagred and Hazel. I was so grateful to them for defending us from death and hoped and prayed they were safe.

Elhian, Elhian, Elhian . . . I breathed. *I hope and pray you're safe, too.*

Alexia hadn't spoken about Darj or her children since I'd sent our husbands after Telitha. It was too painful for me to speak about my family, and I assumed it was the same for her. It seemed we were both coping by not thinking or talking about it.

We covered a significant distance by the afternoon, but the sky filled with threatening, black clouds. A menacing wind slithered past us as the clouds bathed us with a mixture of rain and snow.

'A bad sign,' Alexia said with a shiver.

The storm rapidly grew worse. Rain and snow trickled down my spine. Soon, we could barely see a few steps in front of us.

'It's no good,' I said. 'We need shelter.'

If Alexia responded, I didn't hear.

We walked along a rocky ledge that had risen above the edge of the creek, heading up a small hill. I thought I saw a lamp shining through the sleet and blowing in the wind. I took a step towards it, but my foot landed on nothing. I tumbled forward and fell. A moment later, I was completely buried in soft, white snow.

The next thing I knew, Alexia was frantically shoveling the snow away from my face and neck with her bare hands. Her teeth were chattering. The ice and cold probed my skin like scalpels. My whole body seized up, and my vision darkened. Alexia's black hair was covered in sticky snowflakes and kept flicking around her face in the growing wind. She heaved as she tugged at my arm. I was still buried up to my waist. She dug away more snow, muttering my name over and over. The skin around her lips was turning blue. She took my arm and heaved again. She succeeded at last and dragged me towards the flickering lamp and inside the mouth of the cave. She collapsed with me to the ground, just inside the entry, and draped Bobban's fur blanket over us. How long we lay there, shivering, is known only to Ru'ach.

'Darj and Elhian . . . ' I began. 'It will be hard for them to find us in the storm.'

'The storm will pass. I will get you out of here. You must . . . must finish Mors and Telitha.'

The wind howled past the opening of the cave, expressing its anguish with a swirl of snow.

'Do you . . . remember when you came to visit me at the palace for my father's birthday?' Alexia asked some time later, trying to keep us awake. The wind had tempered a little.

'Which time?'

'The time we went riding in the Yellow Forest. Ethaniel was with us. He had just started courting me.'

I remembered. The sun had been warm that day, a pleasant thought. It was the middle of autumn, and the beautiful Yellow Forest had lived up to its name. I'd felt a bit left out as the young lord and princess rode closely together behind me and shared private laughs. A small part of me had resented him for taking up all of my older cousin's attention. I must have been about ten at the time. 'Yes, I remember.'

'I asked what you thought of him afterwards,' Alexia said. 'Do you remember what you said?'

I shook my head. The cold was fighting with all other thoughts.

'You said that your horse was more handsome and interesting than he.' She gave a soft laugh.

I smiled. I did have a rather good horse at the time.

'He kissed me that day,' she said, poignantly. 'It was the first kiss for both of us.'

She took off her signet ring and tucked it into her shirt. She pulled the blanket up to my shoulders, and we fell into a frosty sleep, thinking it was the end.

31
ALEXIA'S SACRIFICE

The next time I woke, my eyelids were ice-covered, and I was lying on something unforgiving. I couldn't place where I was at first. The icy rock walls looked as if they'd been shaved back with rudimentary tools, and they formed a large room within the cave. I could hear a chipping sound somewhere in the distance—a pickaxe repeatedly bouncing off an unrelenting rock.

We made it. I'm alive.

Other men and women sat against the walls, hugging their knees with frozen hands. Brown hair and eyes, pale skin—they were Casmodians. There was a small fire crackling. Several women sat around it, their fingers hovering close to the flames. Most of their lips were cracked and bleeding. They were young and broken. Beyond them was a pool with steam rising off the top—a hot spring.

I slept some more. I attempted to move the second time I woke but felt restricted. I tried to move my hands, but they were manacled so tightly that my wrists felt raw. My ankles smarted against their metal binds, too.

I can't move.

I pulled against all four manacles again, and they rattled.

Something tightened around my upper arm. A hand. Alexia was crouching beside me.

She's alive.

I attempted to part my lips and felt some of the skin pulling. I tasted blood in my mouth as I forced them to separate. I tried to speak Alexia's name but had barely formed the 'a' sound before she shook her head at me. Her grip on my arm tightened again. *She wants me to be quiet.* I didn't need any further persuading. Confused and weary, I felt like my spirit wasn't quite resting with my body. My knees hurt. I rested my head again and fell back to sleep.

It was impossible for me to track how much time passed as I drifted in and out of consciousness. At one point, I heard a man yelling, women screaming.

Garrow.

I tried to pay attention to the sounds around me. Garrow was definitely there. I recognised his low, gruff voice. He was directing these men and women like they were dogs. I remembered that Alexia had said they were Casmodian prisoners from Ignallia.

The next time I woke, I could feel the heat of a fire, and Alexia was kneeling beside me again.

'How long have I been like this?' I asked.

'Two days.'

'Is that all?' It felt like a week had passed. 'He still hasn't killed us?'

'He doesn't know we're here.'

'Why am I bound while you're free?'

'Because I am able to work and you are not. Those of us who work are almost always supervised. You are often left alone. I don't know where they keep the key. Garrow has hundreds of Casmodian slaves here, mining for gold, just like I said. His foremen found us, but he doesn't know who we are.'

Alexia kept her eyes at the tunnel opening behind me like she wasn't speaking to me at all. There was that heightened agitation in her tone again. I wondered if we would both be broken before the end. 'Garrow hasn't inspected us yet, and I've been trying to be subservient so as not to draw his attention, at least not until you're well enough to escape.'

'That must have been hard.' It was my flat attempt at humour.

Alexia rewarded me with a slight smile. 'Garrow is violent with his slaves and forces them to work in these conditions with little food and warmth. He punishes them if they don't keep up. I've had to work a shift.' She raised her hands, showing ten fragmented nails and bleeding fingertips unbefitting for a queen. 'You haven't because the foreman believes you are in a perpetual state of unconsciousness. I don't want him to see you awake. You're not fit to do anything but breathe.'

'What's wrong with my knees?' I asked, noticing the pain again.

'When they found us and dragged us in here, they threw you down, and your knees hit the rocks. They are both bruised.' She pulled back the rags that covered my legs, and I saw the black and blue patches for myself.

'How . . . how did you get better?' I asked. 'Better' wasn't the right word—Alexia was clearly cold and exhausted, with several lacerations and bruises visible on her arms. But she was awake and functioning a lot better than me. The warmth of the fire was finally reaching my core, but I was still too weak to hold my head up or fight against the manacles.

She shrugged. 'I think when he brought us in, I was placed closer to the fire, that's all. But we're going to get out of here, Adaliah, and with everything we need.'

'How?'

She met my eyes properly for the first time. 'Garrow is waiting for Telitha to bring the other part of the sword so they can destroy it. So, I've made up my mind. I'm going to kill him.' She fingered a small knife, which had been hidden in her palm. 'Today.'

It wasn't until some time later, after Alexia had managed to steal and feed me some bread pieces, that I glimpsed Garrow in action for myself. I lay on the rocky ground and shut my eyes when I heard him coming. I didn't move, not even when someone threw a log on the fire and some of the sparks landed on my arm.

'We are running out of time!' he yelled. 'Your group has been lazy today.'

'Please, Your Majesty . . . ' one young-sounding girl whimpered. 'Please, we did our best.'

Garrow grumbled and slapped her. I opened my eyes just enough to make out her figure falling backwards onto the rocks. Alexia sat next to me. She was tense, but somehow I knew it was anger, not fear.

Garrow struck the girl whilst she was down. I couldn't see what he was using, but from her cries it sounded like a sharp object. The shrill screams echoed around the cave.

Alexia stood. I raised my head a little. Her signet ring was back on her finger.

'Stop hitting her.' Alexia made the simple sentence sound as fierce as a blade. Several people gasped at her boldness.

Garrow's face was haggard with grit-filled wrinkles. He hit the girl a second time, and the screaming stopped. His mouth tightened as he stepped towards Alexia. He hadn't recognised her. The dirt-covered and poorly dressed woman before him was certainly a long way from the queen he knew. Tucked into his belt was the hilt of my sword.

Alexia didn't flinch, not even when he raised his arm to strike her. I glimpsed what he had used to slay the other girl. It was a short, round stick with pieces of leather sprouting out of the top. Each one was tipped with sharp, curved pieces of bone, designed to cut deeply. Some were white, but most were bloodied.

He brought this instrument of torture down against Alexia. She ducked and stabbed him in the leg with the small blade. Garrow screeched with pain and annoyance. It was a quick blow, and she took the knife with her as she stepped behind him. Alexia gave a defiant shout as she lodged the knife in his back and twisted it. The slaves gasped again, and some screamed.

Garrow thrust himself back with an even louder cry. He turned to Alexia and bared his teeth in a grimace. She stared severely at him, her shoulders heaving as she fought to catch her breath.

'I should have shot you in the heart the first time,' she said. 'It led you to Anash a long time ago.'

His face filled with realisation. He roared at her, and then he saw me. 'You! You will not touch the sword.'

He raised his arm again, and I realised with horror that he was going to strike me—on my front side.

'No!' Alexia cried.

I struggled against the manacles but couldn't break free. I tensed and pressed my eyes shut, preparing for the coming, death-bringing blow. Instead, I felt the sudden weight of someone dropping on top of me, forcing all wind from my lungs. There was the sound of a thrash, followed by a harrowing shriek right by my ear.

Alexia had taken the blow for me.

Garrow swore at her. 'If you want to take a beating, I am happy to oblige.'

The whip connected with her back for a second time. Her body shook.

'Stop,' I said, barely able to form the word. My arms trembled as I tried to lift them against the manacles again, as I tried to do something to protect my cousin.

Garrow raised the instrument to strike her for a third time.

'Alexia!'

She rolled over and off me. Garrow's arm was mid-strike. She reached up and lodged the knife in his chest. They were nose to nose, grimacing in each other's faces. He dropped his weapon. Alexia withdrew the knife and pushed him away with a grunt. Red spit dribbled from his mouth, and he fell to his side, dead.

There was a moment of stunned silence as the Casmodian slaves stood and tried to comprehend what had happened. I heard a cry of surprise and disgust as another man came into our area of the cave, presumably the foreman who had been helping Garrow. The slaves didn't move but stared at him with growing hatred. He bristled. 'Anash will take care of you,' he said, taking two steps back before turning and running.

My cousin lay on her side, her face ashen, her body shaking. I couldn't see her shredded back, but I could see the blood that was trickling down her side and across her stomach.

'Alexia . . . '

'It's . . . not so bad,' she said softly.

'Why . . . why would you do that?'

She met my eyes. 'You were there for me, and I'll be there for you, always. Remember?'

Tears dripped down my face. 'You are my ledzagor.'

My friend even in the face of death.

An older Casmodian woman ran to Alexia's side. 'I have never seen such valour,' she said in a frail voice, touching the queen's arm. Alexia's lips were coated in sticky blood, and she was now unconscious.

'Please, help her,' I said.

'There are two beds in a cavern further down the path,' the woman said to one of the others, 'where Garrow and his foreman slept. Zana, help me carry her there.' The two women lifted the queen as carefully as they could. Blood had thoroughly stained her threadbare clothes.

'Get her warm and try and stop the blood flow with whatever you can find,' I said.

Please, don't let her die.

'Of course,' the first woman said.

The image of my cousin's flayed body lying limp in their arms as they carried her away would remain with me forever.

The knife Alexia had used was on the ground nearby. 'Can someone use that to break my manacles?' I asked with a nod towards it.

While most of the others stood about with white, stunned faces, a young man picked up and fed the bloodied knife through his fingers. He stabbed the lock on my right hand repeatedly until it broke all together and my hand was free. 'Almost there,' he said as he moved onto the next one.

Once he went to work on the manacles around my ankles, I tried to pull myself up into a sitting position. My back griped. One of the other Casmodians saw this and gently helped me until I was upright again.

I sat there and let the blood inside me rearrange itself for a minute or two, until my head cleared and my ankles were freed.

The next task was to stand. I rolled onto my stomach first. I fixed my hands against the ground and gradually pushed myself up. Every frozen muscle in my arms protested. Sweat beaded on my forehead as I finally rested back on my legs. The pressure was then on my knees; I quickly shifted so I was sitting on my buttocks. Two Casmodians gripped my arms to pull me to my feet, but I knew it would be too painful for my joints. The tiniest movements were agonising.

I remembered the hot spring. *The heat and the water will soothe my knees.* I couldn't think of any other way to quickly reduce the pain and help me move properly.

'We can just carry you to bed, like they did your friend,' one of them said.

'The longer I lie still, the worse it will become. Please, I need to do this.' *And I need to be able to move before I face Mors.*

Two of them pulled me as carefully as they could across the icy gravel and eased me into the hot springs, feet first. It felt so good that I let go of them and slipped in, despite their cries of alarm. At first, there was confusion. The sound of bubbles filled my ears, and I wasn't sure which way I was facing. My feet rested on the rocky shelf beneath. I pushed up and resurfaced. That was when relief filled me. For the first time in days, I felt truly warm. The cold ran from my body like a frightened enemy. I shuddered as every muscle relaxed and calmed. I dipped underneath, ran my hands through my hair, and rubbed the wounds where the manacles had been. The mineral water stung slightly, but it was worth it as the dirt and blood faded away and I finally felt clean.

'Are you all right?' one of the Casmodians asked me.

'Much better, thank you.' I hurriedly massaged the muscles around my knees, my eyes searching the expanse of the cave. Where were the beds? We needed to build a fire. Where was the wood? I spotted a disheveled pile lying in the snow. Would it be dry enough to burn? What would we all do for food? There was some meat hanging on a row of hooks and a loaf of bread lying on the ground.

I floated myself back towards the edge of the spring, and the same two Casmodians helped me out of the water. The chilled air shocked me, but another Casmodian had rushed to find me a blanket, which I used as a towel before wrapping it around my shoulders. The real test was whether I could stand. I already knew I had more movement in my joints, but could they support my weight?

The Casmodians gradually lifted me until I was on my feet. I grimaced, but the thought of my cousin bleeding to death gave me the courage I needed.

With a Casmodian propping me up under each arm, I took a step. *I can do this.*

I broke away from my supports. I was unsteady and weak, but I could walk. I staggered over to Garrow's body and took the hilt of my sword from his belt.

'Take me to her.'

Each step was difficult as I followed them down an uneven, icy path. I passed a few side caves—one was filled with crates; another was used as cells. It was the fourth one that had the two beds in it. To my great relief, they had already laid Alexia down on her front and wrapped her legs and feet in the same fur blanket Bobban had given us. They attempted to bandage her back with rags. One of them had lit a small fire and was carefully placing additional pieces of wood upon it. Feeling lightheaded and feverish, I sat down on the other bed and tucked the sword hilt under it. Our helpers finished doing what they could for Alexia. They looked as exhausted, frozen, and hungry as I felt.

'Please, go and take care of yourselves. Build up the fires, eat what you need to, take what clothes you can find. Don't go outside into the winter until you're feeling stronger. We'll be all right. We just . . . need to rest.'

I lay down, promising myself it was just for a minute.

'How pretty they are.'

The leathery voice drew me out of unconsciousness.

'How fragile they are.'

A sharp fingernail stroked my cheek. It sent a chill through my body, and a familiar fear tightened my chest. I opened my eyes. Mors was leaning over me, and beside him was his High Zalem. Telitha had red eyes, tears on her cheeks, and an expression like a vicious animal about to tear its prey apart.

'You killed Garrow,' she said, seeing me awake. 'You killed—'

'Now, now, Telitha,' Mors said gently. The red scales on his arms shimmered. He stroked my cheek again, his long talon pressing into my skin. I shrunk away from him, both repulsed and terrified. 'It wasn't this one who killed him. This one is as innocent as a dove, aren't you?'

I frantically searched my mind for any idea that would lead to escape, but there was nothing I could do to defend Alexia or myself. I had no strength and no weapons.

'Seeing you lying here with your poor knees, so weak, I can almost forget that you destroyed the power of my four swords and the Dark Orb or that you killed Jag, Odavan . . . '

Alexia hadn't moved and was a deathly white. The fur blanket had fallen off her, and her back was covered in fresh blood. She needed help immediately. It was possible it was already too late.

'Who killed Garrow, if not this one?' Telitha asked.

'Where is the broken blade?' Mors asked me, suddenly fierce.

I glared at him, anger rising in my blood. 'I don't know.'

I wondered about the Casmodians. Had they escaped in time?

I didn't get to find out whether Mors accepted my answer or not. Telitha had drawn out a dagger and raised it above Alexia. Tears streamed down her face.

'What are you doing?' Mors asked.

'If Adaliah didn't kill Garrow, this one must have.'

'Yes, she did,' Mors said matter-of-factly. 'Kill her if you wish, but just know that if you do, we will lose the opportunity to make her a Ghost. And I have been enjoying the thought of her soulless enslavement. She escaped it once before; she won't again.'

'I have wanted to kill her since we first met,' Telitha said. She pointed the dagger down at Alexia, even though Alexia looked as if she had died hours ago.

I rolled myself off the bed and reached for Telitha. 'Don't you touch her!' I said, but I could barely get my body to move.

Mors calmly reached for Telitha's arm. 'There is no reward when she is like this. Don't you want to give her orders and see her lose herself, see her serve everything she has fought against?'

'But I hate her so much,' Telitha said again, sobbing as she lowered the dagger. 'I hate her the most.'

'You can kill her after she becomes a Ghost, if you still haven't changed your mind,' Mors said comfortingly, disarming her of the dagger. 'I will not take that away from you, I promise, not if it's what you really want.'

The way he was calmly discussing the murder of my cousin was unnerving. 'How . . . did you become like this?' I asked.

'How does anyone become the person they are? From their childhood, of course.'

'A thousand years of tormenting the world because you were jealous of your older brother?'

Mors sneered. 'Don't be ridiculous. That is only the beginning of things—the seed, the idea, the foundation. From there, we make a choice, and then another choice, and then choice upon choice until we rebirth ourselves into something terrible and glorious. My brother was given everything: my parents' love, my father's kingdom . . . He was praised for his looks and his knowledge, revered wherever he went. Whenever he did something wrong, they beat me for it. Sometimes, he would do the wrong thing just to watch me be flogged by my own father, the king. And now he is dead, and I live. And what's more, I will soon be the master of death. We each receive our just rewards.'

'If we are not going to kill them now, we may as well go,' Telitha said angrily. 'We do not have time for this sentimentality. We came to get Garrow and his part of the sword, and we have failed. Let us be on our way, or I will kill Alexia.'

Mors stood and roared at Telitha, but there were no flames. 'Shut up, woman! Do not forget whom you serve.'

Telitha raised the dagger again and stepped back towards Alexia, apparently prepared to defy Mors.

I wanted to say something that would alarm them into submission, but my throat was sore and dry.

'There!' a new, much braver sounding voice said. 'You, stop!'

I raised my head and fought back the urge to sob at the sight of my Elhian, chipped ear and all, and Darj beside him.

Darj's face was more thunderous than I had ever seen. He pointed his sword at Telitha. 'Get away from my wife.'

'I am going to cut her in two,' Telitha said, baring her teeth at the prince-general.

Darj threw his sword at Telitha. She ducked, and it lodged firmly into the cave wall. Telitha raised a sword to strike him, but Mors stepped forward and clicked his fingers. Darj's and Elhian's hands flew to their foreheads as if they were experiencing the worst headaches of their lives. They slowly dropped to their knees, their creased faces full of indescribable agonies. The cave echoed with the sound of their muted groans while Telitha's expression changed from anger to delight.

'Elhian,' Darj said behind gritted teeth. 'The blade!'

My head hurt. I couldn't keep my eyes open.

Elhian . . .

Exhaustion took over again, and I melted back into the bed.

32
HELP

'Adaliah?'

Elhian? He's alive?

I wanted to get up, but I couldn't move. My face felt wet, and I realised I was crying.

'Adaliah . . . '

I opened my eyes. Elhian had knelt next to me, and there was no sign of Mors and Telitha. My husband's face was shining with sweat and dirt. He had thrown some wood on the fire, still fighting to catch his breath.

'We need to get them warm,' he said.

'Alexia!' Darj was by her side. 'No, my darling, what did he do to you?' His hands shaking, he picked up the fur blanket and wrapped it around Alexia's legs and feet again.

Elhian helped me back onto the bed, and I lay down. He hurried to the queen and took her limp hand in his. 'Cousin, can you hear me?' There was no response. He put a finger against her neck. 'She's still breathing,' he said, but his face failed to conceal his worry.

'She lost a . . . a lot of blood,' I said. My throat was raw.

I drifted in and out of consciousness again as Elhian propped my head up on a pillow and covered me in blankets. His cold hand gently rested on my forehead. 'She's burning up.'

'Alexia, too,' Darj said.

'Can you hear me?' Elhian asked. I nodded. 'Can you take some warm water with honey?'

I nodded again. A minute later, a cup appeared at my lips. Elhian helped me lift my head and held the cup while I drank as much as I could. The honey brought relief to my sore throat, and I felt the liquid run all the way down to my stomach.

I rested my head again, wanting to cry. It was amazing to me how such simple things could bring such comfort. A bed and pillow. A blanket. A warm cup of honey water. Someone to help Alexia. And a balm Elhian put on my lips, soothing the aching.

Elhian brought over some bread and nuts. 'Eat if you can. I must help Darj with Alexia.'

'Garrow is dead,' I said.

'Yes, we saw him,' Elhian said.

Darj had already moved Alexia's head into a more comfortable position on the pillow and peeled back the bloodied rags on her back. Tears ran down his face, but I don't think he was aware of them.

He and Elhian gently wiped away the blood from Alexia's back with damp cloths. Soon, the many deep cuts inflicted upon her lay open, seeping, and raw. Elhian felt for her pulse again. White-faced, he ran his hand over his mouth. 'She is in considerable danger.'

Darj swayed on his feet; Elhian took his arm and helped him sit at the end of her bed. 'Just do your best for her,' Darj said, catching his breath.

'For all of us,' I whispered. 'Please, I couldn't bear it if she died, especially if it was because of me.'

Elhian left to get his saddlebags.

I hadn't heard any other noise beyond our particular cavern for some time. 'Elhian,' I called as he returned, 'there were Casmodians here. What happened to them? Did they get away in time?'

Elhian and Darj exchanged looks. 'Adaliah,' Elhian said, 'Mors killed them. Every one of them.'

'He didn't just kill them,' Darj said lowly. 'He dismembered and disemboweled them.'

I sensed it was not a sight either of them would recover from quickly. I turned my face back towards the ceiling, shuddering and fighting off the desire to sink into a dark and weepy mess. My talk of safety and home had been followed with the very brutal torture I had hoped to save them from.

'You can only imagine what state we feared we'd find you two in,' Darj said as he turned back to Alexia, brushing away his tears. 'What can I do, Elhian?'

'You must do the hardest thing of all now, my friend. Nothing.' Elhian went to work blending some herbs from the saddlebags he'd brought in until he had formed a paste. He began to apply it to each of Alexia's small but deep wounds with delicacy. By the time he finished, Alexia's back was thinly covered in what looked like dry, green mud.

'Here,' Elhian said, handing Darj a pile of clean bandages. 'These can't be applied without compromising her modesty.'

'I need you to lift up her shoulders.'

Standing at her head, Elhian complied. Darj wrapped the bandages around the queen's upper body while Elhian looked away.

'All we can do now is let them sleep,' Elhian said.

'I'll get more wood,' Darj said.

What followed were several days of coughing and strenuous breathing. Alexia remained insensible, but I heard her groaning from the fever. I felt like I was alive in a dream world. Elhian later told me he had to restrain me more than once when I sat up, ready to fight anyone who would take me on. At other times, I wept for Alexia. Worst of all was the disempowering exhaustion that followed. I even kept my eyes closed to refrain from blinking. I had never before felt so ill.

Elhian massaged my legs and knees before bandaging the joints. He cleaned and redressed the wound where Mors had torn me. He and Darj nursed us continuously. I wondered if they ever slept. I wished for the misery to end more than once, but finally, I woke with my head a little clearer.

'Welcome back,' Elhian said, gently stroking my hand.

'Elhian.' Somehow it was easier to talk. My lips weren't as chapped, and my throat wasn't as sore. 'How long . . . ?'

'We've been nursing you for five days now.'

'Five . . . days?' I tried to calculate how many days were left until Mors' birthday. *Seven.* 'A-Alexia?'

'I believe there is cause for hope,' Elhian said. 'See for yourself.'

I turned my head and saw her sleeping on her side.

My dear cousin.

'Her fever broke earlier than yours,' Elhian said, 'and her wounds are healing without infection. We have thankfully been able to keep her adequately warm.'

'She lives because of Elhian,' Darj said as he appeared at my side. His face was unshaven, his eyes outlined with dark shadows. I had never seen him look so wretched. 'I will never forget what you've done for her.'

Elhian gave him an understanding nod.

'What happened with Telitha and Mors?' I asked them. 'What did he do to you?'

'He brought to mind all of our worst memories,' Elhian said. 'But they didn't feel just like memories. They were so real, it was like they were happening again. The pain was just as tangible and as crippling as it was before, but Darj reminded me I had the blade of the Life Sword in my boot, which we had managed to steal back from Telitha. We'll tell you about that later. I pulled it out and pointed it at Mors, just as you did by the river. He ran, Telitha on his heels.'

'A coward, then.'

'They always are, aren't they?'

Darj's eyes were upon his wife, ever watchful. 'I didn't get to tell you, Darj,' I said. 'Alexia . . . She was so brave. She threw herself in front of me. She risked her life for mine.'

Darj gave me a crooked smile, and his eyes reddened again. 'May Ru'ach honour her for her love.'

A few minutes of silence later, a breeze filtered into the cavern. It wasn't the first time fresh air had come to us, the wind presumably picking up outside from time-to-time, but this breeze felt comfortingly warmer. As it softly swirled around us, Alexia's chest rose like she was taking a particularly deep breath. Her mouth opened with a small gasp. Darj kneeled next to her and put his hand on her forehead, brushing her hair back. 'Alexia? Can you hear me?'

She opened her eyes and gave a slight nod. 'Where are we?' Her voice was hoarse and thick with mucus, but we all felt such joy to hear it. Elhian blinked away tears, more relieved than I think he could say.

'Still in the cave,' her husband said. 'Try not to move too much. Your back is tender.'

'It's not so bad.'

Darj brought her hand to his lips, a tear dripping down his face. 'You don't always have to be so brave, you know.'

She squeezed his hand. 'I know I am glad I chose you.'

33
QUEEN OF THE WHITE ISLES

'Elhian?' I asked a little later.

He sat on the edge of my bed. His hands had smudges of ash on them, and he smelt comfortingly like smoke from the campfire he had just been building up again. Drips of water echoed around the room as the ice-covered ceiling yielded to the warmth.

'What is it?' he asked, tucking a stray piece of hair behind my ear.

'There's something I need to tell you.'

Darj had just eased his wife into a sitting position and given her a tankard of warm tea he'd brewed earlier. Alexia was frail, even ghostlike in her appearance. The battering both from Garrow and the fever had taken a significant toll on her strength and health. I knew she would bear the stripes Garrow had left on her back forever.

Elhian was waiting for me to speak. 'Tell me,' he said when I hesitated again. 'I don't think there's much left in this world that could surprise me now.'

I wasn't convinced of that, but I pressed on anyway. 'When we were in Semanez, in the library, I found a letter from my mother to yours. It's in my saddlebag with Bagred somewhere; otherwise, I would show it to you.'

'What did it say?'

Darj and Alexia were watching, waiting for my answer as well.

'Telitha is Cades' daughter.'

Elhian's blinked. 'What?' he asked calmly, as if he had simply misheard me and would hear a more reasonable statement instead.

'Cades forcefully lay with a Jazmardian lady called Ida, and Telitha is the result.'

Elhian's face paled. A tense silence followed.

'I'll, ah . . . I better go and check on our horses,' Darj said, not quite hiding his astonishment.

'Help me up, and I'll come with you,' Alexia said. Darj put an arm around her waist and carefully assisted her out of the cave room.

'Why didn't you tell me at the time?' Elhian asked. He was still trying to sound calm, but I could tell he was hurt, even angry.

'There's hardly been an opportunity.'

'You could have found one for something like this.'

'I have now. Please, I don't want to fight about it. I'm not sure it even changes anything.'

'She could try and claim the crown.' His mouth dropped. 'She has already stolen the crown.'

'The physical crown, yes, but not the rule of the kingdom. She's illegitimate and younger. Her claim to rule would be a thin one and only valid if . . . '

'If something were to happen to me.' Elhian's face aged before me. His eyes—normally bright and the colour of chestnuts—were troubled and dull. His thick, brown hair needed a wash, and he had a short but growing beard.

'What are you thinking?' I asked when he didn't say anything further.

'She's evil.'

'Yes.' I told him about her relationship to Kadram and how she had allowed him to die.

He unfolded his arms and stood up. 'It all makes sense. The way Telitha is behaving, the way she fights, the way she hates you and Alexia . . . It reminds me of him. It reminds me of how much I hate him.' Elhian kicked a smoldering log that had the audacity to fall away from the fire. The fire spat as it accepted it back within its flames.

'Don't,' I said, sitting up. 'Don't let the memory of his evil poison you. This is exactly why I was worried about telling you.'

'How could he do that to my mother? How could he? He killed my mother. I killed him. Now, we have to kill Telitha. That's what it is to be a part of my family.'

For the first time in days, I stood. My knees ached but were much better than they had been. My confidence grew as I realised they could support my weight. 'Your father did the things he did because he was evil.' I put a hand on his shoulder and made him face me. 'But you are not.'

Anger still shadowed his eyes. 'Adaliah, I don't hate them for their sake. Don't you see? I hate them for yours. I hate them because they keep trying to hurt—'

'I don't want you to hate them or anyone for my sake. I would never want that. I am a Targian. We always seek to choose love. You and I are among the sons and daughters of the Great Spirit. Hate is not his way. This keeps coming up and haunting you. It has to stop. You have to forgive him, Elhian, and stop defining yourself by him. You have just brought the Queen of Targe back from the brink of death; there's no imagining what that might mean for our world. You bring healing and hope where there is none. That is anything but evil.'

'How can I forgive him when even now, I keep finding out more and more about his depravity?'

'Alexia forgave him, and he committed many foul deeds against her, too. You know how much happier she has been. This hate for him will only eat you up. Forgive him and Telitha for your own sake. It won't free them from the consequences of their actions, but it will free your heart. Then we will go out there and defeat her and Mors for everyone's sake.' The mention of Mors reminded me of what the dragon had said about Elhian's self-doubt. 'You are tormenting yourself,' I said. 'You must fight back against the thoughts that plague you. *You* are good. You do have what it takes. We will win this war.'

A few days earlier, I wouldn't have thought those last words myself, let alone spoken them. Now I was filled with such passion and hope that I was convinced of it. I wanted—needed—Elhian to be convinced of it as well.

He faltered, but then he took a deep breath and straightened. He closed his eyes. 'I am not him,' he breathed. 'I am not him.' He opened his eyes. 'I'm sorry.' He kissed me. It was tentative at first but rapidly grew in intensity. I wrapped my arms around his neck. When we drew apart, his eyes were filled with spirit again. 'It actually makes me sad now,' he said.

'What do you mean?'

'She is what I could have become, if not for my mother or King Amaz.'

'You are the result of your choices, just as she is.'

He rested his forehead against mine. 'Tell me truly,' he said, drawing back, 'have you been unhappy as my queen?'

'Of course not,' I said, stroking back his hair. 'I've just felt that my role as your queen wasn't all that was awaiting me, and it's been hard to find meaning in day-to-day life.'

'I haven't been sure what my role is or how to move forward, either, not after everything we've been through. But I think now you go on by realising that every day, there are differences to be made. You search for them and fight for them until something inside you learns there is just as much value in the small victories as there are in the big ones.'

'Yes,' I said, feeling something inside me settle at his words, 'you are exactly right.'

'And when we are done fighting wars, we will fight to improve the lives of our people in whatever way we can, just as Alexia does and just as Amaz did before her. That, I think, is what we're here for.'

'And that is just the kind of battle I want to fight.' I kissed him again, leaning into his strong frame.

There was a self-conscious cough, the sort Darj made whenever he was embarrassed. 'Well, I'm glad you two sorted that out,' he said. He and Alexia stood in the doorway with reserved smiles. Darj held the cape Elhian had given me and Alexia's bow and quiver. 'Guess who we found outside,' he said.

'Bagred and Hazel,' I said.

Despite Alexia's raw back and hacking cough, Darj decided we had to move in the morning. When Darj decided action was needed, action usually followed. But first, in a rare victory against his determination, I made him and Elhian explain how they got the blade.

As Darj told it, he and Elhian had chased Telitha all the way back to Levanna. They travelled right behind her at first but decided to drop back to give the appearance they'd given up on the pursuit. They cut across the land towards Levanna and picked up her trail again on the outskirts of the battlefield. They watched from afar as she met with Hanequin and gave him care of the blade. The battle still underway, the forces at Levanna were yet standing thanks to Darj's earlier precautions; but the Bone Hordes were, as Alexia had said, innumerable.

Darj and Elhian saw Hanequin pass the blade to a soldier, who, with four others, ran with it away from the battle and over a small hill. Darj and Elhian followed at a distance, their cover aided by the night. They came in view of a large tent; three of the soldiers went inside, including the one with the blade. The other two stood at the tent's door with their swords drawn. It became clear they intended to guard the blade in shifts. Darj and Elhian guessed that Telitha didn't want the blade anywhere near Mors for fear of his safety and planned to take it to Garrow as soon as the battle was over and won.

Darj downed the two guards at the door with dagger throws, which Elhian described as reminiscent of Alexia's skill and aim. After that, it didn't take them long to sneak through the grass, enter the tent, and kill the remaining three soldiers.

But there was a man inside they did not expect.

'Cordale was sitting in the corner behind a table,' Darj told me, 'in the dark, dressed in a thick, black cloak and scratching away in his book. He didn't even look up when we killed the men about him. Once they were dead, he told us we were too late, that Garrow already had the greater weapon in his possession and would destroy it.'

'The hilt?' I asked.

'Presumably.'

Darj went on to explain that the blade was sitting right before them on the table. 'Cordale told us to take it if we wished. He told us he would consider it a favour if we were to deliver it to Sapphires Hold for him. That was the first time he raised his gaze to us, but even then, it was like he was seeing through us.

'Cordale returned to writing in his book while Elhian took the blade, weighed it in his hands, and asked him how he had escaped at the end of the last war. Cordale laughed and said, "That was easy. You all thought the threat had died with Bylon and Sirvan. You forgot about me, and I simply walked away."'

'When I asked him what he was writing, he told me it was none of my concern,' Elhian said. 'I asked him if it was a work of fiction, like the blade. He'd forgotten I have one of the swords myself and can tell when one is a copy. This one was definitely a forgery, and a poor one at that.'

'Cordale stood and flipped the table towards us, making a run for it towards the tent door with his book in hand,' Darj said. 'Elhian launched himself at Cordale, and they collided into the side wall, the tent almost coming down upon us. Cordale fell to the ground; Elhian scrambled over the top of him. He saw the true blade tucked in a pocket on the inside of Cordale's cloak and shouted to me.

'Elhian continued to wrestle with Cordale, pinning his hands down while I quickly took the true blade out of the Zalem's cloak and stepped back. Elhian got up and pulled Cordale to his feet. His book still in hand, Cordale opened it and turned the pages towards us. It was as if an incredible coldness came upon us, and yet not a coldness we felt in our bodies. It was like something in our spirits had frozen. We became fastened on the spot, and in that moment, Cordale escaped. But not with the true blade, thanks to Elhian.'

Darj added that he and Elhian briefly met with Xander and Yorella on the west side of Levanna, away from the battle. There, Elhian told them to meet us at Sapphires Hold as soon as they could and to bring Wolfgar with them so he could repair the sword. Like a true Casmodian, Elhian had faith that we would be able to give Wolfgar both pieces.

'Several men of the Bone Hordes followed us,' Darj said. 'I held back to slay them and sent Elhian on with the blade. I was worried that one or both of you might need a physician, but I was able to catch up, thankfully.'

'When we arrived in Sapphires Hold,' Elhian said, 'we had no idea where to go, but a man named Bobban saw us in the street and asked if we were the husbands of two respectable women who had passed through earlier. It was he who showed us the way, getting us here in time.'

'So, we just need to find the hilt,' Darj said.

'It's under this very bed,' I said, 'the hard work already done by the queen.'

Elhian sighed with relief. 'Thanks be to Ru'ach it hasn't all been for nothing.'

Elhian and Darj tried to bury Garrow's body, having safely retrieved his signet ring. The ground was so hard, it took them nearly two hours with picks to make it deep enough. They wrapped the body in cloths, laid him in his grave, and covered him with broken stones. The hundred or so dismembered Casmodian bodies were more difficult to deal with. Elhian and Darj laid them in rows and covered them with any cloths and blankets they could find before Alexia or I would have to see them.

As they took care of this, we dressed in our proper leather armour, which Darj had found attached to our saddles on Bagred and Hazel. Elhian re-discovered the fur-lined boots Bobban had given us, which, although a little big, Alexia and I were able to wear against the savage winter outside. We weren't at our full strength, but we had enough to ride. We walked past the covered bodies and outside, all of us anxious to leave. I greeted my horse with a hug around his black neck. Hazel looked grand standing in the white snow, waiting uncomplainingly for her rider.

We left Chimeric Cave forever. In the years that followed, pilgrims came to see the site where Queen Alexia had killed Garrow and laid her life down for me, but no one dared step foot inside. The people came to believe it was a cursed place, inhabited by Anash and the disembodied spirits of those murdered. We could almost feel them watching us as we rode away.

In the clear weather, it didn't take us long to arrive back in Sapphires Hold. Bobban must have seen us coming. He ran out of his house and dropped to a knee to the side of the road. We halted our horses. 'Thank Ru'ach you have returned safely,' he said, his eyes on the road.

'Thanks also in part to you,' I said.

'If I'd had more to give you for your journey, I would have given it freely.'

'You gave us all that you had before you even knew who we were,' Alexia said. 'Prince Darj, please compensate him on my behalf.'

Darj reached into his saddle bag and brought out a small bag of gold coins, which he passed down to Bobban. Bobban tentatively opened the drawstrings. His eyes widened when he saw how much was inside.

'This is more than I earn in a year,' he said. 'It's too much.' He raised the bag back towards Darj, who didn't move.

'It's yours,' Alexia said. 'An infinitesimal price to pay for the kindness that helped save my life.'

We continued down the road until we arrived at a small tavern. Hitching our horses to posts out the front, we walked inside and found a handful of miners. Captain Xander sat alone at a separate table. His eyes glistened with tears when he saw Alexia and me, and he didn't refrain from hugging us both.

'I am so pleased to see you safe, if not quite well,' he said, taking Alexia's hand and kissing it.

'I owe my life to Alexia,' I said softly with a thankful nod towards her.

'And I owe mine to Elhian,' she said.

'Where is Yorella?' Elhian asked.

'She is asleep upstairs, and Wolfgar is getting the local blacksmith ready to repair the sword.' Xander led us into the kitchen, where we could talk in private. It was a quaint room with onions, lavender, and sage hanging from the ceiling and several barrels of wine lining one of the walls. A square, wooden table was in the middle of the room with four unpadded seats. We each took one except for Darj, who stood behind Alexia.

'What happened with Garrow?' Xander asked.

I flinched at the memory of Alexia taking Garrow's blows in my stead. The image of her lying on her side and shaking was ever present in my mind.

'He is dead,' Darj said. 'Yorella is Queen of the White Isles.'

We spent more than an hour updating Xander on all that had happened. Somehow, it helped to speak to an old friend about it all.

'I can tell you that Fenton and his men were able to stop the Bone Hordes from entering Levanna,' Xander said, 'thanks to your preparations, Darj. But rather than engaging in a long siege, I suggested they draw the majority of the forces there out of Levanna's tunnel and up to Liane. Garrow's Islanders have already been sighted on their way there, no doubt directed by Mors. It's only a matter of time before he gives up on Levanna and directs the Bone Hordes there, too. Liane is the prize they have wanted all along, and together, they will make a formidable army.'

I sensed that by 'formidable' Xander meant 'undefeatable'.

'What is the plan, then?' Alexia asked.

'I told Lord Fenton to give us two weeks,' Xander said. 'I said if we don't arrive or he doesn't hear from us within that time, he is to get the children out of the city . . . and surrender it.'

'How long does that leave us?' Alexia asked.

Xander gripped his palms together. 'Six days. Just enough time to get to Liane, if you leave first thing tomorrow.'

I gulped. *And six days to defeat Mors, too.*

A tentative knock at the door interrupted the foreboding silence, and Yorella came in. The afternoon sun streamed through a window behind her, giving her an angelic appearance, but her face was full of dread.

Alexia stared unblinking at the floor. She hadn't expressed any remorse over Garrow's death, but then she'd hardly spoken about the incident at all. Now faced with his sister, she seemed unsure what to say or do.

'Come in, Yorella,' Elhian said gently.

She stepped towards us, looking nervously from one face to another.

'The king is dead,' he said, taking her hand. 'Blessed be the queen.' He pushed the white signet ring onto her trembling little finger and kissed her cheek.

She waited for an explanation. I knew we had to tell her how it had happened—as detestable as Garrow was, he was still her brother—but I also knew our confessions would seriously test her allegiance. I wondered if she would turn against us and decided not to blame her if she did.

Alexia swallowed. 'I killed him,' she said, lifting her eyes from the floor to the young girl. 'It was necessary, but I hope you can forgive me.'

Yorella's small frame trembled as she stood before the two women who had killed her father and brother. We waited tensely for her response. She had no reason to trust us and certainly no reason to fight alongside us.

'Did he hurt you?' she asked in a small voice.

Alexia's expression didn't change, but I unwillingly visualised her shredded back again. I turned my wrists over in my lap. The bruises from the manacles were faint and fading, but they were still evidence of our trial.

'I am so sorry,' Yorella said.

'You're sorry?' I asked, amazed.

'I know what he was like, how brutal he could be. If he harmed either of you, then I am truly sorry and'—her voice broke—'ashamed.'

Alexia stood, crossed the room, and embraced her. 'Don't you dare carry his shame,' she said.

Yorella rested her head against Alexia's shoulder and sobbed. 'I don't know what to do,' she said.

Alexia held her close in the way of an older sister. 'You can take your men back to the White Isles if you wish, or you can stay and fight with us. You are the monarch now, I'm afraid. You must decide what is best for your people.'

Yorella drew a deep breath and stepped back, looking somewhat puzzled. 'I don't understand you,' she said. 'As Garrow's slayer, you could have claimed rule of the White Isles. You could have claimed Casmodia, Jazmarda, and Delya, too, when their kings were slayed. You could have named yourself empress of the Rhea Lands by now.'

'The potential for great power has never tempted me,' she said. 'My only goal is to protect the inheritance my father gave me and keep my people safe. Had I pursued rule of these kingdoms, I would have only brought more war and devastation upon them and my people. Mors rightly described me as a follower of Ru'ach, the protector of life. It is not in me to deliberately invite death upon my people through offensive warfare and selfish ambitions.'

'I wonder if you may wage war to protect people beyond your kingdom one day,' Yorella said. She looked out the window. 'I had never directed my people to war until now, but if you ask it of me, I will continue to do so until the battle is over and won.'

'Mors hasn't been sighted since he fled Chimeric Cave,' Darj said. 'Xander's had word that Telitha is back with Hanequin and the Bone Hordes, but we've heard nothing of Mors at all.'

'Where would he go?' I asked.

'He knows you have the Life Sword, yes?' Yorella asked.

'Yes, he fled when Elhian threatened him with it, even though it was broken,' I said. 'I'm sure he knows we will repair it.'

'Then he is already afraid of you, and he will go wherever he thinks you will be at your weakest and wait for you to come to him.'

I later came down the stairs to find Darj and Alexia standing together by the hearth in the tavern's foremost room, temporarily emptied of townsfolk. Both had washed and dressed in clean clothes, and it encouraged me to see Alexia looking a little stronger. She'd eaten a proper meal earlier and slept for a few hours, but she was still too thin and pale for my liking, her ordeal not yet far enough behind her. Darj looked more like himself, his thick, black hair only hanging across his forehead a bit lower than normal.

'Do you think I don't notice when you drift away?' he asked her, gently kneading her hand. 'And now, after what Garrow did to you . . . '

Alexia leant against the mantelpiece as the fire crackled beside them. 'His actions don't distress me, Darj. He has paid the price for his cruelty, and it is done. But there is something I'm afraid of.'

I stood on the stairs as Darj's face lightened. 'What is there in this world that you, Queen of Targe and Dauntless Archer, are even remotely afraid of?'

She swallowed. 'Of you dying in my arms as Ethaniel did. The image torments me, both when you are in danger and when you are not. I am worried that Hanequin is going to avenge himself upon me by killing you, as Kadram said, and I couldn't bear that.'

'Alexia.' He tucked a stray tress behind her ear. 'That is not going to happen.'

She turned her face away. 'I am also afraid that life with me will destroy you in some way, and that I couldn't bear either.'

Darj frowned, confused. 'What do you mean?'

'I know you're not happy, that you regret—'

He put a finger under her chin and brought her face back towards him. 'I have long feared I am not worthy to be your husband, that's true, but I regret nothing. I love you, and I will stand by the oath we made to each other until death. Now that you have recovered, that is not going to be for many years yet, I promise.' He caressed her cheek. 'When I first saw you in that cavern . . . ' The memory brought tears to his eyes. 'It only made me more aware that you are the best choice I've ever made. I'm never so happy as when I'm with you.' He grinned. 'And, after seeing how Lord Fenton looks after a few sleepless nights, I've decided I'm your best choice, so I no longer care what the court thinks.'

Alexia laughed quietly. 'What brought on this change?'

'Adaliah. She helped me to see how stupid I've been.'

'I don't think that's the word I used,' I said.

They both smiled when they saw me descending the stairs, Darj shaking his head with amusement. 'I should have known you were listening, A'zyon Eavesdropper.'

'It's not my fault you have private conversations in public areas.' I stopped at the bottom of the stairs.

'The location doesn't usually stop you,' Alexia said dryly.

'True.' I clasped my hands behind my back. 'Now, Darj, it is customary to kiss your wife after making such declarations.'

'I may have already had you not interrupted,' Darj said.

I raised my palms. 'I shall prevent you no further.' I walked towards the kitchen and glanced back over my shoulder. Happily, Darj had already taken Alexia into his arms and met his queen with a loving kiss.

That night, I watched as Wolfgar worked in a small forge in the village to reconstruct my sword from the two retrieved, broken pieces.

'You were right,' I said. 'Telitha did have it.'

'People are not so mysterious,' he said. 'Most of our behaviour has something to do with gaining power over that which we fear.'

'Do you think Telitha fears us?'

'Wouldn't you, if you were in her position?'

I hadn't thought of that, but our success would mean her demise, most likely even her death. Her fate was just as insecure as ours.

Wolfgar put the sword on a workbench. I drew both comfort and courage from the rhythmic taps of his hammer on the moldable steel. Having dwelt in hot coals until it was ready to be reformed, it glowed red and responded well to Wolfgar's coercions. The occasional spark flew into the dark night.

Sweat beading on his forehead, Wolfgar leaned in close to examine his work, ensuring that each tap contributed to restoring the blade to its former glory. 'It's like a warrior in the heat of battle,' he said, 'the fire bringing out its greatest strength.' The word *Life*, engraved just below the stone, glowed orange. I left the artisan to it and considered with mixed feelings that by the morning, the Life Sword would be ready to slay a dragon.

34

THE KEEPER OF KEST

You are first the Keeper of Kest.

I contemplated Kadram's last words just before dawn as I walked to the bloodied, burning Kest River—my river, the river of life that Mors had polluted with death.

Somewhere on the other side, to the northwest, was the Keep where my father and I lived as I grew up. He had died there and was buried there with my mother and brother. After my marriage to Elhian, Captain Darack Symes and a small host of men managed the Keep while I visited whenever I could.

I missed the sense of home. I longed for the carefree days of my childhood—reading stories with my father, fishing with him, learning to wield a sword without any thought of actual battle, racing him on horseback through the forests and mountains, and travelling with him to the great city of Liane to visit our family, the king and princess. Those days were warmed with dances and banquets and festive tournaments. I could remember laughing from my father's shoulders as he carried me across the river and brought me home at the end of each day, just the two of us. I had not been a royal princess like Alexia, but I had been his princess.

It's time to breathe life back into the world.

The words were spoken in my spirit, as if from Ru'ach himself.

'Adaliah,' Elhian called. I heard his footsteps approaching me to the left and greeted him with a kiss on the cheek.

He had my cape in his hand, which he clipped back on my pauldron. 'We have to get back to Fenton,' he said. 'Otherwise, he will forfeit Liane.'

'I know,' I said. 'But I can't come with you.'

He took my hand. 'Adaliah, please. You've suffered enough. We've lost enough. I beg you, no more.' He leant his forehead against mine and shuddered. 'I can't bear it,' he whispered.

He sounded so exhausted, so stressed, that I was filled with pity for him, but not for myself.

'I must,' I said calmly. 'Elhian, you whom I love above all others, you know I must.'

We wrapped our arms around each other, slowly and quietly accepting that we had to once again part without any certainty of seeing each other again.

I thought about the conversations I'd had with Alexia over time, how I disagreed with her about putting one's kingdom ahead of one's family. But when it came to it, she risked her life—the rule of her kingdom—to save me. And here I was about to do the very thing I dreaded: risk losing everything, including the right to raise my own sons and to love my husband until we were old and ready to depart the world naturally. I was preparing to give all that up for the people, for the Rhea Lands, for all that was good.

But it was in that moment I finally understood. My sons were part of my kingdom, part of my people, just as Alexia's children were part of hers. In making sacrifices for our people's future, we were also protecting our children's future. *That* I could live with. After all, both actions came from love.

'Please, tell Karlen and Jovan how much I loved them,' I said to Elhian, blinking away tears. 'Tell them I will love them always.'

Yorella had said that Mors would go where he felt he could defeat me. Somehow, I knew in my heart he had gone to the Keep—my home. He had said he wanted to kill me because I was the Keeper of Kest, the protector of life—the thing he hated most. The Keep was where I lost my parents and brother, a place of both sadness and happiness for me, but not one of weakness as he supposed.

He's waiting for me.

Darj and Alexia joined us by the river. The sun rose, but before it had a chance to provide any warmth, white clouds tumbled across the sky with the promise of more snow. My cape fluttered in the wind.

'The Bone Hordes and Garrow's Islanders have been seen travelling north,' Darj said. 'We will meet them at the battleground before Liane and wait for you there, but we will not go into battle until we know you have succeeded. We haven't had a true victory since Mors reappeared, and now his power is too strong. Fighting against his army whilst he is still alive will only bring defeat. It will take us about five days to get to Liane and about the same for you to get to the Keep. If you haven't rejoined us at Liane by noon, eight days from now, we will take the children, retreat to Jasteria, and save as many people as we can. That should be enough time for you to deal with Mors and travel back to us from Kest.'

Darj hugged me closely. I rested my chin on his shoulder, his beautiful but war-laden wife standing behind him. She needed the one thing we couldn't give her—time to convalesce. I wondered briefly if any of us would ever fully recover from the things we'd done and seen.

'Take care of her.'

Darj drew back, his eyes shining with tears. 'Always.'

Alexia stepped forward with her hands outstretched. In them lay the re-forged Life Sword. It seemed longer, shinier, and sharper than before. 'Wolfgar has given it two-edges,' she said. 'It will cut whichever way you wield it. The greater weapon.'

I took it from her and briefly held it in my hands before sheathing it by my side. 'You don't have to go into battle again, you know,' I said. 'You've done enough. More than enough.'

'Are you afraid I'm not strong enough?' Alexia asked.

'I am afraid of losing you.'

'And this coming from the woman who is about to leave me and face the embodiment of all evil?' she asked, more fiercely than I think she meant to. She took a deep breath and held me against her. 'I will not lay down my weapon while ever there is a threat against my people or my family.' She stepped back and met my eyes. 'That is a choice we have both made, A'zyon Warrior. But please—' she hugged me again, now with desperation— 'please come back to us.'

I mounted Bagred. Having already shed enough tears to last a lifetime, I pressed them back and gave a final nod. 'I love you all.'

I rode along the east bank of the river for the first two days before I came to a bridge known as the Dewr Crossing. Normally, I could have traversed the water at any point as that part of the river was wide but shallow, but I didn't want to risk hurting Bagred by riding through Mors' everlasting flames.

After passing over the bridge, I began the ascent into the Kestian Mountains. Over the next few days, a beautiful white view of the

Valley of Kest grew behind me, and beyond that, Targe. I could just see Liane in the far distance and the naked Yellow Forest bordering the river further upstream. It was a scene I had gazed upon many times.

This was my home.

There were a few different ways I could get to the Keep. Reaching the small shack and tracking through the tunnels Elhian and I had discovered in the Northern Invasion would have been the most covert, but I didn't feel up to facing the small, dark spaces. Instead, I took the longer but most used route: the road that led right up to the front door.

A longing and a sadness came upon me when I first saw the Keep. The great, white stone fortress was built into the side of the mountain like it had grown there. Kest River could be heard and seen at the bottom of the mountain, below the Keep, washing quickly through a deep ravine that didn't widen until the Dewr Crossing. I could see the flames and blood that had replaced the water. The Keep itself was covered in vines that were leafless for the winter, and the road was buried in snow as deep as Bagred's knees.

Ahead, I saw a man sprawled face down in the snow, the snow about him stained with blood. A few steps closer, and a mound of dead bodies came into view, piled against the mountain. They were the men charged with caring for the Keep in my absence. The first body was their captain, Darack.

I closed my eyes, the futility of their deaths settling on my shoulders along with the memory of so many others.

But they have not been dead long. Mors is here.

To the left of the road was the opening of the cave where my parents were entombed. I dismounted Bagred and walked into the darkness. Inside, I found the stone coffins of my parents, side by side. I knelt before them and brushed the grit away from the inscriptions:

Here lies Prince Bagred Elryane,
Son of King Jepath Elryane,
Beloved husband and father,
Keeper of Kest.

And next to him, a much older inscription:

Here lies Princess Cassondra Elryane,
Beloved wife and mother,
And Lord Jepath Bagred Elryane,
Treasured son.

The first I had known and loved until my seventeenth year. The other two I had not known at all.

'Family define who we are, even when we are old and frail. But they are also our weakness.'

I stepped further into the cave towards the voice. There was a figure holding a single unlit torch. Mors.

'Yes,' I said, standing. 'But they are not the only things that define us, otherwise we would cease to exist when they leave us.'

I pulled the Life Sword out of my sheath. Mors saw it and straightened. 'Today is my last day as a nine hundred ninety nine-year-old man. Do you truly think you can defeat me before sunset? Do you truly think you can bring to end a scheme one thousand years in the making?'

'I must.'

He ran his finger along the top of my mother's coffin. 'Why don't you just give up?' His question seemed genuine, like he wanted to understand me.

'The world you desire is not one I can accept for my children, our people, or myself. You are already responsible for countless deaths and must be stopped.'

'That is true,' he said, 'but you are hoping, in vain, to touch upon my conscience. The problem for you is I feel nothing—not regret, guilt, or anything else. All I feel is hungry for more. Death is deeply satisfying but never satisfying enough.'

I lowered my sword. 'Which is why I found you amongst my dead loved ones.'

'Yes. I feel quite at home here. This room is filled with loneliness and shortened lives.' He rested his elbow on my father's sepulchre. 'Now, I have gathered all my power back to me so that I might kill you, and with you, the spirit of five kingdoms.'

'You need that much power to defeat me?'

'That is your one failing, Adaliah,' he said. 'You have no idea how powerful you are.'

I paused. 'Are you afraid of me?'

'No. I am afraid of my own death, but I certainly do not believe you are capable of bringing it to pass. Why else would I risk meeting you before turning one thousand?'

'Because you have to see me dead for your power to take effect.'

'There is that.'

We spoke evenly as if we were simply passing the time of day. He seemed rational, even insightful. It was almost possible to forget he was the dark spirit's incarnation on earth. Almost.

'So, what now?' I asked.

He sighed wearily. 'Well, now, one of us must die.'

He clicked his fingers, and a sharp pain filled my head. All the grief I had ever experienced rushed to the forefront of my mind. Horrific images of the deaths of people I cared deeply about overtook me. There was Cades impaling Ethaniel from behind, and Alexia weeping helplessly over her first love's dead body. There was Jag killing my father, not far from where I was now. Lezan, succumbing to poison as we watched over him. Zavad, taking a dagger to save Darj, his little body shaking from the impact. Thane, dying at Dawfield just after he had saved my life. Kadram, falling down in flames. Other painful images forced their way into my consciousness—Alexia almost dying after I gave her the cure to the Zalem's Bane, Elhian killing his own father, Darj so assaulted on the battlefield that he was unrecognisable, Alexia flogged by Garrow . . .

Stop!

'If Ru'ach's purpose is to protect you,' Mors said, 'why didn't he save you from all this? Why didn't he save them?'

I tried to regain control, tried to force the memories away. I tried to remember nice things, tried to bring to mind the good to force out the bad. Elhian proposing to me. Falling in love with him for a second time. Jeri running into his mother's arms after three years of separation. Alexia inviting Darj into marriage after he had loved her in silence for years. Meeting my sons for the first time.

I couldn't hold onto the joy. The images morphed into visions of them dying—dying because I wasn't there to protect them. I saw myself alone.

'Ru'ach is not here, Adaliah. He has no power here.'

A part of me was aware that Mors was laughing at me, but it was coming out as a deep, rumbling roar.

Stop . . .

I saw myself at seventeen, trapped in the underground cell in Liane, going mad, screaming, throwing myself at the walls.

No . . .

The light had completely gone from the cave. I was trapped in a dark, airless space.

'Welcome to the kingdom of darkness.'

My heart quickened. I clutched at my throat. It felt like it was closing over and suffocating me.

Adaliah, what are you afraid of?

The gentle thought came out of nowhere, and I tried to pin it down.

I'm afraid of inescapable, evil spaces.

No.

The response wasn't mine, but it appeared in my mind just as the first question had.

I'm afraid of dying.

No.

I groaned with frustration.

I'm afraid of letting my loved ones down. I'm afraid of losing them—and of being alone forever.

A pause.

But I am here, always. Now, get up and fight for those who live.

I opened my eyes. Mors' torch was now aflame. He was watching me with a loathsome sneer. My heart was still racing, and I grew angry at my fear. For years, it had controlled me, reminding me of the prolonged torment I had suffered at the hands of Cades' men. Izak had been right. Because of this fear, I was still giving them power over me, giving Mors power over me. He was using it against me now. And I was giving into it. This was not the life my father had taught me to live, nor the one my mother would have wanted for me. I had fought and won many battles, yet continually lost the battle of the mind.

'Enough!' I shouted, rising to my feet. I finally meant it. 'I've had enough. I can do this. I am powerful. I am the A'zyon Warrior. I will not be afraid!'

The change was immediate. A dark presence fled from me. My heart slowed to a normal rate, just a little hastened from adrenaline, and I realised something that made me feel more empowered than ever.

For the first time, I was truly fearless.

For the first time, I was truly the A'zyon Warrior.

35
THE DRAGON AND THE BUTTERFLY

I ran across the cave towards Mors, the Life Sword high, sharp, and ready to impale him. Mors had blocked the entry where I entered and snuffed the torch he'd carried. We were in darkness again. My eyes adjusted, and I could soon make out his figure. He seemed undeterred by my transformation and met my swinging blade with his own. I saw his shoulders heave in the way they did whenever he was taking a deep breath to send fire back out. He lit the torch again; I slid to the ground, and his flames flew across my head. In the light, I saw that Mors had drawn a black cloth across the entry of the cave. I hadn't been trapped at all.

I ducked under it and ran outside. Bagred snorted when he saw me. My boots sank in the snow, but I trudged through it, away from the cave. I heard Mors following and turned. In the light, I realised again how ugly he was. The red scales that covered his hands and arms were shining from sweat or snow, giving him a snakelike appearance. The long talons that draped over the sword he was holding were brown and dirty but sharp. His large, brown irises left almost no whites in his eyes, and the horned crown that was melted into his head, a molten mess of the five Rhea crowns, seemed to be sinking deeper and deeper into his skin. It was a sickening sight.

'Attack!' he yelled.

I was confused—was he describing the action he was about to take or talking to someone? Then hordes of men rushed out of the Keep's every orifice. Some jumped out of windows into the snow. Others rushed out the front door. They came like wasps swarming from a disturbed nest. I couldn't take in how many there were but guessed at least two hundred had been waiting for the call to action. And now they all ran towards me.

Somehow, I wasn't afraid. Alexia's voice was with me. *Anyone who chooses selfless, moral courage when they could flee can turn the tides of battle.*

I raised my sword against the first attacking Bone Horde, whose blade was edged with tarnished animal teeth. I blocked his strike and pushed him backwards. He lost his balance, and I brought my sword down upon him, this time driving him into the ground and impaling him. I deflected another's strike and thrust my sword straight through the attacker's stomach. The others were upon me by then.

Mors was out of my sight, but I could hear him shouting, 'Kill her! We will dismember her in Liane before everyone!'

Not today.

I downed another horde member, and then another. Their bodies started piling up at my feet. I moved backwards, giving myself some space and the chance to unsheathe my tree-blade.

Now doubly armed, I raised both swords. 'Come on!' I yelled.

The Bone Hordes ran at me for a second time. I drew my swords against the chest of the closest one, slashing him to the ground. Outturning both blades, I slew two more who had come up on my sides. I threw the tree-blade at a man running front-on towards me. He doubled over with his upper body parallel to the ground. I ran towards him, stepped up on his back, and launched myself at the men behind.

I had never before fought so many men entirely on my own. I retook the tree-blade as soon as I had the opportunity and fought the hordes until there were only a few left. My face was hot and sweaty, and every part of me ached, but I felt stronger than ever.

'Cowards!' Mors called when the last few men ran from the Keep.

I could see him now. He had climbed part-way up the cliff above my parents' tomb. He threw himself off and landed in front of me.

He raised his sword—the flaming torch back in his other hand—and we resumed our fight away from the dead bodies. The Keep loomed in my vision behind him. The sun was falling lower in the sky, but the world darkened faster than it should. I pushed Mors away and turned to see what was happening.

The moon passed slowly across the sun. The world filled with an eerie red before darkening completely. The chill in the air felt particularly sharp. The sight of it brought to memory another unsettling sky I had seen once before, when the last High Zalem blocked it with storms and black clouds. Somehow, this was even more disturbing. A ring of fire encircled the moon.

'The beginning of the end,' Mors said, laughing.

I brought my sword down upon him as hard as I could. It clanged against his and held. He pushed me back and struck at me in turn. I matched his blows for strength but struggled to keep up with the speed at which he was delivering them. The only way I could was to stop thinking about what I was doing altogether, to respond instinctively. This meant ducking and sliding to avoid the occasional outburst of flames and smoke while still deflecting his sword.

'I don't know why you're bothering with that,' I said when he breathed smoke towards me again. 'It can't harm me.'

Snarling, he dropped the torch and struck me across the face with his fist instead. I fell into the snow, the taste of blood filling my mouth. He kicked me in my side, right where he had dug his talons into me. I cried out in agony. Delighting in my pain, he kicked me several more times until I managed to roll out of the way and get back to my feet. I spat out a mouthful of blood. He struck at me with his sword; I deflected it, but the tip still nipped my upper arm.

Every part of me hurt.

I had to get on the offensive if I was going to end this and get back to Liane in time—if I was going to survive. I waited for a chance to breach his guard. When it came, I struck at him so hard, he stumbled backwards. I moved forward and made my first attempt at impaling him with the Life Sword. He slashed it away so forcefully, it slipped from my fingers. Black smoke poured out of his nostrils, and he snarled at me again. I moved to retrieve the sword. Mors stuck out his foot, and I fell face-forward into the snow. My left eye, which had taken the brunt of one of his kicks, struggled to remain open. My nose bled, and my knees ached. I couldn't get up.

A flash of light drew my attention back to the sky. Several terrifying streaks of lightning glistened across it. Thunder followed, so forceful and loud it seemed to shake my very being.

'I was wrong to wait for a public death,' Mors said to himself. 'I should have killed her days ago. I can still take her broken body back to my army. Yes, I can still make her people celebrate her demise.'

Mors grunted as he prepared his first death-bringing attack. I made another reach for the Life Sword, desperate to deflect him, but it was no good. I could not move fast enough. I pressed my eyes together, awaiting the fateful blow.

Hooves cantered towards me. I opened my eyes in time to see Bagred knock Mors away. A moment later, Mors thrust his sword firmly into Bagred's side.

My horse tumbled to his front knees. I opened my mouth, but no words came.

Bagred dropped to his side. Mors sniggered as he withdrew his sword.

I scrambled over to my beloved horse and draped an arm over his neck, not caring about the blood that was staining everything, including the snow. He breathed heavily a few times and then stopped. His large, black form lay still.

'No, no, no . . .'

He can't be dead!

But his brown eyes were open in stunned silence. I buried my face into his mane and sobbed, exhausted.

'He was an innocent horse,' I said.

'You keep expecting me to care, Adaliah, but I simply do not.'

The sky rumbled, lightning splitting it in several places again. 'It's not over yet,' I said breathlessly.

'Adaliah, Adaliah.' Mors squatted in front of me. 'Didn't you know? Didn't you guess? This was always going to cost you your life. That is the price you have always been destined to pay.'

'What?'

'When King Amaz failed to produce a second child, I tasked Cades and Jag with killing your father to put an end to the Keeper's role and all they represent—all that comes against me. But the Keeper's power inexplicably transferred to you, defying a thousand-year tradition of passing the power from the second born to the second born. This made the butterfly far more deadly to you than any other Keeper of Kest once Eva was born. But the direct transition also made you the most powerful Keeper to ever live.' He shook his head. 'I have known from that day to this that you would be the one I would face here, now.'

I again recalled my father falling to his knees, Jag's sword in his side. *But his power came to me, stronger.*

Darj's words came back to mind: *You are the one, the only one, who has exactly what it takes.*

I wiped my face on my arm and staggered back to my feet. Grasping my sword with both hands, I brought it against the Supreme Overlord once more. He ducked my blade and rammed me into a tree. The force of it shook the snow out of its branches and onto both of us. He shoved me to the ground and struck at me, his claw deeply gashing my left upper arm. I cried out but managed to block his descending sword with mine. He pushed his sword harder and harder against mine, baring his teeth in the effort. I struggled to keep my sword up, my arms trembling as his blade dropped closer and closer to my throat.

I gave a great shout and pushed against Mors with all I had. He fell back from me, took his torch, and used it to send another breath of flames towards me. I felt the heat of it, but the flames were weak, and the toxic fumes did me no harm. My immunity to Dragon's Breath remained.

It was not all without effect on Mors, though. He doubled over in pain and dropped to one knee, struggling to breathe. 'What is wrong with me?' he asked, his voice rasping.

I pulled myself upright until I was resting on my knees. The black sky shuddered, the wind swirling about me with growing speed.

'What's wrong with you is that you have always sought power from death while trying to evade it. You inhale Dragon's Breath to kill others, but it is killing you. I have immunity because I bring life, but a pact with Anash only ever leads to this. Each time you act to bring death and darkness, you drain your own life because that's all they are—a drain on power, not the source of it. You are so lost in it all, you don't even know who you are anymore. You are the Ghost, Mors.'

I picked up the Life Sword.

'You're too late,' he said, his voice rasping. 'Did you think I wouldn't take precautions? That I would let the Zalems become extinct after a thousand years? Telitha has already made the same pact with Anash that I did. If I die, my quest will simply transfer to her. Killing me now will only make you a murderer.'

I narrowed my eyes at him. 'Killing you now makes me the A'zyon Warrior and the Keeper of Kest—both defenders of life.' I thrust a sword point under his chin, tilting his face back up to me. 'I know who I am.'

And with that, before he could say anything else or regain his strength, I ran the Life Sword into his side.

36
THE UNITED RHEA LANDS

When I withdrew my blade, it was covered in blood, just like it would have been for any other person. Mors showed no emotional reaction and didn't even look at me. For a minute or so, it was as if nothing had happened at all. He didn't move, make a cry of pain, or fade.

My confidence waned. Was I too late? The eclipsed sun was low but not gone. Should I impale him again? Did Wolfgar not repair the sword properly? Had we been misled to think the sword was the answer to defeating him?

Then the moon passed away from the setting sun, returning light to the world. The colour in Mors' eyes weakened, and so did the redness in his scales. Wrinkles regrew on his forehead in just the same way as before, and his bone structure shrank so much that he was soon like a small child at my feet. In truth, he was an old, little man with no power at all.

Once again, I was amazed that such a pathetic creature had caused us so much heartache. He shriveled up and slowly died in front of me like a worm left out in the sun. All I could think was how pointless it had been. He had inspired the deaths of our loved ones and through his servants brought war after war upon us. All of that knowledge and power he had was wasted on darkness, and now he was leaving the world just like an ordinary man.

The sun was completely free from the moon's temporary prison. Snow drifted through the trees like nothing had changed, just as it would every winter until the end of time. The world was going on around us, and I was struck with a sense of insignificance.

What has all this been for?

Mors groaned and twisted in agony. That stopped, and there was silence. Everything around me was still.

Mors, the Supreme Overlord, was dead.

The crown, which had detached from his skin, was now too big for him. It fell away.

I picked up Mors' frail remains and carried him towards the edge of the mountain, where the burning river flowed in the ravine below. I dropped him into the river of fire and blood. There were a few slow moments as he fell, and then his body made contact with the water. This time, the effect was immediate. The river bubbled and burst upwards. Bloodied water and flames shot up so high, they almost reached me, halfway up the mountain. A mighty wind screamed upwards through the trees, blowing my hair back from my face. Another immense wind rose up from behind me. They clashed above my head, causing a loud crack of thunder that made me fall to my knees and cover my ears. It shook the ground. Snow fell out of the trees as they swayed severely from side to side. There was a weak hiss as if the first wind had been deflated. It seemed to settle on the crown, which shuddered. There followed a gentle breeze and a clearing sky.

The river swirled and churned. The redness gave way to clear, ice-blue water, and the flames flickered their last and were gone.

My river was back, as beautiful and life-giving as ever.

And I am alive.

I stepped through the snow back to my horse. Bagred was already covered in a layer of snowflakes. I collapsed beside him and buried my face into his mane again, taking in his scent and giving him as much love as I could in this final goodbye.

'I'm so sorry,' I whispered. 'I'm so sorry I wasn't quick enough to save you.'

I unclipped his bridle and saddle, moved them to the side, and kissed the top of his head. 'Thank you for being my friend, for saving me.' I wished I could bury him, but there was no time and no way I could move him on my own. 'I will come back for you,' I said. 'I will make sure you rest in peace.'

The Keep, the steadfast edifice that had been my home, now overlooked a graveyard. Covered in blood, my body was wearied, and my muscles ached beyond anything I had felt before. My childhood room was just a few steps away. I wished more than anything that I could crawl into my old bed and sleep, but Alexia and the others would soon forfeit Liane if I didn't return to them with news of Mors' death. They would surrender to the Bone Hordes. If what Mors had said was true, Telitha could well take up his mantle. Targe, as we knew it, could still be lost. It wasn't over yet.

'I don't know if I've got the strength,' I whispered to myself. 'I don't even have a way of getting to them.' With Bagred gone and no nearby village, my only option was to return on foot, and that would take me days. I closed my eyes, trying to rally something within me that would inspire me to keep going, to find a way, but I felt nothing.

I saw the crown lying in the snow. *Maybe destroying it will strengthen me.* I picked up my sword and stepped towards it.

'Adaliah.'

I stopped. I knew that voice. I was standing almost where I had last heard it.

I slowly turned around.

My father stood before me.

I blinked, sure I was imagining it. Or perhaps I was dead, after all. But I was definitely breathing, and he was definitely there: ethereal and transparent, but otherwise my father as I remembered him. He had a sword in hand. It was sharp and bloodied. He looked so strong and handsome, so in control and full of faith. And he was smiling at me, just as he used to. Another figure appeared beside him. It was my mother—I recognised her from the portraits I'd seen. She was beautiful and armed with a used sword as well. I felt such a longing for her, wanted more than anything to talk with her, to hug her. A third figure appeared, a boy who looked a year or two younger than me and a lot like my father . . . And even more like me.

My brother.

Tears ran down my face, but I was hardly aware of them.

More and more figures appeared. Soon, there stood Ethaniel, and King Amaz and Queen Jenethea, and King Thane, Raggin, Zavad, my paternal grandparents King Jepath and Queen Clair, a younger Kadram and, beside him, Lezan. Behind them were many more I either couldn't see or didn't recognise, but I sensed they were my ancestors of old. I tried to take it all in, tried to engrave the memory of their faces on my mind, and I felt overcome with emotion—a mixture of sadness and love and courage.

They held weapons as if they were ready to fight or had been fighting all along. My father opened his mouth, and I saw the words he spoke before I heard them. 'My dear girl,' he said. 'You defied Anash once again.'

I wiped away my tears, but they kept coming. 'Are you all right?' I asked. They all smiled and nodded at me. I sensed such strength and joy in them. 'And you are with me?'

'You are never alone,' my father said. 'Remember us, but keep fighting for those who live.'

I nodded and took a step towards the crown.

'No, Adaliah.' This time it was Uncle Amaz who spoke, his voice august and kind. 'You are not the greater weapon, my dear. If you were to try and destroy it, it would only destroy you.'

'The greater weapon is a person?' I asked.

'Of course.'

The child Zavad, who seemed a little taller than when he had died, pointed to something behind me. I turned. Brzina stood by Bagred's body. The great, silver horse looked magnificent in the snow. Zavad waved at me, and they all began to fade. I wanted to weep at their parting but still felt such a joy from having seen them at all. It was a memory that would give me courage for years to come—my most treasured gift from the Great Spirit.

I walked to Brzina, again awestruck at her height. I raised my hand to her nose and let her sniff me. She lowered her head, her long neck stretching down as she sniffed Bagred as well.

I covered Mors' crown with a piece of cloth I took from his clothes. Even as my hands passed near it, I felt a coldness fill my heart. It made the hairs on my arms stand on end. Shivering, I secured it to Brzina's saddle, gripped her mane, and lifted my foot up to the stirrup. I settled into the saddle and looked back at the Keep one last time, where my loved ones had been just moments before. I took a deep breath.

I can do this.

I had never before ridden such a fast horse. Bagred had been strong and quick, but Brzina could have outrun him. We reached the river by midnight. Almost asleep in the saddle, I forced myself to stop. I covered myself in a fur blanket and slept unmoving until I was woken by the warm, mid-morning sun. My body swollen and bruised in many places, I quickly washed the blood from my wounds, including the new claw mark on my arm. Then, Brzina and I glided together through the clean waters, Brzina coming to the other side without a second thought. She galloped to the Yellow Forest, and we rode on beyond sundown and into the night. There was no more time to sleep. I only had until noon the next day before the others would surrender and retreat, not knowing Mors was dead and his power broken, not knowing I was alive.

The sun rose strongly and felt warmer than it had in weeks. Nearby, I saw some green grass peeking above the snow.

Brzina carried me through the rest of the Yellow Forest, and we came out onto the Targian plains. Soon, Liane appeared on her hill in the distance like a glistening gem.

Not much further.

It was another hour or so before the battlefield came into view. Our soldiers stood in lines to the northwest of Liane, across a stretch of meadows. Coming up behind them, I could see Izak with the Jazmardians he brought to fight with us. There were several battalions of them, their red banners waving high in the wind. The Casmodians Elhian had sent for were standing next to them. Then there were the white anchor banners of the Islanders, the yellow banners of King Ren and the Delyans, and at the vanguard, the fearless Targians. The kingdoms of the Rhea Lands had united.

Brzina battered the ground towards them. In the distance, there stood the Bone Hordes and the remainder of Garrow's Islanders, still loyal to Telitha and Mors. There were yet thousands upon thousands of them, a sea of enemies still threatening to sink us. Many of them carried the flag of the broken butterfly. But Mors was dead and broken, not us. Not me.

The gap between us shrank further. I heard the sound of a horn. It wasn't the sound of victory or of hope, but the call to retreat, to surrender. It was coming from our side.

No!

'Please,' I whispered in Brzina's ear. I dug my heels into her sides again. Brzina tossed her head and thrust herself forward.

Now, I was nearly upon them. Some of the soldiers turned as they heard Brzina galloping up behind them. They jumped out of the way, not quite comprehending what was happening until someone shouted, 'It's Adaliah!'

Suddenly, thousands upon thousands of people were turning my way, yelling, cheering, thrusting their swords and spears and shields into the sky. The soldiers in front of me parted as Brzina and I charged through the middle of the army.

I unsheathed my sword and raised it high. The amethyst stone in it, a replacement of the original which I thought to be unremarkable, came alive and shone brightly. We hadn't seen anything like it since the end of the Northern Invasion. The soldiers continued to cheer my name, and the sound seemed to resonate across the entire kingdom.

Elhian, Alexia, and Darj were at the head of the army. They raised their weapons to me and cheered, too. Darj brought the horn to his lips again, and this time, he sounded the call to attack.

'Arjla divala!' My cry resounded across the army.

I lowered my sword until it was pointing straight ahead. I came to the front of the army. Without stopping, I rode ahead and towards the enemy, eighty thousand soldiers shouting as they followed me into battle.

37

THE BATTLE OF LIANE

Elhian, Darj, Alexia and I rode abreast. Our horses fell into rhythm with each other as we charged at the enemy. Alexia shot arrows into the barbarians before us, her legs clinging to her golden horse as she rode hands-free. Darj and Elhian drew their swords.

Hanequin stood at the front of his men wearing an iron helmet and breastplate that set him apart from the rest of his men. Alexia shot an arrow directly at him. He raised his shield and blocked it, but the impact made him stumble backwards. He shouted at his men, and they raised their shields. Hanequin yelled something else. Garrow's Islanders didn't move, but the Bone Hordes faded away from us.

Telitha appeared, riding at full speed towards Hanequin. She held a long sword. I wondered whether she intended to use it, to fight alongside the people she had called common.

Perhaps now she's desperate enough.

She yelled and made large gestures, urging the Bone Hordes to face us again with Garrow's Islanders.

'We haven't been paid enough for this!' Hanequin shouted at her.

'I have the gold, I promise!'

They heeded her but barely had time to gather themselves before we were upon them. The Targian cavalry rode through their front line, leaning down to swipe them with swords and making way for the rest of the army to follow.

We waged war from our feet, except for Elhian, who left to circle the battle with the Casmodians and later flank the enemy. To my left, King Ren and his dagger fighters pushed against Garrow's Islanders. To my right, Izak fought with a sword and shield, leading his men into the thick of the Bone Hordes.

I was fighting two of them when I saw Hanequin walking to Alexia, swiping his large, spiked mace at any enemies in his arm's reach. 'Who are you?' he asked, spraying spit towards her. Alexia's arrow was still lodged in his shield.

She fought by her husband's side as he slew soldier after soldier, a sword in each hand. Alexia alternated between swinging her bow to strike the hordes directly and shooting them when she had more space. She downed two soldiers with a dual shot before turning to Hanequin.

He ran at the queen and swiped his mace at her. Alexia ducked in time but lost her footing and fell backwards on the damp grass. She cried out when her tender back made contact with the ground. Hanequin raised his mace to flatten her with it. I gasped, and there was an almighty yell as Darj tackled Hanequin from the side and into the ground.

'No!' Telitha yelled again, drawing my attention back to her.

'Surrender!' I called to her. 'Surrender and save these men's lives.'

She answered by bringing her sword against me. I deflected her blow with my blade and struck at her in turn. Darj wrestled with Hanequin, and the horde leader was large and strong. Darj struggled to contain him. Two horde men ran to assist their master to kill Darj. Alexia shot them down with her last arrows.

As I fought against Telitha, I was struck with a pang of sadness as I again recalled that this woman was Cades' daughter but also Kadram's— and that she could have led a different life.

Telitha attacked me again. I blocked her once more, and we stood with our blades raised above our heads, pressing against each other, both trying to push the other down.

'I know you killed Mors,' she said, 'but I will not let him down now. I cannot! You can try and kill me, but you will not succeed. You are not the greater weapon!'

'I know.' I grunted as I pushed harder against her blade. It dropped from her fingertips. 'But I can still fight you, and you still have a choice,' I said. 'You can choose right now to turn away from all of this. You can still choose a different path.'

'Is that what you will teach your sons? To abandon everything they believe in when it gets hard?'

'I will teach my sons to know right from wrong.'

'Did you really think I wouldn't go after them?' she asked. 'Did you really think your children would be safe in Liane?'

'What do you mean?' I asked.

Darj managed to get Hanequin face down in the snow, while Alexia came over to me, her quiver empty. Her face glistened with sweat.

'How do you think we knew you had changed the medallion to wedding rings?' Telitha asked. 'How do you think we stole your crowns? How do you think I got my men into the castle the night Hazaka died?'

'You had an agent,' Alexia said.

'Yes. Cordale, but he also used the Casmodian boy, Finn. They are with your children right now, and if I die, they will take them and kill them.'

What?

We had trusted Finn and his sister to care for our children all these weeks. How could that skinny, nervous boy collude with villains like Telitha and Cordale, risking the lives of the very heirs to the

Casmodian and Targian thrones? Had Cordale really manipulated him into infiltrating our homes and stealing Alexia's and Elhian's crowns, directly delivering power to Mors? I realised how they must have known about Elhian's and my rings: Finn must have eavesdropped on my conversation with Alexia about them in Dawfield. I felt sick. I looked towards Liane, towards our children, praying it wasn't too late.

Telitha picked up her sword and swung it at me. I fought hard against her and within a few blows had her lying on the ground with the point of my sword pressing into her neck. Exhausted in every way, my hand was shaking.

'Get away from me,' Telitha said.

Alexia stepped forward and scowled at her. 'Didn't you see the horse my cousin rode to get here? Mors is dead. Garrow is dead. It's over. Get up!'

Tears rolling down her face, Telitha gingerly got to her feet, my sword still at her throat. She spat in my face. I blinked. In that moment, she dodged my sword and ran towards Brzina.

I didn't understand—was she planning to steal Mors' horse and flee from us? No, she had her own horse for that, and he was closer than Brzina. Then I remembered what was hanging from Brzina's saddle.

The crown. She's after the crown!

Hanequin managed to throw Darj off and retake his mace. He was shouting and waving the mace at both Darj and Alexia. The queen instinctively reached for her quiver, forgetting she had no arrows until none came into her fingertips.

'Here, Your Majesty!'

Wolfgar ran across the field with a handful of arrows. He raised his arm to throw them towards Alexia; Hanequin raised his spiked mace, and it landed in Wolfgar's side. We watched in horror as Wolfgar flew through the air and crashed to the ground several steps away, bloodied and broken.

Hanequin charged at the queen for a second time. Darj scrambled to his feet and ran after him, his face red and covered in dirt. He tackled Hanequin to the ground once more. Hanequin lost his grip on his mace, and it fell away from his hand. Darj picked it up and, with a great heave, threw it across the field.

I kept running, but Telitha reached Brzina and ripped the crown from its tether. She raised it to the sky with a wild grin before lowering it towards her head.

I'm not going to make it!

Alexia ran to Wolfgar's body, picked up the arrows, and swung them into her quiver.

Telitha laughed as the crown touched her head, but as soon as she shifted it into place, she twisted, flinched, and cried out in pain. The crown squeezed her skull and burnt her skin. I stopped running and watched in horror and confusion. Soon she was on her knees, trying to rip it off, her hands burning as well.

Anash has not accepted her.

She crumpled to the ground, yelling, 'Get it off! Get it off!'

Her screams sent chills down my spine, and her army dispersed in terror. For the first time, I experienced what Alexia and Elhian had already felt for her: pity.

I reached out to take the crown from her head, to free her from the pain and darkness. As soon as my fingertips touched the foul object, my hands were sucked in against it. It molded to my palms, burning, searing, and enfolding me in the gravest darkness. It was as if I had been transported to a world of death, somewhere without light or joy or anything green and life-giving. My vision darkened, the colour in the fields around me melting into shades of black and grey. It affected the people around me, too. All soldiers nearby, including Hanequin and Darj, fell to their knees with agony in their faces. Somehow, only Alexia remained standing.

Someone called my name as a serpentine voice filled my head.

Accept the crown, and I will give you power over death—power over all the kingdoms of the world.

I tried to rip my hands away, but it was no good. It had seared itself to me.

I could give it to Telitha . . . But you could do even greater things with it. You could be the next Supreme Overlord.

I sensed that all I had to do was stop resisting, stop fighting, and the darkness would overtake me, become part of me. A coldness spread through my body as a vision filled my mind of people from every kingdom and tongue bowing their knees to me—a dark queen, mighty and terrible.

The vision gave way to a memory of Alexia as the High Zalem. She had been tempted with dark power and had risen above it.

The second verse of Cazine's poem rushed back to me:

> *But a greater weapon was forged*
> *When her light made the shadow flee;*
> *Now blessed to split the hateful crown,*
> *May love's sacrifice set them free.*

It's Alexia!

It was she who had wrestled and overcome the darkest of trials, brought on by the Zalem's Bane. It was she who had sacrificed herself to the Zalems for her people. It was her love that had led her to sacrifice herself for me. Jeri hadn't been far off when he'd suggested the greater weapon was her bow, but in the midst of everything, it hadn't occurred to me it was Alexia herself.

But Telitha had said the crown could only be destroyed by Mors or one empowered as his High Zalem.

Alexia was empowered as a High Zalem once, I realised. And when she overcame the darkness with good, she became more powerful than any High Zalem. Powerful enough to split the crown and defeat Telitha.

That's why she was still standing. She'd already overcome the darkness. Now, she was impervious to it, just as I was to Dragon's Breath.

Just a few moments had passed. The crown was twisting my hands, but I forced myself to my feet and pulled Telitha up with me.

'Alexia!' I shouted, standing as far back as I could from Telitha to give her a clear shot. The pain in my hands was agonising. 'You can set us free. You have power over the darkness. Hurry!'

Telitha composed herself enough to shout at her, too. 'Yes, hurry up and kill your cousin!' She dropped to her knees again, pulling me down with her.

'Do it!' I called. 'It's your duty. You are the greater weapon!'

I could tell by the look on Alexia's face she was beginning to understand.

'You are nothing!' Telitha shouted. 'You are nothing but a queen who fouls her throne with a common husband, nothing but a shame and a disappointment to your father—'

Alexia raised her bow and nocked one of Wolfgar's arrows. This time, it was Telitha who froze.

'I hate you!' she shouted.

Alexia drew back the arrow, her eyes focused.

I tried not to imagine her arrow piercing my hand, or worse. It would be a near-impossible shot that left me unharmed.

Just stay still.

I heard the flick of her bow and pressed my eyes closed. At first, there was nothing but the sound of my own breath, and then it was as if a mighty force hit me, stronger than I could have ever anticipated. A wave of searing pain coursed through my fingers, right up to my head. I thought Alexia's arrow had indeed gone straight through my hand at first, but it had pierced the ugly, ten-horned crown at Telitha's temple, right between my thumb and forefinger. A perfect shot. There was a slow moment as it hung there, quivering, and then the sound of a great crack, like an ancient tree falling. The crown exploded into five pieces, flinging me away and sending forth a force of wind so strong that the entire battlefield of soldiers fell to the ground.

Once again, only Alexia remained standing, bow in hand, dauntless.

I lay in the dirtied snow, thinking I would die. Then, I realised how blue the sky looked. My head began to clear. The serpentine voice was gone. I was neither a Ghost nor a Supreme Overlord. I tentatively raised my hands to my face. They were red and blistered but intact.

Crumpled in the snow beside me with Alexia's arrow lodged in her skull, the Queen of Jazmarda lay dead, her frightened eyes open and unblinking.

The battlefield was soundless and still. Across the field, Hanequin got to his feet. Darj stood up behind him and pressed his sword point into his side.

'Who are you?' Hanequin shouted at Alexia. His voice cut through the heavy silence.

She turned to face him, breathless.

'That is Queen Alexia of Targe, daughter of King Amaz,' Darj said. 'And I am her husband, the commander of all the men who come against you this day. You have trespassed here long enough.'

Alexia gave him the slightest nod, and Darj ran his sword through Hanequin's middle. The Bone Horde leader teetered on his feet, and then he, too, fell down dead.

I stood, and the earth swayed before me. I reeled forward. Darj and Alexia ran for me, the former catching me before I fell and gently helping me down to my knees.

Alexia grabbed me by my shoulders, so pale I thought she might faint, too, but there was yet fire in her eyes and fierceness in her grip. 'I thought I was going to kill you,' she said. 'How could I have borne that for the rest of my life?' She shook me. 'Don't ever put me in that position again!'

Darj gently drew her away from me. 'She's safe, Alexia,' he said. 'It's over.'

She shook her arm free of Darj and pulled me towards her—affectionately this time. We slumped against each other, both spent.

'Show me your hands,' she said as we drew apart. I obliged. 'They are only a little red and blistered. The crown did much more damage to Telitha.'

'Anash didn't want Telitha to have it,' I said. 'He asked me to supplant Mors instead.'

'Clearly he didn't know he was dealing with an Elryane woman,' Darj said warmly.

He unclipped the horn from his belt and sounded the call of victory. The men of the Rhea Lands cheered. Darj collected and thrust

Hanequin's mace into the sky. 'Arjla divala!' he shouted, and the men echoed him. He sounded the horn a second time. 'Blessings upon the queen and the A'zyon Warrior!' he called, and the men chanted our names until the sound seemed to fill the sky.

Darj considered the two dead soldiers who lay nearby with arrows in their hearts, the ones who had initially run to kill him and save their master. 'For the record,' Darj said to his wife, pulling one of her arrows out and pointing it at her. 'I would have got them, thank you very much.'

She smiled. 'You were taking too long.'

There was a pause, and then the three of us laughed. I raised my arm to Darj; he took it and carefully pulled me to my feet.

She's dead, I told myself, letting a little relief settle in my heart. I turned my eyes upwards, hoping our fathers felt as proud as I did. *Now we can save the children.*

The Bone Hordes and Islanders raised themselves to their feet, too. They shouted at each other in their various tongues, inflaming each other back to war, but it was then that a Casmodian trumpet sounded to our right. Leuk soared over the crest of a small hill and landed masterfully as he and the King of Casmodia charged towards the enemy's flank. The hooves of a thousand Casmodian horses followed as they rode to slay anyone who dared to yet stand against us.

The Bone Hordes fled towards their barren lands. The Islanders who had fought with them for Garrow dropped to their knees in a collective, humiliating surrender. Yorella and her Islanders commenced the work of binding their hands, while Ren and Izak searched for survivors with what was left of their men.

Darj, Alexia, and I found Wolfgar's body. Having seen the blow he had taken bringing our queen the arrows of our salvation, I knew there was no hope of life within him, and I was right. His entire left side was completely ripped open and broken.

'He would have been dead before he hit the ground,' Darj said quietly. 'A noble sacrifice.'

I knelt beside him and gently closed his eyes. 'Great Spirit,' I said, my hand resting on Wolfgar's forehead, 'may this man find joy in his brother's presence and pass peacefully into your eternal care.'

Elhian rode back towards us. He passed Telitha's body before dismounting at our side.

'I am so sorry,' Alexia said to him, 'I know she was your—'

He raised a hand. 'You three are my family. I would have conquered her myself, if it came to it. But that dubious honour fell to you, and you satisfied it to perfection. Casmodia is in your debt, Alexia, and yours, Adaliah. You have both saved the Rhea Lands from the Zalems, once and for all.'

'Not quite yet,' I said. 'We must get back to the palace. If Telitha was truthful about Cordale and Finn, the children could be in danger. Can you help me up onto Brzina?' I asked Elhian.

He lifted my foot into Brzina's stirrup and pushed me up towards the saddle. Alexia called for Hazel, who trotted over to us, while Guntar answered the prince-general's call.

'Xander!' Darj called to the captain, who we spotted amongst the men. 'Help Ren and Izak in the search for survivors, and then bring these soldiers home.'

38
FAMILY

The people in Liane cheered as we passed through the northern gate into the streets. The battle had been visible from the city's walls, so they already knew we were victorious, that the battle was over. Under other circumstances, I would have delighted in the celebration of it all, but first I needed to see that my sons were safe. We galloped towards the palace, Brzina taking the lead.

The four of us dismounted in the courtyard and hurried inside. Master Rowan was already coming down the flight of stairs to meet us. 'Thank goodness, Your Majesty,' he said, giving Alexia a quick bow and stopping us in our tracks. 'There has been a major conflict between—'

Shouting upstairs interrupted him. Darj pushed past Rowan, and we ran up the stairs, following the sounds of the yelling until we came to the door of the guest room where Karlen and Jovan had been staying.

'Oh no you don't,' a familiar, female voice was saying inside. 'You just sit there and do what you're told!'

I opened the door. Inside, there was a crowd of people. One was a large woman in the process of tying a terrified Finn to a chair. Reyna cowered in the front corner of the room, crying. The other adult was a fair-haired man, untangling more rope to give to the woman.

'Rosana?' Darj asked, greeting his sister with the same air of amazement as when he first reunited with her in Tiathi. All of her children were in the room, too. A fire burned in the hearth.

She gave him a toothy smile. 'Darj. Oh, I'm so glad you made it. Oh no you don't!' she said crossly when Finn struggled against his binds. 'Franc, use that rope on his hands.'

Her husband obediently tied Finn's hands as tightly as he could.

'They made me do it,' Finn said, shaking. 'I didn't want to. I didn't want to!'

'He is nothing.' Cordale stepped out of a dark corner, drawing our attention to him. His black book was clasped firmly in his hand. Rosana and Franc took a step back in unison. 'Do you really think this boy did anything on his own? He merely gave me information. I was the one who stole the crowns. I was the one who found out about your wedding rings. I was the one who gave great power to the Zalems.'

'And now they're all dead,' I said.

'I am not. Not all power is held by those who wield a sword. It was a scribe like me who wrote the curses in Dragon's Breath ink to bring about your deaths.'

'The curses that Cazine corrected, allowing us to redeem our lives?' I asked. 'Thereby not bringing about our deaths at all? Yes, you really did bring great power to the Zalems.'

Cordale flinched at my derision. He thrust his black book towards me. 'There is power yet in this!'

'What power?' I asked impatiently.

Cordale's face darkened. 'Mors believed that power is the answer to fear. I believe that power is *found* in fear. In this book is written every memory, every experience, every incident that caused you and every other Zalem enemy to tremble. Here it is recorded to be used against you, fed to me and to Mors through the Great Spirit of Anash, brought to mind at the simple click of the fingers to torment you and destroy you. Fear, my friends, is the greatest and most powerful weapon of them all.'

I snatched the book out of Cordale's hand and threw it into the hearth. 'Not anymore.'

Cordale cried out as the book fell into the flames. He attempted to run for it, but Elhian grabbed him by the shirt and dragged him out of the room.

'Don't worry, Cordale,' he said. 'You won't be the first Zalem to experience a Targian prison cell.'

Realising that the danger had passed, our children came out from amongst Rosana's. Alexia cuddled Nichole and bent down to kiss Jeri's head. I knelt and put an arm around each of my sons. They all seemed healthy and unharmed, if a little bewildered.

'What happened?' Darj asked his sister as Princess Eva snuggled into his chest.

Rosana had been momentarily silenced, but she quickly gathered herself. 'We were in Egra. Weren't we, Franc?'

'Beautiful city,' Franc said. 'Beautiful!'

'But we had been staying in the inn for quite some time and had grown tired of it. We didn't want to return to the White Isles while there was so much unrest, so we moved on to Chettona. There we heard a group of men talking over their ales—you know what you men are like.' She rolled her eyes. 'One of them was prattling on about how you had sent the children to Liane with one of Telitha's spies.' She gave an indignant snort. 'Well, I told him—didn't I, Franc?—that he had better give me the whole story and tell me who the spy was and what they were going to do with the children. I told them that my brother is the grand commander of all the armies and is married to the Queen of Targe!'

'She did,' Franc said admiringly. 'She told them just like that.'

'As it turned out, he was Garrow's foreman and had fled when he saw Garrow dead. He was on his way home, deserting like a proper coward. In his drunkenness and anger, he told me how Garrow had spoken openly about Finn, how Finn had been charged by Telitha to get his sister a job at Tiathi Castle and use her as a spy, and to report everything back to him and Cordale so he could then report to the Jazmardian queen. When you asked Reyna to follow you to Dawfield, Finn took his opportunity to seem helpful, but he really was just trying to save his own skin. He was given the chance to be with the children, and he sent word to Cordale as soon as he could to say he was with them. Garrow had known all about it.'

'He'd been telling his foreman about it,' Franc said, breaking in while Rosana took a breath, 'saying that victory was assured because Cordale could take the children and use them as leverage against you all.'

'So, we reported the foreman to Captain Hawl,' Rosana said, 'who very helpfully locked him in irons, and we came to Liane straight away. I knew you were all too busy with battle and wouldn't even know the danger your children were in. I said to my Franc, "We can help them; we can do this". So, we packed up our children and came here, and I told them here at the palace who I was and that I had come to see my nephew and nieces, the prince and princesses.'

'I think she made Master Rowan nervous,' Franc said with a loving laugh.

'I don't care,' Rosana said. 'No one's going to interfere with my family.' She gave a resolved nod, and I saw perhaps the only traits she shared with her brother: stubborn courage and fierce loyalty.

'Thank you,' Alexia said, kneeling with her arms around all three of her children. 'I can't begin to imagine what would have happened had you not been there for us.'

Rosana beamed. Darj hugged her, and they held each other tightly.

'I'm sorry I let you down,' Darj said quietly, 'when our family died. But I have missed you, and I am very grateful for what you have done for us.'

'Oh, Darj,' she said as she drew back, keeping her hands on his arms. 'I'm sorry I left when you were still so young and that I let us be apart for so long. I know I can be a bit silly sometimes, but I've only ever wanted to be there for you when it matters.' She gently jabbed his arm. 'I am still a Ryder at heart.'

39

REDEEMED

The next day, I found Ren and Yorella sitting together in the palace's dining hall. They were the only two there. Ren poked at several strips of fried meat with an air of melancholy, Yorella gazing at him like she was finding the silence uncomfortable but wasn't sure what to say.

'How are you this morning?' she asked me.

I opened my mouth to give a cheerful answer, but in truth, I was weary in every way and wanted to sleep for a week before I had to confront any of the things I was feeling. 'I'm all right.'

'You have slayed the king of all evil,' Ren said, raising his eyes to mine. 'You should be more than all right.'

'I will be,' I said. 'That's probably the most any of us can hope for right now.' I wrapped my arms around myself. 'We have lost a lot.'

Ren and Yorella returned to gazing at their breakfast. They had each lost a brother. One had been loved; one had been despised.

'And what do we do now?' Ren asked in a barely perceptible whisper. 'I was not born to be king. That was never meant to be my path.'

'Mine either,' Yorella said as she tucked her slender fingers around a warm mug of honeycomb. 'Most of my army has been slaughtered, and the ones who remain are wounded and exhausted.'

I sat down at the table next to Ren and covered his hand with mine. 'I don't know if you know this,' I said, my voice shaking a little, 'but your brother died protecting my life. He was so brave, and I owe him everything.'

Ren blinked away tears. 'He loved you, you know,' he said. 'He would have done that gladly. He always regretted not coming to assist you personally in the Zalem Crisis.'

I remembered Thane's touching declaration as he died. 'But he loved you, too, and he believed in you. He was so sorry to leave you, but I know he would want nothing more than for you to take up his sceptre. Yorella, I believe the same is true of your father. You were his pride, not Garrow.'

Ren nodded and buried his face in his hands. Across from him, Yorella quietly wept as well.

Liane was busy and full of energy. Everywhere, there were people celebrating, dancing, and drinking in the streets. News had spread of my victory over Mors, and the people were also talking about the defeat of Garrow, Hanequin, and Telitha. With so many guests at the palace, there was hardly a quiet place to be found, and I desperately needed one. The events of the past few days—weeks—were bearing down on me, and I felt on the edge of physical and mental collapse.

After lying awake beside Elhian in bed that night—he had quickly fallen into a deep sleep—I remembered Alexia's Secret Room. Sleep was still far off, so I carefully got out of bed and wandered through the now-quieter palace towards the library. There I found the small passage that led to the hidden chamber.

I opened the door and found a candle burning inside. Alexia was on one of the chairs, also in her bedclothes, her hair damp from a recent wash. I hadn't meant to impose, and it was her special room.

But before I could speak or retreat, she reached her hand out to me. I took it, sat beside her, and rested my head on her shoulder. She leant her head down on mine, and we said nothing for a long time.

'When you came riding through the army on Brzina,' she said eventually, breaking the silence, 'I don't think I have ever felt so proud of anything in all my life. We saw the storm on the mountains but had no idea whether you lived or died. It wasn't until we saw you on Brzina that we all knew you had defeated Mors, that we had won.' She lifted her head and met my eyes. My face, particularly my left eye and upper lip, were still bruised from the encounter. 'Every artist will be painting that scene for the next century.'

'You're the hero,' I said. 'You defeated Garrow and Telitha. They'll be singing songs about that. You named your heir after a courageous targarn; people will name their daughters in honour of you.'

'I had help.'

'So did I,' I said. 'Your father was a great man, Alexia, but today, you surpassed even him. No one else would have had the valor or skill to make that shot. I know Uncle Amaz is proud of you. I'm sure all of our ancestors are.'

'I hope so,' she said shyly. She poured me a mug of honeycomb, and we settled in for the lengthy talk we both needed. 'What about you?' she asked. 'Confidence has slayed doubt, I hope.'

I leant into her shoulder again. 'Yes, that battle is finally over and won. I was just afraid of letting you all down, afraid that Mors would prove right and that I wouldn't be found worthy.'

'All Mors did was point out that we have all been defining ourselves by our roles, ancestry, and positions. And he was right. That is a weakness because none of that matters. We are first and foremost

Adaliah and Elhian, Darj and Alexia, sons and daughters of the Great Spirit and fighters for all that's good. Everything else we do is informed by that, not the other way around.' She shared one of her warming smiles—the image of her mother's, which I had seen at Kest—and I couldn't help but return it.

I told her all about what I had seen at the Keep, and she listened in quiet wonder.

'I wish I could have seen them,' she said. 'To think, if I'd had a younger sibling, the Keeper's power would not have transferred to you the way it did. It would not have been strong enough to defeat Mors. Ru'ach has been taking care of us all from the beginning.' She squeezed my hand. 'But I do so miss our parents.'

'They are here with us even now, I'm sure,' I said. 'They always have been, I think.'

I told her how Elhian and I sent Finn off to Tiathi Prison to await trial but let Reyna go free. We were confident she had been a mere pawn in a much greater plan. She would not continue to work for us, however, and was being escorted back to her family in Casmodia. Alexia told me how she had already pronounced judgment on Cordale. His trial and execution had been swift and his burial a lonely one.

'Izak spoke to Hazaka's scribe when he went to Jazmarda to gather his men for war,' Alexia said. 'He told me over dinner.' We had told Izak about the concordat Hazaka wanted us to sign and how we never had time to read it before it went up in flames. The scribe told Izak the concordat started out very nobly and was all about uniting to defeat Telitha, whom Hazaka mentioned by name. Clearly, he had known her intentions. 'I believe she found out that he knew what she was up to,' Alexia said, 'and that's why they argued the morning he died. She killed him to protect her cause, and he died trying to protect ours, even sending us the note to direct us to Cazine's writings. But he hadn't been so honourable at first.'

'What do you mean?' I asked.

'The scribe said that at the end of the agreement, Hazaka requested tribute from each kingdom as payment for his help—five thousand Jazmardian xaws from each kingdom for five years.'

This was an exorbitant amount that would have indeed redeemed Hazaka and his kingdom from his debts but practically driven the other kingdoms into insolvency. Each monarch would have been required to provide him with the money, regardless of whether they could afford to or not. He had never mentioned that when trying to get us to sign.

'That is just like Hazaka, isn't it?' I said. 'Half-noble, half-selfish. Hopefully, Izak will be different and raise Mirza in the true Jazmardian way—the way of Lezan and Kadram.' Alexia had already told me that Izak found Mirza and his brothers in Etarbelec, Telitha having sent them there, out of the way, after the Winter Council. In just a few weeks, Izak had become both a regent and a father.

'I believe he will be honourable,' Alexia said. 'He and Yorella have already spoken about how they will help each other. Jazmarda will supply her with timber for stronger ships so they can settle more islands in the east, and the White Isles will supply them with as much fish as they can get. I believe Izak will do fine and that he is honourable enough to carry the original Cazinian Papers home with him. They belong to the people of Jazmarda and should be returned to their care.'

'And hopefully we have had need of them for the last time,' I said.

The following afternoon, I walked with Darj across the palace grounds towards the barracks. We came upon Lord Fenton along the way. He saw us and awkwardly glanced over his shoulder like he was hoping for an excuse to avoid us. He hadn't had the opportunity to speak to Darj or his wife since he'd made his impertinent comment to Alexia in Levanna.

'Fenton,' Darj said curtly.

'Ah . . . On your way to the barracks?' Fenton asked. He bowed his head to me. 'Shall I accompany you there?'

'I know the way to the barracks,' Darj said. 'It's a place I plan to still visit regularly.'

Fenton took his meaning, and his face turned pink. 'Darj, I must apologise,' he said. 'I don't want there to be ill feelings between us or between the queen and me. Please, I have nothing but the highest respect for you both. I saw the way you saved the queen from Hanequin's blow. So many of us had tried and failed to even scratch him, but you defeated him almost effortlessly. You are every bit deserving to carry both the title of "prince" and "general". Everyone in the court is saying so.'

'I appreciate that,' Darj said politely.

Fenton gave a bow and continued his walk in a different direction.

I grinned. 'All hail the prince-general,' I said. 'Conqueror of the court!'

Darj shook his head at me with a long-suffering smile.

We found Xander inside the barracks inspecting several outfits and weapons collected from the bodies of those they had failed to keep safe, determining which ones could be repaired.

'If Wolfgar had survived,' Darj said, 'I would have had him stay on to improve our armour. His arrows worked perfectly on the crown and Telitha. We can only hope our fletchers can replicate them.'

'He was a Casmodian and would have come home with us,' I said.

'In the one conversation I had with him,' Xander said, 'at the camp near Semanez, he spoke of his love, Josselyn, and how he was going to ask her to be his wife when he returned. Now, she will never see him again.' Xander picked up a helmet, which was completely bent from a blunt blow. 'He would have loved to have seen the queen's last shot. She was perfect, truly dauntless, but those arrows were also powerful because of his skill.'

'And because he got them to her in time,' Darj said.

'And now, he is gone.' Xander tossed the helmet onto a pile of other damaged pieces that were beyond repair. 'Such is the price of war.'

'This isn't a job for a captain,' Darj said. 'Why not have some of the soldiers do it?'

'No, I want to do it,' Xander said, picking up a bloodied green tunic with twelve gold stars patterned across the front. 'It ensures I never take for granted those who fight under my authority, or those who died for their kingdom. We are safe now, yes, but thousands across the Rhea Lands are dead. Thousands of families must adjust to a life without the ones they loved.' He paused. 'It's like losing Raggin all over again.'

There was nothing Darj or I could say or add to that. It was all true—unfairly, unjustly true.

'What happened to the pieces of the crown you collected?' I asked Xander. He had taken the initiative to bring them back into Liane for us.

'There.' He indicated a bag sitting on a bench. 'Is it true you believe the water will redeem them back into the five crowns of the Rhea Lands?'

'I believe so, yes,' I said. 'I've seen the river redeem many other things, my own life included. Ru'ach's spirit is strongest there, and that is what we need if we are to breathe life back into something so corrupted by evil.'

Xander stopped what he was doing. 'Mors said that when you cleansed the swords, the darkness in them reverted to him. The despair, the fear, the hate, and the death.'

'Yes,' I said. 'He poured all of those things into his grotesque crown to represent all that he is and where he got his power from.'

'Exactly,' Xander said. 'I think you will need all four cleansed swords to counter his darkness—the Jazmardian Hope Sword for the despair, the Casmodian Faith Sword for the fear, the Targian Love Sword for the hate, and the Kestian Life Sword for the death.'

'What are you saying?' I asked.

'I think you will need to take the swords to the river with you and place them in the water along with the crown.'

'What if it destroys them?' Darj asked uncertainly.

'The time for war has passed, I hope,' Xander said. 'Everything they represent should be imbued into the crowns. Their power will live on and will be given to all the kingdoms of the Rhea Lands, not just three of them and Kest.'

'But Wolfgar reformed the Life Sword so beautifully,' I said sadly.

Xander put his hand on my arm. 'And it served its purpose beautifully, with much thanks to you.'

Two days later, just before dawn, Alexia's ladies-in-waiting fixed my hair and made some last-minute adjustments to the amethyst-coloured gown my cousin had found for me. I watched from my window as several battalions from all kingdoms rode out of Liane on their way to free the south of Targe and Delya from the Bone Hordes. King Ren led them, and I knew it would be to victory. It was generally agreed the Bone Hordes had already retreated to their own lands, especially now that all of their leaders had been killed. Ren carried the Targian gold Garrow and Telitha had collected to pay Hanequin, which had been found in one of their camps. Under the queen's orders, Ren was to give it to the people of Fenellar, Rorinhall, and the other southern towns to help rebuild the homes that had fallen. As for those of Garrow's Islanders who had survived the last battle, Yorella's most trusted captains escorted them to their homeland as prisoners of war.

I met Elhian, Darj, and Alexia in the palace forecourt, the queen wearing a long, teal gown with golden embroidery stitched around the hem. Her hair lay down her back with some tresses curled in a pretty way, and she was crowned with a delicate, gold-leafed headpiece adorned with pearls. She seemed so different from the woman who had killed Telitha on the battlefield just a few days before—beautiful, calm, and, like all of us, still in need of rest.

The four of us rode through the quiet streets of Liane and back to the battlefield. Thousands of bodies from all kingdoms lay in lines on the ground before us. Our soldiers had tended them in preparation for their burials, having sung songs of goodbye in the Targian way as they covered them in cloth and prayed for their swift release to Ru'ach. Now, great crowds gathered on the grass around their lost loved ones, waiting solemnly in the cold dark.

The four of us dismounted and walked to a white stone pillar—a memorial built especially for the occasion. A bowl of oil burned steadily on top. The queen knelt before it, and everyone else followed. Together, we watched in silence as the sun rose once more.

As it warmed us, Alexia stood to address the people. 'While we mourn those who died,' she said, 'let us rejoice that it was not in vain. The Zalems are defeated!'

The people thrust their arms and weapons into the sky, cheering.

A warm, gentle breeze strewed around us. Alexia closed her eyes and breathed it in. 'We can now live the life of peace and safety we have long fought for.'

Afterwards, we collected Izak and rode to Kest once more, reaching the river at the Yellow Forest at dusk. Alexia, Darj, Elhian and Izak watched as I took the bag that held the five pieces of the broken crown from Brzina's saddle. The river was higher and running faster than when I'd passed through just days ago, the snow from the mountains above yielding to the forthcoming spring.

Darj and Elhian arranged some of the rocks under the icy water to form a small pool. While they did so, I unsaddled Brzina and removed her bridle.

'Go on, girl,' I said, running my hand down her silvery neck. 'Live your life in the freedom you deserve.'

Brzina tossed her head with a soft grunt.

'Go,' I said again. 'And thank you for all you did for me.'

Brzina nudged me with her nose, turned, and trotted off into the forest. She paused and looked back one last time before cantering away from us forever.

I opened the bag and tipped the contents into the pool. The five pieces of the crown sank to the bottom of the river.

Nothing happened.

Alexia took the Targian sword with its green stone and placed it in the water. Elhian and Izak did the same with their swords. The water rolled over them in gentle waves while I unsheathed the long and glorious Life Sword. I held it in my hands briefly before laying it in the water beside its friends. A glittering white light rose out of the river and shone gently into the evening sky.

One of the broken pieces of Mors' crown twisted and glowed and floated upwards. Deformed and ugly no more, it transformed into the crown of the White Isles, exactly the same as it had been before. The Jazmardian crown followed, then the Delyan and Casmodian. Elhian carefully took them out one-by-one and set them on the bank to dry. Alexia's crown was the last to appear. The twelve gold stars emerged first and when Elhian picked it up and the water dripped away, it shone in all its former glory. The five crowns were cleansed and reborn.

'They seem to be the same,' Darj said, kneeling down and peering at them. He turned the Islander crown and frowned, looking closer at something inside the headband. He reached out with his fingertip to touch it. When his skin made contact with it, he yelped like it had burnt him.

'What is it?' Alexia asked.

Darj inspected his finger. 'It's . . . it's like the stones in the swords used to be, only touchable by the Ordained. The crowns must only be touchable by the monarchs and their heirs.'

Alexia collected her crown and held it in her hands just as she had done many times before. It brought her no harm. 'It must be to protect our right to rule,' she said.

Elhian picked up his crown and then the Jazmardian one. He handed the latter to Izak. Neither of them were harmed. 'What were you pointing at?' Elhian asked Darj.

'There was a tiny butterfly engraved inside Engres' crown,' Darj said.

'It's Yorella's now,' Elhian said.

Izak checked his. 'There's one here, too.'

Alexia gasped when she found one inside hers as well. 'These weren't here before. They must be here because of you, Adaliah, because of all you've done for us.'

I looked down at the pool again and realised the swords were gone. They had withered away in the water. That this had happened so quietly and without any of us noticing filled me with sadness.

I saw something else glistening on the riverbed. I scooped it up with my palm. Whatever it was, it was small and light.

I stretched out my fingers. 'I forgot these would come back, too,' I said, looking over at my husband.

Elhian saw the two rings comfortably overlapping each other on my palm.

'Are you ready to be married again?' I asked as he collected and examined his.

'Oh, I don't know,' Elhian said with great deliberation, 'it's been a much more stressful experience than I anticipated.'

'I suppose if anyone needs a Medallion of Courage for a wedding ring, it's the husband of an Elryane woman,' Darj said.

'Perhaps you should have the other one, then?' Elhian said. Alexia gave them both a half-hearted glare.

'Do you think it's been safe and easy for us?' I asked, and we laughed. Elhian slipped my ring onto my finger, brought my hand to his lips, and kissed it.

'Look,' Izak said, pointing back towards the water.

Something else appeared. We held our breath as it slowly emerged. It flew upwards, water dripping off its wings. It was delicate, beautiful, strong. We all knew what it was, and we were all too amazed to utter the words.

A new Armoured Butterfly.

But there was a difference. It didn't just have purple wings like its two predecessors, but wings mixed with all the colours of the Rhea Lands.

'Why?' Darj asked, breaking the silence.

'Because it belongs to all of us,' I said.

As it hovered in the air, hundreds of living white butterflies rose out of the frosted grass around us. We watched in awe as they fluttered about us almost like snow. They gleamed in the moonlight as the Armoured Butterfly flew away into the night sky.

'And so begins the next era of the Rhea Lands,' I said.

40

THE CROWNED GUARDIANS

Liane Cathedral is beautifully situated on a rise in sight of the palace. It was carefully crafted from the same light stones, sparing it from being overbearing or oppressive. While many cathedrals house beautiful, story-telling stained glass, the large windows in Liane are crystal clear, giving entrance to streams of pure sunlight.

It warmed my back as I stood at the front before a crowd. Every seat in the cathedral was taken. Lords and ladies from Targe and many nobles from the other kingdoms had come to see the five monarchs of the Rhea Lands re-crowned. I waited for them to arrive, standing before the thousand or so people. I wore a long, sparkling gown that left my shoulders bare and high white gloves that reached my elbows. I was crowned with my circlet of old—the Kestian diadem that was made of silver threads, interwoven to create a pattern of never-ending swirls, with a purple stone sitting in the small rise at the front.

To my right and a few steps back, Darj stood with his hand resting on the ceremonial sword sheathed by his side. His sister and her family were in the front section before us, all of them with big smiles, and by them were our children. Eva's fifth birthday had just passed.

The doors at the other end of the cathedral opened majestically, and the choir, which was above us, began to sing.

As the longest reigning monarch in the Rhea Lands, Queen Alexia entered first, wearing an elegant velvet gown that flowed several steps behind her. Her black hair was up with two feminine braids meeting at the back of her head and long, diamond earrings emphasising her slender neck. Now rested and well, she was perfectly regal. Darj's general expression was indistinct, but the look in his eyes was one of adoration.

King Elhian followed her up the aisle. A blue sash was tied around his waist, and he was decked with gold braid. A golden brooch on his chest secured his white-edged blue cloak. It moved masterfully behind him. He seemed more settled within himself than ever. I couldn't help but beam at him, and the warm smile he gave me in turn reminded me of my love for him all over again.

Ren, who had returned after ensuring his home was free of the Bone Hordes, came in next followed by Izak and then Yorella—the last to rise to her throne. The three of them had never participated in a coronation, had never committed the rule of their people to Ru'ach. Now they would do so together.

The five kings and queens formed a line before me and kneeled—not to me, but to Ru'ach. The choir's song came to an end, and everyone in the cathedral bowed their heads. There passed a sacred minute of quietness and trust.

'Yorella, spear maiden of the White Isles and daughter of King Engres,' I said, addressing the youngest and most innocent of the monarchs. 'Rise.'

She tentatively got to her feet. Darj stepped forward and picked up the cushion with the Islander crown on it. I moved my gloved hands towards the crown, unable to touch it with my skin. I held it above her head. 'I crown you, Yorella Loren, Queen of the White Isles. May you protect your people with grace.' The crown settled on her head as if it had been made just for her.

'Izak, desert hunter and ledzagor of your people, rise.' The Jazmardian man seemed the most solemn one of them all and was staring at me intently. 'I crown you, Izak Tan, Prince Regent of Jazmarda and protector of King Mirza Cazren until he comes of age. May you protect him and your people with hope.' The Jazmardian crown was heavy, but Izak carried it well.

'Ren, dagger fighter of the Rivermen and brother of good King Thane, rise.' The Delyan youth stood before me, his face showing a range of emotions that I recognised as nervousness, sadness, and expectation, all mixed together. 'I crown you, Ren Markus, King of Delya. May you protect your people with strength.' I took the crown from the cushion Darj was holding and set it on his head.

'Elhian,' I said, turning to my husband as Darj picked up the cushion with the Casmodian crown on it, 'sword-wielder of the icy north and King of Casmodia, rise. I return to you your rightful crown. May you protect your people with faith.' I placed it on his head, his deep brown, unblinking eyes conveying all that he felt, all that it meant.

'Alexia, Dauntless Archer and Queen of Targe, rise.' My cousin, who had been kneeling in the middle of the five, gracefully rose to her feet. Her sky-blue eyes flickered towards Darj with a sparkle. 'I return to you your rightful crown. May you protect your people with love.' The Targian crown was the heaviest and most impressive of them all, but Alexia wore it like she always had: with great ease and authority.

'Together you are the Crowned Guardians of the Rhea Lands, charged with leading your people into peace and prosperity under the guidance of Ru'ach, protector of all the living. Do you promise to do so until all breath leaves your body?'

Without hesitation, they answered as one, 'We do.'

'Then sign your names as evidence of your promise.'

They each stepped forward and signed their names to a long scroll that detailed how they would support each other across the kingdoms—an agreement like the one Hazaka had hoped for, but with complete honesty and integrity.

We called it the Concordat of the Crowned Guardians.

Epilogue

It was a warm spring morning when we rode into Kest, racing and laughing through the Yellow Forest. I saw new life in the flowers that peeked above the foliage, the leaves that unfurled in the sunlight, and the rushing of Kest River, which was near bursting with the melted snow from the mountains above. We dismounted as we came to the front of the Keep.

'Come on,' Alexia called back to our children.

Straggling behind us was Prince Jeri, now twenty and as handsome as his father had been. Nichole had already dismounted her mare, and our Jovan held her horse's reins for her.

'Come on, Brielle,' Karlen said, helping my seven-year-old daughter down from Leuk, where she had been riding with Elhian. I reflected poignantly how we had been told that after the complicated birth of our twins, we would never have another child. Brielle Cassondra Alexia was our miracle.

'Race you to the front door,' Jeri called to Darj and Alexia's youngest. Amaz Naythan had been looking in his saddlebags for something to eat, but he abandoned his quest and took off after his brother.

'Rosana's here already,' Darj said to Alexia beside him, pointing to the Odinel carriage. He met his wife's eyes and, on impulse, drew her in for a kiss.

She took his hand with a smile. 'Wait,' she said. 'Where is she?'

'I'm here, Mother.' Princess Eva was leading her horse up the road behind us. 'Her shoe came loose.'

The princess was only just sixteen, but she was already as lovely as her mother. Her blue eyes were made all the more vibrant from the sapphire cloak she wore, and her long, black hair flowed freely down her back. She carried herself with grace but blushed as we all watched her.

'What?' she asked.

'Are you ready?' I asked.

Eva nodded, and I knew she was both nervous and excited.

As we walked towards the Keep, we passed a moss-covered headstone that marked the spot where a beloved friend had been buried.

Here lies Bagred,
The warrior horse of Adaliah,
Who gave his life in the battle against Mors.

Soon after Mors' defeat, Alexia and I arranged for the Keep to be refurnished, with a new set of soldiers put in place to guard it. We had gathered there many times for holidays over the years, and in many ways, it was still the home of my heart. Franc, Rosana, and their children, who had moved to Jasteria after the Battles of Mors, soon began to join us. There had been a time when Alexia and I could only count each other as family; now, family filled every room.

Jeri and Amaz stood in front of the main hearth when we came inside, warming their hands while Rosana pinched and kissed Amaz's cheeks. Jeri ducked when she tried to catch him next; her laughter filled the house. The staff prepared a light meal, which we ate before gathering together in the living room. Once everyone was quiet and settled, Alexia and I walked to the front of the room next to Tomek. He proudly held a cushion with a precious item I had been saving for the princess. It was the last crown I had to place: the circlet of Kest.

'Your Highness,' I called.

The young princess walked to the front and stood before me while our family and the Keep's servants watched on with reverence. I collected the circlet from Tomek and carefully held it over Eva's head.

'Eva Jenethea Adaliah Elryane, today you become the Keeper of Kest,' I said. 'May you serve as the cornerstone of peace between the kingdoms of the Rhea Lands.' I placed the circlet on her head and kissed her cheeks.

'I promise to honor the Great Spirit in all that I do,' she said, bowing her head to me. She turned to her mother and curtsied low. 'I pledge allegiance to you, my queen, and promise to do my part to keep your kingdom's alliances safe and strong.'

'May Ru'ach guide and bless you in all your ways,' the queen said warmly.

'Those present, do you promise to support Princess Eva in her endeavour?' I asked.

The room answered together, 'We do.'

'Then so be it,' I concluded, and everyone clapped, none more loudly than Rosana and Franc.

'I'm so proud of you,' Alexia and I said to her together as the others talked amongst themselves.

I saw a reflection of the three of us in a nearby wall-length mirror. I remembered briefly how this young girl had come into the world, almost slain by Cades at birth. The scars Garrow and Jag had given her mother were visible on her back, although faded with time and mostly hidden by her dress. Echoes of Mors' claw marks were still on my side and arm. Sometimes, it seemed amazing that we had all survived.

'Can I go and show the others?' Eva asked.

'Of course, darling,' Alexia said.

Eva moved towards the only man she had known as her father but stepped back and gave her mother a hug. 'Thank you,' she said to us both.

Alexia and I watched as the princess showed Darj her circlet. 'The Keep belongs to her now,' I said, 'until Jeri's second child is born and ready to inherit.' I tilted my head. 'And on it goes.'

'Yes.' Alexia reached for my hand. 'But you, cousin, will always be the A'zyon Warrior.'

As she spoke, a flash of coloured light passed one of the windows, briefly filling the room with it. By the time I had turned, whatever it was had gone. I linked my arm with Alexia's, and the two of us walked back to our family, smiling.

For more information about
Trudy Adams
&
The Crowned Guardians
please visit:

www.trudyadams.squarespace.com
www.facebook.com/trudyadamsauthor

For more information about
AMBASSADOR INTERNATIONAL
please visit:

www.ambassador-international.com
@AmbassadorIntl
www.facebook.com/AmbassadorIntl

*If you enjoyed this book, please consider leaving us a review on
Amazon, Goodreads, or our website.*

With a mom in forensics and a dad on the police force, it's no wonder fourteen-year-old Bailey McKenzie has her sights set on working in law enforcement. When she and her friends are given the opportunity to be junior forensic interns for the summer, Bailey jumps at the chance. But investigating a murder scene takes a turn when the team comes under attack and their lives are placed in danger. Will Bailey's dreams of fighting for justice never become a reality?

When Ari finds herself with a job offer to work undercover and find her purpose again, she can't resist. But as her undercover case deepens, she discovers that the voices in her head aren't as imaginary as she thought.

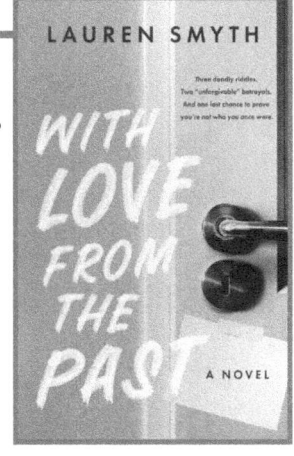

Thirteen-year-old Jason is on the cusp of manhood, striving to find his place at school and at home. When Jason and his father encounter a bear, they shoot and kill it, not realizing they have left a cub without its mother. When Sasquot of the Penobscot Tribe, discovers what they have done, he decides that Jason needs a lesson in caring for God's creatures. Thus begins a year Jason will never forget as he begins to care and train the cub in order for it to survive.